CARRIE NEWBERRY

WHEN THE FUR HITS THE FAN, DUCK

BOOK THREE OF THE ETERNAL SPRING, INVISIBLE FOREST SERIES

EDGE SCIENCE FICTION AND FANTASY PUBLISHING
An Imprint of HADES PUBLICATIONS, INC.
CALGARY

When the Fur Hits the Fan, Duck
(Book Three of the Eternal Spring, Invisible Forest series)

Copyright © 2025 by Carrie Newberry

This is a work of fiction. Names, characters, places, and incidents are the products of the author's imagination or are used fictitiously and are not to be construed as real. Any resemblance to actual events, locales, organizations, or persons, living or dead, is entirely coincidental.

EDGE SCIENCE FICTION AND FANTASY PUBLISHING
An Imprint of HADES PUBLICATIONS, INC.
P.O. Box 1414, Calgary, Alberta, T2P 2L6, Canada

The EDGE Team:
Producer: Brian Hades
Cover Design: Jamie Ty
Cover Art: 100 Covers
Book Design: Mark Steele

ISBN: 9781770532441

EDGE Science Fiction and Fantasy Publishing and Hades Publications, Inc. acknowledges the ongoing support of the Alberta Foundation for the Arts and the Canada Council for the Arts for our publishing programme.

Library and Archives Canada Cataloguing in Publication
Title: When the fur hits the fan, duck / Carrie Newberry.
Names: Newberry, Carrie, author.
Description: First edition. | Series statement: Book 3 of The eternal spring, invisible forest series
Identifiers: Canadiana (print) 20250174197 | Canadiana (ebook) 2025017491X | ISBN 9781770532458 (hardcover) | ISBN 9781770532441 (softcover) | ISBN 9781770532434 (EPUB)
Subjects: LCGFT: Fantasy fiction. | LCGFT: Novels.
Classification: LCC PS3614.E815 W44 2025 | DDC 813/.6—dc23

FIRST EDITION
(20250401)
Printed in USA
www.edgewebsite.com

Publisher's Note:

Picture this: a moonlit forest shrouded in whispers, where shadows ripple with secrets too dangerous to reveal. A woman stands on the brink of two lives— one bound by loyalty to her pack, the other haunted by an unspeakable act. She is Kellan Faolanni, a shape-shifter, protector, and unwilling mother-to-be. Somewhere in the depths of her heart lies a fragile truth she dares not face: the child she carries could be her salvation—or her undoing. Beyond the trees, magick spirals wildly, a force as chaotic as the emotions tearing through her. Justice falters, betrayal festers, and danger stalks her every step.

But this is not just Kellan's story. It is a mirror held up to those who dare to confront their fears, who understand that survival is a choice, not a guarantee. The question isn't whether she will prevail—it's what she will lose in the process.

Step into her world. Feel the forest's pulse. Taste the danger in the air. And ask yourself: what would you sacrifice to protect what matters most? This is When the Fur Hits the Fan, Duck—a journey that will leave you breathless.

Brian Hades, publisher

Dedication

To Mom and Dad. Thank you for always being ready to tell me how much you love me and believe in me. Love you. So much.

Chapter 1

KELLAN

Wolves do not play with yarn. I was a wolf. I stared at the fluffy ball on my table. Oh, fuck, no. "What's that?"

Finn sighed his you're-an-idiot sigh. "It's yarn." As the second-in-command of the Sankhain, protectors of an invisible forest that held a fountain of youth, Finn had many opportunities to give me, his subordinate, that particular sigh. Or as he sometimes liked to call me, his insubordinate. Hilarious, he was.

A growl escaped my throat. I was a shape-shifter, half-wolf, half-human, which made that growl a significantly scarier sound than anything a human throat could create. Finn didn't even blink, although my dog, Galen, shifted his position on the bed so he could glare at the man who was prompting me to growl. "I know it's yarn," I said, the growl bleeding into the words. "Why is it here? In my cabin?"

"You're going to learn to knit."

I was suddenly glad that Tony, my live-in something-or-other, wasn't there, because he would've been laughing his ass off. Personally, I was hoping I misheard. "Come again?"

"It's very relaxing," Finn said, in his pompous, I-know-what's-best-for-you tone. "You need an outlet."

"That's what running is for." I picked up the sticks – needles? – and tried to figure out how to hold them. I liked pointy objects, but these weren't really made for stabbing.

"Yes," Finn said, "and you've run yourself to skin and bones." He gave me a distinctly judgmental up-and-down gaze. "You need a different option."

That's not why I'm so skinny. It's because I can't keep food down, because I'm...because... I growled again. I could probably stab him with the knitting stick if I jabbed it in his eye. Examining it closer, I tried to assess whether it was long enough to pierce his brain, if I shoved it up his nose. With enough force...

"Kellan," he said, in his impatient, pay-attention-to-the-superior-being-sitting-in-front-of-you tone.

Another outlet. "Kickboxing. I'll do more kickboxing. And weight-lifting."

"You need a nonathletic outlet."

Knitting, though? "I like athletic outlets."

"Kellan." Now his tone was soft, sad, almost. He touched my wrist. Just that little touch made me jump, and it was enough to draw my attention to what he saw. The bones jutted against the skin, making me look fragile. A small amount of sinew wound around my forearm. Not as much as there should be. He wasn't wrong. He wasn't. I needed to burn fewer calories, because all the exercise was helping to whittle me away. It wasn't the whole story, though, and I'd be damned if I was going to tell him the whole story before I could even say it to myself.

"I have muscle," I said.

"Not what you should," he countered. "With the amount of weight-lifting you do, you should be quite muscular. You either need to resume eating meat…" I tried to hide my shudder, but I knew he saw it. I gave up meat last fall, after being tortured by a psychopath. It was a long story. "Or you need to cut back on the physical activity until you can regain some weight. Ever since Christmas, you have been pushing yourself far too hard." The unspoken question hung in the air – what the hell happened at Christmas?

I shied away from the question and stated, "It's impossible for a shape-shifter to starve to death." The only thing that could kill me was an instant killing blow – a bullet to the heart, decapitation, something like that. I couldn't die from my body turning against me. I was pretty sure.

"Perhaps," Finn said. "However, must you try so hard to test that theory?" A tiny bit of emotion wove through his scent, a warmth that wasn't like his seared-earth angry smell. It was more like sun-warmed, fresh-turned earth. Concern.

Finn never allowed what he considered "softer" emotions to play in his scent, where he knew I could smell them, as a half-wolf. That he was letting me smell his worry said he was very, very worried.

Heat built up behind my eyes. I would not cry. Lately, it seemed like I burst into tears over a hangnail. "Knitting, though. Come on. I have PTSD, not angina." I felt grateful for the annoyance that warmed me. Annoyance was a kissing cousin of my favorite emotion, anger. I could get through this, using annoyance. "Are you going to teach me?" I sneered. I doubted he would do anything so prosaic as crafting, but if he planned to teach me, I was fairly sure I would soon find out if the knitting sticks could double as a weapon.

Someone knocked at the door. "I don't believe that would be in the best interests of anyone," Finn said wryly. He got up, opened the cabin door, and let Smack in.

Smack was one of the Sankhain's younglings, street kids we rescued like stray dogs and trained to be warriors. She was also one of my favorite people. Galen's, too, as he hopped off the bed and trotted over to her for a pat. "You?" I said. "You knit?"

As she scratched behind Galen's ears, she gave me a little smile. "I know. You'd think it's such an old white lady thing. Really, it's kinda cool. You don't have to do doilies and shit." Finn cleared his throat, a mild admonishment on the language. Smack muttered under her breath, too quiet for Finn to make out, "Yeah, cuz she ain't said shit ten times worse before I got here." As I struggled not to laugh, she raised her voice to a normal level. "Sorry, sir." She looked back at me. "Yarn comes in some pretty awesome colors, and you can make cool sh- cool stuff. I knitted Ryder a skull-and-crossbones hat for his birthday."

I saw Ryder, another youngling, wearing that hat yesterday. It was, as she said, cool. I wavered.

"Here, you don't hold the needles like that. Didn't he show you how to hold them?" She sent Finn an almost too brief to see glance of accusation.

"Wait, you really knit?" I asked Finn. He inclined his head in a halfway nod. I felt my ire rise again. "He didn't show me anything. Just came in here and told me how relaxing it would be. Do I look relaxed?"

She snorted and muttered, "No, but that's cuz he's here. He always pisses you off." She looked up at Finn with a beatific smile. "Sir, maybe you could leave us now."

With a nod, Finn left. He wore a self-satisfied smirk that made me want to see if I could throw the knitting stick hard enough to pierce his brain stem.

"Look," Smack said. She did something with her needles, too fast for me to follow. "There isn't nothing to it. You hold 'em like this. Not like you're gonna stab with 'em. More like you're gonna write with 'em."

And thus began my first lesson in knitting. By the time we were done, I managed to cast on and knit two rows.

As Smack packed up her knitting things – she managed to knit half a scarf in the time we spent together – I sighed. "I'm not relaxed."

"That's cuz you don't know what you're doing yet. You kinda suck at it, and that's not relaxing." Only Smack could get away with saying something like that to me. "You'll practice and you'll get better, and pretty soon, you'll start to like it. It's kinda addicting, but it's better than drugs, cuz you don't come down from it."

I wondered if it would be better than cutting myself. That was my other outlet, currently my only nonathletic outlet. Cutting always made me feel better, then was inevitably followed by shame and emptiness.

I picked a piece of lint off the yarn ball. "Do you knit with the other younglings?"

She shook her head as she pulled on her coat. From his spot by my feet, Galen watched her. He liked watching humans transform into puffy winter dwellers. He particularly liked scarves. I think he always looked at them with the belief that they would make great tug-of-war toys. "Nah," Smack said, answering my question. "I mean, a couple of them knit. Most of them think it's lame."

I made a strangled sound, and she laughed.

"It's not lame." She narrowed her eyes and studied me. Her voice flipped from amused to dead serious. "Sometimes you reach a point where you gotta know that what you're doing isn't working. And I gotta tell you, what you're doing isn't working. Ma'am."

She was right. I knew it. Because sometimes when I bent over, it seemed like my ribs rubbed against one another, because there wasn't enough meat in between them to provide a cushion. And the problem wasn't just the exercise. Sure, I ran too much and lifted weights until I couldn't lift my hand. This was nothing new. The difference was, I wasn't eating enough. I forced myself to eat as much as I could, because without it, I wouldn't be able to run or lift weights or heal when I cut myself. Half the time, though, I barely got food past my lips before I started puking it back up. Didn't exactly make the idea of food enticing.

Then there were the nightmares. I never needed as much sleep as humans did. I slept shorter and deeper. Lately, I dreaded the moment sleep overtook me. It was a constant shadow hanging over me, the knowledge that eventually, I would need to sleep, I would need to eat. I avoided it until I couldn't anymore. And I knew the effects were beginning to show.

Show. My skin going cold, I clenched my fists to keep my hands from wandering to my lower belly, which was the only spot on me that carried extra weight. It wasn't much, but I could tell there was a paunch. I didn't want to admit to myself why that was. Fortunately, the extra-large hoodie that I wore twenty-four seven hid that. For now.

I forced myself back to the current conversation. "Thanks for trying to teach me," I said.

She smiled. "Not trying. I am teaching you."

I looked at the product of my labor – two lumpy rows. Which were bright pink, because apparently, that was the only color of yarn Finn could find. Yeah, right. More like it was the most obnoxious color Finn could find.

"Something else people like to do when they knit," Smack said. "People talk. It's called stitch-n-bitch, and it's a whole thing. Like a movement or some shit." She shrugged and muttered, "White people." She said it with the same unfathomability that I sometimes said, *Humans.* "That's probably something else Sankha Finn was hoping for. That you'd talk."

I swallowed, feeling a little claustrophobic. Maybe it was time for a run. "Talk, sure, well, maybe next time. Thanks again." I started moving toward the door. As soon as she was gone, I could change into running clothes. I knew it was a bad idea, but I needed it. Too much feeling building up like steam.

She studied me with an intensity that made my skin crawl a little. It was the same sort of intense stare that, when it came from our head honcho, Janus, it meant he was reading my mind. Smack couldn't read minds. At least, not as far as I knew. Just as I was about to kick her out of my cabin, the door opened. Tony walked in.

Fuck. He would put up a stink if I told him I was going running. He was even more worried about my weight loss than Finn, probably because I wasn't doing a good job of hiding how much puking I was doing.

He smiled and said hi to Smack, and he greeted Galen, who trotted over to say hello. Then Tony stared at the knitting sticks and Pepto-bismal yarn on the table. He glanced up at me, one eyebrow cocked.

I shrugged. "Finn said it's relaxing and I need an outlet."

His mouth did that twisty-turny dance that meant he was trying not to burst out laughing.

"Bite me." I picked up the knitting junk and threw it in the bottom drawer of my dresser.

"We'll try again tomorrow, 'kay, Sankha Kellan? G'night." Smack eased out the door.

"Smack's teaching you to knit." Tony pulled a chair out from the table and plopped down into it. He sighed and rubbed the back of his neck. He was wearing a black slouchy hat. For the first time, I wondered if someone made the hat for him.

He looked exhausted. Before Christmas, I would've gone over to him, maybe rubbed his shoulders or kissed his cheek. I was getting better at touching and being touched, despite my Disorder, which was how I referred to PTSD. But now, I didn't dare move. I didn't want him to touch me, because then he might figure it out.

Instead, I just itched to go for a run. I didn't move, because I didn't want to argue. Especially since the dinner discussion was coming up next.

"You eat yet?" he said. Yup, there it was.

"No." I walked over to the television and popped a DVD in the player, one of my zombie DVDs. Zombie shows relaxed me. I didn't try to explain it. I just went with what worked.

Zombie shows also had the added benefit of grossing Tony out, thereby postponing the dinner discussion for a bit. Or usually, they did. Not so tonight.

"All right," Tony said, pushing to his feet. "I'll go get something for you from the mess hall. Gina made vegetarian chili and this spicy black bean soup. There's about four hundred loaves of fresh-baked bread, too. I bet I can steal a couple of those for us to keep here. Which soup sounds good to you?" He waited for my answer, a stubborn look on his face that said there would be an answer, if he had to drag it out of me.

Soup, sawdust, what was the difference? I gritted my teeth and said, "Surprise me."

"Okay, both then." His fake-chipper tone made me growl. "I'll be back in a few minutes."

"Can't wait." The second he was out the door, I pulled out my running shoes. I didn't take time to change clothes, just switched from my hiking boots to running shoes and hit the track. Not that we had a track, we just had a dirt path that the younglings ran, a figure-eight around two of the practice yards. Younglings kept it shoveled in the winter, so while there was a little ice on the path, it was free of snow. The practice yards were old horse paddocks, both fairly large, so one figure-eight came to about a half-mile. Galen and I were on our third figure eight by the time Tony caught up to us.

He came running up the track from the opposite direction, planting himself in my path. I didn't see him coming, because my vision was going grey around the edges and it took all my energy just to keep moving forward. As a result, I skidded to a stop just before slamming into him. "I just – need – a run," I spat out between heaving breaths. My knees felt way too wobbly. Passing out would not help my case.

"Did you eat lunch?" Tony glared at me. "Gina said you didn't come up for anything today."

"I – had a protein bar." The grey edges of my vision were turning black. Rage flared at the knowledge that he was checking up on me. That they were conspiring to –

To what? Feed me? Jesus. I was really fucked up.

When the rage left in a whoosh, I was left feeling weak, cold and empty. Not cold because the air was about twenty-two degrees. Cold inside. I forced out grown-up words. "I've asked you not to do that. Check up on me."

"Yeah? Well, I asked you not to consider a protein bar a meal." His shoulders slumped a little, and I knew he was tired. Tired from working all day in the cold, teaching younglings, and also, tired of me.

"I just forgot," I lied.

His jaw clenched. He knew I was lying. All he said was, "Let's go. The bread smells really good. It's got cinnamon and raisins and nuts in it. I grabbed some butter for it."

The idea of raisins made me gag a little. Why? Who the fuck knew? I couldn't explain the things happening in my body right now. I did my best to hide the gag, to hide everything going on inside me in that moment. "Sure." I clucked my tongue at Galen, took a step into the snow, and promptly fell flat on my face. My legs just gave out. Shit.

Galen nudged me with his nose, his way of telling me to get up. Tony stood there for a second, staring down at me. Almost like he was debating whether to help me up or just leave me there to freeze. Then he reached down, took my hand, and pulled me to my feet. Too fast, because it made my head swim. He held onto my arm until I was steadier. My cheeks heated with shame, but I needed the help.

He waited until we were walking again to say, "Guess maybe a real lunch would've been a good idea, after all."

I clenched my jaw and swallowed the *fuck you* that begged to be said. I didn't want to fight anymore. I really didn't. Sometimes, though, it was easier to fight than to face the worry that he wore like a cheap cologne these days.

Back at the cabin, Tony warmed bowls of soup for each of us in the microwave. I made coffee, then sliced the bread and slathered butter on four thick slices. Two for each of us. We sat at the table and ate quietly. It was a struggle. I waited too long between meals. I noticed that I had a threshold, and once I crossed that threshold, if I tried to eat, everything made me gag. It took everything I had not to vomit.

I started to feel better as I finished my bowl of soup. Tony looked like he was about to fall asleep in his chair, and the last of the anger, the fight, left me. "How'd it go today?" I asked quietly.

"Hmm?" He blinked at me like he forgot I knew how to speak. "Today. Um, good. The archery class got cut short when Tia got scared and ran away again. Something about the arrows flying around freaks her out. It's the third time it's happened."

The black bean soup was actually good. So spicy that I forgot it was food. I served myself seconds. Tony raised his eyebrows, but wisely didn't say anything. "So let her quit archery for a while. She's what, seven? She's so itty-bitty, she probably can't even draw a bow."

"She can't. But Valentine is really good at archery." He sighed and stared at his food, not like he was seeing it, like he was judging whether the bread would make a comfy pillow. "Tia insists on being wherever Valentine is. She's gotten really clingy lately."

Valentine was Tia's sister. Or at least, that's what they told us. They were living together in a squat in Atlanta when we found them, so they might actually be related. It was also possible they simply glommed onto one another because they didn't have anyone else.

"After class, Valentine asked me if she could quit archery." He rubbed the back of his neck again. It was his tell, the sign that he was drained mentally and physically. He looked like he aged twenty years in the last month. The last month since Christmas. The cold inside me thawed further, as I felt a pull to help him.

"Maybe I could work with them one-on-one. Two on one. Whatever," I said. The surprise on his face made me feel ashamed, because I knew how selfish I'd been. Pulling away from him, letting things get so out of control. The shame made me start to babble. "I mean, that way, there wouldn't be as many people or arrows. And maybe she wouldn't get so scared. That way, Valentine can keep learning. I know I'm not as good at archery as you or some of the other instructors –"

"Kellan, that's a great idea. I'll go talk to Finn about it after dinner." Tony smiled, and I thought some of that sudden aging fell away. He grabbed a piece of bread and ate it in three bites. The bread was really good, as long as I didn't think about the raisins. Just that thought made my gorge rise, but I managed to swallow and set down the rest of my slice normally, not like it just bit me. I went for more soup instead. No raisins in there.

His smile broadened, and my shame deepened. "I'm sorry," I mumbled.

The smile disappeared. "For what?" His tone implied that there were so many things I should be apologizing for, he didn't want to guess which one I referred to.

"I've been a butthead."

He laughed, and I wondered when the last time was that I heard that laugh. "No, Kell, you haven't. I appreciate you saying that, though. It's been a rough few weeks."

Like Finn, he didn't ask the question, and like with Finn, I could feel the weight of the question hanging between us. *What happened?* I didn't owe Finn an explanation. I probably owed Tony one. "I just…" I couldn't tell him. *I think I might be…* Fuck. No. I couldn't tell him that. He didn't want to have children. He said it before, multiple times. And what if it wasn't his baby? What if it belonged to…? No. I couldn't tell him. So I used another incident that happened around the same time. "I started having more flashbacks."

"I noticed." His tone was a little wry and a lot cautious.

I cleared my throat and started to shred my piece of bread. That made me think of my friend Darcy, who had a tendency to shred whatever was at hand when he was nervous. Darcy was an outsider, a human who ended up becoming my packmate after I saved his life. Normally, thinking about Darcy made me feel warm and fuzzy inside. This time, my brain took a different road. I thought instead of the psycho faery who was hunting him last year, which made me think of the reason for my Disorder: I volunteered to be Aza the psycho's victim for two months, so that he would leave Darcy alone. Let's just say that, as a shape-shifter who could heal almost any damage Aza inflicted, I was a much more appealing victim than a human like Darcy. Aza leapt at the chance, especially since I was the daughter and heir of the king of the faeries, whom Aza hated. It was a win-win for him. Not so much for me.

And now, I was fairly sure I was…god, I couldn't even think it, much less say it. And the fucking kicker was, I really wasn't sure who the, well, who the father was. There was a chance it was Aza. And if it was Aza's…shit, I might just have to kill myself.

I looked at Tony, feeling the bleak emptiness yawn inside me. He wouldn't push, as much as he wanted to know why the setback happened. But he put up with me and never stopped trying to help me, no matter how awful I was. And I could be pretty awful when I wanted to be. So I owed him something, even if I couldn't tell him the whole truth. "You know how we had a bunch of Sankhain come home for Christmas?"

He started to nod, then went utterly still. "Did one of them do something?"

"What? No. Fuck, no." Christmas was like a family reunion. Most of the Sankhain lived away from the forest, traveling around to monitor supernatural activity across the country and keep their ears peeled for the slightest rumor about the existence of the Spring. I normally loved it, getting to see friends that I missed. This year... "It wasn't like that. It was just so stupid."

I could see tension at the corners of his mouth, his eyes. He was having a harder and harder time staying silent, not asking questions. I knew I was really torturing him with this slow release of information. All he said, though, was, "If it affected you, it wasn't stupid."

"Yes, it was!" It was, really, and yes, it triggered some flashbacks and nightmares, but that would all have happened anyway because what if it was Aza's...offspring inside me? *Fuck.* "All that happened was, Paul was wearing cologne. It...it was the same cologne Aza likes to wear. And I smelled it, and..."

He closed his eyes. Was he going to call bullshit on me? What about the vomiting, the fact that I insisted on wearing a bra to bed now, not because I felt more secure like I let him believe, but because my breasts were too sensitive to go without support for even short periods? What about the fact that I hadn't needed a tampon in months? My period was more like a wolf's than a human's, only happening once or twice a year, but still. We lived together, he must've noticed. No way he was going to believe that this was all that was bothering me.

He opened his eyes. "Kellan, I'm so sorry."

Tony's scent always reminded me of fresh-baked bread. He didn't smell like the spice of anger, frustration or even annoyance. He smelled like the sourdough of worry, the cinnamon sweetness of compassion, the almost-nothing white-bread scent of grief.

I didn't know what to think, much less what to say. He actually bought it. That this was all that was wrong. I should've let it go, let it lie and thanked my lucky stars, but I wasn't that smart. "It was just a smell. That's all. And I've been horrible to you, to everyone, ever since. I'm a fucking menace."

"Kell —" His voice sounded dangerously thick, and I caught the scent of tears. Was this the part where he told me he'd had enough? That he was walking away, he was leaving me? If so, then he better not fucking cry while he did it. No fucking way I was going to feel sorry for him as he walked out the door. "Jesus, Kell, I'm sorry I didn't put it together. Smell triggers memories like nothing else, and for you, with your nose...Jesus. No wonder you've been in so much pain."

He started to get up, then stopped himself and closed his eyes again. I knew what that meant. He wanted to touch me, and he was stopping himself. Because I didn't let him touch me anymore, for fear he'd figure out what I was really hiding. Fucking hell.

He wouldn't be able to tell I was pregnant by touching me. As long as he didn't go near my stomach, it would be fine. I forced myself to stand. Forced myself to walk around the small table, stand by his chair, lean down, wrap my arms around his shoulders, an awkward motion made all the more awkward because he was once again utterly still. Afraid to move, as if the slightest reaction would spook me. I hated that. But part of me was also grateful, because it meant I could touch him without worrying about him taking it any further. I wasn't sure I could afford to go any further.

I released him, walked back to my chair, sat down and shoved a spoonful of soup past my teeth. I didn't look at him. While I wasn't sure what I was afraid of, fear was definitely the prevailing emotion.

"I'm sorry I've been pushing you so much," Tony said.

That shocked me, because he didn't have anything to apologize for. I really needed this conversation to be a little less intense, so I said, "Yeah, you've really been a dick." Then I snorted.

Tony must've understood why I said that, because he then changed the subject. "How's Darcy doing?"

"Good, I think." This time, the reminder of Darcy made me smile. Maybe because it was Tony asking and not me remembering. Darcy was a librarian who stumbled into a supernatural shitstorm last spring. He was also an endangered species – a genuinely nice person who said please and thank you and gosh. And he was an alcoholic. "He says he's been going to meetings and he found a sponsor and all that shit. He's at a library conference this week. Whatever the fuck that is."

"Probably a bunch of people talking about books. Sounds right up his alley." He smiled.

When the food was gone, I felt like I should thank Tony for bringing it home. I tried to find a way to say thank you without actually having to say it. I failed, so I said, "Thanks. For the food. And stuff." And stuff like pushing me, making me stop my run and eat, listening to my crazy talk and acting like it wasn't crazy at all.

"You're welcome," he said nonchalantly, and he started to reach for the bowls.

"Nope, I got cleanup. Why don't you relax?" I carried the dishes to the sink and started rinsing them.

"I should go talk to Finn," he said.

"Stop it. Just relax." Standing at the sink, I watched him out of the corner of my eye. He didn't get up from the table, though he did lean back in his chair and close his eyes. I felt that pull inside me again, like I wanted to help him. Like I wanted to make him feel better. I set down the bowl I was holding and walked over to him.

I started to massage his neck and shoulders. He tended to bunch up his shoulders when he was stressed, so they always needed loosening up. And as a shape-shifter, I possessed enough strength to give really good shoulder rubs.

At first, he tensed, once again like he didn't want to spook the wild Kellan. Very quickly, though, he started to melt. He slid down in his chair until he was about ready to slide off. I smiled as his scent went from tired, bland whole wheat bread to something sweeter, warmer. "Thank you," he said, and his voice was thick like he was already half asleep.

I leaned down and kissed the top of his hat. It was like I was scared of what would happen if I kissed his skin. Not because I didn't want to. Because I did. I wanted so much to relish every inch of him. But I couldn't. It was irrational, but I genuinely feared that physical contact would give away my secret. And if he found out, he might leave me. He felt very strongly about people who should never have children. And while he never said anything about me being one of them, I mean, come on. I didn't take a shower without a knife on me. Baby, me? Shit, no.

I hated that a kiss on the hat was as good as it got, but there you have it. Shit happened and changed the way the world worked. I lived two centuries so far, and world-changing shit was one of the few constants.

"Go get some sleep," I said softly, like a loud word might break the tenuous bond. It was barely nine o'clock, but Tony was up really early that morning to teach. He nodded and stumbled to the bed. He didn't even bother to change clothes, just kicked off his boots and crawled under the covers.

Tony understood how Aza changed me, because he came from his own nightmare. The son of a crack addict who sold him to her dealer for drugs, he ended up in the hands of a sadistic pimp for several years. Then we found him. Without him, I probably would've found a way to kill myself at some point in the past few months. He stayed through a whole shitstorm of trauma. But this might be the one thing that pushed him too far, made him leave. I couldn't risk that. Not yet.

Galen must've smelled a change in my mood, because he leaned up against my leg. When I looked down at him, he was gazing up at me with big, soulful brown eyes. I smiled and he wagged his tail. All better? No. A little better? Definitely.

Chapter 2

KELLAN

Once Tony was snoring loudly, dead to the world, I took the dirty dishes and my dog and headed for the mess hall. I wanted some quiet, some space. Just me, my dog, and the thing growing in my uterus.

I left a note for Tony, so he wouldn't think I was trying to sneak in a run. The mess hall was locked between meals, but I had a key. All the Sankhain had keys to the mess hall and the other buildings. And since we taught the younglings to pick locks, the lock on the mess hall was kind of pointless. Humans, however, have this thing about principles. It's the principle of the thing, Kellan. It's dumb, was always my response. Of course, a lot of human quirks were dumb. At least, from a wolf's point of view.

I put the dishes in the huge kitchen sink, which was full of soapy water and soaking pots. Then, after a stop at the bathroom, my eight hundredth pee for the day, I started a pot of coffee. I could've had coffee in our cabin, but the sound of Mr. Coffee would've woken Tony up. He needed to sleep. So Galen and I settled in the dining room at one of the tables with a steaming mug and a plate of fudge-striped cookies.

Should I be drinking coffee? Caffeine was bad for pregnant women, wasn't it? Fuck that. There was no way I was going to survive without coffee. Maybe that was one of those fads, like how they could never decide if butter is good or bad for you. What did humans know about that shit, anyway?

The dining hall was never quiet at meal times. After hours like this, it was almost eerie. The haunted dining hall. I drank my coffee and petted Galen and tried not to think about anything. I let my mind wander. Maybe running didn't count if I ran in my wolf form. Maybe Tony wouldn't mind that. I laughed a little at the mental image of the conversation where I tried to justify that.

Quickly, though, my mind started down a familiar path. What if this thing inside me belonged to Aza? Could I live with that? I mean, truly. Being a responsible parent was probably beyond me anyway. Could I really manage to raise a baby that came from *him*?

I didn't know. And that was the number one reason why I didn't want to talk to anyone about it. I could tell myself all I wanted that I was worried Tony would leave because he didn't want kids. But that wasn't the problem, not really. Tony would never abandon a child. Aza was, and always would be, the boogeyman lurking in the shadows. And once I said those words out loud – "I'm pregnant and it might be Aza's baby" – I would have to deal with those words. All of them.

I suddenly felt chilled and alone, despite Galen and the coffee. Even though I didn't want to say those words out loud, even though I wasn't sure I wanted to say anything out loud, I pulled out my cell phone and hit Darcy's name on my favorites list. While the phone rang, I refilled my mug with fresh, steaming brew. I took a sip just as a sleepy voice on the other end of the line said, "H'llo?"

"Oh, shit, were you sleeping?" I glanced at the clock on the wall. It was only 10:00. Darcy was usually up much later than this.

"Mmm. That's okay." I heard a rustling, and pictured him sitting up in bed. "It's always good to hear from you."

"You're the only person in the world who ever says that to me." The knowledge that he was sincere when he said it, too, managed to warm me when the coffee could not.

"I doubt that." I was pretty sure I could hear him smiling.

"No, it's true, trust me. Anyway, how are you? How's the library conference thing?"

"Good. Really good. There was a cocktail thing tonight, though, so I just went back to my room. I was reading and must've dozed off." He started to talk about books and AI and e-books and other things that I didn't care about at all, except that he cared about them, so I tried to listen. "And because we already have to screen constantly for self-published books, now the idea that we'll be dealing with books generated by AI, too, has people all up in arms."

I tried to picture librarians up in arms. Would they be toting machine guns? Or wooden rulers and extra-heavy books?

"But you didn't call to hear me jabber on about that stuff." Darcy's voice softened, like he thought there was some other reason why I called.

Darcy didn't know about the...in my uterus, either, but he knew something was up, just like Tony did. The urge to spill was much stronger with Darcy, because I knew he didn't have a personal stake in the outcome the way Tony would. But Darcy was a great listener and often gave solid advice, which was a problem for me, because I knew what his advice would be. *You have to tell Tony*. I didn't want to hear that, so I didn't tell him.

"No, I didn't really have a reason for calling," I lied. "Tony asked me how you were doing, and that made me want to talk to you. That's all."

He was quiet for a minute. "You should talk to Tony about what's going on."

What? I didn't tell Darcy anything, precisely so I wouldn't have to listen to that advice. A growl rumbled in my chest. "I did talk to him tonight."

"If you told him all of what's bothering you, then you wouldn't be hiding it from me still." Darcy was entirely too smugly smart for a human.

"Whatever. Listen, I'm glad your conference is going well. And I'm proud of you for skipping the cocktail thing."

I heard a sigh, then the sound of water being poured. Probably making a cup of tea. Darcy liked tea. It was one of those weird quirks that I learned to tolerate, despite my assertion that leaves should never be boiled in any context.

"Tony loves you, Kellan, and he wants to be there for you."

I scowled. "Have you two been talking?"

"No, but I know him well enough to know that. Whatever it is, he would want to help. Just like I do." The gentleness in his voice made my throat close up and tears prickle my eyes again.

I cleared my throat and downed a gulp of hot coffee to wash away the lump. "What kind of tea are you drinking?" An artless change of subject, but I really didn't want to talk about me anymore.

"Chamomile, of course."

"Did you bring it with you, or did the hotel provide it?"

"The hotel only provides Lipton. That stuff is end-of-the-world stock, not late night comfort."

"End of the world stock?" I found myself smiling again.

"Yeah, you know. If there was a cataclysmic event and all the good tea was destroyed, I would drink Lipton if it was the only tea left on Earth. But that doesn't mean I would like it."

"Oh, okay, I get it. Like instant coffee."

"Does instant coffee taste like boiled socks?" He sounded curious, not at all sarcastic. One of the many things I loved about Darcy was that he asked questions like that with a genuine desire to learn the answer.

"More like motor oil scraped off the pavement."

"Ah. Well, Lipton tastes like boiled socks."

"And Lipton doesn't make chamomile?"

"No, they make Lipton," he said solemnly. "Actually, that's not true. They do have a line of herbal teas. But I've never been brave enough to try them."

I laughed. "Well, good thing you brought your own."

We talked a little while longer, long enough for Darcy to drink his tea and me to polish off the last of the pot of coffee. By that time, I had to pee again, and I also remembered my promise to Tony that I would talk to Janus and Finn about working with Valentine and Tia. "I should go, I told Tony I'd talk to Janus about me doing some individual instruction with a couple of the younglings."

"Really?" The disbelief in his voice made me growl again.

"Yes, really."

"You just haven't mentioned doing anything like that in…" His voice trailed off. Either he was trying to remember the last time I stepped out of my self-involved funk, or he was realizing there was no way to end that comment that didn't make me sound like a selfish bitch.

Whichever it was, he wasn't wrong. "Yeah, I know. I guess it's time to pull my head out of my ass."

"I'm proud of you, too, Kellan."

And just like that, I was all choked up again. "Okay. I better go."

"Talk to you soon."

"Yep. Soon. G'night." We hung up.

I hit the bathroom again, washed the coffee pot and added my dishes to those soaking in the sink. Then I stepped outside, locking the mess hall behind me, with Galen by my side. I was heading to Janus's cabin, when I saw one of the younglings leaving the cabin I shared with Tony.

If it had been anyone else in that cabin, I would've worried that a Sankha was sleeping with a youngling. Since it was Tony, I knew there had to be a good reason why a youngling would be visiting his cabin at eleven o'clock at night. Janus could wait. I detoured back to my cabin.

Galen and I walked in the door to find Tony searching frantically for something. "Where is it?" he muttered over and over.

"Hey, what's wrong?"

He turned to look at me, and I could tell from his eyes that he wasn't fully awake. He had that uber-panicky, bleary look that meant he'd woken suddenly from a sound sleep and couldn't quite shake the nightmare.

Something about seeing me seemed to help him wake up. He blinked a few times, rubbed his hands over his scalp, and took a deep breath. "Kell."

Well, he recognized me, at least. I repeated my question. "What's wrong?"

"I – um, it's Smack. She – something – um, happened." It wasn't sleepiness stopping him from speaking. I was almost certain he was about to tell me what happened, then stopped himself short.

Which meant it was something bad, if Tony didn't want to betray the younglings' confidence.

"I can't find my hat," he said. I could smell the panic edging back up again.

"Tony, sit." Yes, I gave him the order in exactly the same voice I would've said it to Galen. And both males gratifyingly obeyed. Galen plopped his butt on the floor, and Tony sat down on the bed. "Good. Now, talk."

"I – I have to..." His voice trailed off.

"Is Smack in the bunkhouse?" The younglings had two bunkhouses, one for boys and one for girls.

He hesitated, and from the pained expression on his face, I guessed he was trying to evaluate how much to tell me. "Yes."

"Male Sankhain aren't allowed in the girls' bunk. I'll go."

"But –"

I growled, getting impatient. "What happened?"

"I – she – fuck." He slumped. "She tried to slit her wrists."

"WHAT?" That was impossible. I just saw Smack, four hours ago. What could've changed in four hours to make her...? She seemed fine.

"Valentine bound the wounds and sent Tia to get help. Tia – she came to me."

Gradually, Tony's dilemma sunk in. The girls entrusted him with this situation, and him alone. His personal moral code dictated that he be the one to help. Tony wasn't a delegator. We didn't have time for moral codes.

The problem was, Tony was much better at fragile situations than I was. And if this was true – how could it be true, I just saw Smack, she was just here – the situation was about as fragile as it got.

"All right," I said. "I'll go get Simone, and –" Simone was our healer. She could take care of any wounds.

"No!" He smelled so much like fear, like I was holding a knife to his throat. He still wasn't a hundred percent awake. "They – they don't want Simone. She'll have to report it to Finn. Finn will..."

What did he think Finn would do? As far as I could tell, the worst Finn was likely to do was say something completely insensitive and make Smack want to turn the knife on him. Time to cut through the bullshit. "Tony, we have two options. We both sit here and do nothing, or I go to the girls' bunk. You can't go. That's nonnegotiable." I gave him a second to think about it. "I'm going." I hesitated, then leaned over and gave him a quick hug. I felt like a douchebag – I should've kissed him, I knew that, but a hug was better than nothing. I hoped.

"Text me." He looked up at me with big, sad eyes, and I could smell that strong sourdough scent of his worry.

"I will," I said, and ran out.

Chapter 3

KELLAN

I double-timed it to the girls' bunkhouse, Galen at my heels. The building was about as elaborate as the name "bunkhouse" implied. Another log cabin, but about three times the length of the other cabins. It slept twenty girls. Not that we had twenty female younglings at the moment. I was pretty sure there were six, but I couldn't swear to it. Numbers weren't my thing.

The second I entered the bunk, I could smell the blood. Not a lot of blood, though. Not a life-threatening amount. And it was definitely Smack's blood. Her blood smelled a little different than the typical human's – a little too sweet, like she had some fey in her.

I felt my eyes heat, and I knew they were glowing as my enhanced night vision kicked in. Once my eyes adjusted, I saw a small cluster of bodies around one of the beds in the far corner. The bunks closest to the door were always empty. Younglings – and Sankhain, for that matter – tended to prioritize safety over ease of access.

"Girls?" I said quietly, not wanting to startle them.

They jumped anyway. "Um, Sankha Kellan." It was Gina, and I relaxed instantly. If Gina was here, she could handle the majority of the tears and wailing. I could focus on sorting things out.

"You're a Sankha now, too, Gina, you don't have to call me that anymore." Why would they ask both Gina and Tony to come to the bunkhouse? Especially since Tony wasn't even allowed in the building. Maybe two of the girls went looking for a sympathetic Sankha, and Gina got there first? Gina and Smack were close friends, so that made sense, but none of that changed the fact that Tony couldn't enter the bunkhouse. Maybe Tia forgot.

It also didn't escape my notice that the Sankhain they approached for help were the two newest. Tony became a Sankha barely a year ago, and Gina only passed her tests in November. Did they think Tony and Gina were most likely to be good allies, since they were younglings themselves not that long ago?

I approached the group, sorting through scents as I did. There was surprisingly little fear, although I could smell a fair amount of worry. That told me I was right about the amount of blood - Smack wasn't in danger of bleeding out. "I heard you might need some help with bandages."

"We don't need help." That was Smack's voice. I felt anger flare. This was why Tony didn't want me here. Anger was my go-to emotion. Only helpful in very select situations. Probably not in this one, so I did my best to tamp it down.

"Well, too late," I said. "I'm here. Might as well take a look. Girls, I'm going to turn on the light."

Galen bore down on the group of girls. Little Tia skittered away, but the others offered him a pat or a hello. He headed straight to Smack, and with typical doggy certainty that he could help, he stuck his head in her lap. She stroked his head, because it was impossible not to.

When I reached the group, I took stock of Smack's wrists. Clumsily bandaged in roughly five hundred yards of gauze, her arms looked a healthy color, and she appeared alert, if a little agitated. Not shocky. All good news.

I did, however, see blood on her sheets, and a knife lay on her bedside table, not discarded, but carefully centered. Like the person who put it there expected the table to be jarred and didn't want the knife to fall and hurt anyone. This was no accident.

I stared at that knife like I never saw one before. It wasn't the first time a youngling hurt herself. They came to us with a lot of traumatic baggage. But it was the first time I was the one called to the scene. This really wasn't my bag. I always heard about it later, from the more emotionally evolved Sankha who handled the situation. I didn't know what to do. Should I take the blade? Hide it from sight and pretend it never existed? Forbid Smack from ever handling sharp objects again?

I chose a different route. Picking up the knife, I assessed it. "Well, if you want to slit your wrists, I probably wouldn't choose a paring knife." Beside me, Gina made a strangled sound, but she didn't try to stop me, so I kept going. "I mean, I suppose this'll do in a pinch for stabbing someone in the neck, but it's way too dull to really get the job done in this case. You'll probably get bored with the whole thing before you manage to hit a vein."

I set the knife back on the table, placing it carefully just so. Then I looked around and saw identical shocked and angry faces glaring back at me. Except Smack's. She scowled, but also nodded slightly, as if acknowledging my point.

"I think what she means," Gina began, but I interrupted.

"I really thought we taught you better than that, but oh, well." Ignoring glares and mutterings, I focused on Smack's reaction, which this time was a snort of almost-laughter. "I'd like to look at your arms now."

Smack tensed, casting sidelong glances at the other girls without actually moving her head.

I took that to mean she didn't want an audience for this part. How could I get them all to leave? With a bright smile that matched nothing in the room, I looked at Gina. "Hey, listen, I'm starving. Is there any more of that bread, the one with the raisins in it?" Just the word raisins made me gag. Being knocked up was so much fun.

Gina hesitated. Probably didn't want to leave me alone with Smack for fear I'd give her wrist-slitting lessons. I looked Gina in the eye and wished she was a dog so I could communicate nonverbally. But she wasn't, so I hoped the steady eye contact showed her I was in alpha mode and not about to let anything happen to one of my cubs. Gina took a deep breath, and though she didn't sound happy, she said, "Yes, of course. There's plenty."

"Great. Maybe you ladies could go and get some for us? And maybe on the way back, you could stop at the infirmary and pick up more gauze. Looks like you used up your whole first aid kit with this, um, spectacular bandaging job." I tried to telepathically convey to Gina that I was going to call Simone. The girls didn't want that, but this was bigger than my limited capabilities. I doubted Gina got the message, although looking at Valentine, I got the eerie feeling that she heard my thoughts. I wasn't sure if I liked Valentine or found her creepy. It was about fifty-fifty. "Thanks, ladies."

I turned back to Smack and listened for their departure.

They left, taking their glares and mutterings with them. With not a small amount of relief, I breathed a sigh. I didn't like an audience, either. "All right. Just give me a second." I pulled out my phone and sent a text to Simone, the Sankhain healer. *Girls coming to get gauze. Need you to come back to bunkhouse with them.* "Can I sit down? It'll be easier to look at your arms." I was dying to demand what the fuck happened, but I forced myself to focus on other things.

Smack shrugged and shifted slightly to the side, making room for me on the bed. Now that it was just the two of us, I could smell the sourness of her shame. I really wanted to know what happened between our little knitting lesson and now. Or did nothing happen? Was she planning this even as she patiently tried to teach me how to cast on stitches?

I pushed the questions away and started to unwrap the gauze. It took a few minutes. I could've tried to cut it, but it was wrapped so tight around her arm, I probably would've cut her in the process. She'd spilled enough blood for one night. When I got to the last layer, I saw the girls hadn't applied any ointment or padding, so the blood stuck the gauze to the skin like someone superglued it there. My stomach flopped over like a dying fish as I looked up at Smack. "This is going to hurt." The thought of causing her pain made the ever-present nausea rise.

She returned my gaze with eyes so tired and dead. Those eyes scared me more than the blood, more than the knife, more than the act she committed. Those eyes said, What could you do to me that's worse than what's already been done?

They also said, I'm going to try this again as soon as you leave.

Fuck. What happened? I should ask, I knew I needed to ask, but I was so scared that the answer would be more than I could handle. I should've brought Tony with me, rules be damned.

My stomach flopped again. "I know. Come with me over to the sink. We'll run some warm water over it. It'll loosen up the gauze. Come on."

"Just rip it off." Her voice, dead as her eyes, was barely audible. Usually, when Smack spoke that softly, it was a scathing insult or commentary on the stupidity of her superiors. I wanted to do something stupid, just so she'd say something Smack-like.

Instead, I led her over to the sink. I couldn't just rip those bandages off. Turning on the water, I let it run until it was a nice lukewarm temperature. Then I held her wrists under the spray and gently worked the bandages until they came away from her skin.

As I expected, the cuts were ragged and raw. The paring knife made a pulpy mess of her skin. Smack might not have succeeded in her efforts, but not for lack of trying. I swallowed hard. It bled a little as the bandages came off. None of the cuts were deep, though, other than a puncture on her right wrist.

"You were right. I got tired of not getting anywhere, so I tried poking a hole." Smack spoke so quietly, a human wouldn't be able to hear her. I could barely hear her with my wolf hearing.

I glanced over at the knife with its sharp tip. I didn't want to react, but I also didn't want to ignore her words. "I'm guessing that's where most of the blood came from." It was too big. Like maybe she stabbed herself and then twisted the knife. I tasted bile in my mouth and hoped to god that Smack wouldn't see any change in my expression.

"Yeah."

"All right." I tried to think of something to say. What would Tony say? What would Darcy say? Shitfuckmotherfucker. Yeah, probably not that. "Let's change your sheets. Unless you want to switch to a different bunk for tonight?"

A shrug. The most apathetic shrug I ever saw, and I worked with abused teenage runaways on a daily basis for years, so I saw more than my share of apathy.

"Yeah, let's just get those sheets changed. We can swap out the sheets with one of the bunks that isn't being used, and I'll get those dirty ones soaking overnight." Overnight? Over the next week? Shit, maybe we should just burn them and be done with it.

The girls didn't go to Simone because they wanted to keep this quiet. They didn't want the higher-ups to know. One, because the younglings operated like a pack of their own. Close ranks and handle problems themselves. But also because younglings that chose suicide over asking for help could be ostracized. Not intentionally. But Sankhain culture valued toughness, strength, the ability to fight through anything. If word got out that Smack tried to end things, she would be treated differently. Like she was less than she was. It was wrong in all kinds of ways, but life tended to be that way.

People were going to find out. The camp had one laundry facility. There was no way to keep this blood a secret in the washroom. And the problem with burning the sheets was fire tended to attract attention. If I started a bonfire without clearing it with Finn first, he'd hustle over to see what the hell was going on. And if I tried to hide them, either in my cabin or my truck, I risked someone seeing me carrying bloody sheets. Nope, people were going to find out.

I reached a decision. "Smack, I texted Simone. She's going to be with the girls when they come back."

She looked at me with those dead eyes again and muttered, "Course you did that. Traitor."

I ignored the accusation and forged ahead. "Look, I'm shit with first aid, and judging by the bandaging job your friends did, they're not much better. They get high marks for quantity of gauze, but that's about it. Simone will fix you up, and she can take the sheets and soak them in the infirmary. No one else needs to know they came from your bed."

Smack smelled a little less empty. A little more like the heat of anger. Was that good or bad? I continued my one-sided conversation. "We're going to have to report this to Janus. With his mind-reading abilities, he'd figure it out anyway. But I think it would be better if you and I go to him together. I can be a buffer. And it'll all go over better if we volunteer the information, rather than waiting for him to find out some other way. He'll respect that honesty." I hoped. "How does that sound?"

She shrugged again, though the anger scent grew stronger.

"All right, well, you can think about that while Simone fixes you up." I was really beginning to hate the sound of my own voice. Maybe that's why Smack's scent kept getting angrier – she was tired of listening to me, too.

Fortunately, the other girls and Simone burst through the door at that moment, saving me from spouting more inane chatter. As the girls sniped at one another – they seemed to be blaming each other for catching Simone's attention when they tried to sneak into the infirmary – Simone looked around, taking in the scene with the efficiency of a six-hundred-year old healer. As she led Smack over to a bunk, she said to me, "You should go outside."

The look she gave me told me there was something outside that needed to be dealt with. "All right. I'll be back and we can decide what to do next, okay, Smack?" I didn't expect an answer, which was good, because I didn't get one.

Even before I stepped outside, I knew by the scent in the air why Simone sent me out. Tony paced at the edge of the forest, far enough away that he wouldn't call attention to the girls' bunkhouse, while still close enough to keep an eye on the place. I could see from the jerkiness of his movements that he was half frozen.

I trotted over, Galen at my side. "What are you doing?"

"I – is she okay?" He wasn't wearing a hat. He wasn't even wearing a heavy coat, just a hoodie and a down vest. Drinking from the Spring didn't protect him against hypothermia or frostbite.

I bit my tongue, literally, because it was the only way to prevent myself from saying something mean, like, Do you see a body bag? He was being nice. He was being Tony. He couldn't go inside, so he held a vigil outside. That was what he needed to do. But for fuck's sake, the wind chill had to be below zero at this point.

When I trusted myself to speak, I unclenched my jaw and allowed words to come out. "She's going to live. Which I would've told you the second I could send you a text." I wasn't just angry at him for taking such poor care of himself. I was also, I realized, more than a little hurt that he didn't trust me to handle the situation. I couldn't blame him – I didn't trust myself to handle it. His lack of faith in me still hurt, though.

"Oh. That's – that's good. I – I saw Simone rush in there, and I know the girls didn't want her there, and…" Now that he wasn't pacing, he started to shiver. His teeth began chattering. With a growl, I put my hands on his shoulders and steered him back toward our cabin.

"Go inside."

"No, I'm –"

"What? You're what?" The dam burst and my rage poured out. "You're fine? You're plenty warm? You're just going to stay out here a little longer and enjoy some fucking fresh air?"

He dug in his heels and, while I could still push him, he obviously planned to make it difficult.

I dropped my hands from his shoulders, instantly forming fists. Not to hit him. Just to…I didn't know. But fists felt right. "Tony, I promised Smack I'd be back. I have to convince her to come with me to talk to Janus. The others are pissed that Simone found out, and once I tell them I was the one who texted her, they're really going to hate me. I'm fine being the bad guy, but it's a little hard to do when I'm worried about you freezing to death."

He turned, and I braced myself for argument, for frustration, for lashing out. Because if Tony needed it, I could be the bad guy for him, too. As long as it meant he stormed back to the cabin afterwards.

Instead, when he raised his hand, he reached up, tucked my hair behind my ear in the sort of familiar gesture we both avoided over the last few weeks, and he laid his (very cold) forehead against mine. I jumped a little, but maybe he would believe it was because of the cold, not the touching. I managed not to pull away, reminding myself he couldn't possibly tell I was pregnant by touching his forehead to mine.

He didn't say anything for a moment, just stood there, forehead to forehead. I relaxed slowly and started to enjoy the closeness of his scent, pressed against my skin. Finally, he said, "All right," and turned to walk away, and I didn't want him to walk away anymore.

I glanced back at the girls' bunkhouse. I should go face the reckoning for calling Simone. I ran after Tony instead. I followed him into the cabin, and once he was safely inside the warmth, I pulled him into a hug. He stood stiffly, probably shocked and confused and borderline hypothermic, which slowed reaction time. Finally, he wrapped his arms around me, gently at first, then fiercely. And it felt good.

The hug only lasted a moment before he released me and took a step back. "You should go. It's a good idea to get her to talk to

Janus. If he finds out any other way, he'll be upset. Particularly if he finds out you kept it from him." Then he turned, walked over to the space heater, cranked it up to high, and settled in front of it, warming his hands.

He was right, but it took me a second to push myself to move. I missed touching him. Wolves liked touch. We didn't want to be alone. Darcy was right. I needed to talk to Tony. But what if he ran away?

With a sigh, I said good-bye and left. When I entered the bunkhouse this time, Simone's voice greeted me. From what I could hear, she was explaining first aid to the girls. How to properly bandage your friend's wrist after she tried so unsuccessfully to slit it. Exhaustion washed over me, almost knocking me to the ground.

Oh, god. What if she succeeded?

Galen whined, pushing his nose against my hand. I felt the dampness on my cheeks and realized I was crying. I wiped my face on my shirt and sniffled, then walked over to the group.

"Oh, good, Kellan, I'm glad you're back. You could use a lesson in this, too." Simone gave the girls an eye-roll that made a couple of them giggle.

I made a face, because that was the expected response, but really, I wanted to start crying again. The sound of those giggles broke something inside me. But I shored whatever it was back up with duct tape and chewing gum, and told myself to hold it together until I was alone.

"Well, that does look much better than I would've done," I said, surveying the new bandages on Smack's wrists. They looked great. Smack's eyes? Still dead. "All right, you ready to go talk to Janus?"

At this, the girls started arguing, a chorus of bird voices telling me I couldn't do that. I heard more than once, "We never should've trusted you!" Not a word from Smack herself. I met Gina's gaze. Her shoulders slumped, but she nodded. She knew that we needed to disclose this.

"Girls, it's time for you to go to bed," Gina said. "Or you could all come back to the kitchen with me and peel potatoes for tomorrow's dinner. And the next night's, and maybe the next night's, too. We could peel potatoes until your fingers all fall off, if you'd rather."

It was the same threat the cooks used when I was a youngling. Humanity's hatred of potato peeling was timeless, apparently. Smack put on her coat, and Simone took Smack's hand and led her toward the door, while Gina herded the other girls to bed.

Simone carried a garbage sack that probably held Smack's sheets. I followed them.

"Thanks, Simone," I said when we were outside. "I've got it from here." The fewer bodies in Janus's cabin, the better. I didn't want him to feel like we were trying to protect Smack from him.

Simone hesitated, then nodded. "I healed the wounds, Smack, you don't really need the bandages, but you will have scars, and these bandages will give you a little time to get used to the idea. Also, wearing them shows Janus that you sought help from me. That's a sign of strength, asking for help."

Smack tugged at her sleeves and stared at something over Simone's shoulder. Simone glanced at me, shrugged, and left. I started walking, but Smack didn't. "What's he gonna do?" she whispered.

I turned to look back at her. "Do?"

She scuffed the toe of her boot on the ground. "I stole the knife and…did stuff we aren't supposed to do. What's he gonna do?"

She thought he was going to punish her. I wondered if this wasn't the first time Smack tried to end things. I wondered what happened when the man who held her captive discovered what she did.

"He's not going to do a damn thing, Smack. I promise. He'll be concerned, and he'll want to come up with a plan to help you cope. But he's not going to punish you. And if I'm wrong and he tries, I'll knock him on his puny ass." Not that he would or I would, but I needed to reassure her that I had her back.

"Cope." The anger was back in her scent. Why did that particular word make her mad?

"Smack?" I didn't say anything else, hoping she'd open up and tell me what was going on.

She didn't, just started walking. The death row prisoner on the way to the gas chamber, back straight, shoulders square, only a slight dragging of feet to show reluctance.

The idea of coping triggered anger in her. Why? Because she would be forced to do that now? Because she hoped she wouldn't have to anymore? And now that plan was foiled, and all eyes would be on her, or at least enough eyes that she'd have to really work to find another opportunity to kill herself.

In that moment, I realized I should've sent Simone with Smack to Janus's office. Because I was so very much the wrong person to be here.

Chapter 4

KELLAN

But we were at Janus's door now. Too late to go running for a Better Person. When we stepped into the reception area, the outer office that led to Janus's inner sanctum, the youngling on desk duty, Cat, looked at us with surprise. "Oh. What's -" She stopped herself. Cat's usual assignment was patrolling the border of the forest, making sure no outsiders wandered into our land. She was one of our best archers, and she loved being outside, perched in the trees. Finn decided, though, that she needed socialization, like a puppy, so he assigned her to act as Janus's secretary for a month. I could tell from her twitchiness that the assignment rankled.

"I will announce you. Please wait here." She stood stiffly and slid through the door leading to Janus's chambers.

I glanced down at Smack. She looked exhausted and pale. Maybe she lost more blood than I thought. "Why don't you let me go in first? I'll talk to him. Maybe you won't even need to go in."

She blinked, then raised her dead eyes to glare at me. "No. I'll go in."

Why didn't you say something? I wanted to ask. She spent the entire evening teaching me to knit, like everything was fine. Then she left and tried to kill herself. I knew that it most likely wasn't a spontaneous act. The idea was there already. How could she pretend to be normal and then go and...

"You can go in." Cat stood by the door, waiting for us to walk through. Like she was a butler, which, I guess, she sort of was at this point.

I gave her arm a squeeze as I walked past. I'd talk to Finn. This was torture for her, and a flat-out waste of her talents. And let's face it, she was better socialized than I was. I acted like a feral dog half the time.

Then we were inside, and Janus was there, and I focused on the task before me.

Janus usually waited by the huge fireplace, backlit and dramatic. But tonight, he was just inside the door. I met his gaze and knew that he already knew what happened, that he probably heard it in my thoughts the second I stepped within range.

Janus was a sorcerer, and his magick hid the forest and the Academy from the eyes of the modern world. He kept us invisible. The only way to see the forest was to step within its borders. But Janus could also read minds, a skill that normally annoyed the shit out of me. Tonight, though, I was grateful. I didn't want to have to tell him about the evening's events, particularly not with Smack listening in.

Smack's anger filled the room, the way cooking curry permeated an entire building with its strong scent. Her usual assignment was as Janus's secretary, so she knew his gifts as well as I did. Which meant she, too, probably understood that he knew.

I glanced over at her, worried that she might fix that dead glare on him. But no, she was staring at the floor, appearing contrite while clenching her fists.

I rolled my shoulders back and returned my focus to Janus. "Good evening, sir."

"Good evening, Kellan. Smack." I heard the familiar distaste in his tone. He didn't like the name Smack. From day one, he wanted her to pick a different name, but she refused. He attempted to assign her a name, but she feigned deafness whenever someone addressed her as Serena. I couldn't blame her. She definitely wasn't a Serena. Eventually, Janus relented and agreed to call her Smack. But that didn't mean he had to like it.

As the silence grew and stretched thin, I realized I might not need to tell Janus the whole story, but I needed to say something. "Sir," I began, then glanced at Smack. Despite her anger, her shoulders were starting to sag. I wasn't feeling too chipper myself. "May we sit down?"

Janus waved us to the conference table, a huge oak monstrosity that probably weighed more than my ancient pickup truck. Each of the chairs required two hands to pull it away from the table. Solid, dark, and surprisingly comfortable. Smack sank into a chair and I chose the one next to her. Galen settled between us with his head resting on my foot.

"Thank you, sir." I wondered if it would be too forward to ask Janus for some coffee. I decided it probably would, and I pushed the thought from my mind. Then the door opened and Cat entered, carrying a tray laden with coffee, mugs and Gina's cranberry orange scones. I guess he really could read minds. Clearing his throat,

Janus met my eyes with a slight smile and an almost imperceptible nod.

That smile made me relax. I poured coffee for Smack and me. I didn't bother pouring one for Janus. He almost never drank the stuff. He was more of an organic green tea kind of person. But he indulged my addictions without judging. Much.

"Actually, I believe I will also have a cup." He waited while I poured him one, then he settled across the table from us. Not in the throne-like seat at the head of the table where he usually sat, but here, among the little people. When I realized my mouth hung open, I quickly shoved a bite of scone in it to cover my shock.

Why were cranberries okay and raisins weren't? Just another great mystery. "Sir," I began again.

Smack interrupted me. "I slit my wrists. Or I tried to. Which you already know. So what now?"

If Janus was shocked by her bluntness, he didn't show any sign. His only expression was a slight grimace at the taste of the coffee. "What now, indeed?" He glanced at me. "Why do you enjoy this drink so much? It tastes like acid."

Said the man whose drink of choice was basically boiled grass. "Well, this brew is a little weak. I'll make it for you next time you want a cup."

He snorted delicately and set his mug down. "Thank you, but no. Smack, why did you do what you did?"

She shrugged and started picking at the grain of the table.

"That is a distinctly unsatisfying answer." Despite his words, his tone wasn't imperious. He sounded warm and a little sad. The old man had a soft spot for Smack. "Why did you do it?"

This time, she didn't even bother to shrug. The scent of Janus's sadness grew. "Until you can give me a better reason, I must remove you from classes that involve sharp objects. You may continue in your hand-to-hand combat classes, as well as your computer skills class and your kickboxing. Weight training and the like shall continue as well. But no knives, swords, guns, et cetera."

Smack didn't speak, didn't move. Decorum dictated that she respond with, at the very least, a yes, sir. But she didn't. And Janus didn't prompt her to say it, which was almost as weird as him drinking coffee.

I felt compelled to fill the empty space. "Sir, I believe we should…" What? What insight could I offer? What could we do to help Smack? To convince her not to try this again? "There must be something we can do besides keeping her away from weapons."

He looked at me and shook his head so slightly, I questioned whether I really saw his head move. "Until Smack gives us more information on how we may help her, this is the only course of action. She will report to Ethan twice daily for counseling sessions. I believe you will have time in the morning between breakfast and your computer class, then again in the evening after dinner." Ethan was another Sankha, a trained shrink who recently moved back to the Academy to act as our resident therapist. "I believe that is all we can do. Unless there is anything else..." Janus said, almost hopefully, watching Smack.

I studied her. She didn't want help, I could tell. She didn't want counseling or anything else. What happened? What changed to send this tough, resilient kid down this path?

She raised her eyes and looked at Janus. "I was tired. I wanted to sleep." She said it like it explained things. Like just lying down and closing her eyes wouldn't cover it. I understood that. Sometimes, lying down and closing your eyes just made it worse.

He cocked an eyebrow. "People do not use knives to fall asleep. You could seek sleep aids from Simone. You could drink chamomile tea or count lambs."

"Sheep." I murmured the correction, not wanting to interrupt, but unable to let the mistake go.

Janus waved his hand, dismissing it. Close enough, that wave said. He studied Smack, and I wondered what he heard in her thoughts. I wondered if she let him see what was really in there, or if she tried to hide her feelings from him. Apparently, Janus heard something he didn't like. "I believe that for now, it would be best if you spend your nights in the infirmary."

I pictured the infirmary, with its sterile surfaces and its wide assortment of cutting tools. Janus met my gaze and raised his eyebrows, as if asking if I had a better idea. And miraculously, I did. "The infirmary's so chaotic." That was a better word than "well stocked with sharp things." "And Smack said she wants to sleep. Maybe spending the night with a Sankha in a private cabin would..." How to say suicide watch without actually saying it? "Provide her an opportunity to rest."

She stared at the table like I wasn't talking about her. Like she wasn't even in the room anymore. Janus, however, puffed up and gave me a proud smile before turning his expression thoughtful. At least I was pleasing someone tonight.

"Yes, that sounds like an excellent idea. Do you have a particular Sankha in mind?"

I couldn't just exclude Smack from the conversation. This was getting ridiculous. "Smack, do you want to stay with me and Tony? Or would you rather stay with Gina?" I hesitated, then said, "Or, if you'd prefer the infirmary, I'm sure Simone would be able to provide earplugs so you don't get woken up by any emergencies." I was more worried about the scalpels, but if anyone was qualified to administer suicide watch, it was our healer. I just didn't like the idea of adding to Simone's plate.

Smack gave another shrug. "You should ask Gina before you volunteer her."

Which I took to mean Gina would be her first choice. "Gina ran to see you when she found out what happened." How did Gina find out what happened? Tia went to get Tony. Did another girl go in search of a Sankha, too, and find Gina? Another question for later. "I think she'll be good with it. But I'll text her and ask, if you want." Younglings weren't allowed cell phones, but as a newly initiated Sankha, Gina now possessed her own phone.

Yet another shrug. I was starting to get annoyed with the silent treatment.

"Super," I said, after unclenching my teeth. All this tact and thoughtfulness was really starting to grate on me. Eager to end this meeting before I lost what little self-control I had left, I sent Gina a text. She responded instantly. "All right, Gina says she's good with that. So let's go gather up some stuff for you and we'll head to Gina's cabin."

Smack stood and walked to the door, where she waited, staring at the doorframe. We needed to be dismissed before we could leave.

I sighed and drained my coffee. "May we be dismissed, sir?"

Janus was watching Smack with a scent of cold fall air, just before a rainstorm. He cared about Smack, probably more than all the other younglings combined, and seeing her so disengaged made him sad, I could tell. I felt a sudden and shocking urge to hug him. Instead, I repeated my question in a softer tone.

He blinked, as if coming out of a trance. "Yes. Yes, you are dismissed. Have a restful sleep." Janus's version of sweet dreams.

"Thank you, sir." As close as I could come to saying it would be all right.

Smack and I left. Cat watched us go. She might not know what was going on, but an idiot could tell it wasn't good.

When we got outside, Smack said, "I'm not stupid, I know what you guys are doing."

"What?" I glanced at her.

"You're putting me on suicide watch."

Well, yeah. Part of me wanted to point out that suicide watch in her friend's cabin was a hell of a lot better than suicide watch in the busy infirmary. But all I said was, "What did you expect?"

She stopped and glared at me. "I expected to die."

The air whooshed out of my lungs and I couldn't pull more in. When I didn't answer, Smack started walking again. *I expected to die.* I forced my feet in motion, jogged over to her, but I still couldn't think of anything to say, so we returned to the bunkhouse and packed a bag with Smack's things without saying another word to each other. I did break the silence to tell the other girls where Smack would be sleeping. Everyone was wide awake, but I said, "Time to sleep now. If you need anything, come get me."

I looked at each face and heard the words "suicide cluster" pop up in my head. I wanted to pat them down, make sure there were no other hidden weapons. I wanted to camp out in their bunkhouse to make sure each and every one was safe tonight. But instead, I said good night and left with Smack.

In keeping with the theme of angry and awkward silence, Smack went inside Gina's cabin without a word to either of us. Gina met my gaze and turned the corners of her mouth upward in a grotesque attempt at a reassuring smile.

I repeated my earlier words. "If you need anything, just call." I felt my shoulders slump a little under the weight of emotion. "Not like I'll be sleeping tonight."

Gina gave me a quick hug, said, "Try to get some rest," and went inside.

I stared at the door, then at the brightly lit windows of the cabin. Gina hung white twinkle lights in the windows, a whimsical touch that surprised me, but made the cabin look more like a home than any I ever stayed in. Maybe I should get some twinkle lights.

Galen leaned against my leg and I jumped. Through everything, he stayed by my side, a vigilant shadow. Now he looked up at me, waiting to see what was next. I might've just stayed outside Gina's cabin all night, if not for Galen, but it was much too cold to keep my dog out all night. I suddenly understood Tony's need to wait outside the bunkhouse for me.

"All right, buddy, let's go." We walked slowly back to the cabin.

Tony met us at the door, like he watched for us out the window. Which, knowing Tony, he probably did. The scent of his worry, which to my mind smelled like fresh-baked sourdough, filled the cabin. That smell, the warmth of the cabin, the waiting coffee that smelled fresh and strong, all combined to take the starch right out of me. I almost went down in a puddle, but I managed to walk over to the table. Tony brought us both cups of coffee, then he went to get Galen a little kibble. I was so tired, I probably should've skipped the coffee, but I needed the comfort.

"Smack's staying with Gina for now." I answered the question that I knew was on his mind. "Thanks for the coffee." I sniffed it. "Is this decaf?"

"Half caff. For my sake. I'd like to sleep sometime tonight, but I figured you'd want some."

I grunted and sipped. My stomach gurgled. The baby wasn't impressed with half caff, and I set the mug down without taking another sip.

I expected him to ask how Smack was, so I was busy trying to come up with an honest answer that wouldn't upset him too much. What he actually asked was, "How are you?"

"Huh?" I squinted at him as I tried to make sense of the words. I wasn't the one that mattered right now.

"That had to be hard for you." Tony held his mug, but didn't drink from it. If he wasn't going to drink it, why the hell didn't he make real coffee for the rest of us? "Are you okay?"

The real answer, the answer I hesitated to admit, was yes, I was okay. I was exhausted and tense, a little nauseous and I needed to pee again, but for the first time in weeks, I felt like me. Like I was finally forced to step out of my own selfish head and focus on someone else, which made me feel better.

What kind of monster felt better after attending to a suicidal girl? The kind of monster that sure as shit shouldn't reproduce.

I finally answered, "Yeah, I guess so." That sounded adequately lacking enthusiasm. "I have to pee," I said suddenly, and escaped to the bathroom briefly. Hopefully, that would give him time to get over any judgement at my lack of emotional response. On the way back to the table, I grabbed a piece of bread from the counter and nibbled at it while I sat across from him. "Um, are you okay? Are you warm?"

He ducked his head, and I could see the rims of his ears darkening as he blushed. "Yeah. That was stupid. I'm sorry about that."

"No, I get it." I told him about standing outside Gina's cabin, wishing I could keep watch overnight. "I'm sorry I got mad."

His mouth quirked up, and the sight of that almost-smile relaxed me incrementally. "It was kinda nice, actually."

"Me getting mad?" I heard the confusion drip from each word.

He laughed a little. "You getting mad at me for not taking care of myself. Usually, you're mad at me for trying to take care of you."

"Oh." Fuck. Did it really happen often enough to qualify as "usually?"

"Honestly, as shitty as tonight was, I'm actually feeling pretty good." He hesitated. "It's nice to know what happened. At

Christmas. I was just so scared. I thought maybe…I did something. You know. To make you…"

I wanted to slink under the table. I made him feel that. It was my fault. "I'm so sorry."

"No, don't do that." He sighed. "It's not your fault. I shoulda asked sooner. I shoulda tried to get you to talk instead of just trying to manage you. But like I said, I was scared of what the answer might be." He cocked his head slightly. "Have you talked to Paul?"

Paul? Oh, yeah. I reminded myself that he thought this was all about cologne. "About the cologne, you mean?"

He nodded.

"It doesn't matter," I said firmly. "It wasn't his fault, and he left again on another assignment right after New Year's. He probably won't be back until next Christmas."

"Of course, it wasn't intentional, but he'd want to know. Most people don't wear cologne once and say, well, that was nice, and never wear it again. They keep wearing it. So he'd want to know if it was causing you problems."

I shook my head. I couldn't do it. I couldn't admit to anyone else that I still had flashbacks. That Aza still affected me.

"Kellan, if it was happening to me, if something you did triggered me, you'd want to know, right?"

I felt sick. "Did I? Ever trigger you?"

"No," he said, not even giving it any thought. "But if it happened, I would tell you, so you could be aware of it."

I wasn't sure I believed him. When Tony was a youngling, he was a cocky little shit. I really enjoyed knocking him in the dirt. How could I have managed to avoid triggering flashbacks to his abusive past? That didn't seem possible.

"None of us come from happy childhoods, Kell." Tony kept talking and I struggled to follow the flow of words. "We get it. We all have triggers, and sometimes shit happens, and you get triggered, and there's nothing you can do, except ride it out. But sometimes, you can ask someone not to make things worse."

That sounded completely selfish and unreasonable. "Can we stop talking about this? I'll give you a thousand dollars to pick a different topic."

He snorted. "Like you have two nickels to pay me with."

"I bet I could find two nickels, if you're willing to bid that low."

He took a drink of his coffee, then grimaced. "This is cold."

I ran my fingers over the top of Galen's head, stroking his surprisingly silky ears. His coat was fairly rough, but the hair on his ears was like satin. "Tony, if you want to leave, you should do that." Where did that come from? But I knew where it came from. This was my greatest fear. More than anything, I was terrified of facing things without him.

But if he knew what I was really hiding, he'd leave for sure.

He tore his gaze from his coffee mug to stare at me. "What?"

I forced myself to keep going. I knew my comments seemed out of the blue to him, but these thoughts lurked in the back of my mind constantly. Because let's face it. If he treated me half as badly as I treated him, I would've kicked his ass to the curb ages ago. So why wouldn't he want to leave? "If you aren't happy, you should go. Be with someone, you know, who isn't so…" Awful? Broken? Bitchy? Fuckered? Pick your adjective.

Tony looked at me for an excruciatingly long time. Then he stood up, took both of our mugs to the sink and dumped the cold coffee down the drain. "You're right, half caff sucks." He turned off Mr. Coffee and the light over the sink and walked to the bed. "I'm so tired, I bet even your zombie shows won't keep me awake tonight."

Was that supposed to be an answer? Fuck that. I finally worked up the courage to say something out loud, and I wasn't going to let him ignore it. "Tony, did you hear me?"

In the middle of pulling off his hoodie, he stopped. He was facing away from me, and I couldn't detect a scent to clue me into what he was thinking. "Yes, Kellan, I heard you." He finished pulling off his hoodie and laid it on top of his dresser, so that he only wore his undershirt.

I looked away before he moved onto changing his pants. I wanted to scream. I wanted him to answer me. I wanted him to say he was leaving, so I could get it over with. Like Smack with the bandage. Just rip it off.

Galen whined a little and nudged my hand with his nose. I absently started petting him, even though I felt like I was coming apart at the seams.

I heard the scuff of Tony's socks on the wood floor. He came very close to me, then stopped, but I didn't look up at him. I couldn't. I closed my eyes and told myself to listen to the sound of his voice, to let the words wash over me and just be sounds.

"Kell, it's been a long night, so I'm just going to say this and then, hopefully, we can go to bed. I can't say I'm happy, because it's been such a rough few weeks. Months, I guess. But I'd be a shit-ton more unhappy if I wasn't here with you. I don't want to leave. So I'm going to bed. You can join me, or you can stay up and torture yourself. Your choice. But I'm not leaving. G'night."

Scuff, scuff, scuff. I loved that sound. That I'm-too-tired-to-pick-my-feet-up,   here's-hoping-I-make-it-all-the-way-to-the-bed-before-I-fall-asleep sound. I felt the dreaded damp heat at the back of my eyes, and pressed my fingers into my eye sockets to prevent tears from falling. I never wanted to not hear that sound. Because even if I couldn't look at him, I knew what that sound was. I knew what he looked like when he dragged himself from one side of the room to the other, after exhaustion set in and made each movement that much slower, that much less graceful, that much more cozy. Next came the sound of the bedsprings as he lowered himself onto the mattress. Then the soft sigh as he stretched out. The deeper sigh as he rolled onto his side, already mostly asleep.

Tears escaped anyway.

Chapter 5

TONY

As I rolled onto my side, I wished she would just tell me. I didn't doubt that what she said earlier was true. That she was triggered by Paul's cologne at Christmas. Kellan hated lying and wasn't particularly good at it, so she avoided it whenever she could. So I believed her, and I believed, too, that she was worried about me wanting to leave. But that didn't mean it was the whole truth. It might explain why she cried at the drop of a hat these days or why she shied away from my touch, but it didn't explain the way she insisted on wearing a bra to bed or why she was puking all the time, or why the only pants she wore now had an elastic waist. She who used to say that yoga pants were a sign of the collapse of civilization. That all started before Christmas.

No. This was something else. I knew that. It was obvious, no matter how hard she tried to hide it from me. Shape-shifters like her couldn't get sick, so she must be pregnant. An idiot could see that. But why wouldn't she just tell me? We needed to talk about it, god damn it. How did she feel about it? I mean, she just found out her sister had a kid, and now Kellan's pregnant? Did she even want kids? Did she want a baby?

Did I want a baby?

I tried to imagine it, even as sleep tugged at me. I couldn't. I had no idea how to be a father. I never knew mine, and my mom wasn't role model material, either. Even the good memories – what few I had – were only good relatively speaking. Listening to blues after she smoked her pipe, because she was happy and sweet when she was high. The special treat of a McDonald's breakfast when she had some extra cash. A disc of hashbrowns in a paper wrapper was the closest I had to a mother's cooking. No, I didn't know shit about being a parent. I never even changed a diaper before. Pretty sure Kellan never did, either. I couldn't think of two people less prepared to be parents.

But did I want a baby? And was the baby even mine? All hope of sleep fled. There was another possibility. Another possible father for this child. What would we do if this baby belonged to Aza?

I forced myself to focus on breathing. In and out. I could only control what I could control. We'd figure it out. Breathe. In and out.

My eyes drifted shut again. A miniature Kellan. Her first word would be fuck. That thought made me smile as I dozed off.

《》

KELLAN

I couldn't fall asleep. I tossed and turned and kept seeing Smack's sheets, her dead gaze, her stiff spine. Finally, Tony rolled onto his back. "Turn on a DVD."

"What?"

"For the love of fuck, just turn on one of your damn zombie shows. Then maybe at least one of us can get some sleep." I knew what he meant by that. If I turned on the TV, he might not sleep, but I would. Guilt crept up on me, but I still put in a DVD. I couldn't take the images in my head. I needed to see something normal, like a zombie apocalypse.

Sure enough, I fell asleep almost before the opening credits finished rolling. It didn't last, though. I bolted awake. I couldn't remember specifics of the nightmare, but I knew it was bloody.

Tony sat up and pulled earplugs from his ears. This was our compromise on zombie nights. He would wear earplugs, even though he hated them. He flipped on the lamp and studied me. He didn't ask if I was okay, though. The answer was obvious. I was practically hyperventilating.

Galen crawled up from the foot of the bed, until he stretched between us. Tony shifted slightly so there was more room for my dog. I inhaled their combined scents, and started to relax.

I turned off the TV. The show didn't cause the nightmare, but I also couldn't stomach the sounds of violence right then. Tony's eyes flicked to the dark screen, then back to me, a silent *Are you sure?* I swallowed and nodded. "You can turn off the light. I'm okay," I said. Okayer, anyway.

He only hesitated a moment before turning off the light. My night vision kicked in, making my eyes feel warm as they glowed in the dark. I stroked Galen's fur as Tony lay down, facing me this time, and closed his eyes. His muscles relaxed slowly, making him look warm and comfortable and...

Oh, shit. Oh shit oh shit oh shit. I wanted to touch him. Not just touch him. I wanted to kiss him. I wanted to...oh, shit.

I closed my eyes tight, clenched my fists, tried to force my lungs to expand. But breathing meant smelling Tony's scent, and that made everything worse. His scent while he slept was so sweet. Almost like French toast. A vanilla-y cinnamon-y kind of sweetness.

I really needed to go for a run.

But I couldn't do that. If I got out of bed, he would wake back up, and I already woke him once. He needed to sleep. I needed to stay in place.

My fists were clenched so tight, I whimpered a little. Which woke him up. He pushed onto his elbow and looked at me. "What's wrong?"

"Um." I tried to think of a reason for my distress that didn't involve sex. But I was tired, too, and my brain balked at the mental cartwheels I attempted. "Oh, shit, I don't know."

He turned the lamp back on. I watched him look me over, take in the hands still clenched, the stiff way I sat there. "You want to sleep with the light on?"

Sure, then I can see you easier. That's a great idea. "No. I, um, want to go for a run. I'm trying to relax instead."

He sniffled, rubbed his eyes, and once again looked at my hands. "Doesn't look like it's working so good." His voice was low, gravelly, a sound I could just roll around in, preferably naked, and...Fuck.

Since he was awake, I pushed out of bed. "I'm just going to read for a while. You go back to sleep. I'll – I'll come to bed in a bit."

Instead, he sat up the rest of the way, leaned back against the wall. "Is it what happened with Smack?"

Oh, god, please stop talking. I felt tears heat my eyes for the ten thousandth time that night. I didn't want to cry. I didn't want to feel any of this. I didn't want to *be* this. I just wanted to go back to normal. Normal, un-knocked-up me. I forced myself to speak. "I'm feeling some things. Things that are making me want to – that are making sleep difficult." I looked at him, the way his t-shirt clung to his muscles, and felt a hunger that had nothing to do with food. I blinked and forced myself to look away.

He frowned for another moment, then his eyes widened. Guess he figured out what I meant. "Oh."

"I don't know what to do. So I'm going to stay over here at the table for a while."

He sat very, very still. The room filled with the scent of sour, moldy white bread, the scent of hurt feelings, swirling unappetizingly with the chocolatey scent of desire. Laying down, he rolled over on his side, arms wrapped around his middle like he was trying to hold himself together. I couldn't just sit there and let him hurt. And, I once again reminded myself, I was barely showing. The teeniest little baby bump, which could be explained by too many slices of bread. He wouldn't be able to tell I was pregnant by looking at me or touching me. Probably. And I could turn off the light. Like most humans, his night vision was shit.

Still, my heart pounded with irrational fear as I walked back over to the bed, turned out the light, and crawled in behind him. He stiffened. The scent of his desire flared, calling out to me, pulling me closer. I pressed against his back and wrapped my arm around him. I pulled one of his hands free and entwined my fingers with his. We were both tense. There was nothing pleasurable about this embrace. But I was trying.

He shuddered and slowly relaxed against me. He didn't roll over, didn't turn to look at me or try to kiss me. I didn't know if I felt relieved or disappointed.

"It's okay," he said. His voice sounded thick, like he had a lump in his throat. Or maybe I was just projecting. "You don't have to touch me. I understand."

Fuck. Just like that, tears began to stream down my cheeks. I buried my face in the back of his t-shirt, breathing in his scent with a greed that I hadn't allowed myself to feel for weeks. "I want to." I pulled back from his t-shirt so I could speak. "I just can't promise it'll last. I can't promise I won't fall apart. I can't promise anything."

He shuddered again, and I realized he was crying, too. *I just keep making it worse*, I thought. *He's miserable and I'm making it worse.*

So I was shocked when he rolled over and took my face in his hands. He started to lean in, then stopped himself. I didn't. I pushed him on his back, climbed on top of him, and kissed him. Not a kiss on the forehead, not a tentative peck. A real, full-blown kiss that robbed me of my breath and made my vision go all blurry.

When I pulled away, we were both panting, which made me laugh. He smiled and closed his eyes, like he was reveling in the sound. He raised himself up a little, using only those amazing abs, and gave me a soft, lingering, close-mouthed kiss. "Thank you," he whispered.

"Oh, I'm not done with you yet." I pushed him back down, and pulled off my shirt. For a second, I faltered. Would he see? The cabin was dark, but not absolutely dark, and my pale skin glowed like, well, like a pale white chick in the middle of a Wisconsin winter. Could he see more than I thought? Would he figure it out? But his expression never changed. One of his hands rested on my thigh, and he started tracing circles with his finger. A gentle, aimless movement that never went any higher toward a danger zone, but felt relaxing and comfortable. And slowly, I forgot all the fear, everything but the man in the bed.

I kissed him again, hungry, and slid my lower body down so that my groin pressed to his. He gasped, and I took that sound into my mouth and kissed him deeper. I rubbed against him, feeling the friction build and build until I tipped over the edge. When I opened my eyes, he was smiling at me. "I never thought I'd hear you make those sounds again," he said.

I could tell from his tone that he thought we were done. Which made it that much sweeter as I reached down, slid my hand into his shorts, and wrapped my hand around his penis. His expression was so open, so surprised, that I laughed again.

I didn't go down on him. Part of me wished I could, seeing that look on his face, but my gag reflex was way too strong these days. But with the hand job, I brought him to orgasm within moments. Normally, Tony had marvelous staying power, but I guess that was what happened when a guy forced himself to be celibate.

We took turns cleaning up in the bathroom. I was grateful. I needed a few minutes to absorb what just happened, without any questions or "let's talk" coming at me. It wasn't sex, but it was the closest we'd come in a while. It felt huge, even though it only lasted a few minutes. I tried not to think about what this might mean. I cleaned up first, then I just listened to Tony, humming in the bathroom, and I curled my body around Galen, because his scent was the definition of normalcy for me.

I had the lights off, though I lit some LED candles. The gentle flickering lights and Galen's scent kept all the worries from sneaking up on me again.

When Tony came out and saw me, though, he apparently thought something was wrong. His steps faltered, and I could smell worry and sadness from across the room. I forced myself to untangle from my dog and sit up. I smiled a little. "I didn't want Galen to feel neglected."

Tony smiled a little back. "I hope you didn't take care of him the way you took care of me."

I made a face. "Yuck. No. He's a brother, not…no."

Tony came back toward the bed. He was wearing fresh boxers, but didn't bother with a clean t-shirt. His upper body was bare, and that body was a work of art. If Michelangelo saw Tony, he would've tossed David out the window and devoted himself to sculpting the man before me. And for the first time in a long, long time, I let myself just look and enjoy.

His steps faltered again when he saw the look on my face. I stretched out on my back, pulled off first my clean shirt, then the shorts and underwear that completed my pajamas. The bra was the last thing to go, and I tried not to wince as I touched my breasts. I lay there, bare and vulnerable in more ways than one, and hoped that he accepted my silent invitation. Because if he made me say something out loud, I might chicken out and run away.

I watched him run his gaze over my body. Could he see? Could he tell? But all I smelled was a renewed surge of desire. He swallowed hard and dragged his gaze up to my face. "Are you sure?" he asked.

I nodded, still unwilling to speak.

He didn't wait for me to change my mind. He joined me on the bed. I wasn't sure he'd be ready again so soon, but he was, and when he entered me, he did it so slowly, like he was memorizing each sensation. And I let him, because it felt so damn good. It lasted a little longer than the hand job, but I think because we were both so sensitive to each touch, it was still over pretty quick.

Afterward, we had to clean up again. This time, we shared the bathroom. I took a quick shower while Tony cleaned up at the sink. He didn't try to talk to me. Maybe he didn't want to break the spell. Whatever the reason, I was glad. I was much too tired to form words.

As we left the bathroom, though, he slanted a look at my breasts. "Damn. If I didn't know better…Are they bigger?"

I felt my face flush and hurried to put my bra and shirt back on. When we crawled back into bed, my hair still dripping wet, we were both asleep within seconds.

I had two more nightmares. Tony slept through both, which showed just how exhausted he was. Neither dream was too terrible, but they were enough that I didn't feel rested in the morning, and sleep abandoned me long before the sun came up.

Tony was still dead asleep when I got up. I wanted to go for a run or at least go lift weights, but I felt like I should be there when he woke. That seemed like the kind of thing that would be important to him. So I stayed, did some squats, push-ups. I almost started doing crunches, then stopped. It was weeks since my last abs workout. I had an image of the baby, squashed and deformed, all because of too many crunches. Stupid, maybe, but there you have it.

When Tony finally woke up, I was already seated at the table with a cup of coffee and a book. The sound of him sitting up in bed made me jump.

He looked over at me and smiled a slow, sleepy smile that made me clench up inside. I looked at him, his abs bunching, his triceps prominent as he propped himself up. He was beautiful. I heard a small, annoying voice in my head, telling me I needed to tell Tony about the baby, and I told that voice to fuck off. "Good morning," I said. "There's coffee. I didn't go get food yet. Are you hungry?"

"Starving," he said, never taking his eyes from my face. He sounded like maybe he wasn't just thinking about food. I felt heat creep up my neck and spread over my face. He laughed. "I love that I can make you blush. If there's any bread left, do you mind toasting me a piece? I gotta get dressed. Archery class at nine."

With a nod, I went over to the toaster. I glanced at the clock. 8:52. Well, at least we didn't have time for a long, drawn out discussion of our feelings. Except part of me wanted to at least have a short discussion of things. I felt like I needed to remind him that I couldn't promise anything. That last night didn't mean I was back to normal. With another look at the clock, I decided eight minutes was enough time to spit that out.

"Tony, look, about last night, that was great and all, but I can't promise that, you know, that…" Maybe eight minutes wasn't long enough, since "spitting it out" seemed a lot harder than I expected.

I heard a soft chuckle, which annoyed me, since I didn't find my discomfort very funny. But I kept working on the toast. I spread peanut butter on it, because he really should have some protein before spending the morning out in the cold. Shuffling footsteps approached, and Tony reached around me without touching me to grab one of the pieces of toast. "It's okay, Kell. It was great. I wouldn't trade it for a million bucks. But I know how huge it was for you, and I don't have any expectations. If you want to do it again, awesome. But until then, we're cool."

His Zen acceptance made me wish I could do the same. I didn't feel Zen, though. He didn't know the whole story. Fuck, he didn't know any of the story, not the important bits. But I could smell his sweet, sweet scent, which made me want to turn, bury my face in his neck, and breathe it in. I couldn't bear the thought of losing him because of this…baby.

I glanced at the clock again. Tony now had five minutes to eat, and he probably wanted a little coffee to go with his toast, so I handed him the other piece and then poured some coffee into an insulated mug.

He beamed at me like I handed him a pot of gold. "Thank you."

I hated lying to him. I stood on tiptoe, intending to give him a peck on the lips. But he smelled like peanut butter and like Tony, and that peck turned into a kiss that ended with the toast falling on the floor and me sitting on the counter with my legs wrapped around his waist. He pulled back and looked at me. "I have to go."

I felt my face heat again. "I know. I'm sorry."

He leaned in and kissed me softly. "Don't ever, ever apologize for doing that. Ever." Laughing again, he left with his coffee in hand.

Still sitting on the counter, I glanced at Galen, who looked back at me guiltily. I knew the second Tony dropped that piece of toast, my dog would've eaten it. I didn't hold it against him. He was just doing what felt good. I smiled a little. I guess I was doing the same thing.

Chapter 6

KELLAN

After I fed Galen a proper breakfast, we wandered into the forest, where he could lift his leg until he dehydrated like a piece of dog jerky. And where I could avoid running into younglings on their way to their classes. I chose a tree and leaned against it, closed my eyes and breathed.

The forest in the winter smelled like a paler version of itself. The carpet of leaves and pine needles on the ground were covered by a layer of snow and ice. No smell of earth or decay, just the frozenness of it all. But it didn't matter. After a decade of living in the city, I now woke up every morning to this. I could breathe all day and never get a hint of exhaust or cigarette smoke. The forest smelled like home, even when it didn't smell like much of anything.

Galen finished marking and trotted over to me. He looked up at me, tail wagging. Run? I could almost hear his thought as if it were my own.

I shouldn't. Finn didn't think I should shape-shift where the younglings could see. But god, it was a perfect morning for it. Cold and dry, the air hung still, just waiting to be disturbed by the sound of a howl. I grinned at Galen and darted inside a thicket of brambles. I'd end up with scratches, but it was the closest spot with privacy.

I started to strip, then heard footsteps crunching on the snow. It was one thing to shape-shift when the woods were empty. Another thing entirely when I knew younglings were nearby. Fucking hell. I pulled my shirt back on and emerged from the bushes, bipedal and cranky.

"Sankha Kellan?"

I whirled around. Valentine stood behind me. She glared at me, silently judging me for something. "Hi," I said, when it became clear she wasn't going to say anything else. "Do you need something, Valentine?"

"You didn't try very hard." Her tone was accusing for such vague words.

I had to bite the inside of my cheek hard enough to draw blood in order to keep from snapping at her. My voice sounded strangled as I said, "What do you mean?"

"Smack. You didn't try to find out why she did it."

A wave of anger washed over me. I did try. And I hated that I failed. "Do you know something about it?"

"Maybe. But you should talk to her again. She wants to tell. She just can't."

"Vallie? You ready?" Another youngling, Dirk, came up behind Valentine. She looked up at him and lifted the corners of her mouth in a little smile, the sort of smile that says, *I don't feel like smiling, but I care about you, so I'll at least try.* Dirk didn't seem like the kind of kid who would inspire that kind of smile. He also didn't seem like the type to use nicknames. But he smiled back at her, like she was his little sister. It was nice.

Dirk nodded at me. I noticed he unconsciously ran a hand over the place where a nocturne stabbed him, a nocturne my sister brought into the camp. Nocturnes were another kind of shape-shifter, a long-time enemy of the Sankhain. My twin, Mal, used them in a complex plot to escape from the hold of Janus. She told me she did it for her daughter, which I gave up trying to understand. People got hurt in the process, Dirk being one of them. An old, familiar shame heated my cheeks. "Good morning, Sankha Kellan," he said. "My apologies for interrupting, but we have border patrol. We need to go relieve the others."

"Of course." I started to tell Valentine something, that I'd go talk to Smack, that I'd do something. But she was already gone. The girl was like a ghost, only quieter.

Dirk lingered. "I have to go."

"Okay." I thought we already established that.

"You should talk to Smack."

For pete's sake, how did he know about Smack? And why did everyone think it was my job to fix things? "Youngling, your partner already chastised me for that. You can go now."

He nodded, started to walk away, hesitated. "You have to stop him. Please." Then he hurried away.

"Whoa, whoa, whoa." I ran after him and caught him by the arm. "What do you mean? Who? Did someone – did someone hurt Smack?"

Dirk glanced at a tree several yards away, and I saw Valentine sitting in its branches, watching us. "It's not my story to tell," he said. "Please don't make me." His voice sounded small and vulnerable.

I realized how hard I was gripping his arm, and released him. "I'm not going to make you do anything, Dirk. I'll handle it. I promise you."

He nodded again. I thought maybe that was Dirk's way of dealing with uncomfortable things, a way of feeling in control with an affirmative head bob. He headed off into the trees, and I left him to watch our borders with Valentine.

And Tia. I saw her as I turned away. I remembered what Tony said, how the little girl needed to be with her sister at all times. She was hiding behind a nearby tree. She looked like she overslept. Her hair wasn't brushed and her boots weren't tied. Of course, she was up almost as late as I was last night.

"Hey, Tia," I said as I approached. "Did you get breakfast?"

She shook her head in a jerky movement. "I'm okay," she whispered.

I wondered where she was supposed to be right now. We kept the younglings' days pretty heavily scheduled. They had free time, but not a lot. As I studied her, I thought that if I asked, she would either lie or run away. Probably the latter. She looked as skittish as a dog that just got hit. I didn't want her running away from the forest, so I decided letting her stay near Valentine was the lesser evil. "Listen, I'm going to get myself something to eat. How about I bring you back something? What do you like?"

She stared at the toe of her boot and shrugged, just as jerkily as her head shake.

I couldn't take it. I knelt down and tied her boots. "There, now you can run faster and safer. You have a hat? You're going to get cold on border patrol without a hat."

"I'm not on border patrol," she whispered, like she expected me to yell at her. That little voice broke my heart.

"Looks to me like you're Dirk and Valentine's backup. And backup can only help if they don't freeze to death. I'll bring you a hat and some mittens, and maybe a peanut butter sandwich?"

She didn't scream, "NO!" at the prospect, so I figured peanut butter must be acceptable.

I leaned over and whispered conspiratorially, "Maybe a thermos of hot chocolate?"

That got her. Her gaze darted up to my face and she almost – almost – smiled. I smiled big enough for both of us and left on my quest.

As I walked away, I shook my head. Tying younglings' boots and offering to bring them hot chocolate? Since when did I become Donna Reed's heavily armed doppelganger?

Since I got knocked up, I guess.

The mess hall was one of the largest buildings on our little campus, but still only the size of a convenience store. It was its usual chaotic mass of bodies. We only had a dozen younglings and a few resident Sankhain, not counting Finn, Janus, and me, but somehow, mealtimes always felt like a huge cafeteria. Maybe because the mess hall was one place the younglings could hang out and just be kids. No rules of decorum, no grammar checks or salutes. Just food, drink, laughter.

And Smack. There, in the corner, smiling, talking with Cat. She looked fine. Normal. No trace of the dead-inside girl from last night. This was the Smack who was in my cabin yesterday, patiently teaching me how to knit. But I had a feeling that the dead-inside girl was just below that smiling surface.

Stay focused, I told myself. I would talk to Smack as soon as I delivered the promised items to Tia. One thing at a time. From the kitchen, I grabbed a thermos full of hot chocolate and four peanut butter sandwiches – two for me, two for Tia. Then I went to the laundry and found two hats and a couple pairs of mittens that looked like they might fit Tia. All the younglings got their clothes from us. They didn't have uniforms, but they also didn't have a lot of choices. Finn refused to order special clothes for each kid. I was working on changing that, per Tony's request, but convincing Finn to change was like convincing a tree to do the hokey-pokey. Anyway, in the laundry, we kept a stash of unused hats, mittens, coats, socks, underwear – spares in case something got lost, damaged, or became otherwise unusable. The items I chose might be too big for Tia, since at age seven, she was the smallest youngling we had since Mal and I were her age, but that was why I was bringing extras. In this weather, doubling up on warm clothes made sense.

I could've gone into the girls' bunkhouse and found Tia's stuff, rifled through it and found her hat and mittens. But that felt like an invasion of a girl who probably got invaded way too many times in her short life.

I stuffed everything into a cloth sack, and jogged back to the forest. I helped Tia put on the hats and mittens, then we realized she wasn't going to be able to eat wearing two pairs of mittens. So the mittens came back off, though I extracted a promise from her that she would put them back on as soon as she finished her breakfast. Once Tia was devouring her sandwiches – she gave me another almost-smile, a little bigger this time – I returned to the mess hall. Of course, by that time, Smack was gone, but I had to check.

Rather than searching for her, I headed to the old horse paddock that we converted to our archery range. Tony was teaching there.

In addition to duties like border patrol, the younglings attended a rotation of classes. Archery, hand-to-hand fighting combined with knife work, and gun safety, as well as math, English, computer skills. Tony taught the combat skills, while another Sankha, Maya, taught the schoolish stuff. I didn't bother trying to keep track of the schedule, because Tony had a freakish ability to remember each youngling's schedule. Even if Smack wasn't in his archery class, he would know where I could find her.

I didn't enter the archery range. Never surprise younglings learning to use weapons. Instead, Galen and I stood at the fence, caught Tony's eye, and waved to him. He jogged over. "Hey," he said, his scent warm enough to roll around in. He greeted Galen, too, reaching between the fence rails to rub the top of my dog's head.

Seeing Tony made me want to kiss him and maybe do a little warming of my own. But I had more important business. "Hi. You wouldn't happen to know where Smack's supposed to be right now, would you?"

Instantly, he radiated worry. "You can't find her?"

"Well, no, but I also don't know where I should be looking."

"Ummm…" His eyes watched his students as he thought about it. "Hang on. J.C., I see you point an arrow at anything other than a target one more time, you're gonna be in solitary for a week." The offending student shrugged with teenage indifference and lowered his bow. Tony shook his head. "Smack's in computer class right now. Then she has a shift in the kitchen, doing lunch prep, then this afternoon, she has hand-to-hand with me. She works the rest of the day at Janus's." How the hell did he keep track of all that? Freakish. Suddenly, Tony yelled, "J.C.!"

I looked over and saw a dead squirrel with an arrow through it. J.C. protested that he wasn't the one who shot the squirrel, but it had to be him. The other three students were focused on their targets, not wildlife. I was simultaneously impressed by the shot and creeped out by the kid who made it. J.C. didn't smell right to me. Never did.

"You gotta go," I said to Tony. "Good luck. I'll let you know when I find her."

"Thanks," he said without a glance back at me. He was already loping back to the students. As much as my morbid curiosity wanted to stay and make sure he followed through on his threat to J.C. – Tony had an annoying tendency to believe excuses and justifications, and let offenses slide – my guilty conscience spurred me toward the computer lab.

Our computer lab was just another cabin like the one Tony and I lived in, retrofitted with extra outlets for computer stations. It contained the Academy's Wi-Fi setup, along with two desktop computers, fairly new, and two laptops that Abe Lincoln used at his law practice. My understanding was the younglings fought over who got to use the desktops, and whoever got to class last had to work on the laptops. They were slower than a dead snail, or at least, that's what Smack told me once.

She liked computers, I knew that, which was one reason why Janus liked assigning her to be his assistant. He couldn't even turn a computer on, so when Smack was right outside his office, he could ask her to Google all kinds of shit for him. The man could hide an entire forest from the world, but he couldn't operate a smartphone. Of course, I wasn't a hell of a lot better at it.

Because this was an area of strength for Smack, I was surprised when I walked in the classroom and saw her sitting at one of the laptops. It shocked me that she would've allowed herself to arrive late enough to be stuck on one of the ancient machines. She might've looked normal at breakfast, but she obviously wasn't.

I sent Tony a quick, "She's here," text, then I pulled up a chair and sat next to her. She ignored me for three heartbeats, then turned and met my gaze. There, there was the dead-inside girl from last night. Apparently, she didn't feel the need to hide it from me now, the way she did with her friends. "I'm busy. Sankha Kellan, ma'am." The respectful address was muttered under her breath, negating any illusion of respect.

I looked at her screen. It was blank. The computer wasn't even on. "Yeah, I can see that."

Smack hit the power button, and the laptop made an awful grinding noise as it struggled to boot up. I detected an odor of over-taxed electronics, and scooted my chair a little further away, in case the computer blew up.

"How about we give the laptop time to…do whatever it needs to do, and you and I go for a walk?" By the sound and smell of things, we had at least half an hour before the screen even lit up.

"I'm busy. Ma'am," she said again, a little more pointed.

"Yeah, I really wanted to pretend this was a request, but you and I are going for a walk now." I looked up at the instructor, a woman who looked like she was barely thirty, but was actually descended from real Mayans. She was one of our oldest Sankhain. Her chosen name was a little joke for her. "Maya? I need to borrow Smack for a bit."

"Sure," she said. "And the next time you see Finn, remind him we're waiting on those new laptops."

"You bet." Fat chance. I'd mention it, but Finn clung to the belief that electronics could live forever. We had a whole closet full of toasters that he refused to throw away, in the hopes that one day they'd rise from the dead.

I waited for Smack to pull on her hat and coat, which seemed to take a thousand times longer than it took Tia to polish off three sandwiches (I gave her one of mine). Galen looked up at me. He heard "walk" and probably didn't understand why we were still standing there.

When we finally got outside, I headed for the trees. I knew exactly where I wanted to go. Smack trudged along beside me, like I was leading her to the gallows. Galen pranced, like I was leading him to a giant bowl of kibble. Actually, I led the way to the Spring in the heart of the forest.

The Spring was a sort of fountain of youth. When humans drank from it, they remained eternally at their current age, which was why Janus looked like he was in his forties and all the rest of us looked like we were in our late twenties. When a supernatural being like me drank from it, we remained our current age and received some fringe benefits, like heightened senses and increased strength. Janus told me once that he was always a powerful sorcerer, but after he drank from the Spring, he could do things no sorcerer should be able to do. I found that impressive and scary and hoped that I never gave him reason to demonstrate those things.

It was really more of an aquifer-fed pond than a spring, but "aquifer-fed pond" was too fucking long to keep saying when you lived for centuries. It looked like a little lake, one that never froze, no matter how cold the winters got. I didn't understand that, but then, a magickal spring could probably do whatever it wanted.

I wiped some snow off one of the nearby boulders and sat down, gazing at the water. Janus kept magickal safeguards around the place to ensure that no younglings decided to help themselves until we deemed them ready. We also kept a guard there 24-7, like our border patrol. But if you could ignore all that, it was a very peaceful place to sit and think. Or talk.

"I thought you said we were going for a walk," Smack said, her tone resentful.

I ignored her for the moment, glancing up at the hide where the youngling guard sat. "Who's on duty?"

A face appeared. It was one of the girls, so she already knew about Smack's suicide attempt. Still, it might make Smack more talkative if we were alone. I searched my memory for the girl's name. "Naia. Do me a favor and go take a coffee break."

"I'm not supposed to leave," she said, while looking like she desperately hoped I could override that order.

"I'm here. I'll keep watch. Go get yourself something hot to drink."

That seemed good enough for her. She clambered down the ladder and took off at a jog before I could change my mind.

I nodded. "Better." I returned my attention to Smack. "I know I said we were going for a walk. Now, we're sitting and talking. Come on. You can't tell me you'd rather be sitting in that classroom, waiting for that computer to spontaneously combust."

The corners of her mouth quirked slightly, the only indication that she heard me.

"Fine. Stand." I stared at the water and petted Galen.

After a few minutes, Smack sat down on the rock to my right. "What do you want?"

I decided to go for the direct approach. "I want to know why you tried to kill yourself. What do you want?"

"I want you to leave me the fuck alone to do whatever I want."

"Well, that's not going to happen." I ignored the cursing, ignored the disrespect. No one was here to witness it, and I personally didn't give a shit about that right now. "I like you, Smack. I like the world with you in it. Without you, the world would be..." I floundered for a word. "It would be less."

"Less what?"

"Just less, you know." I could hear frustration start to creep into my voice, and I took a deep breath to squelch it. "All right, so eloquence isn't my thing."

"Shocker," she muttered, so quietly, I barely heard her.

I snorted.

"Why doesn't matter," she said in a normal volume. "I didn't do it, so it doesn't matter why."

"Actually, it does. You were fine when we were knitting, and then you suddenly wanted to die. Something must've happened."

"How do you know I was fine? You think you know everything about me?" Her voice jumped an octave, startling me, and I decided to move a little more cautiously.

"No, you're right, I don't." I watched Galen move to Smack's side. She started petting him without even seeming to see him, and instantly, her scent calmed. I cocked my head to one side. "Were you fine? Or were you already planning to kill yourself after everyone else went to bed?"

"No, I wasn't plannin' it. If I was plannin' it, I woulda picked a better knife." She sounded insulted that I would think a paring knife was her big plan to off herself.

"Okay, that's fair. So what happened that you needed to do it right then, so badly that you tried to make do with that piece of crap blade?"

"I told you, it don't matter." As I opened my mouth to correct her, she shouted, "Doesn't!"

When anyone else shouted in my presence, Galen went into protective mode. But this time, he laid his head on Smack's lap and gazed up at her, like he was encouraging her to focus on him, instead of whatever caused her pain.

"It does matter," I said again. "It matters to me. And it matters to Valentine and Gina and all the other girls you'd be leaving behind. It matters to Tony. It matters to Janus. I'm not sure about Finn. He's kind of a selfish dick."

Smack laughed, a brief, involuntary sound that appeared to just sneak out. Then she clamped her mouth shut, probably to prevent any other sounds from escaping.

As I watched her work so hard at not reacting, I realized I wasn't going to get answers by asking questions or deflecting with humor. Maybe it would help if I shared something of my own experience. Not all of it. The last thing Smack needed was a recounting of Aza's torture. But maybe just an acknowledgement that I empathized.

"Smack, you remember when I was gone for those couple months last fall?"

She shrugged, which I took as a yes. "Sankha Finn told everybody you were on an assignment." Her tone told me she knew that was bullshit, confirmed by her next statement. "You didn't take Galen."

"Yeah. I – I was in a bad situation. It was to save someone, so I had my reasons, but it was…bad. I can't even tell you how many times I wanted to die."

She snorted again. "But you didn't, and it gets better, so I should just hang on, because this, too, shall pass. Right?" Her voice dripped with disdain at my pitiful attempt to share.

"They tell me it gets better. I'm not sure yet." Her eyes narrowed at my honesty, as if she was trying to see the trick behind it. "But I never thought about ending my life before that happened. That's what I was trying to get at. So I'm guessing whatever happened to you was probably worse, because I'm pretty sure you're stronger than I am. Emotionally, at least."

Her hand started to shake. She clenched it into a fist. "If I was strong, I wouldn't'a done that."

"I said stronger." I emphasized the "er." "I'm not saying you're the Superman of emotional strength, but I think you've got me beat. I just don't set the bar real high on that." Her other hand formed a fist, too. "You know, I'm a big fan of fists. They make me feel strong. But sometimes, it's nice to pet Galen instead. Particularly without gloves on." I tugged off one glove, leaned over and gave the dog in question a scratch behind the ear.

Smack's hands stayed clenched. I fell silent. I couldn't think of anything else to say. I was tapped out.

I could feel the cold of the rock I sat on seep through my clothing to chill my skin. And if I was cold, Smack was probably freezing. Shape-shifters ran warmer than humans. I was about to suggest we start walking back when Smack murmured, "It was supposed to be over."

She was so quiet, I wondered if maybe I heard wrong, maybe I missed some vital part that would make the sentence make sense. But I was terrified that if I asked her to repeat herself, she'd clam up again. "What was supposed to be over, Smack?" Please don't say your life.

I could actually hear her blood rushing to the surface. I could hear her heart start to pound, and I imagined anger and pain and every other emotion under the sun heating her skin and causing her whole body to start shaking. I knew that feeling, and it was impossible to clench your whole body to hide the shakes the way you could when it was just your hands.

"The touching," she spat. "No more, that's what Trini told me. I wasn't gonna have to do that anymore."

Trini was one of the Sankhain who rescued Smack. As her words sunk in, I felt cold, the kind of cold that comes from inside, from shock and fear. And rage.

Smack couldn't smell my emotions, so she just kept talking. "But it's never gonna be over. There'll always be another man. Another dick stickin' its way into me. That's why, if you want to know so bad."

Fuckfuckfuckfuckfuck. "Who, Smack? Tell me who, and I'll kill him for you." It never occurred to me to say anything else. Whoever did this would die. Period.

"Nuh-uh." She shook her head. "No way I'm snitching. I tell, and he knows it was me. No way."

"Smack, you have to –"

"NO!" She jumped up and ran away. I chased after her, glancing back at the Spring that I promised I would watch for Naia. Fortunately, as we ran, I saw Naia heading back toward her perch with an insulated mug in hand.

When I caught up to Smack, I didn't touch her. I didn't dare. She'd been violated enough.

"Smack, even if he stops hurting you, even if you manage to kill yourself, he's not going to stop all together. Please. I need to make sure he doesn't hurt anyone else. Because you're right. This shouldn't have happened. It's never happened before, and I need to make sure it never happens again. You're supposed to be safe now. You're right, Trini should've been right. Please. It won't matter if he knows you told, because he'll be too dead to do a damn thing about it. I promise you."

She wiped her cheeks and stared straight ahead. "I'm late for computer class. I gotta change clothes, cuz my butt's all wet from sitting on that rock. I gotta go."

I let her run ahead of me, but I followed. I waited outside the bunkhouse while she changed clothes, then I followed her to the classroom cabin. I stayed out there for a long time, wondering what I should do. Where should I go? Who could I tell? How could I discover the identity of Smack's abuser without her help?

I glanced at Janus's cabin. I thought I could see him standing in the window, watching me. Maybe I should just think it at him. He could read my mind, I wouldn't have to say anything, and he could take over responsibility. But like Tony last night, I felt it was my responsibility. The younglings seemed to be trusting me to take care of things. I needed to at least try.

Younglings raced out of the buildings, using the time between classes to run off some excess energy. Smack emerged from the cabin before me and met my gaze with dead eyes. Yes, I needed to at least try, and I had an idea where I could look. I took off for the trees, Galen keeping pace at my side. There was one person who might know the identity of the man who…god damn it. I couldn't even think the words.

I reviewed the Sankhain instructors as I ran. It wasn't Tony, obviously. He would never. It couldn't be Finn, he was a prick, but not that kind of prick. Janus was even less likely than Tony. The only other male Sankha staying at camp was Ethan, and I dismissed him as quickly as the others. Ethan struggled with physical contact. I brushed up against him once and he jumped a foot in the air. I couldn't picture him touching another person voluntarily, much less having sex. The thing was, I couldn't really picture any Sankha doing this. They were my family, my pack.

But sometimes, family turned ugly like that.

Chapter 7

KELLAN

I reached the forest and slowed down slightly. If I fell and broke an ankle, it would slow me down while it healed. But I still pressed my pace a little harder than I probably should have, as I made my way to the outer border of the forest, where Valentine and Dirk would still be on patrol.

I couldn't see Tia. I hoped she was somewhere warm, but I suspected she was just hiding that well. Finn probably intended for the girls to get some time apart, putting Valentine on border patrol. That obviously wasn't working.

Another problem for another day. "Valentine, come down here, please. I need to speak to you." I waited and didn't hear movement. "Now!"

Valentine shimmied down from her tree, and so did Dirk. Tia emerged from the inside of a hollowed-out log. How did she even fit in there? So small. So helpless.

Would she be next?

I shook my head and focused on Valentine. "I talked to Smack. You want to do this in private?"

Valentine fixed me with her laser gaze. "They know what's been happening. Everybody knows. 'Cept you guys." You guys, meaning the adults. The ones who were supposed to be protecting the younglings.

Something else she said hit me. She said, "what's been happening." Like it didn't happen just once. How long had this been going on? I felt a flash of impotent anger. "If everybody knows, then why is nobody saying anything?" It wasn't her fault, I reminded myself. It wasn't her fault I felt this way. So ashamed of my cluelessness. So useless. But still, the anger coursed through me.

Dirk stepped up behind Valentine. "Vallie." He rested a hand on her shoulder, and she shrugged it off.

"She won't tell me who did it," I told them. I looked from one to the next. What's been going on. Were there others being abused? Was Smack really the only one? Could we bring damaged people together into a community and be dumb enough to expect that we'd all just live in harmony? The anger left me in a whoosh, and I felt weak, like rage was the only thing keeping me upright. "I need you to tell me who did it."

Valentine stayed silent. But that stubborn glint in her eye faded a little, like she wanted to tell.

I wanted to scream. "Please," I said, the effort that went into not screaming making my voice raspy. "Tell me who it is. It's not Ethan, is it?"

She looked at me like I was a simpleton. "Sankha Ethan wears gloves in the summer so he doesn't have to touch anybody."

"I know that," I snapped. Ethan and I practically grew up together. But again, I forced myself to speak quietly. "I didn't think it could be, but I don't know who else...was it one of the Sankhain who visited over the holidays?" But then why would Smack have reached her breaking point now?

Tia moved soundlessly to her sister's side and wrapped her arms around her. Valentine's arms snaked around Tia's shoulders. Valentine leaned down as Tia whispered something. Then Valentine looked up at me. "She says I should tell you."

Suddenly so happy I brought Tia hot chocolate, I said, "She's a smart girl."

Valentine studied me a moment more, then seemed to reach a decision. "It's not a Sankha."

An outsider? Someone made their way into camp without us knowing? I shivered. Was it Aza? Was he back? Finn said he was keeping track of him, but what if Aza returned and...?

No. There was no way someone could enter camp without Janus knowing. He set up spells to alert him to everything, like motion detectors. I think he only bothered with border patrol to give the kids practice sitting still for long periods. But then who did that leave?

As the realization hit me, my already-weakened knees gave out. I found myself kneeling in the snow, trying to breathe. Another youngling. One of our younglings was victimizing another. I looked up at the three before me. "Who?" was all I could manage to say, as I flipped through the faces of the younglings like a mental deck of cards. Which one?

Tia whimpered a little, and I watched Valentine tighten her hold. "It's J.C. Now what're you gonna do about it?"

J.C. The same kid who was giving Tony trouble in archery class. The one who just killed a helpless squirrel. That was a bad sign, right? Torturing animals. That was a sign something was really wrong.

J.C. always gave me the creeps. He was always polite, always helpful, and yet I could always smell rage on him, like a cologne. He came to us when he was older, already sixteen. Usually, Janus didn't take in younglings that old. Younger kids were easier to work with, easier to acclimate to our hierarchy. But Tony and Ethan lobbied for J.C. I think they saw some part of themselves in him, and Janus caved, took him on. He was eighteen now, so technically, he was an adult, but when you count your age in centuries like I did, it was harder to see them that way until they started acting like adults.

I realized I was still kneeling on the ground, still being stared at by three kids. I pushed to my feet. I needed to get to J.C., get him locked up while I explained to Janus and Finn what he did. But first, I said, "Thank you." I never uttered more heartfelt words in my life. These kids stood up for their friend. They were exactly what younglings were supposed to be. "I'm really proud of you three. Thank you."

Then I ran again. Of course, J.C.'s archery class was done, just like Smack's computer class, so I had to ask Tony for another youngling's schedule. When he saw my face, his scent went to immediate alarm. I wondered briefly what I looked like, as I asked him for J.C.'s whereabouts.

"Oh, okay, um, I think he has kitchen duty right now. Why?"

No fucking way I could explain why I needed to know. Not without privacy, a shit-ton of time and a big fucking bottle of whiskey. Instead, I promised I'd tell him later, thanked him and took off for the mess hall, ignoring him as he called my name.

Halfway there, I skidded to a halt as I realized something. Kitchen duty. Wasn't that where Smack was going after computer class? I felt my body go pale, like all the blood drained from me. Run, run, run.

I couldn't bring Galen into the kitchen with me. I mean, I could, I did it all the time, but I wasn't about to bring Galen into a potentially volatile situation. I left him on a down-stay outside and ducked through the back door into the kitchen.

Smack and J.C. were the only two younglings on lunch prep with Gina. Smack was across the room, washing dishes. J.C. stood inches from Gina, his back to me. She must not know the identity of Smack's attacker, I thought. Valentine said everyone knew, but maybe that didn't include Gina, now that she was a Sankha. There was no way Gina knew J.C. raped Smack. Even Christian Gina wouldn't let J.C. live if she knew what happened.

Gina saw me and glanced down at my side, obviously registering that Galen wasn't with me. "Hi, Kellan."

At those words, both Smack and J.C. stiffened. Smack just froze, but I saw J.C. reach for a carving knife on the cutting board next to him. "Hey, J.C., leave the knife and come with me, all right?" I said. Gina kept looking from me to him, me to him. Confusion clouded her expression, but after glancing at Smack, she moved to the girl's side. She might not know what was going on, but she could obviously tell her friend was in distress.

J.C. stayed absolutely still for a very long minute. I could see the tension in his shoulders, the way his hand twitched like he really, really wanted to grab that knife. Then he turned and smiled at me. "Hello, Sankha Kellan. May I get you some coffee?"

"No, thanks, J.C., I just need you to come with me for a bit. All right? So let's go." I held my breath as I waited to see if he'd come voluntarily. I almost blacked out, he kept me waiting so long, but finally, he walked over to me.

"Of course, Sankha Kellan." The scent of his rage overpowered all other scents, a massive feat in a kitchen. I took his arm, my grip a little too tight to be comfortable, but he didn't say another word until we were outside. "So the little cunt talked, huh? I should've known, after she tried to off herself last night," he said, in the same friendly, easy-going voice.

Before I realized what I was doing, he was lying face-down on the ground with my foot on the back of his neck, pressing down so he was probably inhaling snow. "Shut. The fuck. Up," I growled. Part of me hoped he would so I could get him to the cells without a scene. But most of me hoped he said something, anything, else.

He didn't, just laughed a little as I hauled him to his feet and led him roughly to the solitary cells. Galen trailed along behind us, watching my prisoner with the focus of, well, of an akita whose person was radiating hatred for the boy in her custody.

Our solitary cells were free-standing brick structures about the size of an outhouse. They had strong doors, and the only windows were tiny, up by the ceiling and opened with a crank. The cells weren't the sort of place anyone would want to spend any amount of time, which was the point of a cell, really. I shoved J.C. into the first cell and slammed the door. I bolted it and leaned against it, breathing hard, and realized I could smell his scent. The door was solid, but not airtight. His scent escaped through the cracks, trickled out to me. He smelled…young.

Teenagers had a particular smell. Beyond the normal body odor, I could smell the overflow of hormones charging through a teen's body. J.C. had that scent. He smelled angry, he smelled wrong, but he also smelled young. And scared. Then I heard something that made my legs drop out from under me again. Sniffles, and the scent of tears. J.C. was crying.

I started to shake, as I realized how close I came to ripping that boy's head off with my bare hands. I wasn't a stranger to violence. I didn't have a problem killing when it was necessary. But this was the first time I wanted to kill a child. I tried to tell myself he was eighteen now, much too old to be called a child. But those sounds on the other side of the door said differently. This was a boy, a broken kid. It didn't excuse his actions, but he wasn't born this way. He was made.

I stayed sitting outside J.C.'s cell long enough for my butt to start hurting from the cold ground. I reminded myself of what Smack had been through. It was worse, so much worse. And we couldn't allow J.C. to stay, to live with us. He was a rapist. He took his pain and rage out on one of our younglings. But fuck it all, the sound of him crying would haunt my nightmares, I knew it would.

He wasn't Aza. He was just a boy.

I didn't smell Gina approach, but when she knelt beside me, I could smell the stew meat she must've been preparing before she left the kitchen. A few months ago, that smell would've made me gag, but now, it just made me wrinkle my nose.

"What did he do?" she asked.

I met her eyes. "He – Smack. He..." I still couldn't say it, but Gina just kept staring at me. "He raped her," I whispered.

She paused, seeming to absorb this. "And he's still alive?" The venom, the rage, sounded foreign coming from Gina.

"For now." I promised Smack he would die. I intended to make good on my promise. No matter what.

I heard a shuddering breath behind the door, the sort of breath you take after crying too hard for too long. Fuck.

"You should've told me. I never would've left Smack." Gina leapt to her feet and ran off.

I forced myself to stand, to slowly back away from the cell. Because I couldn't turn my back on it, I realized. On him. I would have to kill this boy, but I would force myself to also witness his pain. That was only right.

I didn't want to leave. But I realized there was someone I needed to inform of the day's events. Someone who might not appreciate me taking a youngling into custody without running it past him first. With Galen at my side, I headed for Janus's cabin. I kept glancing back at J.C.'s cell, though. As if he would somehow manage to get the door open. *Did I bolt it properly? Was I sure it was secure?* I knew it was, I knew I bolted it and there was no way J.C. could get out. But paranoia made me run back to double-check. Then I raced for Janus's cabin, because I felt the weight of his potential disapproval hanging over my head.

Technically, it was possible Janus already knew. With his mind-reading abilities, he could monitor all the goings-on at the Academy. But with almost twenty people on the premises, it drained his energy too much to watch us all. He tended to shut down that part of his abilities and focus more on close-contact readings and the more important magick of keeping the forest invisible.

As Galen and I reached the cabin, I found myself again hoping he would read my mind and I wouldn't have to say anything out loud. Normally, it pissed me off when Janus invaded my mind, but now? This was becoming a habit, first last night with Smack's suicide attempt and now this. Of course, eventually, I would have to say it. Tony couldn't read minds, and he would want to know what happened. Eventually.

First, though, I needed to make sure Smack was okay. I called Gina's phone. As soon as she answered, I asked, still out of breath from my run, "Is she with you?"

Gina said yes. I didn't ask if Smack was okay. That seemed like a stupid question. But at least she wasn't alone. I thanked Gina and hung up. Then I returned to the task at hand. I carefully opened the door.

Tevin sat at the reception desk. He told me I could go right in. Janus was expecting me.

That sounded ominous, but when I stepped inside Janus's inner sanctum, I didn't smell anger. Concern, curiosity, maybe a little anxiety. But no anger. "Good morning, sir." I stopped inside the door, gaze lowered, and waited.

"I saw you escort J.C. to a holding cell."

So that was why he was expecting me. I should've known he would see. "Yes, sir. I'm sorry I didn't consult you first. I just..." Then I told him what happened. I didn't bother to wonder if he knew any of it already, if he picked up anything from my thoughts. I just rattled off the events. I stumbled a little over J.C.'s words as I took him into custody, but I managed to say them. When I finished, I said, "My deepest apologies for not getting here sooner, sir."

He looked pale, shaken. Basically, he looked like I felt before going in search of J.C. To think that one of our younglings could rape another...well, it was unthinkable. Except it wasn't.

This never happened before. I didn't think so. But what if it did? Would we know? The younglings didn't want to tell us this time. They kept secrets from us, from the adults.

I felt like the earth shifted under my feet. My knees threatened to give out, and I slumped into a chair. Janus quickly followed suit.

A knock at the door, and Finn stepped inside. "What's happened? I heard that…" His voice trailed off as he got a look at us. "What's happened?" he asked again, his voice a little lower as the realization that This Was Bad seemed to set in.

I didn't know I was crying until I felt drops of water hitting my wrist. I rubbed my cheeks, trying to hide the evidence, but more tears kept falling. Finally, I turned away, so Galen was the only one who could see my face. He placed his head in my lap, and that helped me get a grip on myself. I sniffled, wiped my eyes one last time, and turned back to see two very uncomfortable-looking men, staring at me like I just sprouted rabbit ears and whipped out a giant carrot. "Sorry," I said.

That seemed to break the spell. Janus reached out to me, just a brief brush of his hand on my wrist, and Finn retrieved a dusty box of tissues from the bathroom. You didn't go through a lot of tissues after drinking from a Spring of immortality, not unless you had allergies like Tony. The dust made me sneeze, which only made the snot situation worse. Suffice it to say, it took me a few moments to pull myself together the rest of the way.

Finn waited a whole two seconds after I blew my nose the last time, an act of compassion, as far as he was concerned. "Will someone kindly explain to me what has happened?" He emphasized "what" and "happened," as if to remind us this was the third time he asked. Finn compassion looked a lot different than normal-person compassion.

Which I guess could also be said about me. "I need to kill J.C." Because that was how I could be compassionate. It might break something inside me to kill a kid, a youngling, especially after listening to him cry, but I would do it, because Smack was like my kid sister. Nobody was going to hurt her that way.

Janus cleared his throat as Finn's jaw dropped. "You see," Janus said, and he explained the situation. As Finn listened, he slowly lowered himself into a chair and even more slowly lowered his head into his hands. He stayed that way for the duration of the tale and for quite a while after.

Then he raised his head and addressed Janus. Not me. Definitely not me, because what he said was, "We must have a hearing before enacting any sentence," and he wasn't dumb enough to say that to me. Knew if he said that to me, he'd find himself with a broken nose and maybe minus a few precious parts.

"A hearing? Fuck, no. There's only one way to –" I was just gathering steam when Finn raised his hand to silence me. I shot to my feet, sending my chair clattering as I advanced on him and drew back my fist.

But Janus spoke before I could murder anyone. "That's enough. Finlay, Kellan has suffered a shock. We all have. I believe it would be in everyone's best interest if we spoke of next steps at a later time."

"Fuck that," I said. Janus hated when I swore. I knew I was pushing my luck, but I couldn't stop myself. "You guys want a hearing? Fine. Convene it now. I'll tell you how Smack looked this morning when she thought word might get out about who hurt her. Better yet, let's get Smack in here. But we better have J.C. in here, too, right? He has the right to defend himself. Right? Maybe he can call Smack a cunt to her face. Maybe we can even let him demonstrate some of the things he did to her?" I spat the words at them, wishing they were poison darts, or at least acid.

"Kellan," Finn said.

This time, I didn't let him silence me. "We robbed that girl of her last safe place. We promised her something and we didn't deliver. You really want to make her testify about what she went through? Really. God, I knew you were bastards, but come on." I knew instantly that I went too far. But fuck, I made a career of going too far. It was worth it if it meant I could protect Smack from the trauma of a hearing.

"If you would allow me to continue," Finn said, "I believe I may be able to explain my intention." He smelled pissed, which was fine. I'd rather fight with a pissed-off Finn than a passive, entitled one.

Because misery loves company, I waited for several moments before nodding, like I was giving him permission to speak. That ratcheted up his anger, which made me perversely happy.

"We must have a hearing so the younglings see we are being fair." He swallowed hard, and his temper cooled, like he was too busy keeping his breakfast down to bother with anger. "We have never been in this position before. It's – it's atrocious. And as much as I sympathize with what Smack has been through..." Another pause, another swallow. "We – we made the same promises to J.C. We must be absolutely clear that we are giving him the same consideration that we give her."

I felt the ground shifting under me. I didn't like this version of our world. We weren't a fucking democracy. We were a monarchy, damn it, and Janus was the one and only vote that mattered. That was one of the many things I liked about this life. The Sankhain were built like a wolf pack. One alpha. Sure, he had Finn as his beta, but Janus's word was law. This whole enlightened, fairness-to-all bullshit wasn't who we were.

And I was damned if I was going to roll over and accept what Finn was trying to do. "Sure. We made those promises to J.C. We made them, and he gathered them up in a pile, shat on them, and set them on fire. He violated everything we stand for. If he was a Sankha rather than a youngling, we wouldn't be having this conversation. None of it. There's one sentence for those who break our laws, who betray our trust to this degree. Death. Period." Even as I said the words, I remembered the sound of sniffling on the other side of the bolted door. I shook my head violently to push the memory away.

Janus exhaled a heavy sigh, the kind that slipped out from under the weight of the world. I was winning, I realized. He knew I was right. Well, fuck me.

Never one to quit while I was ahead, I kept talking. "You want to show the younglings that you value them? Show them that we'll protect them, but only as long as they respect one another. We can't have predators in this pack. Not ones who prey on our cubs. These children need us to at least give them that much. J.C. made a choice. He knew exactly what he was doing, and he wasn't sorry." Was he? Did it matter? We couldn't just send him back to the outside world. No one other than the Sankhain were allowed to know of the Spring's existence. Well, except for Darcy, but the only reason Darcy was allowed to live was because I guilted Finn and Janus into it, and because he was the most trustworthy human ever to walk the earth. Not so with J.C. If J.C. wasn't going to be a Sankha, then he would have to die.

I took a deep breath, then plunged ahead. "You didn't want him here. Neither of you. If you listened to your instincts, none of this would've happened. If you listened to what you knew to be true, Smack wouldn't have been reviolated on our watch."

Finn paled at this, and I knew I had them both.

"Fuck fairness. Show these kids that we'll protect them from threats, inside and out." I sat back in my chair, exhaustion closing over me.

I heard a throat clear. I looked at the doorway and saw Tony there. He was staring at me like he never saw me before. No, worse, like I was something slimy that just crawled out from under the kitchen sink. He cleared his throat again and turned his gaze to

Janus. "Sorry, sirs. I – heard raised voices, so I told Tevin I would announce myself, but then..." His gaze swung back to me.

Tony was one of the people who argued to allow J.C. to join the younglings, when he was still a youngling himself. Argued very passionately about saving the boy. And now, he just heard me arguing to execute that boy. Fuck.

"Tony -" I started to get up, but he very deliberately turned away to look at Janus and Finn.

"Sirs, I merely came to check on Kellan. Gina suggested she might – she might need support." He blinked. "Obviously, Gina was mistaken. I will go, if I may be dismissed." He ducked out without waiting for an answer.

I felt something slipping away from me. I looked at Janus with wide eyes, feeling my skin grow cold. He nodded once. "Go."

I shot out of the room. Tony was still standing in the waiting area, staring at the window. At, not out of, because I doubted he saw anything in front of him. "Tony, look," I began, but he cut me off.

"Go away, Kellan." His voice sounded raw, and I inhaled deeply, seeking information. I smelled a torrent of feelings, fear, sadness, anger, and yes, hurt. And I reminded myself how much Tony cared about the younglings. How he was once promised the same things Smack was. Not all that long ago, really. He'd only been a full Sankha for a couple of years.

I hesitated, then went to him. I pressed myself up against his back, wrapped my arms carefully around his middle. He stiffened like he wanted to pull away, but instead he just stood there, not leaving, but not relaxing, either.

"Smack. J.C. He – raped her?" Tony's voice was so quiet, almost timid.

"Yeah."

Silence stretched thick and humid like the air on a July night.

"He's just a kid," he said softly.

The same thing I was thinking half an hour ago, sitting outside the solitary cell, listening to J.C. cry. Just a kid. And I remembered how Tony saw himself in J.C. Tony was a good person who couldn't have known what J.C. would do. But my words to Janus were just as true as my thoughts now. "Smack's just a kid, too."

His breath whooshed out like it was fleeing his lungs. "I know." And those two words held so much pain. So much horror. Part of me wanted to give him a pass. Unlike Finn and Janus, Tony would see his culpability and hate himself for it. It made it harder to be mad at him.

But he was the one who thought J.C. should be one of us. He was even more culpable than Finn and Janus. In my head, I heard Smack saying, *It was supposed to be over.* I never heard her sound so broken, not even when she first came to us. My old friend rage warmed me from the inside out.

I let go of Tony, as the rage settled in to stay, but then he leaned his forehead against the top of the window frame. Because he was too tall to rest it against the window itself. I forgot sometimes how tall he was. Because he was just Tony. And my arms snaked around his waist again.

J.C. would never have a moment like this, I realized. Someone who knew him so well that they forgot to even see what he looked like. And I understood a little of what Tony was feeling. But still... Smack.

"Is she okay?" he asked, and my arms tightened around him as moisture prickled at my eyes.

"No." I couldn't lie. He'd know I was lying, anyway. "But she's with Gina. It'll – it'll be all right eventually."

"You're right," he said, and I knew he didn't mean about Smack being all right. "It's the only thing we can do. I – I knew he was damaged. I knew it. I just – fuck."

Sometimes, fuck was about all there was to say. Which was why it was my favorite word.

"You wanted to save him," I said quietly. He shuddered, and I knew I hit on the truth. Tony wasn't denying that J.C. was a rapist. He wasn't denying the boy had to die. He was mourning the fact that he failed to save J.C. I adjusted my arms because they were getting tired from holding him so tight. But I didn't let go. As much as I was mad, as much as part of me blamed him, I didn't let go.

The next thing I knew, Tony was stepping to the side, sliding from my grasp. "I, um, I think I'll go guard his cell." He moved toward the door.

What if Tony heard him crying? That would break Tony's heart. "I'll go with you."

He turned too quickly and bumped into me. "No. No, I'll go by myself. I just – fuck, Kell, I need some time, okay? I'll see you later."

I stood there, watched him go. If he was somewhere else, I told myself, I didn't have to deal with my rage. I could just let it burn. Rage was so much more comfortable than all the other emotions swirling around right now.

The door to the inner office swung open, and I turned to see Finn standing there. Oh, good. A target for my rage that wouldn't confuse the shit out of my psyche.

"Give him a little space, Kellan." His voice was gentle. Like he pitied me.

Fuck that. "I'll take relationship advice from you when you manage to grow a heart, Dr. Phil. Was there something you wanted, other than to intrude on a private personal moment?"

A slight twitch of the eyebrows was the only acknowledgment that my insult registered. "Janus wishes to discuss the carrying out of the sentence."

"Super. I'll be there in a minute."

"Kellan -"

"I said I'll be there in a minute." I didn't raise my voice, but the growl in my tone made Galen's head dip submissively. I reached down and petted him to reassure him the growl wasn't for him.

Finn nodded and disappeared back behind the door. I took all of two seconds to gather myself and try to calm down, then I followed him.

Chapter 8

TONY

As I strode toward the solitary cells, several younglings tried to stop me and ask me questions. I ignored them. I never ignored younglings, but right that moment, I had to. I wasn't even sure I could speak, and I was certain I didn't want to.

How did things go from so amazing to so horribly wrong? Not that I was feeling sorry for myself. I didn't deserve pity. It was my fault J.C. was even here. What I should be asking was, how could I possibly think I could help a boy who didn't want help? Shit, even if J.C. wanted help, I was hardly the person to offer it. I was just as damaged, just as broken.

Moisture prickled at the corners of my eyes. I sniffed and quickened my pace. *Will not cry in front of younglings. Fuck, I hope they didn't station a youngling to guard the door of the cell.*

They didn't. When I arrived at the cells, I saw Gina standing outside one of them. Didn't Kellan say she was supposed to be with Smack? I wanted to ask what she was doing there when she should be helping her friend. But I didn't, just said, "Hey, I'm here to take over guard duty."

Gina turned to me. Her brown eyes, usually so normal, now appeared to blaze. How could brown look like fire? I didn't know, but her eyes managed it. Then I felt a shift in the air, like a breeze but not, because it was warm, almost hot, and Wisconsin didn't get warm breezes in January. "You. You were one of them. You brought him here."

Her words, the same ones I was using to beat myself up, hit my gut like a heavy punch. I rubbed the back of my neck and felt the tears press against the back of my throat. "I know. I'm so sorry. If I could take it back -"

"You can't." Her voice sounded different, hollow, yet piercing, and I realized what that warm breeze was. I heard Janus's voice go that way before, when the old man raised magickal power. But this was Gina. She wasn't a sorcerer.

Impossible as it was, I felt the pinpricks of magickal energy stab at my skin, like thousands of sparks of static electricity all over my body. I didn't know much about magick, but I was pretty sure this was bad. I tried to keep my voice soothing. "Gina, listen."

"No, you listen." With each word, the pinpricks hit harder, sharper, until I felt like I should be bleeding. "That monster hurt her. And he's going to pay. I'm going to make sure he suffers."

Fear cut through me. Gina wasn't this person. She was gentle, a little acerbic sometimes, but nothing like this. She didn't like violence. It took months of one-on-one training to get her to throw a proper punch. This was all wrong. "Gina, he will pay." I reached out to her. "Come on. We'll go talk to Finn and Janus, we'll -"

"Don't touch me!" She flung her hand out, and I felt something slice through my jeans. A blade? No, her hands were empty. But somehow, blood poured down my leg, hot and fast, too fast. She must've hit the femoral artery. Fuck.

I heard footsteps running toward us. Turning, I saw Kellan, followed by Janus and Finn both.

"Tony?" All traces of rage gone, Gina now sounded scared. Unfortunately, fear seemed to feed the magick the same way rage apparently did. The air still crackled with unnatural heat.

I knew I needed medical help, but I couldn't turn away from her fear. Trying to press my hand against my leg, I stepped toward her. She approached me, reached out to me – and the static electricity followed, assaulting me with a wave of energy that pierced my skin and hurt a thousand times worse than my leg. I yelped in pain, and she backed up.

The world started to narrow and blacken around the edges. Blood loss. I was going to pass out. Fuck. I dropped to my knees, then fell on my ass before collapsing to the ground. Kellan's face swam above me. "Gina," I managed to say. "Help Gina."

"Finn's got Gina." She pressed her hat to my leg, and it was like I felt the wound for the first time. I swallowed a scream. Kellan barked at someone to go get Simone. And that was the last thing I heard.

———— «◊» ————

KELLAN

Blood. So much blood. "No, no, no, no." I pressed the hat tighter to Tony's leg, part of me hoping the pain would rouse him. He was so pale and now his eyes were closed. "Fuck, you will not die on me, motherfucker. God damn it, wake the fuck up."

He jerked from the pressure on his leg, but didn't open his eyes.

"Did you honestly just call him a motherfucker?" Simone pushed me aside. "You have the worst bedside manner I've ever seen." She evaluated the wound. "Keep pressure on it. This is going to feel weird, but I need you to keep pressure there until I can close the artery."

She closed her eyes and held her hands an inch above mine. And I felt heat, almost painful, radiate from her hands toward Tony's leg. Through my hands, into Tony's leg. Fuck. Weird didn't begin to cover it.

Her eyes fluttered slightly. "Okay." She sounded a little out of breath. "I got the artery, now I need you to move your hands and take away the hat. I don't want to fuse your hands or the hat to his skin."

I hesitated. Everything I knew about first aid said don't take away the pressure. But Simone knew what she was doing. I forced myself to move my hands, and then I saw Finn.

He glowed with power. That was the only word for it. He slowly walked toward Gina, speaking softly. His eyes glowed, and his skin was alabaster-pale, but more than that, it looked like he was lit from within. He was frightening and beautiful. The power I sensed in the past from Janus made me want to roll over on my back and pee myself. Finn's power made me want to see how many licks it took to get to the gooey center of the Finn-pop.

I wondered why he was raising power of his own. Was he going to hurt Gina? Then I realized that the power in the air wasn't getting worse, the way it would be if they were both raising power. In fact, the energy was lessening. It was almost like – like he was siphoning the power from Gina, taking it into his own body. Was that even possible?

"Gina," Finn said. His mouth moved, but his voice wasn't coming from his mouth, it came from everywhere. The molecules around us were speaking. I began to tremble, feeling afraid of Finn for probably the first time in my life. He now stood right in front of Gina. "Listen closely and do as I say. You will do as I say. Disobedience is not an option."

Gina nodded, and I found myself nodding with her.

"Strong emotions, all strong emotions, feed into the magick, making control more difficult," Finn said, his own voice devoid of emotion. "You will now focus on your breathing, and let go of those emotions, let go of the energy inside."

Beside me, Galen whined. That drew my attention back to Simone and Tony. Tony's leg wound was closed. Simone looked ready to pass out beside him, but she simply told two nearby younglings to get the stretcher and help her get him to the infirmary. Trusting that Tony was safe, I turned back to the main event.

"Breathe deep," Finn said now. Finn, or God, or someone so powerful, I couldn't help but comply. "As you exhale, allow the energy to drain from your body. Let go. Empty yourself and allow my voice to take the place of that energy."

As he continued in the McGuru vein, I remembered a long ago conversation. Finn once bragged to me that he was able to hold more power inside his body than even Janus could, without disturbing the air around him. That must be why the air was almost back to normal. But Finn also told me that holding power inside the body came with a cost. He never elaborated on what that cost was. Watching him now, it seemed possible he was cooking his organs with the heat of that power. Nothing that shone that bright could possibly fail to burn.

I was so focused on what was happening that when I felt a hand on my shoulder, I jumped. Janus stood beside me. I forgot he followed us from the cabin. Followed us when Finn felt the power being raised and ordered me to come with him. When I realized we were heading for the solitary cells, I started to run, because Tony was there. Tony was there with someone raising magickal power, someone who wasn't Finn or Janus, and all I could think was that J.C. must be a sorcerer and oh, fuck, that would be bad. I never imagined that it was Gina. I almost wished it was J.C. Even sorcerers could be killed, and that little worm was going to die, which would eliminate this magickal threat.

But it was Gina. Oh, shit, it was Gina, and somehow, Tony got hurt, and what the fuck happened?

Janus squeezed my shoulder and pointed to the small crowd gathered around us. I glanced back and saw Smack. Her eyes were wide and shimmering with tears, and I turned my back on Finn and Gina and went to her. "Come on," I said quietly, not wanting to disturb McGuru Finn. "She's okay. Finn will take care of her. Come on."

Smack allowed me to push her backwards, backing away, when suddenly she cried out. I turned to see Gina collapse in a heap. Smack and I ran toward her.

Finn stopped us with an outstretched arm. "She's all right. She needs to sleep." He sounded spent, his voice reedy as the power drained from him, drained back into the earth and the air. That's what he told me, years ago, that magickal power came from the elements, and a sorcerer could draw on it and manipulate it to his will. Or her will, apparently.

He sighed, and the sound was a little too final. The pasty whiteness of his skin made me worry that I was about to have two heaps-of-sorcerer on my hands. Smack knelt beside Gina, shaking her, tears streaking down her cheeks.

Cat and Valentine appeared, followed by Tia. "We'll help them," Cat told me. "You should help him." She nodded at Finn, who was wavering on his feet. I caught him and draped his arm over my shoulder, starting to lead him toward his cabin.

"I'm fine." Despite the stubborn set of his jaw, he sounded ill and his skin felt like it burned from fever. "I'll just go to Janus's office. I'm fine."

I pretended to stumble, losing my grip on him and letting his knees buckle under his weight before I caught him again. Galen pressed his nose to my leg, whining, and I smacked my lips together to tell him I was okay. Once again settling Finn's weight on my shoulders, I kept walking toward his place. "Tell you what. I'm going to take you to your cabin. When we get there, if you feel up to it, all you have to do is walk back over to Janus's. If, however, you can't manage that, you're going to lie down and rest. If I have to tie your moron ass to the bed, you're going to rest." I felt so helpless, which pissed me off, and Finn was always a good target for rage.

He shivered violently, and I almost lost my grip for real. "I'm fine," he said yet again.

"Why did you hold that power inside you? Why siphon it off and then hold it inside? Why not just act as a goddamn conduit and send it back into the earth as soon as you took it from her?"

"I couldn't." His teeth started to chatter. How could he be cold, when his skin was on fire? "She would've drawn it back into herself. She – she was so powerful. I didn't think -" He shivered again, and I stopped trying to walk. Even though I was more than strong enough to support his weight, I was having a hard time keeping us both balanced. He was too tall, the angle too awkward.

"Don't suppose you'd let me do a fireman's carry," I said.

"I don't suppose I would." Even with chattering teeth, he managed to sound haughty.

"Right." I waited for the patience to continue on. Since that might take a while, I asked him a question. "What happened back there? Did Gina – do that to Tony?" Blood. So much blood. I swallowed hard and pushed the memory away. Tony was fine. Simone was taking care of him.

Finn nodded. "I've never managed to do it, but I've tried. Taking magickal energy and focusing it, like turning the air into a blade. I wish I could've seen it. Awesome."

I growled at him, seriously tempted to drop him. He didn't mean awesome in the modern way, but in its true meaning, awe-inspiring. That "awesome" thing damn near killed my – Tony. Which is what I said, when I could find my human voice again. "Yeah. Awesome. Too bad Tony didn't actually die. That would've been so fucking cool."

Finn blinked. "That is not what I meant."

"I know it's not, dumbass." I started walking again. I may have been slightly less gentle than before. "But maybe once in a while, you should listen to yourself talk. Then you'd understand why I think you're an asshat."

"An ass…hat?" His voice told me that he never heard the term before.

"Yeah. Asshat."

He made an inarticulate noise, then said, "I didn't think her powers would manifest. When they didn't emerge at puberty, I thought she must have repressed them."

As I half-carried, half-dragged him, I reviewed the puzzle pieces my brain was pawing through. Finn knew Gina was a sorcerer. I was absolutely sure Gina didn't know about her magickal proclivities, which meant this puzzle was turning into an even uglier picture than before. Typical Finn. It probably never occurred to him to tell the poor girl that someday, she might start oozing magick out her pores like metaphysical sweat. Never occurred to him to teach her what to do before it happened, either. Recalling the terror on Gina's face, the weakness of Tony's voice as he told me to help her while he bled all over the snow, I felt sincerely tempted to stab Finn in the femoral artery and leave him on the ground to rot.

"Did you see what she did?" Oblivious to my feelings as always, he just sounded amazed. "Without any instruction. All that power she raised, without even trying. Her instinctive manipulation of it. It was beautiful."

Apparently, he decided not to listen to what he was saying. Which made me feel justified when I shrugged his arm off my shoulder and let him drop. "Get your own ass back to your cabin. Or don't. I don't fucking care." But when I turned, I saw a trail of younglings following us. And they looked terrified. First, Smack was assaulted, then she tried to kill herself, then J.C. was arrested, then Tony was attacked and bleeding and Gina collapsed. Now Finn, one of our leaders, was lying helpless in the snow. Fucking hell. I didn't want to help him, but I couldn't add to the fear and uncertainty that tainted the air.

That didn't mean I had to be nice about it. I pulled Finn off the ground and heaved him across my shoulders. He bleated in dismay, but I ignored him and carried him to his cabin. I may have narrated the trip with an assortment of four letter words to vent my rage. I may also have jostled him a couple times, just to hear him grunt in pain when my shoulder hit an uncomfortable spot or my hand yanked his leg too hard. Oops.

At his cabin, I kicked the door open and carried Finn inside. Galen followed hesitantly. He didn't like Finn, and Galen was clearly concerned I was falling back into bad habits, intending to have sex with Finn. So not where this was going.

I carried him across the cabin to his cot, upon which I dropped his body with enough force to make the frame – and Finn – groan. "Thank you." His voice was heavy with sarcasm.

"I didn't do it for you. I did it for the kids who have seen too much bad stuff to watch me kill you."

His eyes fluttered closed, I assumed from exhaustion. I started to leave when he said, "Kellan."

What did he want now? "If you think I'm going to stay here and wait on you, you are sorely mistaken."

"I'm sorry." That stopped me. I wasn't sure I ever heard those words cross Finn's lips. "Tony almost died. I should have prepared her. I was – I was so wrong. I'm sorry." His voice cracked, and I didn't want to look at him. I could smell the sadness in his scent, like spring rain gathering in puddles on the muddy ground. "There's so much I was so wrong about. I'm sorry."

I could tell he was apologizing for more than the current events. He was sorry for being a dick when we were together. Maybe even sorry for hiding what Mal was doing before she defected, for knowing something was wrong and not telling me. I believed he meant that apology, and I swallowed hard, because I didn't want to feel anything but rage toward him. Our past was complicated. We barely tolerated each other. Yet he was my first in so many things.

I swallowed again and walked over to the closet where he kept the bedding. I carried an extra blanket over and tucked him in, careful not to touch him. He was a dick, but I wasn't exactly Princess Charming. Neither one of us was a dream come true.

"I'm glad we got there in time for Antony," he said quietly. "He's good to you. I'm glad."

My lungs were suddenly the size of kidney beans. Dehydrated ones. "Yeah. He is." Better than I deserved. The truth was, I deserved to be with someone like Finn, someone who would treat me as badly as I treated him. But somehow, I got lucky. My lungs shrunk further, until I could barely draw a breath. "I'm sorry, too. Now shut up and go to sleep." Maybe from lack of oxygen, the words sounded so soft, I wasn't even sure it was me that said them.

I returned to the linen closet and got two more blankets and a comforter. By the time I returned to the bed, Finn's eyes were closed and his breathing was deep and even. As I laid the covers over him, I paused and studied one of the blankets. It was thick and gray and soft, and so obviously not store-bought. Did Finn make it? I glanced in the corner, saw a large wicker basket piled with yarn and a swath of knitted something or other on top. How did I never know he knitted? I looked from the basket to the man on the bed, and for a moment, I watched him sleep. He looked so harmless. So unconniving. Too bad he had to wake up eventually. I left, Galen padding softly behind me.

Chapter 9

KELLAN

I needed to check on Tony. I needed to check on Gina. On Smack. But as I stepped outside into the cold air, the forest called to me, and I didn't fight it. I ran into its arms and allowed tears to fall. I would've climbed a tree, if Galen could've followed. But of course, that wasn't an option, so I did the next best thing. The best best thing, really, because I needed to escape from humanity, and the only way to do that was to let myself be a wolf. I shed my clothes and crouched on the ground. The shift happened so quickly, I barely had time to feel it. Apparently, my wolf half wanted out as badly as my human half wanted to escape.

Now furry and on four legs, I trotted over to Galen. As good as it felt to be lupine, I couldn't help feeling a little guilty, like I was skipping work to go fishing. I would attend to human concerns, I told myself. After a good run.

That's what we did. I tore off into the trees, and Galen followed. We played our favorite game, a cross between tag, hide-and-seek and tackle football. I won, as I always did, and celebrated by tackling my brother and wrestling with him, then letting him go. Because I wasn't one to gloat. Actually, I was, but not with Galen. I never gloated with Galen.

As we walked back to my pile of clothes, Galen kept sniffing my hindquarters. It wasn't an overture, more like he smelled something different, but it was still annoying. After the third time, I whirled around and snapped at him. He regarded me with his head cocked to the side, and I felt icy alarm slice through me. The baby. What the fuck was I thinking? What just happened to the baby when I shifted? What did I just do?

Now I was terrified to shift back. I wasn't even sure I wanted this cub, but damned if I wanted it to die. But I couldn't do my job in wolf form, and there was far too much work to be done. I shifted as fast as I could and dressed rapidly, like putting on underwear would keep the baby from falling out. My clothes were soaked and stiff from the freezing rain I didn't notice falling as we played. As soon as I was dressed, I started to shiver. Damn, I was going to need fresh clothes before I checked on anybody.

As we approached our cabin, I saw Smack sitting on the front steps. She looked cold and lost. I hurried over and pulled her to her feet, instinctively checking her scent for fresh blood. She just had that sort of look, like she was feeling the need to hurt herself again. "Come on, come inside."

As chilled as I was, I started a pot of coffee before I grabbed some clothes and ducked into the bathroom to change. When I came back out, the cabin smelled of coffee, and Smack stood by my dresser, holding one of my daggers.

"Drop it, youngling." Fear made my voice sharper than I intended.

She set it back in the drawer where I kept my blades. Second drawer. Top drawer was the sock drawer, of course. "I wasn't gonna do anything." Her voice was too sad to pull off the sullen teenager routine.

"Good. Because you could do a lot more damage with that than with your little butter knife."

"Paring knife," she corrected me as she walked away and sat down at the table.

"Whatever." I crossed to my dresser and checked the drawer as surreptitiously as I could. All the blades seemed to be there. Good. Retrieving a spare hoodie, I approached the table in my socks, thick wool hiking socks that had arch support. My arches were fine, but there was something so comforting about wearing socks that literally hugged my feet. I handed the hoodie to Smack. "You look frozen. Put this on."

"Yes, ma'am," she muttered sarcastically.

I went to pour us both some coffee, so she wouldn't see me smile. "Now drink this," I said, placing a full mug in front of her. "You still look frozen. Did you eat?"

She stared at me like I was asking if she used her hair to floss her teeth. Why did everyone think that being in a crisis meant you shouldn't eat? Stupid humans. I rummaged around. I'd finished off the bread that morning, but I had some granola bars and Pop Tarts. I set an assortment on the table and tore into a package of frosted strawberry Pop Tarts. I dunked it in my coffee before taking a big bite.

"Where do you get this stuff?" Smack looked at the packaged food like it was gold-plated. "We never get food like this."

"Yeah, well." I had to swallow the mouthful of sugary goodness before I could keep speaking. "Janus hopes that you kids will learn not to eat shit like this and instead choose healthy food. I told him it doesn't work like that, but he doesn't get it."

Smack reverently held a s'mores Pop Tart. "Wow." She took a bite. "Damn, that's good shit."

I laughed a little. "One of the few perks of adulthood. I get to eat what I want. Now what were you doing sitting outside my cabin in an ice storm?"

I expected another "are you really that stupid" glare or maybe some more scathingly muttered words. Instead, Smack set down the pastry and wrapped her hands around her mug, staring into the depths of her coffee like it held answers. It didn't. I knew that, because I often searched for answers in my coffee. Of course, maybe Smack's coffee would be more forthcoming. A girl could hope.

If she found any answers in her mug, she didn't share them. Instead, she said, "What happened?"

Shit. Nobody took the time to talk to her. While I was running around in the forest, Smack was suffering. I sucked.

"Well, to be honest, I'm not exactly sure what happened or how. Or why. I – I guess that Gina heard what J.C. did to you. She went to his cell, to…I don't know what. Instead, she ended up freaking out and attacking Tony." I swallowed hard, the coffee and Pop Tart turning angry inside me as I remembered the scent of Tony's blood soaking the snow. "Seriously, I have no clue. I didn't even know Gina could do magick."

"Gina was – that was magick?" She sounded small. I hated that, so I passed her another packet of Pop-Tarts.

"Yeah, that was magick. It's a kind I've never seen before, but that weird static electricity feeling? That's magick." I did my best to explain how magick worked. Which probably just confused her more, since I wasn't a practitioner and only ever watched it or heard about it second-hand. It occurred to me that there was someone who could explain this a hell of a lot better than me, because she used magick all the time to heal people. Simone.

I took Smack over to the infirmary, explained to Simone what Smack wanted to know, and left them to talk it over. The infirmary held a large, bunk-filled room for when illness ran through the younglings and Simone needed to house a greater number of them. It also had a few small, private rooms. I checked inside each. One was empty. One held a sleeping Gina. I stood and watched her for a while, to make sure she was just sleeping and not dead.

I tried to figure out how I felt. Gina hurt Tony. I should be mad at her. But really, it wasn't Gina's fault. It was like putting a loaded pistol in the hands of a five-year old and then being mad when she shot you. This shitshow was Janus and Finn's fault, not Gina's.

I quietly closed Gina's door and opened the door of the next room. Tony was there, sitting up in bed like he was getting ready to leave. He looked over at me. "Hi," he said.

What a fucking stupid thing to say. He almost died, and all he could say was hi? Fucking asshole. In the back of my mind, a small voice tried to tell me that my anger at Tony was as misplaced as anger at Gina would be. But anger was safer than fear or any of the other emotions that threatened to crush me, so I let the angry voice in my mind drown out the small, reasonable one.

I entered the room and closed the door, because I didn't want anyone to hear us talking. "How could you?" My voice was shaking.

He frowned. "How could I...?"

"You told me to help Gina. You were fucking bleeding to death, and all you fucking cared about was Gina." I shoved him, feeling myself come unhinged, but unable to stop it. "How could you? You weren't even trying to help yourself. You weren't even trying!" At some point, I started crying, but it didn't matter. Tears were inevitable these days.

He pushed to his feet and closed the distance between us, limping slightly. That limp made me want to push him away again, but he wrapped his arms around me. "I'm sorry," he whispered. "I'm sorry." He held me as I sobbed.

What's more ridiculous than me being mad at Tony for almost dying? Tony apologizing for almost dying. Which I told him when the tears subsided and I could speak again.

"Yeah, well, the world's a fucked-up place," was his response. Which made me laugh, which absurdly started me crying again.

He led me over to the bed and we stretched out on top of it. Galen hopped up and lay across our legs, as if to make us stay in one spot, safe and together.

We were quiet for a while, until I said, "I'm so fucking sick of crying."

He snorted a laugh. "It's been kind of a rough couple of days."

I propped myself up on one elbow and stared at him. "I thought you were dead."

"Me, too."

I smacked his shoulder. "Don't joke."

"I'm not." As he stared at me with calm, reasonable eyes, I understood he was telling the truth. He thought he was going to die, and he still told me to help Gina first. I felt my insides turn to jelly, and not in a good way. I hurried over to the sink along the wall and vomited. I heaved until I was shaking and my stomach muscles hurt from the force of it.

I felt his hand on the nape of my neck. Galen's nose nudged my fingertips where they clutched at the counter. Tony reached around me to turn on the faucet, washing my vomit down the drain. "You okay?" he asked.

I started to laugh, but fortunately, that made my stomach ache. Fortunate because the laughter was tinged with hysteria, and if not for the stomachache, I might never have stopped. "It's possible that I'm not as much of a badass as I thought."

"Sure you are." He stroked my hair back. "You're both. Badass exterior. Sentimental center."

I turned and looked at him. "Don't fucking die. You are not allowed to die. Do you understand me? I will fucking kill you if you die."

"Yup. Okay." He kissed my forehead and smiled, treating the threat with as much dignity as it deserved. "How's Gina doing?"

"She's fine," I said grumpily. "Sleeping. Not bleeding. Unlike some people."

"I'm not bleeding anymore."

I grumbled a little more, because I still wanted to be mad. But it was hard to be mad at Tony. Which just meant I needed to go find someone else to be mad at. Luckily, I had a few options. Then something occurred to me. Gina was standing outside J.C.'s cell when she went all Magick Rambo. What if she turned that magick blade on J.C. before Tony arrived? Someone needed to check on J.C.

"I'm glad you're not dead," I told him. "But I should go. I need to see about – about some things." I didn't want to say out loud that I was going to go check and make sure J.C. wasn't dead. That would probably upset Tony.

"I'll go with you," Tony said.

"Like hell you will," Simone said, opening the door.

"Were you eavesdropping?" I scowled at her.

"Yes. That's my job, when I hear someone yelling at one of my patients. Which one of you threw up in the sink?"

"That was her." Tony was quick to throw me under the bus.

"I'm fine," I said quickly. Nothing to see here, just a little vomit. Totally normal. "Too much coffee, too little food. And too much emotion. It's a bad fucking combination."

Simone squinted at me, but didn't argue. She pointed at Tony. "You, back in bed." She pointed at me. "You, with me. Let's go. He needs rest."

"I feel fine," Tony protested.

Simone turned to him with the look that made both Sankha and youngling alike quake in their boots. "You're not. I used a good chunk of my life force, healing you. I'm not about to let you waste it on male pride. Bed. Now." This time, Tony obeyed.

Simone held my hand and led me out, as if she expected me to fight. I didn't. After she closed the door on Tony's room, she looked at me. "You look like crap."

"Um, thank you."

"I'm serious. Don't come back here, looking like that. He's got too much of a hero complex. I'll never get him to rest and take care of himself if you show up looking like crap."

I wanted to be annoyed, but she wasn't wrong. I probably did look like crap, and Tony was too much of a caretaker to put himself first. "Okay. Where's Smack?"

"In Gina's room. Smack asked if she could keep her friend company. I didn't see any reason not to. Now, you want to tell me why you've been throwing up?" She crossed her arms and glared at me, the same look she gave Tony to make him go back to bed.

"I don't know what you're talking about. I told you, too much coffee."

"Kellan, if you're preg-"

"Fuck!" I dragged her into the empty room. "Don't fucking say that. Not where he can hear you. Not where anyone can hear you."

She closed the door, then continued where she left off. "If you're pregnant, then there are things we need to talk about. Shape-shifter pregnancies are tricky."

I didn't want to talk about it. I didn't want it to be real. But somehow, the words came out anyway. "Come on. Let's be honest. Can you think of anyone who would be a worse mother than me? Fuck. I can't even go three seconds without saying fuck. How could I possibly raise a kid?"

"So you are pregnant." She raised her chin triumphantly.

"Congrats for figuring it out. If you're waiting for your prize, keep waiting." I started to leave.

"Kellan. Sit down, please."

I sat, but only because I was starting to shake too badly to stay standing. "I don't know that I'm pregnant."

"Uh-huh."

"I don't. This could all be…food poisoning."

She cocked a brow. "You eat the same food all the rest of us eat. You think you have selective food poisoning? For the last two months?"

"It hasn't been happening for two months." Was it really two months? Shit.

"Fine. That's still not food poisoning, considering no one else is sick. I'm not even sure shape-shifters can get food poisoning."

"Some healer you are. Shouldn't you know that?"

Simone sighed and sat down beside me. "I know you're freaking out. But lashing out at me isn't going to make you feel better."

"Mmm, I'm pretty sure it will." But she was right. I knew she was. "Sorry."

"Kellan, as I said, shape-shifter pregnancies are really difficult. Let me help you."

I narrowed my eyes. "I've never heard you say that before. You always just order people around."

She smiled. "Yeah, I do enjoy that. But in this case, I would really prefer your compliance. It makes the exam less like a fist fight."

"Fuck. Would you have to –?" I gestured at my pelvic area.

She shook her head. "I just want to check things like your temperature, your weight. See how you're faring."

"You said shape-shifter...you said difficult. What do you mean?" Fear fluttered through my already-dicey stomach, and a horrible thought occurred to me. "You're going to make me give up coffee, aren't you?"

"Oh, for pete's sake, just lay down on the bed."

I complied.

"Coffee isn't a problem for pregnant women. That's old-fashioned thinking. So don't worry about that." She examined me, and I sang myself Metallica songs while clenching my hands into fists. "Things seem fine. You can unclench your fists now."

I did, wincing slightly as blood rushed back into my fingers.

"I'm going to get you some prenatal vitamins. We need to talk about your diet. You need more protein. A lot more. Pregnant shape-shifters require an extreme amount of protein to support both your metabolism and the baby's. But you also just need to eat more, period. As many calories as you can stand to eat."

"What if – what if I don't want it? The – the baby?" I whispered.

I expected her to judge me. Instead, she looked at me sympathetically. "I don't do that, and it's now outlawed in Wisconsin, so nobody else around here can, either. But we could take you to Illinois or Minnesota. It would be tricky. Given your ability to heal, we'd have to get you out of there immediately following the procedure so the humans don't see what's happening to your body. But we could manage, if that's what you want."

My stomach roiled again and I tasted bile. "It's not. Not really." I hesitated, then whispered, "I shape-shifted earlier."

Her brow furrowed, making my heart turn to ice. "Well, you're barely showing, which means the baby is probably too small to really be affected by the physical changes to your body. But you shouldn't make a habit of it."

"What happens to the baby? The cub? When I shift."

She gave me a little smile. "I don't know, to be honest. But your mother and the other shape-shifters I've known all avoided shifting once they reached the fourth month. When was the last time you had a period?"

"I don't know. I don't have monthly cycles. My cycles are more like a wolf's. Once a year."

She blinked. "Really?"

I frowned at her. "Didn't you know that?"

"I guess I never asked. Your mom, for example, she was always pretty certain about when she conceived. We wondered a little when she was pregnant with you and Mal, because she got so much bigger so much earlier. But still, she knew when she had sex, so I never had to question."

"Well, now you know, I guess."

"Hmm. Lay back down. I can measure your uterus. That will help tell us how far along you are."

She examined me again. "Well, judging by this, I'd say you're at least five months in. So I would recommend not changing shape until after the baby is born."

Five months. That could've been the start of my time with Aza. Or it could've happened before Aza, when I was with Tony the first couple times. That wasn't helpful at all. Panic started creeping into my chest, tightening the muscles around my ribcage.

One foot in front of the other. One breath at a time. I focused on gazing into Galen's eyes. He assisted me with my efforts by laying his head in my lap and staring soulfully up at me.

"Kellan? Are you all right?"

"Well…" I struggled to breathe. "I'm not a hundred percent sure who the…who the father is."

"Isn't Tony – oooohhh." She covered her mouth with her hand, probably to keep something from flying into her mouth while it hung open for an obnoxiously long time.

"Yeah. Oh."

"Do you think – I mean, could it have been the Horror?"

Yes, please, call him by his awesome nickname. That's going to make me feel better. "Well, he fucked me a whole bunch, so yeah, if I'm correctly understanding how a woman gets knocked up, yeah, it definitely could've been him." A baby that looked like Aza. A baby that *acted* like Aza. Oh, god.

"I'm so sorry, Kellan." Like someone died.

"So basically, you can't tell me anything helpful, other than eat more. Is that about right?" I was being a bitch, but I was ready to move on from this conversation.

"Not just 'eat more.' I mean, yes, that's the only advice I can offer right now, but it's really crucial. When I said your people have difficult pregnancies, I meant that you get so sick that it's difficult to consume enough calories to support the baby. Your cub has just as big an appetite as you do. So consider eating protein part of your job now. Every hour, I want you to eat, and every time you eat, you have to include protein." Just the thought made my stomach lurch. I closed my eyes. She paused. "Kellan?"

I opened my eyes to look at her.

"Being scared is a good thing. If you weren't scared, I'd be concerned you weren't taking this seriously." She paused. "But you need to tell Tony."

I shook my head. He and I talked about this. Late one night, shortly after we started having sex again. He told me he never wanted kids. That the younglings were the closest he ever wanted to come to being a father. I said that was okay, because I would be a terrible mother. Which was still true.

The problem with having a shape-shifter baby? I couldn't exactly offer it up for adoption. Unless...

"Simone, do you think Mal would want another cub?"

She blinked at me. I rarely brought up my sister with her. They had a relationship and broke up shortly before Mal started taking assignments away from the Academy. But Mal had a cub. She already knew how to raise one. And for all her faults, she seemed to really love her cub. Maybe she would be a better mother than I could be.

"Okay, let's just take a breath." Simone ducked her head to meet my lowered eyes. "You don't need to know what to do right now. Just worry about today. We'll get you some vitamins. I don't have prenatals in stock, but I'll order some right away. In the meantime, we need to..." She kept talking, but I stopped listening. *You need to tell Tony.*

This was it. The big thing that I was hiding from him. He knew something was wrong, but once I told him what it was, he'd be gone. That was the only thing that would make this situation worse. If I lost Tony, too.

"…and you're not hearing a thing I'm saying, are you?" She smiled to soften her words. "Look, I'll write it down. For now, just go home and rest."

I snorted. "Rest. Right. I have to go – oh, shit, I was going to go check on J.C."

"Oh. Yes. J.C." She turned solemn. "Yes, that does take precedence. Okay, I'll let you know when I have the vitamins. I have protein powder on hand, too. The younglings who want to put on muscle really like it. That might be an option to supplement your diet. Let me get you a shake, then you can go."

While Simone made my shake, I peeked in Gina's room. Smack was curled up beside Gina on the bed, looking a little like Galen curled up on my bed. Both girls appeared to be asleep now. Hopefully, that was what they needed.

"I'll keep an eye on them." Simone stood behind me, a sad smile on her face.

I nodded and left, protein shake in hand, after promising to rest as soon as I could. I should feel better, letting someone else in on the secret. Instead, I just felt tired and vaguely nauseous. Consuming the protein shake didn't help much. No matter how much you mixed those shakes, they still felt gritty going down. I struggled not to gag as I downed the shake as fast as I could.

Too bad Pop-Tarts didn't have twenty grams of protein in them.

Chapter 10

KELLAN

I swung by J.C.'s cell. Carefully ignoring the blood-stained snow and the memories that threatened to overwhelm me, I knelt and slid open the trap door that we used to deliver food and water to the prisoner. I could see J.C.'s boots pacing back and forth, proof enough for me that he wasn't too injured. When he realized someone was there, he started protesting his innocence, so I slammed the small door shut. But not before I smelled the thread of fear in his scent.

He smelled like a scared kid.

I closed down those thoughts. The thoughts that wondered if there was another way to ensure Smack's safety while still sparing J.C. I didn't really want to let him live. He was a rapist who showed no remorse until he was caught and realized that his crime probably came with the death penalty. He was Aza.

Except he wasn't Aza. He hadn't spent the last several hundred years hunting and preying on innocent people. He was an almost-adult who was really, really fucked up. Was there some way to fix that? Some way that didn't involve killing him?

God, these hormones were really messing with my head. I glanced down at Galen, walking by my side. "It has to be done," I told him. He wagged his tail at me. Thus agreed, now that I knew J.C. wasn't dead yet, I needed to talk to Janus about rectifying that. When I reached Janus's cabin, I was glad to see Finn wasn't there. I preferred to speak to Janus alone, if only to keep my blood pressure from rising.

"Hello, Kellan." Janus looked me over as I entered. I remembered what Simone said about me looking like crap. Oh, well, too late to do anything about that now. At least the day was about the shittiest in history, so I had a decent excuse.

"Hello, sir. We were discussing J.C.'s sentence when… everything happened."

Janus wanted me to carry out the sentence immediately. "We should not wait. It is too important to resolve this matter."

"Okay."

He must've heard something in my voice, some hesitation. Or maybe he read my thoughts. But his eyes narrowed and his brows knit together, and I felt like a bug pinned to foamboard. "What is wrong?" he asked.

I didn't know how to respond. I decided the only option, really, was brutal honesty. "I'm struggling with this one, sir."

"You argued quite passionately for the boy's death."

I felt myself wince at "boy." "Yeah. I did. And I know it's the only way. But...he is, isn't he? A boy. Compared to us, anyway."

"Compared to us, Antony is a boy." Despite the dryness of his words, his tone was kind.

"Ick. Thanks for making me feel like a lech."

He frowned his I-don't-speak-slang frown.

"A lecherous person," I clarified.

"Ah. I see. 'Lech' is catchier."

I snorted a laugh, because there was no other possible response to hearing fussy, uptight Janus uttering the word *lech*.

"I do not believe you are a lech, however. Antony is an old soul. But more than that, he has completed the rights of passage in our little society that make him a man. And I do not believe that Antony would be this happy with a lech."

An embarrassing need came over me, and I said, "Do you think so? Do you think he's happy?"

Janus tilted his head and studied me. "Do you believe he is not?"

I sighed. "I don't know what I believe. It seems to change by the second."

"Perhaps that is related to your current condition."

Fuck. Did he know? My entire body went cold, like someone dumped a bucket of Gatorade over my head. Except I wasn't winning anything. Not today. "My – condition? I don't know what you mean."

"Hmph." He made a very un-Janus sound. Fucking mind-reading bastard. "I believe you know exactly what I am referring to, but I will not pursue it. For now." His expression softened. "But you will have to face it, and soon."

I did face it. I talked to Simone about it. I sure as hell wasn't going to have another heart-to-heart. Not with Janus. "We were talking about J.C."

"Yes. Of course. First, though, in answer to your question, yes. I believe Antony is happy as your partner."

For now. His words echoed in my brain. Pretty soon, I wasn't going to be able to lie about it anymore. Pretty soon, the reality of my condition would be clear to anyone with working eyes.

J.C. Focus on the topic at hand. "I hate having to kill a kid. But he committed an unforgivable act. We can't overlook that." I sighed. "With all your magickal abilities, there's no way for you to erase his memories of us? To magick away the Spring and the Sankhain, and maybe get rid of whatever impulses made him think rape was an okay thing to do?"

The look Janus gave me was so sad, I could almost taste it in the back of my throat. "No. It is not possible. I would not be able to pick and choose what to erase. If I were to try, I would erase all his memories, all his knowledge, everything. He would be left with the mind of a babe, while in the body of a young man."

I nodded slowly. That would've been too easy. I rubbed my hands over my face. "So I guess the only question is, how do you want it done?"

A thread of anger, frustration, wound through his scent. "I do not want this. None of this is what I want."

He wasn't mad at me. I knew that. He was mad at the situation. This wasn't how things were supposed to be here, and Janus liked things to be just so. Still, I was the one who was going to have to kill J.C. I shouldn't have to tiptoe around anyone's delicate sensibilities. But I did. "Sir, I meant no offense. Of course, this isn't what any of us want. However, it is what must be done, as you said. It must be resolved." I could see he didn't want to tell me how to kill J.C. "Perhaps it would be best if I handled the arrangements myself? Since you have a lot on your plate, what with Gina's…magickal explosion and all."

Janus nodded, relief brightening his scent like lemon floor polish. "Yes, we must attend to young Gina." He paused. "She is very powerful, is she not?" He didn't seem to be speaking to me anymore. I wasn't sure he was speaking to anyone.

"Yeah. Maybe you guys should start by teaching her how to avoid slicing people open. Just a thought. Anyway, I better go. See ya." I escaped, because the look on Janus's face, an almost hungry look, creeped the mother-loving shit out of me.

I found Smack waiting for me outside. "Hey, Smack. I thought you were keeping Gina company." And I thought Simone was going to keep an eye on you, I added silently.

She patted Galen hello, then met my eyes. "You're going to kill him now?"

"Are you psychic, too? Fuck. Just what we need, another mind reader."

"I'm not psychic. You just got this look on your face like you're about to go kill someone."

"Pretty sure that's just my regular expression." I started toward my cabin. I needed to get a bigger blade – I only had small ones on me, and it was a lot easier slitting someone's throat with a blade longer than a couple inches. "Anyway, I promised you I'd take him out. That's what I'm going to do."

"I want to be there."

I stopped. Turned. Looked at her. I understood. Believe me, I understood the impulse. But it was one thing to want to see your attacker get his comeuppance. It was a whole other thing to watch another person bleed out in front of you. "No."

"Kellan -"

"It's Sankha Kellan, and the answer is no. You don't need to see that. Fuck, I don't need to see that, but I kind of have to. If you want, I can arrange for you to see his body when it's done. That's the best I can do."

"I don't mean that. I mean, you need backup. He's a slimy motherfucker. Somebody's gotta watch your back."

She might be right. I wasn't at my best. But hell, fuck, and damn, no. No way was I going to let her be the one to back me up. How to get her to go away, though? Because that was what I wanted. A little peace and quiet before I added another nightmare to my collection. No matter how much I hated what J.C. did to her, this would haunt me. The sound of his crying. How we all watched him go from an underweight, scared teen to a...

Fuck. To a rapist.

"Smack, I need someone to look after Galen for me while I take care of this. He doesn't like bloodshed." Which wasn't strictly true. He didn't like it when I was injured, but the list of people my dog cared about that much was pretty small, and J.C. wasn't on it. "Can you do that for me? Please? Tony's still laid up, and I don't know who else to ask."

She narrowed her eyes at me, like she knew I was lying. But I could live with that, as long as it worked. Finally, she spat out, "Fine."

"Thank you." I meant it, even if I wasn't thanking her for taking care of Galen so much as for backing off her request. "Thank you."

She hesitated. "You'll come tell me?" she said in a small voice. "When it's done?"

I wanted to hug her, or maybe cry a little. "You have my word."

She nodded once, took Galen's leash from me, and headed toward the bunkhouse. Galen trailed behind her, looking back at me like he was waiting for me to realize my mistake and call him over. I blew him a kiss and jogged to my cabin.

Once inside, I took a second to lean against the door, as if to prevent anyone else from pushing their way in. I wasn't normally bothered by killing. I mean, sure, it wasn't on my top ten list of how to spend a Saturday night, but it was also part of my training, my upbringing. It was different, though, killing someone so young. Even knowing what he did, even remembering the look on Smack's face last night as she told me she wanted to die. This was the right thing, the only thing to do. But that didn't make it easy.

I shook my head, like I could shake off the thoughts the way a dog shakes off rainwater. It didn't really work like that, but it reminded me to keep moving. Once this was over, it would be done, and I could move on. We could all move on.

I chose my blade, a jeweled dagger that my sister gave me for our fiftieth birthday. It made me feel a little better, having a piece of Mal with me. I slipped the sheath in the kangaroo pocket of my hoodie and headed for the cells. When I got there, my eyes darted to the red, red snow, like somebody spilled a giant, blood-flavored slushie. Tony could have died here. A lot of forces were to blame for that, but ultimately, if not for J.C., it wouldn't have happened. Suddenly, I didn't feel so wishy-washy anymore.

I slid the bolt on the door. I was tired. I was a little wobbly from not keeping enough food down. I should've gotten someone for backup, like Smack suggested, but I forgot to, because my brain wasn't working right these days. And those were only excuses, and weak ones at that. The reality was, I wasn't prepared when I unlocked the door, and so when the door exploded outward and J.C. pushed his way out, I wasted a few precious seconds getting my balance and reacting. And by then, he was in the forest.

J.C. didn't try to be stealthy, so I was able to follow him, but then I tripped on an exposed root and went down. By the time I stood up, the forest was quiet. And dark. It was almost five o'clock, and darkness gathered quickly in Wisconsin in January. I paused. Listened. Sniffed the air. And almost jumped out of my skin when Valentine appeared next to me.

"I tried to shoot him, but I missed." She still held her bow. "He's gone."

How long was I down? Did I pass out for a second? He couldn't have gotten away otherwise. "Don't worry," I said with more confidence than I felt. The idea of losing time really shook me. "I'll find him. I can track him." I glanced at the ground. The snow might've helped me follow his footprints, if we were in a pristine field. But this was a forest, a mix of deciduous trees without leaves that allowed snow to hit the ground, but also evergreens that caught the snow and kept the ground clear. And besides, this was a heavily travelled area. J.C. followed the same path that the border patrol took several times a day. Too many boot prints to find one set and follow them.

Too bad Cat wasn't on duty. She could shoot through George Washington's eyeball on a one-dollar bill.

This would be much easier if I could shape-shift. Follow his scent on the ground and in the air. But…my hand came to rest on my stomach.

Why was I even hesitating? It wasn't like I wanted a cub.

Did I?

Focus. If I wasn't going to shape-shift, then I needed to get moving, because it was a shit-ton harder to follow a scent through the air and a wind was kicking up. "Valentine, this wasn't your fault. It was mine. Please go tell Janus and Finn what happened. Let them know that I'm going to track him. I'll call in when I have him." I paused. "And make sure Tony knows where I am, okay? Galen's with Smack. He can either stay with her or go to Tony. I'll get J.C. Don't worry."

She looked at me with those big eyes. "He left the forest by the downed tree. The one that got hit by lightning last summer."

That gave me a starting point. "Thanks, kid. I'll see you soon." I ran.

⸺ «» ⸺

TONY

Maybe I should have told her I figured it out. I should've just told her that I knew she was pregnant. See what she said. Maybe it all would've been fine if I had just put it out there that I knew. We could've talked about it and she could've stopped pretending.

Just thinking about that made my breath freeze in my chest. Kellan liked her denial. Was I really brave enough to take that away? No. No, I was not. Even with this lie between us, things were good, better than they'd been for months. I really didn't want to ruin that.

Also, if we had the conversation where I told her I knew she was pregnant, we would probably also have to have the conversation where I told her I knew I might not be the father. My heart started to pound and I felt sweat break out. This might be Aza's baby. The thought of her carrying that guy's kid, that this kid could look like Aza. Could *be* like Aza…shit. No wonder she was throwing up all the time.

I shoved down the panic and told myself to man up. It wasn't about me. Kellan was the one carrying maybe-Aza's baby. Once again, my breathing sped up, and I tried to push those thoughts away. It was Kellan's trauma. And until she was willing to talk to me about it, it was none of my business. I needed to…

I heard a scream. "No!" It sounded like a girl, but that was all I could tell. I pushed out of bed, ignoring the fact that my leg still ached, and limped out of the room.

I ran into Simone in the hall. For a second, I thought she was going to order me back to bed, but then she shook her head, said, "Oh, fine, come on," and ran outside with her first-aid bag. I followed before she had a chance to change her mind.

Smack stood in the middle of the grounds, Galen's leash in her hand, the big dog by her side, looking lost. Where was Kellan? Smack let out another pain-filled scream. "No!" Her chest heaved with each breath. What the hell happened?

Valentine rushed over. "J.C. got out. Kellan went after him. I – I shouldn't'a told Smack. I'm sorry."

Kellan went after him. Kellan was out there, by herself, with a violent teenager who was facing a death sentence. The very definition of nothing to lose. And she was so weak and distracted right now. I felt the blood drain from my face. Simone laid a hand on my arm. "I've got them. Go."

I grabbed Galen's leash with shaking hands and headed for the forest. "Find her," I said to Galen. I couldn't track Kellan's scent, but her dog could. "Find her."

Galen took off, like he was just waiting for someone's permission to go after her. I couldn't run, but I could jog, pushing the ache in my leg away like I pushed away the fear. "We'll find her. We'll find her." I said it over and over again. I wasn't sure who I was trying to reassure, him or me. Galen's gaze bounced from me to the path in front of us, like he was begging me to go faster. "I'm sorry, bud, this is as fast as I can go. We'll find her."

Galen wasn't a bloodhound, but he was motivated. He probably wouldn't track anyone else in the world, but set him on Kellan's trail, and he never hesitated. I pushed myself to run faster. J.C. wasn't armed when he broke out, but Kellan was, and she was so weak. What if he got hold of one of her blades? My brain filled with images of her bleeding, dying, and I pushed myself even faster.

My leg was burning by the time we reached the edge of the forest. Simone fixed the bleeding, closed the wound, but that didn't mean I was all healed. She told me that she ran out of juice before she could fully heal the muscle. A little while ago, she said she was rested up and could heal me the rest of the way. I told her no, she saved my life, I could wait for the leg to heal the rest of the way on its own. I wanted her to save her mojo for other emergencies, because the way this week was going, we would definitely need her at full strength. Now I would've given anything for just five more minutes of healing.

Stop whining. Just keep going. Find her.

Stepping out of the forest, I paused and looked around. In an adjacent parking lot, I saw a familiar figure and the breath whooshed out of my lungs. Kellan. We found her, and she was okay. That was all that mattered. I could deal with anything, as long as she was okay.

Galen let out a soft bark, and Kellan turned and saw us. "What the - ?" She ran over, her expression furious. Clearly, she didn't catch J.C. yet, so she was going to take it out on me. Fine. I didn't care. She was alive. I didn't realize until the moment I saw her how scared I was that J.C. would kill her. I was so relieved, I couldn't feel my arms or legs.

"What are you doing here?" she snapped as she skidded to a stop in front of me.

"You need backup." I met her glare with one of my own, not letting my relief show. Oh, god, she was alive. If something happened to her – if J.C. hurt her, when I was the one who fought to let him join us…Galen wagged, looking up at us with his tongue lolling happily. "Yeah, good boy. Good boy. You found her."

"Backup. Why the fuck is everyone telling me I need backup? I don't need fucking backup. I need…" She drifted off, then shook her head like she was trying to toss away a thought. "Go back." She started to walk away.

I followed, starting to limp now that the adrenaline left me. Fortunately, the area seemed deserted. It was late Sunday afternoon, already starting to get dark. Not much happening in the business park. I skirted a patch of ice with a wince. "You're following his scent. Right? Which means you're not looking around you. Not paying attention to your surroundings. You need someone to watch your back. I'm here. We're here. Let us help."

She huffed a sigh. "Like I can stop you. If you're coming, try to be quiet. I'd prefer he didn't hear us coming."

I quickly realized I wasn't wearing any winter gear. When we first set out, the fear and adrenaline kept me from feeling the cold, but now that the relief was fading, the frigid wind sliced through my clothes like they were made of paper. I shoved my hands in my pockets and focused my attention on the area around us. On my job.

"You're cold," Kellan said. It wasn't a question.

"I was in a hurry. Now shut up. Don't want him to hear us."

She raised her nose to the air, moving her head back and forth like she was watching a tennis match. "Fuck."

"Would this be easier if you shifted?" I pointed at the ground. "Galen followed your scent on the ground, not the air. I could pretend I was walking two dogs instead of one."

She glared at me. "I am not a dog."

"No, but most people wouldn't be able to tell the difference. I could say you were a husky." Even with everything going on, I kind of enjoyed watching her seethe over the prospect.

Then something changed. A strange look crossed her face. Did I really offend her? No, this wasn't pissed-off Kellan, this was something else. "I can't. Um, there's no place to hide here."

She was right, we were in the middle of a parking lot. It wasn't even our lot. Not at all safe to be doing supernatural things. But my gut said that wasn't really the reason. A question for another time. Now... "Okay. Lead the way, Cujo."

She flipped me off and started sniffing the air again. I scanned the lot visually. When my gaze hit the far corner of the lot, I saw a flash of movement. "Kell." I nodded in that direction. She turned that way, closed her eyes and inhaled. Just as we heard a car start.

"Fuck!" Kellan took off at a run. I followed, reaching for my gun that, like my coat and gloves, was lying in the infirmary. God damn it.

I saw the car as it pulled away. I couldn't see the driver, but it was an old car, the sort of vehicle a street-wise kid could easily break into and hotwire. It drove off, tires squealing, and Kellan stopped at the spot it occupied.

"Fuck, fuck, fuck," she murmured over and over. She knelt down and sniffed the ground. I looked around, making sure there was no one around to see. "Fuck!"

There was nothing more we could do. Another wave of relief hit me and almost knocked me on my ass. We wouldn't have to fight him. I shouldn't have felt so glad about that, but the truth was, I didn't feel up to fighting a stiff breeze, and Kellan wasn't looking too good, either. And, well...I loved Smack. She was like my little sister. But I didn't want to be there when J.C. was killed. I just...didn't. I empathized too much with him. Hated that we couldn't save him.

Kellan didn't share my relief. She kept saying, "Fuck, fuck, fuck," as she paced back and forth, sniffing and growling.

"Kell, keep your voice down." Just because there was no one in sight didn't mean there was no one to hear. And her voice when she swore tended to really carry.

She turned on me, eyes glowing bright amber. "You slowed me down."

"Your eyes, Kell."

She blinked, as if surprised. Like she didn't know she was doing it. A couple more blinks, and her eyes looked normal again. She jerked one shoulder. "You did. I would've caught him."

"We will catch him," I corrected. "But it's gonna be a little more difficult now. Just – let's just head back. Okay? Report what we saw." Not that I saw much of anything, but I could give them the color and type of car he was driving.

She slumped, like whatever was holding her upright left her in a whoosh. "I failed." Even her face sagged, and I started to worry that I was going to have to help her back to camp.

"We'll catch him," I said again. I had an idea of how to get her moving. "Come on. It's fucking cold out. Galen needs to warm up." It was a low blow. Using her dog to manipulate her. But if it worked, I'd do it.

"I know what you're doing," she growled. "But fine. Let's go."

We walked back to the forest. We weren't supposed to enter or exit the forest in daylight, but since we already broke that rule by exiting, it didn't seem to matter all that much if we reentered the same way. At the edge, I looked around. "I don't see anyone."

She inhaled deeply. "I don't smell anyone."

"Awesome." I stepped over the border and the forest appeared around us. It never failed to amaze me, this weird turn my life took. But now wasn't the time for amazement. On the bright side, the trees broke up the wind and I felt a little less frozen now that we were back in the forest.

Valentine was waiting just inside the trees. "Did you get him?"

Kellan shook her head.

Anger blazed over the girl's face. "You said you would!"

"And we will," I said soothingly. I just got Kellan calmed down, I didn't need Valentine riling her back up. "Is Smack okay?"

"No, she's not okay! Her rapist is out there, running around free, and he knows she ratted him out. Except she didn't. I did, but he's going to kill her, and she knows it."

"Nobody's going to hurt any of you." Kellan's voice sent chills down my spine. She sounded scary. "I will find him. Whatever it takes."

Valentine just looked at her for a moment, then turned and walked away.

Kellan watched her go, her shoulders slumping further, then she glanced at me. "You need help getting back?"

I didn't need it, but had a feeling she needed to feel useful. "Is it that obvious?" I rubbed my leg where the healed wound was.

She snorted something I didn't quite hear, and she took my hand. She draped my arm over her shoulders, then grunted in dissatisfaction. "I gotta stop doing this with guys so much taller than me. Fuck."

"Any help is welcome." I leaned on her just enough to make walking incredibly awkward, but she relaxed as we walked. I was right – she just needed to feel useful. Even if walking like this was going to give me a backache to go along with my achy leg, it was worth it. I relaxed as she relaxed.

"You were right," she said. "I should've taken backup with me. I just – I wanted to get it over with. I'm not used to – I don't normally need help. And then I know I took off without backup, too. I just wanted to catch him. I couldn't – I couldn't let him get away." In her voice, I heard the self-blame. The way she saw it, she let J.C. get away already, when he escaped his cell.

"How did he escape?" I stumbled over a tree root that I didn't see because I was watching her face.

"Stop. Sit." Apparently thinking I was clumsy because of my leg, she pointed to a downed tree.

I didn't want to stop. It was too damn cold to stop. "We're almost there."

"Five minutes won't kill us. We're already cold. Just sit and rest for a second."

So we did. She sat beside me and warmed my hands between hers, although her hands were barely warmer than mine. Normally, her body temp was much higher than mine. I tried to swallow my worry, because if I voiced any concern, she would probably walk away and never look back.

"I was tired," she said, finally answering my question. "I didn't think he'd try to get out. I didn't think. I just opened the fucking door. And he must've heard the bolt, because he came running at the door, knocked me over, and ran. I – it shouldn't have happened."

Tired? She was weak, that was the truth. Shape-shifters needed to eat so much, and she wasn't keeping food down. All over again, my brain flipped through all the ways this could've been so much worse. The harm that could've come to her. All because of this fucking baby who might end up being a constant reminder of what she went through. Anger warmed me, followed closely by shame. It wasn't the baby's fault. But right in that moment, I hated this kid. Hated his very existence, which was putting the woman I loved in danger. I didn't say anything, didn't trust my voice to be steady. Instead, I clenched her hand like I was scared she'd take off again.

"You're frozen," she said quietly.

"Yeah. We should head back." Everything that could've happened. I could've lost her. All because of...

She stood and held her other hand out to me. I looked at her, at how strong she was to stand there and offer to help me, even though she felt like shit. This was the side of her that hid behind the layer of bitchiness. The side that cared about people so much that sometimes, she needed to push them away. I took her hand and she helped me to my feet. I leaned on her again, even though my back was now hurting worse than my leg.

"No one asked you to rush to my rescue," she said.

"You're welcome." I kept my tone wry, because it was what she expected. Even though all I really wanted was to tell her I loved her, no matter what.

"Did I not say thank you?"

"Pretty sure you've never thanked me for anything in your damn life." It wasn't true, but it made her mouth quirk with an almost-smile.

"I have, too."

"Oh, yeah? Name one time." We continued talking as she walked me back to the infirmary.

Chapter 11

KELLAN

I got Tony settled in the infirmary – he wanted to come with me, but I knew Simone would want to check him over. I was a little scared of Simone, so I didn't want to end up on the wrong side of her. I poked my head into Gina's room. She was still sleeping, now with Smack in a chair by her bed. Smack didn't look at me, even though she must have known I was there. I told myself that didn't sting. It was a lie.

I started to leave, but Simone stopped me. She pressed a plastic jug into my hands. "Drink this."

The liquid inside looked green and sludgy. "I don't wanna." I could feel bile rising up my throat, just looking at it.

"Buck up. You need sustenance if you're going to go chasing after escapees." She touched my cheek. "You're cold, and it's not from the temperature outside. Your body doesn't have the calories to maintain its normal temp. Finish that off, then go get something hot from the kitchen. And I don't just mean coffee."

I started to leave.

"But Kellan?"

I turned back and looked at her.

"You need to tell him. He's not stupid. He'll figure it out, if he hasn't already. It's better, coming from you."

"No one has ever been better off hearing anything from me." I took a sip of the shake. "Oh, god, that tastes like monkey ass."

"Stop whining." She disappeared into Tony's room.

I drank the entire shake, because she was right. I needed food. But I didn't go to the kitchen when I left. I headed straight for Janus's cabin. Tevin was on desk duty. As I headed for the inner door, he offered to take the shaker bottle from me. "Don't want to let those things sit around, ma'am. They start to smell. I'll take it to the kitchen."

"Thanks."

"Ma'am?" I turned back and looked at him. "If you need volunteers to help you hunt him down, you won't have any trouble finding them. I, for one, would love to help."

I smiled a little. "Thanks, Tevin. I'll let you know."

Janus was sitting by the fire with his eyes closed. It seemed an odd time for a nap. "Sir?"

He opened his eyes and waved me over. I was a little surprised to see Finn still wasn't there. Janus answered my question before I asked it. "Finlay is resting. This afternoon's difficulties took more out of him than he cares to admit."

Duh. I refrained from responding. "Sir, J.C. took off in a car."

His eyes closed again with a tiny wince. "That is unfortunate."

"Yeah, that's one way to put it. Look, I need help finding him. I don't know how to track a car. What can we do?"

"Do?" His eyes opened and he leaned forward. "First, you will tell me how the prisoner escaped at all." He studied me intensely. "It is time you were honest with me. Enough hiding. Tell me, what is – I believe the phrase is, going on with you?"

I froze. All this time, I thought about how to tell Tony, and it never occurred to me that I would have to tell other people, too. But I couldn't. And besides, didn't he imply earlier that he already knew? Why was he trying to make me say it? "Sir, I was tired, and –"

"Kellan, if you are tired, you drink coffee. This is more than that. I have waited for you to come to me on your own, but I am done waiting. I wish for you to say the words to me. What is wrong?"

"You mean, aside from everything?" It slipped out of my mouth before I could stop it.

Surprisingly, he just nodded. "Yes. Aside from everything. I am seeking a specific answer. You know what that is."

I sank into the chair beside him. The fire felt so good. I didn't realize how cold I was until I felt its warmth.

"Kellan." His voice was gentle with an undercurrent of stubbornness. His fatherly voice.

I raised my head to look at him, and it felt like my skull weighed a hundred pounds. "I'm pregnant." I whispered it, because I didn't want anyone else to hear.

"There, was that so difficult?" Janus patted my hand. "Now go talk to young Antony, because he deserves honesty from you."

I glared at the old man. He already knew. Of course he did – given his psychic powers, it wasn't all that shocking, but did he have to be such a fucking know-it-all about it? Could he at least act surprised? "Sir, I have more pressing matters. J.C. -"

"Is in a car. Not on foot. As you say, you cannot track him. He poses no immediate danger to us. We will formulate a plan and we will find him, but not right this moment."

"Sir..." I couldn't tell Tony. I couldn't. Especially since... "I don't even know who the father is."

He met my gaze unflinchingly. "Even if the child was begot by the Horror," he said, using Aza's nickname, "you must tell Antony. You are a terrible liar, and he is very concerned about you."

Begot by the Horror. He said it out loud. He said it out loud, and the world didn't end. I felt shaky and sick, but I struggled to keep my voice steady. "I am not a terrible liar."

"You certainly are. And it is one of your most admirable qualities. We will speak more later about J.C. Until then, go."

Galen nudged my hand, and I realized I wasn't breathing. I kept hearing those words over and over – begot by the Horror. How could anyone have the child of someone called the Horror? For fuck's sake.

"Go, now. And ask young Tevin to step inside. I have a task for him. Go."

When I stood, my legs felt wobbly. Maybe I should hit the kitchens like Simone ordered me. I needed coffee anyway. I told Tevin to go see Janus and headed for the mess hall with Galen at my heels. I wanted to take action. I wanted to go after J.C., even if I just wandered the streets aimlessly. This was all so much easier when everyone traveled by horse. Horses had individual scents that a wolf could follow. Cars were annoyingly anonymous.

The kitchen was bustling with cleanup from lunch and prep work for dinner. Everyone turned and stared at me. It seemed weird to see meal prep going on without Gina there supervising, ordering everyone around. "I missed lunch," I said to explain my presence. They all went back to their work.

I saw Ethan by the coffee pot. I joined him there. He glanced at me. "Fresh pot. It's strong."

"Did you know I was coming?"

He didn't smile, just leaned his head against the cabinet beside him. "It's all fucked up."

I smelled guilt and shame on him like cologne. I had a feeling I knew what he was upset about. It was the same thing we were all upset about, but Ethan, like Tony, probably felt personally responsible for J.C. He was one of the ones who lobbied for the boy.

I knew I should say something comforting, but all I could come up with was, "Yep."

He sighed heavily, then pointed to a container on the counter. "Leftover vegetable soup. They had it at lunch. If you want it."

"Thanks." I didn't really, but I knew I should eat, so I would. I wasn't sure about much of anything where this stupid baby was concerned, but I did seem to want to keep it alive. Which meant eating more.

Ethan poured coffee into his travel mug, then hesitated. "Tony okay?" Even though he was one of our therapists, he wasn't really much of a talker. Mal teased him once that he took economy of words to an extreme.

The memory of Tony lying bloody in the snow threatened my appetite, but I shoved it away. "Yeah. He's okay."

Ethan nodded and left without another word.

I felt a tug on my sleeve. When I looked down, I saw Tia there. "Hi," I said, surprised. I looked around, but didn't see Valentine.

"She made me go inside for kitchen duty." Tia looked devastated by that fact.

"You do know that kitchen duty is the most important duty here, right?" I knelt so I wouldn't be looming over her. "The kitchen workers are the heroes of every story."

She snorted, a strangely adult sound from such a small girl. "No, they're not."

"Of course they are. Don't argue with me. I'm old and cranky." I smiled to soften the words.

Tia looked around, then whispered, "Smack can find him."

The sounds around us suddenly muted, like someone turned down the volume on the rest of the room. "What do you mean?"

"She can use the computer. She can find him. It's her superpower. But you have to ask her."

"I'm pretty sure I'm the last person Smack wants to talk to." I ruffled her hair. "But I'll let Janus know."

"No. You talk to her." Tia paused. "She's so mad, Miz Kellan. You can take it. Let her be mad at you."

Her voice held so much faith. In me. I swallowed, my throat suddenly thick with emotion. "Okay. I'll see what I can do."

Janus wanted me to talk to Tony. Tia wanted me to talk to Smack. I looked down at Galen. "Food first, right, big dog?" He headbutted my leg, and I almost fell over. Yup, food first.

After three cups of coffee, two pieces of toast and a big bowl of soup, which contained some sort of white bean that soaked up the flavor of the broth and exploded in my mouth like a berry, I headed back to the infirmary. Was Smack still with Gina? I wanted to tell her what the car looked like, so she could start trying to find J.C., but Janus gave me an order. Talk to Tony. Okay, maybe it wasn't an order per se, but he was right. Tony was too smart to believe my bullshit excuses for my behavior. I lived the last few weeks in fear that he would leave me. It was time to find out if those fears had any merit.

Simone was nowhere to be seen, which was kind of nice. I wanted a moment to gather myself before I opened the door to Tony's room, and audiences made it much more difficult to gather myself.

I took a few deep breaths, which did nothing to calm my pounding heart or the albatrosses flapping their wings in my stomach. So much for self-gathering. I opened the door.

Tony was sitting on the bed, reading a book. The way he smiled at me made me feel guilty. People who lied repeatedly over the last several weeks didn't deserve smiles like that. But I loved that smile, so I selfishly tucked it away in my memory. Just in case this scene hit worst-fear proportion.

"Hi." He set down his book and patted the bed beside him. "What's up?"

Of course, he knew something was up. I probably looked like I was about ready to hurl again. Because I felt like I was going to hurl again.

TONY

I felt my smile fade as I looked at Kellan. She was so pale that she looked grey. My first thought was, Well, fuck. What went wrong now?

When I noticed her hands were shaking, I leaned forward and tried to take one of them in mine. She shied away. Uh-oh. This was bad.

"Kell?" I patted the spot beside me again. "Sit down. You look like you're going to pass out."

She shook her head, clenching her shaking hands into tight fists.

I couldn't think of anything that would be so awful, she wouldn't want to sit down. Well, okay, there were plenty of awful things to choose from. "Did someone else get hurt? Smack? Or Gina?" Did Smack try to kill herself again, or did Gina's magick explode and she hurt or killed someone?

"No." She took a shaky breath. "No, they're fine. Well, as fine as they were before. Which really isn't fine, but you know, it's fine-ish. I guess."

The rambling meant she was avoiding something. I was pretty sure I knew what it was. Shit, were we really going to talk about this? My nerves from earlier returned with a vengeance. "Kellan, tell me what's wrong." I sounded sharper than I meant to, but I wasn't sure I could soften my voice. I was too freaked.

She turned a deeper shade of greenish-grey. "I'm pregnant."

The words were so heavy, I swore I heard them hit the floor with a thunk. I sat, staring at the floor in the spot where I figured they must've landed. It was weird, how I waited for this conversation for so long, and now, I didn't know what to say. The angry part of me wanted to say, "Duh." The scared part of me wanted to scream at her to just say it, just say it all. I wanted her to tell me about the paternity, to get it over with. I was so tired of being alone with this. Finally, I just said, "Uh-huh."

She looked at me, her mouth twisting into a scowl. "You know?" Like I betrayed her somehow, figuring it out on my own. She muttered accusingly, "You know. Janus knows. Everybody fucking knows already."

That nudged the scales in the direction of anger. I shrugged. "I wouldn't say I knew. Since you didn't tell me." I couldn't resist pointing that out, even as she winced. "But come on. You're puking your guts out a few times a day. That's not normal for you."

She slid to the floor like her legs gave out. Maybe they did. Seeing the worry and pain on her face, I reminded myself that she was the one carrying this burden. Not just carrying this baby, but also the knowledge of what this baby might mean. What it might be. As much as I wanted to be mad, I couldn't let her suffer.

She didn't seem to want to sit next to me, so I shifted on the bed so I was sitting right in front of her, facing her. I still wanted to scream, "Spit it out," but instead, I said her name. "Kell?"

The corners of her mouth turned down, like Galen's did when he was fighting to keep food down. I reached for the trash can and set it beside her. She touched it with hands that were trembling once again. "You're so nice to me," she said. Tears spilled down her cheeks.

"Me being nice makes you cry?"

She threw her hands in the air. "Oxygen makes me cry. Every fucking thing makes me cry. But yes. You being nice to me when I don't deserve it definitely makes me cry."

I hated this baby. I hated Aza. I hated Darcy, because he was the reason Kellan offered herself up to Aza. I hated all of them for causing her pain. And I hated myself, because what kind of guy hates a baby for existing? "Why do you think you don't deserve me being nice?"

"Because I lied to you!"

I couldn't say that didn't bother me, but it wasn't the really awful part of all this. Maybe because I figured out what she wasn't telling me, I didn't feel like I was living with a lie the way she probably did. I still had a hard time keeping my voice level, because I knew the confessions weren't done. I tried, though. "So what, I should spank you instead?"

Her eyes narrowed, a little color coming back into her cheeks. "You're mocking me."

"No, I'm teasing you. Different from mocking. Less inherent malice. Okay, fine, I hate it when you lie to me. There. Happy?"

"No. Not happy." She pulled her knees up and rested her forehead on them. "There's something else."

Finally. "Something bigger than you being pregnant?"

"It's...related to the first thing, not separate from it."

"Oh." I waited, hoping she was too wrapped up in her own pain to smell mine in the air.

"The, um, the father... I'm not sure... I mean, it might be yours. I want it to be yours. But with the timing of everything, it could be...Aza's."

All words, all the comforting words I practiced when I pictured this conversation, all fled in the face of those words. That name. "Oh," I said again.

There it was. It was out now. We couldn't pretend it didn't exist. Neither one of us. And I realized why it really didn't bother me that Kellan lied to me for weeks. Because as long as she was lying, I could put off figuring out what to do. Now, hearing her say it out loud, the last curtain of denial was ripped away. This was real. And with those words, it felt like she dumped a lead weight on my shoulders. And I maybe hated her a little bit for that.

What if it was Aza's kid? Could I still be there for her? The pain Kellan would go through if it was. Could I honestly stand by and watch that, watch her be constantly reminded of him? Every day? The baby could look like him. Fuck, the baby could act like him. What if this kid wasn't the best of his parents? What if he was the worst? Kellan's stubbornness, her ferocity, combined with Aza's ruthless hunger for torturing others? Could I still be there for her then?

I felt more scared than I ever had in my life. I couldn't say it. I couldn't just say yes, I could be there for her. But she looked as bad as I felt, times a thousand, and I floundered for something, anything, to say. "Kell -"

"And we won't know. Until the kid is born. It's not like Simone has an ultrasound machine, not like she can do a DNA test while the kid's still baking. She doesn't have the equipment for any of that. And I'm not sure when it will be born, not knowing when it was conceived. So it could be a long wait. And I get it if you…if you don't want to stick around for the big reveal." She stared at the floor like she couldn't bear to look at me.

Shit. I couldn't just let her sit there like this. Time to set aside my…everything and just be there for her. I could do this. At least for now. I was ashamed of the truth of that, but it was the only truth I had.

I knelt in front of her and put my hand under her chin and tilted her face up to look at me. She squeezed her eyes shut instead. Stubborn old wolf. So I leaned in and kissed her. That made her eyes fly open.

"Do me a favor, Kell? Stop suggesting that I might want to leave you. It's fucking annoying, so just stop it." I hoped to god I was able to live up to the implied promise that I would stay.

She swallowed convulsively, and I nudged the trash can closer to her to remind her it was here. I really didn't want to be covered in vomit right now. But she didn't throw up. She just stared at me and stared at me. "That position can't feel good on your leg," she said finally.

"It's not too bad." It wasn't, but if my leg gave her something else to think about, something else to focus on, I'd take it. We both needed this fucking conversation to be over.

"Dumbass." She pushed to her feet and reached down to help me up. I pretended I needed the help. Then I wrapped my arms around her. We were both a little shaky.

"I'm sorry," I said, apologizing for my thoughts that she didn't know about. That I couldn't tell her about, because I didn't want her worrying that I would leave her. Not on top of everything else she had on her mind. Maybe I couldn't stay. Maybe just thinking that made me flush with shame. But that was a problem for another day in the distant future. For now, I could be here. I needed to be here.

"What the fuck are you apologizing for?" Her voice was muffled against my shirt.

"Umm…" I struggled for a believable explanation. "I'm sorry that you have to deal with the possibility that this could be Aza's baby. I, um, I know how hard you've worked to put him in the rearview."

A deep sigh shifted her whole body, and she pressed the top of her head against my chest so she was staring at the floor. "Yeah, well. It's just one of the many ways the universe is fucking with me this week."

I snorted a laugh.

"We should probably call it 'her,' not it." She looked up at me.

"Her?" How did she know the sex, if she didn't even know the paternity?

"Yeah. Shape-shifters only have girls. Did I never tell you that?"

I felt a pit grow in the center of my chest. Black-hole size. A girl. A baby who was a girl. Because Kellan was a shape-shifter. So the baby would be a shape-shifter. That didn't mean it wouldn't be anything like Aza. I knew too damn well that "female" didn't mean "nice," or "kind" or anything that you want your kid to be. Shit, what would it be like to raise a shape-shifter baby? When would she start to shift? All these questions that I never asked, because it just didn't seem like something you ask. I pretended Kellan was human, because that's what you do. You don't ask someone what it's like to have a wild animal living inside of her, just like you don't ask the guy in the wheelchair what it's like to not be able to walk. You just don't.

A shape-shifter baby. Fucking hell.

Chapter 12

KELLAN

The next morning, after a surprisingly restful night with Tony in the infirmary, Smack, Tony, Ethan, and I sat around Janus's table. Finn wasn't there. Janus said he was fine, just otherwise occupied. He glanced at my stomach as he said that, which I took to mean Janus told him about the happy news and Finn didn't want to see me. That was fine. I didn't want to see his reaction to learning I was pregnant.

The old man sat at the head of the table. I was still a little annoyed that he figured out I was pregnant and didn't say anything, but that little annoyance was nothing compared to the homicidal rage I felt in that moment.

"What do you mean, we do nothing?" I worked so hard to keep from screaming. "We haven't even tried to track him. We know what car he took. He doesn't have any money, which means he'll probably have to steal that, too. We can check out petty robberies, see what comes of them. We haven't even tried. We need to at least try."

Tony put his hand on my shoulder and squeezed. I wanted to shrug him off, but I still felt really guilty about keeping the pregnancy a secret, so I didn't.

"I did try." Smack's voice cut through the silence.

"What?" I stared at her. When did she have time to try tracking J.C.?

"I been trying all night. While you two were makin' out in the infirmary. Tony gave me the make and model of the car. Found a report of one abandoned by the side of the road. He ditched it. Musta stole another one, but I can't find any reports of stolen vehicles. The trail's colder than a witch's tit on Christmas morning."

Janus made a strangled sound.

Smack glanced at him. "It's a saying. Sir."

"Your colloquialisms are colorful as ever," Janus said carefully. "Please refrain from using them in my presence."

"Sorry." Smack didn't look sorry.

"You are forgiven. Now, we shall keep watching for – what is the word? – leads. For the time being, however, we must exercise patience. While we do so, there is another matter that requires your attention. Ethan, you and Smack met yesterday, yes? What have you learned? Is there anything we can do to help Smack with her recovery?"

Smack tensed, and I could smell both fear and anger coming from her. Ethan, on the other hand, blinked and glanced at me, for some reason. Asking me to intercede? Shit. Janus was in his ruler-of-the-kingdom mode. I hated sticking my nose in. But I understood. Therapy worked because it was private. Ethan didn't want to fill the room in on the things he talked about with Smack.

I took a deep breath. Janus wouldn't hurt me. I was pregnant. Nobody ever hurt the pregnant woman, right? Yeah. Right. "Sir, perhaps Ethan and Smack would prefer to keep their sessions private."

Janus stared at me with an utter lack of comprehension. Ethan's therapy degree was fairly new, and this was probably the first time Janus ever thought to learn anything about the subject. I was pretty sure I knew what he was thinking. He was the boss. There was no such thing as privacy where he was concerned.

"That's the way it works in the outside world, sir," I said quietly. "What's said in therapy stays between the therapist and the patient."

"Client," Ethan corrected me, and it took all my self-control not to snap at him that nobody cared about the semantics of it. Snapping would not be productive.

Janus looked at Ethan. "Is that true?"

Ethan's adam's apple bobbed as he swallowed. "Yes, sir, it is."

Janus continued to stare at him. I saw sweat trickle down the side of Ethan's face. Ethan was never a trouble-maker. I was pretty sure this was the first time Janus looked at him for more than a passing glance. Being very familiar with Janus's stare, I knew what it felt like. But I could smell the old man's scent, and I knew that he wasn't angry. He smelled like a sudden spring rain. He was thinking, considering. There wasn't really a handy way to let Ethan know that, however, so the poor guy had to just sit and tolerate the stare.

"Very well," Janus said, but his mouth twisted with clear displeasure.

I took pity on Ethan. "It's also customary, sir, that the sanctity of the therapeutic bond can be violated if the patient – client – is in danger. Right, Ethan?"

Tony slanted a smile my way as Ethan cleared his throat and said, "Yes. Yes, if I deem Smack is in danger of hurting herself or others, I would be obligated to report that to you."

"And Smack is sitting right here, where Smack can hear every word you're saying about Smack," Smack muttered.

Without even a glance her way, Janus said to Ethan, "Ah. Well, then, that is satisfactory. Very well. Smack and Ethan, you are dismissed."

They left. I started to get up, too, thinking the meeting was over.

"I did not say you were dismissed." Janus pointed at my chair. With a sigh, I lowered myself back into it. Maybe they wanted to talk about Gina. "While I am glad everything is out in the open now, I must express concern at your disregard for your wellbeing and for the safety of others."

My jaw dropped. "What?"

"You were feeling weak and unwell, yet you agreed to take on the assignment of J.C.'s elimination. Because of that, J.C. escaped, putting your life and others in danger."

Tony shifted uncomfortably. "Sir, I think we all know that wasn't Kellan's fault. She only wanted to do the right thing."

I appreciated his loyalty, especially since I was pretty sure he agreed with Janus to an extent. I tried to swallow the rage that rose up my throat. "Fine. What's my punishment?"

"This is not about punishment." The first tendrils of Janus's angry scent threaded their way toward me. "This is about safety. Your safety. The safety of your unborn cub. And the safety of others who seek to keep you from self-destructing." This last with a nod to Tony.

What was happening? "Sir -"

"You are removed from active duty until your child is born. You may still live here, you may assist in everyday duties, but you will not take part in the search for J.C. You most certainly will not hunt for him. Is that clear?"

Rage flared again, making my skin go from ice-cold to feverishly hot in the space of a few seconds. The sensation made me a little nauseous. "So what, I'm supposed to stay home and knit baby blankets while the men do the dangerous work?"

The sarcasm was wasted on Janus. "I understand you are learning to knit. If that is how you wish to spend your time, I take no issue with that. However, if you wish to find other tasks to occupy yourself, I am certain we can find something."

My hand reached for the blade I had strapped to my ankle. Tony intercepted that hand and held it tight. "Sir, I think perhaps Kellan isn't feeling very well. Maybe we could continue this conversation later? We should probably get some food in her."

I knew he was helping me, even if it felt like I was being patronized from every side. That knowledge kept me silent, while Janus dismissed us and we walked outside, still hand in hand. Then I yanked my hand out of his and headed for the forest.

Tony jogged to catch up with me. "Where are you going?"

"To not do anything dangerous or remotely useful."

"Kell -"

"I'm not going anywhere. I just want to walk. Well, what I actually want is to shape-shift. But I can't do that, because a wolf's skeletal structure wasn't meant to accommodate a fucking human baby. So I'm going for a walk."

Galen, who knew the word walk as well as he knew his own name, didn't seem to know how to react. Walk was normally a happy word, but I was so obviously not happy.

Tony smelled worried. What did he have to be worried about? "I'll come with you. But first, you should eat. You look really pale."

"Don't you have real work to do?" A growl edged my words.

"Not really. Classes are cancelled for today, what with Gina being homicidally magickal and J.C. running off. So I'm free as a bird." If a human could growl, Tony would be doing it, as anger mixed with the worry in his scent.

Janus's angry scent reminded me of metal sparking in a microwave. Dangerous and certain to burn the house down. Tony's reminded me of jalapeno-cheddar focaccia bread, which wasn't scary. Heated, but more likely to make me hungry than contrite.

Sure enough, my stomach growled. The hunger pang was immediately followed by a wave of nausea. I ran over to the edge of the trees and threw up in the brush. Frustrated with my body and pissed about the conversation with Janus and all-around lost because I was stuck in this human body for the next several months, I threw my head back and tried to howl. It came out as more of a scream.

I heard footsteps slowly crunching on the snow, approaching me. "Feel better?" Tony asked.

I laughed humorlessly. "No. I feel like I'm going to throw up again. Plus, my throat hurts from all that screaming." My shoulders slumped. "I didn't know how much I depended on shape-shifting until Simone said I couldn't do it anymore."

Tony set his hands on my shoulders, but didn't try to turn me around. I was grateful, because I felt tears encroaching and if I had to see his sympathy as well as smell it, I would probably lose it. "Kellan, you're the toughest bitch I've ever met." Another laugh escaped me, this time a little more real. "You can do this," he went on. He pressed a kiss to the back of my neck. "What sounds good to eat?"

Nothing. But nothing wasn't an option, because the longer my stomach was empty, the worse I was going to feel. "Cereal? Cereal might be okay." Maybe after I ate something, I could down another protein drink. I knew I couldn't face one right away, though.

"Let's go see what we can find."

I gave a shuddering sigh, turned and hugged Tony. "This could very well suck worse for you than it will for me."

"Oh, I know." I heard the smile in his voice. "But I'm pretty tough, too. Don't worry about me."

We headed for the mess hall.

———— «» ————

Regardless of what Janus said, I wasn't about to sit around and do nothing until this kid popped out. After eating two bowls of cereal and drinking a protein shake, I headed for Gina's cabin. It was empty, so I went to the infirmary and asked Simone if she knew where Gina was.

The healer was busy stitching up a youngling. I wondered how the boy managed to hurt himself if classes were cancelled, but I didn't ask. When Simone pointed wordlessly to the same room Gina occupied the day before, I nodded and left her to it.

Worry stirred in my chest as I hesitated outside the room. Gina should be fine by now. Finn took a bigger magickal hit than she did, and he was back to normal. So why was she still in the infirmary? I knocked on the door. Galen waited beside me, tail wagging. I could almost hear him asking, "Who're we gonna visit now?"

When no one answered the knock, I eased open the door. Gina lay on the bed, eyes open and staring at the ceiling. She didn't look at me as I entered and shut the door.

"Hi," I said.

No response.

"How are you doing?"

Still nothing.

"It's rude to ignore visitors."

Gina exhaled a huff of air and turned her head. "I didn't ask you to come."

"Well, no, that's the joy of having a visitor. Sometimes they stop by as a surprise." I smiled stiffly and waved. "Surprise."

She returned to gazing at the ceiling.

I ditched my nice approach and tried a different tactic. "Gina, what the fuck? Why are you still in bed? The world's going to hell in a carry-on, and you're just laying around? Come on. Get up."

"Is he okay?" she whispered. I caught the faintest whiff of salt in the air. She was trying not to cry, and my frustration softened.

"Who, Tony? He's fine. I can bring him here so you can see, if that would make you feel better."

"What happened?" she breathed, even quieter.

Holy Jesus's tack hammer, they never talked to her? Fuck. "Didn't anyone explain it to you?"

She shook her head, cleared her throat, and spoke at a normal volume. "Every time someone comes in, I pretend to be asleep."

So why was I the lucky winner who got to see she was awake? A question for another time. "Listen, I'll go get Finn. He can explain –"

"No." Gina's voice trembled, a difficult feat when uttering a two-letter word.

I sighed. I was really bad at explaining magick, never having done it myself. But for Gina, I would try. "You're a sorcerer. You can do magick. They –" I almost said that Janus and Finn knew about it, but stopped myself in time. I didn't want to upset her with that news just yet. "Finn and Janus can teach you to control it, so that never happens again. It sucks that your introduction was so violent, but really, magick is no big deal."

"No. I don't want it."

Starting to feel irritated, I said, "Well, whether you want it or not, it's a part of you now."

"Evil."

Oh, yeah. Gina was a Christian. Christians thought magick was a devil thing. Shit. "It's not evil. It really isn't. It's just manipulating energy. That's like saying a magnet is evil because it can attract metal. It's a talent you were born with, a part of who you are. And you're not evil. You're the least evil person ever born."

She rolled over to face the wall. "Please leave."

I wanted to keep talking to her, but it didn't seem like the time to push her. So I left. Simone was still helping the youngling, so I didn't ask her to go talk to Gina. As Galen and I crossed the grounds, heading once again to Janus's cabin, I wondered why Simone didn't just heal the kid. I realized I knew very little about how Simone did what she did. I'd have to ask her someday.

But now, Gina was my mission. Smack was now sitting at the receptionist desk. She started to get up when she saw me. I wanted to apologize for the conversation earlier, for the way everyone talked about her right in front of her. But she smelled…solid. She smelled like herself, and I realized that this was the first time since she sat in my cabin, explaining how to cast on stitches, that she smelled like herself. I didn't want to do anything that would upset her again. "I'm going in," I said, and sidestepped around her and through the door to Janus's inner office.

Janus still sat at the table in the same seat as our earlier meeting, but now Finn sat to his left. I watched Finn look at my stomach. Why was everyone looking at my stomach? What did they expect to see? He saw me the day before, and I didn't look pregnant then. Why would I look it now?

I felt my cheeks blaze with some emotion I couldn't name. Did Finn also know that the baby could be Aza's? Probably. Knowing Janus, he wouldn't see anything wrong with discussing my cub's murky paternity. But I didn't like it. I didn't want them talking about me and mine. This wasn't their business, damn it. It was mine, Tony's, maybe even Galen's, but not theirs.

Gina. I was here for Gina. I forced myself to wade past the waves of emotion. I could feel later.

"Yes?" Finn said.

His imperious tone pissed me off. I bent over, like I was bowing at them, only I used the movement to draw the knife strapped to my ankle. Sometimes it's easier to make people listen when you're holding a weapon. Plus, holding a blade made me feel more in control, a feeling sorely lacking in my life these days.

"I just went to see Gina." I watched them for a reaction and didn't see one. "She's awake and she's trying to figure out what the fuck happened to her. You haven't explained it to her? Are you fucking kidding me?"

Janus's eyes narrowed slightly, but Finn raised a hand as if to ward him off. "She has been unconscious."

"No. She's been faking. And considering you two are magicians, I find it very difficult to believe you couldn't tell."

Finn's cheeks flushed slightly. He hated being called a magician. Magicians pulled coins out of bodily orifices. He was a sorcerer. Which was why I called him a magician anytime I really wanted to get a rise out of him.

I tried unsuccessfully to suppress a smile, feeling like I regained some of the power that was stolen away by his probable knowledge of my cub's bloodline. "Anyway, whatever your abilities to detect whether someone's conscious, she's awake now. So go talk to her. Explain to her that she isn't evil, because that's what she's afraid of."

"Evil?" Finn blinked uncomprehendingly.

"Yeah, dumbass. That's what you get when you mix magick with Christianity."

Their faces went blank as they appeared to think about what I said. "Oh, dear," Janus murmured. He stood up and headed for the door.

"I can go, sir." Finn followed him. "You can stay here."

"No. We shall go together. We made a grave error, allowing her to think such a thing." Janus looked at me. "Kellan, will you please bring Antony to Gina's room? She will need to see that he is well. The way the magick manifested will convince her that she is correct, that it is evil. If she can see him, we may be able to convince her otherwise."

"I think it's going to take a hell of a lot more than seeing Tony, but yeah, I'll go get him."

Finn and Janus rushed to the infirmary. I told Smack to follow them, figuring she could provide some much-needed support for Gina. Then I headed for the younglings' lounge. Tony told me he wanted to spend some time hanging out with the kids, to make sure they were okay, so I figured that was where they would be. The lounge was a small cabin on the edge of the campus, filled with board games, a TV and DVD player, and stocked with snacks like fresh fruit and beef jerky. I stopped, though, when I heard voices coming from the archery range. Catching the sound of Tony's voice among the shrieks and giggles of younglings, I followed the noise.

Tony and what looked like ninety percent of the younglings were on the far end of the paddock, behind the targets. They seemed to be constructing a wall, while also engaging in an ongoing snowball fight. I climbed over the fence and trotted across the snow to them.

"Dirk, that's good, keep going." Tony was focused on the kids with tools and didn't appear to notice me until I was by his side. "Oh! Hi, Kell." His gaze dropped briefly to my stomach – him, too? – and his good cheer seemed to falter for a moment. "We're building a wall."

"I see that." I went on my tiptoes and kissed his cheek. "Why do we need a wall on the archery range?"

"Because, Sankha Kellan, we don't want to hurt the animals." Tia waved at me. Her voice was high-pitched with excitement. "When people miss the target, the arrow could go into the forest and hit an animal. This way, the arrow will hit the wall. Then people like -" She stopped herself, instantly turning solemn, but I figured I knew what she was about to say. Only a couple days ago,

J.C. shot a squirrel during archery class, supposedly by accident. "None of the animals will get hurt now," she finished.

"Yup," Tony said. I could hear pride in his voice. "It was Tia's idea. When I asked them if they could think of something that needed work, they came up with this."

Of course, Tony was keeping them busy instead of hanging out watching TV, I thought. He was already a good father. Fuck, I hoped this baby was his. I shook my head and pasted a smile on my face. I didn't want to pull him away, but Gina really needed to see him. "Could someone else take over as foreman for a while?" I asked. "I need you to come with me."

Concern instantly tightened his eyes. "Yeah. Sure." He motioned to Dirk, who was the oldest youngling on site. "Hey, man, I gotta go with Kellan for a minute. Do me a favor and keep an eye on everyone, okay? If anything starts to seem unsafe, then take them all to the mess for hot chocolate." Tony handed Dirk his mess hall key, which Dirk took with wide eyes. Younglings weren't allowed keys to the mess hall, a silly precaution since we also taught them how to pick locks.

"Yes, sir." Dirk's chest puffed up slightly as he turned back to the other younglings. "Watch where you swing that hammer, Tevin!"

I hesitated. "Are you sure he's up to this?"

Tony nodded. "He's basically been in charge of the construction. I've just been here as an obligatory authority figure."

"All right." We watched for a second more, and when I saw Dirk take Tevin's hammer and direct him to the sanding station instead, I finally felt like we could leave.

I filled Tony in as we jogged to the infirmary. He shook his head. "They really didn't talk to her?"

"Don't get me started," I said darkly. "I keep telling myself they're going to make it right. If I have to beat them senseless to get them to do it, they will make it right. But I do think she needs to see you. She's really freaked out that she hurt you."

"I should've gone sooner."

And I should've known he'd blame himself. "Tell you what. Let's put all the blame at Finn and Janus's feet right now. Okay? They deserve it more than you."

We reached the door of the infirmary, and he took my hand. "Deal." We walked inside.

Chapter 13

TONY

When we entered Gina's room, I saw Gina and Smack sitting on the bed, while Finn and Janus leaned against the cabinets lining the opposite wall. The room was too small for all of us, so Kellan and Galen waited outside.

Gina's gaze immediately went to my leg. As I closed the door behind me, I deliberately put weight on that leg. Not even a shadow of a limp. Maybe it was good she didn't see me yesterday, when I was still hobbling a little bit.

Rather than seeming relieved, though, she looked away and studied her hands in her lap.

The atmosphere in the room was tense and awkward, and it was uncomfortably warm in there after spending the last hour outside. I forced a smile. "Sorry to interrupt. I heard Gina was awake, and I wanted to let her know I was okay." I looked at her, even though she wouldn't look at me. "I want you to know that we're okay, you and me."

Her shoulders bunched up, inching toward her ears, in a posture she used to hold all the time when she first arrived as a youngling. It was the first I'd seen her do it for over a year. I glanced at Finn and Janus, waiting for them to start. They were there to explain things to her, right? So why weren't they explaining?

"Yes, Antony, thank you for joining us." Finn's voice, for once, sounded soft and almost kind. "It must have been horribly frightening for you, Gina, to see your magick manifest with such violence. But it does not have to be that way." He paused, as if waiting for a response, but Gina stayed silent.

I saw Smack reach over and take one of her hands, though. That made me smile a little, despite the rising tension in the room.

"Magick is a very natural process," Janus said next. "As natural as breathing, as natural as rain falling or a tree growing leaves.

For those of us who have the ability to work magick, the world becomes a place of immense wonder."

"I hurt someone. You should punish me." Gina's voice was small, but she finally looked up from her lap to meet Janus's eyes.

"No," Janus said. He also sounded surprisingly gentle and, well, more human than he usually did. "You did not intend to hurt anyone. This was not a malicious act. It was an accident. You see, when the magickal ability manifests, it takes the body by surprise. Suddenly, rather than merely standing still, your body absorbs energy from the world around it, like a sponge absorbs water. If you do not know what is happening, then you cannot direct that energy. It builds and builds inside of you. Is that what it felt like? Like a strong emotion filling you up, every cell electrified?"

She blinked at him and nodded.

"Yes." Janus smiled at her. "And then, you see, your body instinctively tried to defend itself. You lashed out, not because you are bad or cruel or evil, but because you were filled with energy that was not yours. Antony was there, and he was caught in the – what is the word? Cross-fire. Yes?"

This was the part that really made no sense to me, so I figured Gina probably wanted more information, too. I asked, "But how, sir? I've never seen you or Finn use magick in that way. How did Gina do that? How did it happen?"

Finn sighed. "I wish I knew. All magick is the manipulation of energy. You somehow instinctively managed to turn that energy into a weapon, a blade that sliced…well, we don't need to go into that. It is a concept I have considered before, but never managed to succeed with. The fact that you did it without even knowing what you were doing —"

I cleared my throat, interrupting him before he could say something stupid, like "wow."

Finn's eyes cut to me, then he nodded slightly. "But just because I do not know how you did it, doesn't mean it's different from other magick. It's the same magick that allows Simone to knit broken bones back together or close a wound like Antony's, the same magick that allows Janus to protect our secret from prying eyes. It can be used to protect lives and save lives. It is a skill, a tool, and like any tool, you will learn how to wield it safely."

"And if I don't want to?" Gina whispered.

"I am afraid you do not have a choice in the matter," Janus said. "This is an ability you have, not a purchase you can return. And it is vital that you learn to use that ability. Strong emotions attract magickal energy, you see. It is why people can sometimes feel the 'mood' in a room. For someone like Antony, that energy simply hovers around him, but for those like myself, like you, who have the gift of wielding magick, when we feel strong emotions, we draw that energy into our bodies, whether we are conscious of it or not. Once that energy is inside of us, it must be used. Otherwise, it will tax our bodies."

Gina was barely breathing. I didn't think this was helping her.

"For example, yesterday when Finlay helped you to let go of the energy, he drew all the energy you released into his own body. That way, you could not absorb it again. You see, your fear and anger made your body a much more appealing home for that energy. So Finlay took it into himself, but holding it exhausted him. Rather like trying to wrap your arms around a horse and hold it in place when it wants to run."

Gina blinked and her shoulders relaxed a tiny bit. She liked horses, I knew that, but did Janus know that? Or was it just a fluke that he managed to stumble on a metaphor that would make Gina feel something positive?

"We will teach you how to calm yourself, how to breathe through strong emotions and release energy back into the earth. And we will explore how you can use your magick to improve your life and the lives of those around you."

Gina pulled her hand from Smack's grasp and seemed to stare at a point on the wall behind Finn. "No disrespect, sirs, but do you mind leaving me alone for a while? I want to…process everything you've told me. Thank you for taking the time to speak to me. Goodbye."

Smack looked up at me, like asking me if she was supposed to leave, too.

I shook my head. I wished I knew. I opened the door, and Janus and Finn filed out. I looked back over my shoulder at Gina. "See you later."

She didn't seem to hear me.

I was expecting to see Kellan and Galen right outside the room, but they were gone. Not for the first time, I wished I could follow her scent trail and find out where they went. I felt so sad for Gina, being thrust into this situation she didn't want. Kind of like Kellan with this baby, which made me want to find her and wrap my arms around her, and just hold her for at least a year.

KELLAN

As I waited outside Gina's room, the adrenaline left me and a wave of tiredness crashed over me. I lowered myself to the floor and leaned back against the wall, listening to the hum of voices in Gina's room and letting my eyes drift shut.

I jerked awake as Simone came down the hall. "It's about time they talked to her," she said.

"You could've sent for them sooner." I wasn't accusing her, just observing.

"I've been a little busy. Your boyfriend's impromptu DIY project led to one severed digit and three nails through hands."

"Jeez." I would've expected Tony to be more careful than that.

"It's hard to keep watch over that many kids with that many tools. But it's been a crazy morning." She slid down to sit beside me. "How are you feeling?"

I snorted. "So far, pregnancy sucks. When does the glowing start?"

"I don't think you're going to be that kind of pregnant woman."

"Yeah, no shit." My eyes drifted closed again. "Why were you stitching up that youngling? Why didn't you magickally heal him?"

"That youngling's name is Nat. And I didn't use magick because magick takes a toll. I exhausted myself healing Tony. So anything non-life-threatening for the next few days will get nonmagickal healing." She sighed. "Which sucks. I hate using stitches on kids."

"I think I better go check on the construction crew. Tony left Dirk in charge." I pushed to my feet.

"That was a good call. Dirk really craves validation. He'll do a good job, watching over the kids."

"But if you had that many injuries with Tony watching over them..."

"Yeah, maybe it's a good idea to go check." Simone was still sitting on the floor.

"You okay?" I asked. She looked more tired than usual.

"Yes." She stood. "It's been a long couple of days. I'll feel better if they're successful with Gina. That's a lot for a young woman to deal with."

I studied her. "Speaking from experience?"

Her mouth tilted in a half-smile, half-grimace. "Go check on the younglings."

"Yes, ma'am." Whistling for Galen, I left, trusting that Gina was in good hands for the time being.

The archery range was deserted, so I checked the mess hall. All the younglings were inside, talking and laughing and drinking hot chocolate and coffee. I went over to the coffee carafe and poured myself a mug. It was weak, but it was hot and caffeinated. I sipped gratefully.

When someone tugged on my coat sleeve, I glanced down. Tia stood there. "Miz Kellan?"

"Yes, Tia."

She motioned for me to come closer. I knelt down and she whispered in my ear, "Your hot chocolate is better."

My eyes were suddenly damp. Fucking hormones. I wiped my traitorously leaky eyes as I said, "Well, see, that's because I use extra chocolate. Most people just use one packet, but that's a mistake. Always use two."

She nodded solemnly, like I was imparting some great wisdom. She glanced around until her eyes settled on Valentine, and then she looked back at me with a smile so beatific, I could almost see her halo. "'Kay. Bye." And she shuffled off back to her sister. I noticed that her boots were untied. I shook my head.

Galen looked up at me longingly. He only ate breakfast a few hours ago, but I felt the need to make someone happy. "Hey, big dog, you want some kibbles? Let's go home and get you some." He wagged his tail furiously.

I half-expected someone to stop us on our way to the cabin with some sort of emergency. It was just that kind of week. But no one did. We went in the cabin, I fed Galen, and sat down on the bed to rest while he ate. The sky outside was grey, which meant the cabin was dim and cozy and quiet. I felt that quiet seep into my muscles, relaxing me. My eyelids drew closed. The next thing I knew, I was waking up to a suddenly brightly lit cabin.

"Oh, shit, Kell, I'm sorry. Were you asleep?" Tony stomped the snow off his boots and flicked the light switch back into the off position. "Go back to sleep."

"No. Come here." I was warm and comfy, with Galen curled up against my stomach, but I did want to hear about what happened with Gina.

Tony eased onto the bed, spooning against my back. "Don't want to disturb the big guy," he rumbled, reaching an arm over me to scratch Galen behind the ears. Galen gave his hand a lick. I breathed in Tony's scent, slightly muted from the cold, but rapidly warming up, like bread toasting in the oven. I caught a hint of sourdough worry.

"What's wrong?"

"Mmm. Nothing." I could hear the exhaustion weighing down his voice.

"I can tell you're worried. Is it Gina?"

He hesitated, then sighed. "Yeah." More worry and something else. Something that smelled like lies. "I just wanted to enjoy this for a second."

Was he lying? "Enjoy what?"

He leaned over and kissed my temple. "You. Not avoiding me."

My skin heated with guilt. "I'm sorry, Tony."

"Don't be. It'll ruin the moment. Just enjoy it with me."

I snorted. I almost asked him what he was lying about, but I didn't really want to ruin the moment, either. I snuggled closer to him. "Like this?"

"Yeah. Just like that."

We lay that way for a while, his breathing getting more and more even, until I could tell he was almost asleep. It was a sleepy kind of day. I gently elbowed him in the stomach, and he jerked awake. "Are you seriously going to make me wait to hear what happened with Gina while you take a nap?"

"You got to take a nap," he teased.

"Yeah, well, I'm knocked up. I get to do shit like that."

"Gina is…resistant."

I rolled over to face him, disturbing Galen, who grumbled sleepily at me. I murmured an apology, but this felt like a conversation that required eye contact. I could feel my eyes glowing as my night vision allowed me to see Tony's expression, which was very serious.

He reached over and tucked a lock of hair behind my ear. "She said she doesn't want it. And then, all of a sudden, she shut down and kicked us out."

I could see how that would be troubling. Maybe Tony wasn't lying about anything. Maybe all I smelled was his concern for Gina. "Yeah, I told Finn and Janus that she thought it meant she was evil. Did they handle her okay?"

"You told them? I should've known." He snorted. "To hear them talk, they figured out her concerns on their own. They talked about how magick isn't good or bad, it's just a skill. All in how you use it. Janus talked to her about how, with practice, she could make sure the power didn't get out of hand like it did when…with me. And I do think it helped, being able to see that I was okay. They pointed out, too, that Simone's healing is a form of magick. That magick allowed her to save my life." He sighed heavily, as if his near-death experience was his fault. "I think it would've helped more if Gina didn't blame herself for my injury, but I think it did help."

"But she still doesn't want it."

"Nope."

I sighed. "Do you think she'll be okay?"

"Mmm-hmm. Gina's a survivor. She's been through worse than this. She'll figure it out. As I was leaving, I heard Smack suggest they go to Gina's cabin. That'll help, getting her out of the infirmary and back into her own space." He rolled onto his back. "Have you eaten since earlier?"

"Do you ever get tired of asking me that?" *Because I get tired of answering that*, I thought.

"Nope. It's what I live for. So I'm guessing that's a no. I'll go get some food." He left, and I rolled back over, so I could curl myself around Galen again. We were both back to sleep in moments.

Chapter 14

KELLAN

Thanks to my nap, I couldn't fall asleep when Tony went to bed. I kept playing the conversation with Janus over in my head. It was a bad track for my brain to be stuck on. All it did was make me mad.

Removed from active duty. Fuck that. I was going to help find J.C. I could do that from here, if what Tia said about Smack's hacking abilities was true.

When my cell phone rang, I grabbed it and hurried outside, pulling on a coat as I went. Galen hopped off the bed and followed me. Tony didn't stir, which I was grateful for. He needed the sleep.

The caller ID was blocked. My stomach clenched and I almost didn't answer. Only one person ever called me from a blocked number. "Hello."

"I hear congratulations are in order." My sister's smooth, strong voice made me close my eyes in longing. I missed her. She was a traitor, but she was my twin, and I missed her.

Damn hormones.

"How did you find out?" I just told Tony – how did my sister know about the pregnancy? How did she know about anything? I started walking with Galen toward the forest. Might as well get in a little exercise while we talked.

Mal ignored my question. "I'm happy for you, Kellan."

I snorted. "That makes one of us."

"You don't want a cub?" She didn't sound surprised by this, but she clearly intended to change my mind about it.

I sighed and ran my fingers over the rough bark of a tree. "Let's just say it wasn't exactly planned. I'm not really mother material. And, well, there's the question of paternity."

She was silent for a long time. I knew she was working through what I just said, that I wasn't suggesting I was suddenly polyamorous. "Okay, I can't say I know what it feels like to have to wonder if the cub is…that faery's. I wish I could just…I wish we could hunt him, you and I. He deserves to die."

This was what family meant to us. Someone threatened you? Someone hurt you? That motherfucker is going down. You and I will do it together. Pack. A wave of longing almost made my throat close up. I had trouble drawing a good breath. And suddenly, I remembered that Mal didn't just defect from the Sankhain. She attacked us. Attacked me. Ran me through with a sword. How did that fit in with our concept of family? A part of me knew that if she wanted to kill me, I'd be dead. She must've been very careful when stabbing me to avoid hitting anything vital. She just had to make it look real. And she did it so that she and her daughter could be free. But still. She ran me through with a fucking sword.

"Kell?"

I must've been quiet too long. I didn't want to say anything about the trip down memory lane. I reminded myself of where the conversation left off, and said, "Not gonna argue. I'd hunt him in a heartbeat if I could."

She cleared her throat. "But as to the other thing, I call bullshit. You're absolutely mother material. Ninety percent of being a mom is protecting your cub. You do that for all those younglings already. And they love you for it." She was silent for a moment. "You did it for me, too. Still are."

"Why do you say that?"

"You're talking to me instead of trying to figure out where I am or running to tell Janus that I'm on the phone."

"That doesn't mean anything. Maybe I'm just lulling you into complacency first."

She laughed, and at the sound, my mouth smiled without my permission. Maybe she was lulling me into complacency.

If she was, it was working. I realized I was talking to the one person alive who knew exactly what I was going through. "I want to shape-shift so bad, I can taste it. How did you do it?"

"It was the hardest thing I've ever done." Her voice was soft, serious. "But you have an advantage over me."

"I do?" I couldn't begin to think what that might be.

"Yes, silly. You have your dog. You can enter his mind, can't you? Let him fill that need for you. Let him run and hunt. You can feel what he's feeling."

"He doesn't really like to hunt alone." I hadn't used my ability to mind-meld with a dog in so long. Could it work? Could it help? "I didn't think of that."

"Because you're too busy avoiding thinking about this pregnancy." She said it like it was fact. Which it kind of was, but the know-it-all thing was annoying.

"I have enough people in my life who can read my mind. Don't you start."

She laughed again. "That's not mind-reading, dear sister. I just know you that well. So what else is playing on your mind?"

I took a breath to tell her, then stopped myself. For a moment, I forgot that she was a traitor. I forgot that I wasn't supposed to be talking to her anymore.

She sighed, the sound a heavy whoosh over the phone. "I suppose I should go."

My heart stopped for a moment as an idea formed. "Wait." A small voice told me to keep my mouth shut, but I was practiced at ignoring voices. "Would you be willing to help us hunt someone?"

Silence. I checked to see if she hung up, but the phone said we were still connected. Finally, she said, "If it's Aza, I already told you I'm in."

The rage, the hatred, in her voice was as familiar to me as the love of a moment ago. And it prompted the same sense of longing. We were a strange pair, but we were a pair. "No, it's not Aza." If I could get a lead on where J.C. went... Mal was out in the world, and she was almost as good a tracker as I was. I'd have to come up with an excuse for where I got the information – I certainly couldn't tell Janus and Finn that Mal helped me – but that was a problem for later. "We...we had a runaway."

"Kellan, you're more than capable of hunting anyone you want. If this is some sort of heavy-handed attempt to corner me -"

"Oh, for fuck's sake. Not everything is about you." I shook my head. "Never mind. This was a stupid idea. But for your information, I've been benched. Janus doesn't want me on the hunt. Because it's my fault he got away in the first place."

I heard a strangled noise as familiar as her laugh, this one meaning that she was angry. "He benched you? You guys have a runaway Sankha, and Janus benched his best tracker? That's insane. Who is this guy, and what happened?"

I was getting cold. The wind was sharp and angry, cutting right through my jacket. I should hang up and go back home. But her indignation on my behalf felt like I had my sister back. I wanted her back. So I said, "Hang on," and led Galen to a vacant cabin two doors down from ours. I plugged in a space heater – we kept them in every cabin, even the ones currently unoccupied – and I settled on the floor in front of it with a blanket from the linen closet.

"Not a Sankha," I told her. "A youngling."

Silence. Then, "What?"

I told her what happened with Smack, finding out what J.C. did, how he got away.

"Kellan, that wasn't your fault."

"Whatever. That doesn't matter. If I can get a lead on where he went, will you find him for me?"

"Only if I get to kill him when I find him." That beautiful rage filled her voice, but for once, I didn't feel the same. All I felt was icy dread, because I could still hear J.C. crying.

I couldn't promise her the kill. Not until I thought about this arrangement further. But asking her for help felt so good, I pretended not to hear her request. "If you agree to this, I'm going to need a way to contact you. No more blocked numbers in the middle of the night."

She was silent again for a while. I could picture her as she thought about it, the risks of giving me a tie to her. Of handing over a small amount of the control she valued so highly. If I was lying to her, I could use this number to track her down. Well, someone else who was capable of doing things like that could use this number to track her down. If I gave it to them. But I honestly had no desire to do that. Mal just wanted to live her life away from the Sankhain. I didn't agree with how she went about it, and even more than the remembered pain of that sword, it hurt like a son of a bitch that she didn't tell me about her kid. But honestly, I didn't see a threat here. I saw no reason we couldn't both live peacefully in this world.

But maybe she didn't, because she didn't say anything for a long time. Finally, I heard a soft, "Okay. You have a pen?"

"Because I keep a pen in my pajamas? Fuck, no. Hang on, let me see if I can find one." We weren't the Radisson, we didn't keep our cabins stocked with pens and paper, but I did find a pencil and a few loose sheets of notepaper in a drawer by the sink. "All right, go."

Mal rattled off her number. Then we both sat in silence, as if neither of us knew what to say after such an act of trust. "I won't give it to them," I said quietly.

"I know," she said, just as quietly.

I felt the confounding dampness of tears in my eyes. Again. "Did you cry a lot when you were pregnant?"

"Oh, god, at every little thing." She laughed. I heard a slight tremor in the laugh, though, like maybe I wasn't the only one feeling impending waterworks.

"It's fucking horrible."

"Worse than the puking," she agreed.

"Well, I don't know about that. The puking is annoying."

After a little more silence, she said, "Love you. Little sis." Because I was born after her.

I had to clear my throat twice before I could answer. "Love you. Shrimp." Because she was always shorter than me.

After we hung up, I stayed in the cabin for a while, petting Galen and letting the hot air from the space heater soak into me. I didn't want to leave just yet, didn't want to risk having to speak to someone who didn't, who couldn't possibly understand what I just recovered. When I woke up from my nap, I didn't have a sister. Now I did. I needed to let that sink in before I tried to go out and be normal again.

Eventually, though, I needed to pee and I was starting to feel hungry. I was learning that I had a narrow window between "starting to feel hungry" and "need to puke right now!" So I unplugged the space heater, put away the blanket and hustled Galen back to the cabin, where I tore into some Pop-Tarts before mixing myself a protein shake. It worked. I didn't puke. Unfortunately, the noise of the little ball in the shaker bottle woke Tony.

He sat up and rubbed his eyes. I saw him glance at the fire I'd started in the fireplace and the wet spots on the floor from the snow on my boots and Galen's feet. "Where'd you go?" he mumbled.

"Just for a walk. I couldn't sleep." Here I was, lying to him again. God damn it. "Actually, that's not true." I drained my protein drink as quickly as possible, then set the bottle in the sink, watching Tony all the while.

His brow crinkled. He still looked half-asleep.

I walked over to the radio and turned on the blues station that Tony liked. An atonal modern jazz song filled the room. I made a face, but left the music playing. I didn't think Janus would try to eavesdrop, but just in case.

"I need you to not tell anyone about this," I said.

His brow furrowed further, but he nodded.

"I got a phone call." I sat on the edge of the bed. "From Mal."

Understanding filled his eyes, but he still didn't say anything.

"She wanted to congratulate me. On the...on the cub. The baby." There, I said it. And maybe someday, I'd be able to actually say it without my sphincter clenching tighter than a virgin's legs.

"Okay," he said slowly. "How'd she find out?"

"Well, I don't think Janus told her." Tony snorted, and I smiled. "And I'm pretty sure you didn't tell her."

"Nope."

"And I didn't tell her. So that leaves one person."

"Simone," Tony said. His voice was soft, like he just realized why I was subjecting us to this god-awful music.

"Unless, of course, my sister has finally learned to read minds, in which case the world is pretty much fucked and we should all surrender now."

He snorted again. "What'd you say to her?"

I hesitated. My answer should've been that I told her to fuck off, but of course, that wasn't what I did. "I told her about J.C. I asked if she would help us find him."

His mouth drooped open. "Kell, she tried to kill you last spring. And she kidnapped you last fall."

No relationship was perfect. "I know. I just…she's a part of me. A part that's been missing for almost a year. And now, I don't know, now that I know her secrets and she knows mine, maybe I can have her back." Saying it out loud to someone so skeptical made me realize just how stupid and risky this was. "And she didn't try to kill me. She very carefully stuck a sword in my side. She made sure she didn't hit anything life-threatening."

He made a sound that was suspiciously close to a growl. "What if you moved at the last minute?"

I didn't answer, because he was right. Mal took a huge risk sticking that sword in me. She was willing to do that. And I was willing to forgive her. Stupid? Sure. But true.

He sighed and looked down at his hands in his lap. "What did she say? About J.C."

"She said yes." I didn't tell Tony about Mal calling dibs on killing J.C. I didn't know if he would understand, and I didn't want him thinking even less of my sister than he already did.

"Okay." I heard something in his voice that made me think he knew Mal would want to kill the boy. He probably did know that, since Mal and I were so alike, and that would normally be my feeling on the matter. I shifted uncomfortably, wishing Tony would look at me again. After a moment, he did, just as some instrument on the radio hit an exceptionally high note. Tony winced. "Can we turn that off now?"

"You're the one who likes this stuff."

"I like blues. Some old-school jazz. Not this."

I switched the station to classic rock, and Zeppelin took the place of the acidic jazz. "This isn't the first time she's called me," I said, watching him for a reaction again.

"Oh." That was all he said.

"I kind of like it that she calls me."

"Okay." He frowned at me. "Were you expecting me to say something? Like tell you not to talk to her?"

"Maybe."

He sighed. "Then you really do think I'm stupid," he said in mock seriousness.

I made a face at him. "Shut up."

"Are you coming back to bed?"

Black Sabbath followed Zeppelin, and I listened to a few lines before turning the radio off and crawling into bed. "So, what, you like big band music?" I asked as I held up the covers for Galen to crawl under them.

"Go to sleep, Kellan."

"Well, you said old-school jazz."

"I like Cannonball Adderly. Louis Armstrong. Billie Holiday, Lena Horne. Big band, not so much."

"Hmm. I'm going to get you a Glen Miller CD."

"Well, I'm sure it would make a very nice coaster."

Around midnight, I fell asleep as the fire slowly died down and my dog and my guy started to snore.

Chapter 15

KELLAN

The next morning, activity resumed as normal. Younglings went back to class, and Gina was back to work, running the kitchen. Tony and I ate breakfast in the mess hall, something I usually avoided because the building stank of bacon for a good hour after breakfast finished. But that morning, the bacon almost smelled good. Almost.

I saw Finn over by the table where the food was laid out, buffet-style. He kept glancing at me, a weird look on his face. Right, because Janus told him about the pregnancy. I decided, since ignore-it-til-it-goes away wasn't working on this baby, I might as well leak the big news. I stood up. "Hey! Attention, please."

Tony watched me, eyebrows raised in an unspoken question.

When the room fell silent, I took a deep breath and said, "Just thought I'd let you know, I'm pregnant. No, I don't want to talk about baby names, and fuck, no, you cannot touch my stomach. The first person who tries that will lose a hand." Loud hoots and applause followed me as I sat back down. No more hiding. No more pretending. It was real.

I hoped it didn't mean I was going to have to endure congratulations from everyone at the Academy.

Gina swung by our table. I wanted to know how she was doing, but first… "If you try to slip me decaf because I'm pregnant, I'll puke all over you."

She gave a wan smile. "Noted." She looked at Tony. "How are you feeling?"

"I'm fine," he said with a smile. "How are you feeling?"

She swallowed and looked away. "Fine. I'll – see you later." She scurried away.

I met Tony's gaze. "She's not fine," I said.

"Nope."

"Are you going to talk to her?" I asked hopefully.

"I have an archery class to teach."

"Maybe Ethan could talk to her. He's the shrink."

"I think he's got appointments with some of the younglings this morning. Aftermath of what happened with J.C. and with Gina."

That was important shrinky stuff. I sighed again. "And I have absolutely nothing constructive to do. By orders of the old man." Which meant I was the logical one to go talk to Gina.

Tony got up, picked up his tray of dirty dishes, and leaned down to kiss me. "Yup. Have fun." He put his dirty dishes in their respective bins and left.

"Fuck." I looked at Galen. "Maybe you want to talk to her?"

He wagged his tail, a look of "what's next, boss?" warming his eyes.

"Yeah. I guess I'll do it. Come on."

Gina was in the kitchen, barking orders at the younglings assisting her. The scent of anxiety was thicker than the scent of bacon. I noticed Tia hiding behind a bank of cabinets.

"Hey, younglings, do you think you could handle the cleanup here if I steal Gina away? I need her on…Sankhain business."

Ryder, one of the younglings handling the dirty dishes, shot me a grateful look before lowering his eyes and saying deferentially, "Yes, ma'am, I think we could."

The others smelled too scared to speak. They just nodded. Gina, on the other hand, stood like a tower of anger at my interruption. Goody.

"Great. Come on, Gina. We need to go…this way." I couldn't think of a good excuse for pulling her away from the kitchen. But I knew I needed to get her away from those poor kids.

"I'm busy," she said through clenched teeth, but she followed me.

"Yeah, I see that." Once we were outside, I took a deep breath of non-anxious air. "You're very busy scaring the shit out of those younglings."

Her steps faltered, and I realized she was probably remembering the incident with Tony. That wasn't what I intended when I told her she was being scary, but before I could say anything, she said, "I was not scaring the younglings."

"Mmm-hmm. Tia was hiding from you."

"I – she what?" I could see her trying to figure out when she last saw Tia. "She was hiding?" Now her voice sounded small and uncertain.

"Yeah. Come on. Let's go lift some weights." With my stomach full of breakfast, the last thing I wanted was to exercise, but Gina clearly needed an outlet.

"Yes, ma'am." She was so preoccupied with her thoughts, she seemed to have forgotten that she wasn't a youngling anymore.

I could work with that. Obedience made everything easier.

The weights room was one of my favorite places in the world. Several years ago, I convinced Janus to convert one of the cabins into a gym. We had a couple elliptical machines, a couple treadmills, and a huge assortment of strength-training equipment and free weights, all hand-picked by me. I had way more fun furnishing the weight room than I did my apartment in the city.

Galen went to stand beside the dish I kept in the weight room, and I filled the dish with fresh, cold water from the minifridge in the corner. After he slurped up a good drink, he settled on the floormats and lowered his head onto his paws. He didn't close his eyes, though, I noticed. He kept a close watch on Gina and me, probably able to smell Gina's emotion just like I could.

I led Gina to the squats machine, because it was impossible to hold onto aggression after doing squats. Not if you were doing them properly. They just tired you out too damn much.

I adjusted the weights, guessing. I wasn't sure how much weight Gina could manage, but I would be there to spot her in case it was too much. "All right. There you go."

She seemed to have regained some of her ire on the walk from the mess hall. "I hate squats." She glowered at me.

"Honey, everybody hates squats. That's how you know they're good for you." I patted the machine. "Have at it."

Like a good spotter, I stood beside her and watched as she performed her reps. She struggled a little toward the end of the set, which meant the weights were just right.

"Good work," I said. I looked longingly at the machine, but didn't take a turn. I had a feeling my breakfast would end up on the floor of the weight room if I tried to lift. "How 'bout some crunches?" I found core work very soothing. Something about connecting to the center of my body calmed me.

"I hate crunches almost as much as squats." But she got on the incline bench and started crunching. When she reached a point where she was sweating and breathing heavy and seemed unable to raise herself up off the bench, I sat down on the floor near her head. Galen stood up, shook himself, and trotted over to curl up against my side.

I petted him as I said to Gina, "Good. Now talk."

She closed her eyes. I watched her breathe in and out. Gradually, her breathing slowed and she opened her eyes. She got off the bench and sat across from me. Plucking at a piece of lint on her yoga pants, she said, "Do you ever wish you were normal?"

I took no offense to the implication that I was less than normal. "No. But I was born knowing what I was. This must be a lot harder for you."

She sighed a weight-of-the-world heavy sigh. "I'm afraid of myself. I hate this."

My old friend Anger stirred inside me again as I thought about how much easier it would be for her if Finn and Janus would've just told her what she was. If they would've prepared her, so it wasn't such a shock when magick exploded from her. This was their fault. "I think you should talk to Finn and Janus some more. Start training."

The air grew thick with magickal static electricity. She apparently didn't like that idea much. Strange that this conversation made her magick rise, when all that anger in the kitchen didn't. I should've been scared after what happened to Tony. I wasn't. Gina might be unhappy, but I felt fairly confident that she wasn't lash-out unhappy.

"I know it's not what you want. But I think learning how this works is the only way you'll ever feel better about it." I touched a twenty-five pound dumbbell that someone left sitting on the floor. "It's like learning how to weightlift, or how to spar, or do anything, really. It's daunting at first. You don't think you'll ever feel better about it, ever feel comfortable with it. But it gets better the more you do it."

She sighed again, and the thick air slowly dropped back to normal. "If I say okay, will you quit offering me advice?"

I scowled at her, but inside, I was smiling. "What, you don't like my insights?"

"You sound like the mom on a family sitcom. Just the right touch of inspirational metaphor."

I laughed. "Pretty sure that's the first and last time anyone's ever going to accuse me of being inspirational. No, wait. Tony called me that once."

"Ew. I don't want to hear about your foreplay."

"It wasn't foreplay!" It was a pep talk, and it was sweet. Of course, it seriously weirded me out at the time, but looking back on it, it was sweet.

"Whatever." She pulled her knees to her chest and wrapped her arms around her shins. "I didn't mean to do that to him, you know."

Duh. "Of course, I know that. It took you two years to learn how to throw a punch. Like you're going to suddenly start craving bloodshed? Please." I cocked my head. Her scent was tense. It reminded me a little of Janus's angry scent, but this wasn't anger. This was worry, maybe even fear. "Let's go." I stood up and held out my hand to her. Galen hopped to his feet, clearly eager for the next adventure.

Dogs were so much more enthusiastic than people. Gina hesitated briefly, then took my hand and rose. "I thought you would be mad at me," she murmured. "You seem angry."

"That's just my personality," I said, and she gave me a look. Was Gina able to read minds like Janus? No, if she could read minds, she would know who I was mad at. So how did she know this wasn't just me being pissy? "Yeah, okay, I'm mad, but not at you. It's -" I stopped. I was pretty sure Gina didn't know that Finn and Janus were aware of her abilities before they manifested. She needed to trust them if she was going to get through this. Nobody else here could teach her how to control this magick. Then I had an idea. "It's this whole J.C. thing. I'm mad at myself for letting him get away, and I'm pissed that we're not doing more to find him." Which was true, it just wasn't the anger she was currently picking up on.

She laid a hand on my shoulder. "That wasn't your fault. He's an evil bastard. He'll get what's coming to him."

There was that "e" word again. I didn't like it. People used it to wash their hands of things. Nothing I can do about it, he's just evil. But this time, I could use that stupid word to turn her fears on their heads. "You're right. He's evil." I paused for dramatic effect. "You're not."

She jerked her hand away. "There's more than one type of evil."

"Yeah," I said, and started walking. She followed, and I was glad. The conversation was going my way, and I wanted to get her to Janus's cabin before I screwed it up. "But see, you've never done anything evil."

"I almost killed Tony."

"That was out of your control. That's like saying you're evil for sneezing."

She blinked, seeming to process that.

I pressed my advantage. "That's why you need to study magick." We arrived at Janus's cabin, and I held the door open. "So you can control it. So you can have a say in how that magick affects you and the people around you."

"Everybody keeps saying that." She met my eyes, and I knew she was going to agree. "I still don't want it."

"Yeah, well." I thought of the cub growing inside me. "Want it or not, it's here to stay."

She swallowed, nodded once, and walked inside. Tevin was sitting at the reception desk. I gave him what I hoped was a reassuring smile, and said, "Gina needs to see Janus."

Tevin nodded and got up to knock on the inner door. "Sir? Uh, Sankha Kellan and Sankha Gina are here to see you."

"Enter," came Janus's voice.

Finn was there, too. He sat in one of the armchairs by the fire and didn't look up when we entered. Great. Finn was in a snit. Fortunately, I was, too, and with pregnancy hormones backing me up, I had way more snit than he did.

"Sirs," I said. "Gina's ready to start training." That brought Finn's attention to me, but his gaze skittered away almost as soon as it met mine. Great. More drama. Just what I needed.

"Very good." Janus looked at me with his eyebrows slightly raised, as if asking why I was there. "Thank you, Kellan. You are dismissed."

"No, I want her to stay," Gina said. Then she apparently remembered who she was speaking to. "Please. Sirs."

This time, Janus's expression was definitely skeptical. Like I asked for this. I shrugged. I didn't ask for it, but if it made Gina feel better, I was happy to do it. It wasn't like I had anything else to do. With a wry twist to his smile, Janus said, "Very well."

Through all of this, Finn was silent. That was just weird. I had enough weird in my life, I didn't have room for more. "Sir? May Finlay and I be excused for a moment?"

Gina and Finn had almost identical horrified expressions.

"I'll be right outside," I told Gina. "I just have something I need to discuss with Finn. We'll be right back. If that's all right, sir?"

Janus looked at Finn, as if he knew where Finn's horror came from. I wondered what they were talking about before Gina and I arrived. After a moment of Finn looking beseechingly at Janus, the old man turned to me. "Yes, certainly. Gina and I will simply talk until you get back. No magick until you return."

Gina, at least, looked slightly less terrified. Finn still looked about the same as we went outside. I left Galen on a down-stay in Janus's office, since he hated Finn so much. This would be easier without my dog constantly growling at the guy.

Finn looked like he lost ten pounds in the last forty-eight hours. He looked better than right after the magickal confrontation, but not by a whole lot. Why was that? "You still look like shit," I told him.

"Thank you," he said dryly. Still wouldn't look at me, though.

"What's wrong with you?"

He sighed. "I have not been sleeping well."

Poor baby. "So why won't you look at me?" I crossed my arms over my chest and waited.

He inhaled deeply, then let the breath out slowly. "Congratulations."

Of course, this was about the pregnancy. Everything these days was about this damn pregnancy.

My past relationship with Finn was…complicated. We didn't love each other – we usually didn't even like each other – but we were exclusive sexual partners for over a hundred years. That ended long before Tony and I started, but still, I probably should've personally told him I was knocked up.

"I should've said something," I said lamely.

His mouth twisted and his tone turned self-deprecating. "It's none of my business, really. We aren't involved anymore."

"Yeah, but still. It was a jackass move. I'm sorry."

He examined his cuticles and blushed a deep shade of red. "We never used protection. Why - ?"

Understanding gradually dawned. Oh, for fuck's sake. He wasn't jealous that I was with another guy. He was jealous that some other guy got me pregnant when he never managed to. This was some fucked-up virility pride thing. "Jesus. You – ya know, it's probably some sort of natural preventative measure. It's bad enough that this poor kid has me as one of its parents. Can you imagine if it was stuck with you for the other one? Forget that any attempt at coparenting would end with one of us killing the other. Let's just be grateful that Mother Nature was smarter than we were, and move on." Of course, the world didn't work like that, and even Finn would be a better baby daddy than Aza, but in my effort not to murder Finn, I let logic fall by the wayside.

His head shot up, eyes blazing. Whatever he saw in my expression – probably a whole lot of rage of my own – cooled him right down. He gave another twisted self-deprecating smile. "Yes, I suppose so."

Eager to exit this conversation, I motioned toward the cabin, where Janus and Gina were waiting. "Shall we?"

He nodded and led the way inside. After a few deep breaths, I managed to follow.

Chapter 16

KELLAN

As we entered the room, Janus was saying, "So you see, I do not even need to be awake for that particular spell to work. I must be awake and aware to work new spells, but I can maintain already existing magick through all states of consciousness. Which is truly good, because magick drains the sorcerer's energy. Proper rest is essential."

Gina seemed to be listening calmly, but she looked a little too happy to see me. I sat down beside her and wished I had a cup of coffee.

Janus met my gaze. "Perhaps young Tevin would be so kind as to bring us refreshments?"

"Great idea. Why don't you ask him?" Now that I was sitting down, I felt exhaustion close in on me again and I wanted to stand back up like I wanted a rectal exam.

Gina's mouth dropped open slightly, and I remembered we weren't alone. Shit. I needed to be more respectful of Janus when other ears were listening. "I'm sorry, sir. What I meant was, I'll go ask him."

I pushed to my feet and trudged to the doorway. After asking Tevin to go get snacks and coffee – lots of coffee – I slowly walked back to my chair. If I felt this heavy and tired now, what the hell was I going to do when I was the size of a house?

When I sat back down, Gina reached over and took my hand. Her palm was cold and clammy and she stank of fear. The longer they waited to start having her do magick, the more her imagination could run rampant. I squeezed her hand and leaned forward. "Sirs, maybe it's time to do a little hands-on work? I think Gina would appreciate your words of wisdom better if she had more practical experience than just that incident with Tony."

Janus nodded as if he was just getting to that. "Of course. Gina, may I come over and take your hand?"

Please, take the one I'm holding, I thought. The clamminess of her skin was making me think of dead things, and that was making my stomach very unhappy. Unfortunately, Janus picked her other hand.

"Very good. Now, I am going to draw a tiny amount of energy into my body from the earth. Because we are touching, you will be able to feel it, but it will not go through you. Do you understand?"

I wanted to say, she's a novice, not an idiot. But I held my tongue and hoped that I didn't feel too much of whatever they did. I had my fill of magick for the next century.

Gina nodded, and I watched her. I couldn't feel it, but I knew exactly when Janus started raising the energy. Gina's eyes grew wide and her fear scent increased. Then something changed. The air grew thick and warm, until it became uncomfortable to breathe. Galen broke his down-stay and approached my side, his head down and his tail tucked. Scared.

I felt the pinpricks of magickal energy on my skin like static electricity, and I pulled my hand free of Gina's. It didn't help. The energy level in the room just kept rising. I glanced at Janus and Finn, just in case one of them was doing it. Judging by their identical flummoxed expressions, I figured this wasn't their magick. Damn it all. The last thing Gina needed was another out-of-control experience.

"Do something," I growled at Finn. Galen joined me in the growl.

Finn nodded. "Gina, you are drawing a huge amount of power into your body. That power wants somewhere to go. So I'm going to help you ground it. Okay? First, though, I need you to let go of Janus's hand."

That made me look at Janus. He was pale and getting paler by the second. What was going on? I wanted more backup. I pulled out my phone and texted Simone. "Janus cabin. 9-1-1. Come now!"

Finn approached Gina, but was very careful not to touch her. "Good," he said gently as she dropped Janus's hand. "That's good. Now, because you're new to this, it will be easier for you to ground if you're actually touching the ground. So I want you to get out of your chair and sit on the floor. I'll do the same. See? Very good. Now place your hands palm-down on the floor. One hand by each hip. Like this. See?" Finn demonstrated everything and Gina complied immediately. Her fear was rank.

"Excellent. You're doing great. Now, I want you to imagine a light inside of you. A bright white light. Are you doing that? Good. That light is the magickal energy you've raised. Now, on your next exhale, I want you to send that light down, down through your palms and into the earth. I've raised a little power, too, so that we can do it together. Are you ready? Good." As he exhaled loudly, Finn pressed his hands harder against the wood floor. Gina followed suit, exhaling and pressing her hands to the floor, and immediately, the energy level in the room dropped. No, not dropped. Disappeared.

Both Galen and I took a deep breath, the air suddenly feeling breathable again.

"Good. Gina, that's very good." Finn's voice sounded strained, like he was getting tired. He exchanged a glance with Janus, who nodded. "Now Janus and I are going to each take one of your hands." I looked at Finn, alarmed, remembering what happened when just Janus held her hand. He shook his head at me, as if telling me to stay silent. I did, but I was more glad than ever that I texted Simone. I had a feeling Finn and Janus would be in a puddle by the time this was over.

Janus knelt on the floor and took Gina's right hand. Finn took her left. They each sandwiched her hand between theirs. "Very good, Gina." Finn continued to do the talking, maybe just to keep things consistent, maybe because Janus, for whatever reason, wasn't able to talk at the moment. I couldn't tell. "Very good. Now, what Janus and I are about to do is called binding. We will construct a wall around you, metaphysically. We are using our own energy to build a shield that will prevent the energy from accessing you, and you it. It is a temporary measure. The wall will need to be rebuilt regularly while you are learning. We will be able to remove one brick of this wall, allow in a trickle of energy to teach you how to control it, how to direct it without it overwhelming you. We can gradually allow more and more energy through, until you no longer require the wall and you can wield your abilities with confidence and safety."

He and Janus were both breathing heavily, like they were jogging or lifting a heavy weight. Why did magick have to be so damn invisible? The door opened and Simone entered. She took in the scene silently, and mouthed, "Thank you," to me. I guess I did the right thing by calling her here.

Lines appeared around their eyes and mouths as Finn and Janus did whatever they were doing. The lines deepened, like the men were in a great deal of pain. But they kept holding Gina's hands, while the air grew thick with energy once again. Was Gina raising magick again? No, I didn't think so. My skin tingled, which I was pretty sure meant the men were doing something with that energy, maybe manipulating it to do whatever they were doing to bind Gina's powers. I buried my hands in Galen's fur in an effort to comfort us both as I watched helplessly.

Then, all of a sudden, the energy disappeared and my ears popped painfully. As one, Finn and Janus released Gina's hands and crumpled bonelessly.

Simone ran to Janus first. I went to Finn. He wasn't breathing. I didn't know shit about first aid, but I knew CPR. I started chest compressions while Simone worked on Janus. Gina sat and stared at us all. She seemed to be in shock or something. Worrisome, but not as worrisome as the lifeless body under me. Finn still wasn't breathing.

"Let me take over. Kellan, let me take over." Simone placed her hands over mine. Her hands were scalding hot, and her eyes glowed with otherworldly energy. She moved my hands and laid hers on Finn's chest. Her eyes closed and her hands grew bright red. Three long seconds later, Finn took a raggedy breath.

Only then did I glance over at Janus. He was propped up against a chair leg, looking weak, but conscious.

Simone looked like she was going to be the next one to pass out, but she waved me away when I reached out to her. "I'm fine. Just...tired." She nodded her head at Gina, who was staring at her hands. "Maybe you two could bring us some stretchers. I'd like to take these two to the infirmary for observation." When I didn't move, Simone gave me a pointed look and again glanced at Gina. "Now would be good."

She wanted me to get Gina out of there. I didn't want to leave. Finn almost died. No, he did die – if Simone wasn't such a kick-ass healer, he would still be dead. He was still lying on the ground, eyes closed, pale as, well, death was the word that came to mind. Why did that bother me? I shook my head. If I'd been a wolf, I would've shaken my whole body, trying to shake off unwanted thoughts and unwelcome emotions.

Because it did bother me, and I didn't want it to.

That, more than anything Simone said or did, prompted me to get up off the floor. Galen stood beside me, his gaze glued to my face. I took solace in that gaze, even though nothing else felt right or good.

"Gina, come on," I said. "We'll need some help with those stretchers. Let's go find Tony." Tony and Ryder could take one of the stretchers. Ryder was the only one who could match Tony's height. Maybe Dirk or Tevin could help me with the other stretcher – they were both about my height. Stretcher-bearers, like pallbearers, worked best without major height discrepancies.

Pallbearers. Why the fuck would that pop into my head?

When we stepped outside, I saw Tony running toward us. "Kell? Valentine just called me and said —" He stopped and stared at me. "Are you okay?"

I didn't know how to answer that question. "Stretchers."

"What?" He touched my arm. I resisted the urge to shake him off. It took all my self control to let his hand rest there.

"We need stretchers. Can you find younglings to carry them? I'll go get the stretchers, we just need —" I almost said pallbearers. Fuck, fuck, fuck. Then his words registered. "Wait. Valentine? Is something wrong?"

Tony shook his head. "She saw something weird at the border. Maya's on her way there, I just wanted to let Finn and Janus know."

Finn and Janus weren't in any shape to be receiving reports. "Yeah, okay. I need stretchers."

"What the fuck happened?" Tony studied my face, then looked at Gina, who still looked shell-shocked. "Never mind. Yes, I'll go find some people to carry stretchers. You got it." He ran off.

I took Gina's hand and pulled her toward the infirmary. "Kellan?" she said as we ran to the infirmary. "Oh, my god." She skidded to a stop and started to hyperventilate. "I almost – I almost killed them. I – I almost –" Her breath came and went in short, ragged gasps. Galen stared up at her like she was going to explode. Maybe she was.

I didn't know what to say. I went with, "They're going to be fine." They would be. They had to be. I might not always like Finn and Janus, I might not agree with the way they handled a lot of things. But I didn't know what the world would look like without them in it. They would be all right. They would be, damn it.

"But –"

My patience gave out. "Gina, I get it. I'm freaking out, too. But we have a job to do." I heard the snap in my voice, and wished that I was alone with my dog, not talking to this vulnerable young woman.

She blinked, and then said, "A job. Okay." She still looked shocky and not all there, but we were moving again. We reached the infirmary and went inside for the stretchers. By the time we came back out, each dragging one, Tony was there with four younglings.

He directed the younglings to take the stretchers back to Janus's cabin. Smack appeared from somewhere, I didn't know where, and took Gina's hand, leading her toward her cabin. Good. I needed one less thing to think about. Smack could take care of Gina for now.

All of this because Finn stopped breathing for a minute. The memory of the feel of him under my hands, so still and cold…

My stomach lurched, and I ran into the sanctuary of the trees. Bracing myself against a trunk, I vomited up breakfast and probably last night's dinner, too. Then I had to nudge Galen's nose away from it before he tried to help with cleanup. I turned us away and stared deeper into the forest, catching my breath for a moment, grateful for Galen's solidness beside me. "Come on, bud. Let's go make sure they don't need help."

When we emerged from the forest, I saw four younglings carrying two stretchers bearing Finn and Janus. Simone held open the door, clearly moving under her own power. That was good.

I looked around, a little lost. I was no longer needed. I didn't know what to do.

When Tony appeared next to me, I jumped a foot in the air. "Sorry," he said. "Didn't mean to scare you."

"'S okay." My teeth started to chatter, and I realized I was cold.

"Come on. They've got this under control. Let me take you inside."

I didn't want to go inside. I wanted to make sure everyone was okay. "The border. What happened?"

"Uh. Valentine said that a guy walking by stopped and stared like he could see the forest. But then he blinked and rubbed his eyes and squinted, like he couldn't see it anymore. Almost like the forest flashed him." His mouth quirked in a half-hearted smile. "Her words, not mine. Kell, you're shivering."

"I'm fine." The forest flashed? Did that happen when Janus lost consciousness? Or did his heart stop, too, and that was what caused the glitch in the invisibility spell? "Someone should check that we're not visible. That our defenses aren't down."

"It's already being done. Maya was between classes, so I sent her to talk to border patrol, and I sent two other younglings to the far end of the forest to step out and check the situation. It's under control." He paused. "Kellan, Galen is cold."

"What?" I looked down at my dog. He looked fine to me, but what if Tony could see something I wasn't seeing? "We should get him inside."

"Good idea," Tony said, placing a hand at the small of my back. I stepped away from his touch, because I wasn't an idiot who couldn't find her own way home. We went to our cabin. Once inside, Tony led me to the table, pulled out a chair, and, his hands putting pressure on my shoulders, forced me into it. I pulled Galen against me and started rubbing him down. His coat was definitely cold, but we'd been outside for longer without him getting overly cold. He should be okay, I decided.

Tony was making coffee, which wouldn't help Galen any. I would've thought that it wouldn't smell good to me, either, but despite my recent vomiting, the scent started to perk me up. Tony set a mug in front of me, along with a box of granola bars. I ate one and immediately felt better. I drank some coffee and felt even better. More solid. More real.

"Wanna tell me what happened?" Tony looked at me with the patience of someone way too damn good to be my partner. I sighed. He deserved better than me, but I couldn't force him to see that. He seemed to think he wanted me.

Weirdo.

I drank my coffee and related the events of the morning. "Wow," was all he said when I was done.

I snorted a laugh and got up to refill my mug. It was getting dark outside. "What time is it?" It felt like it should be bedtime.

"Eleven o'clock."

"In the morning?" I said doubtfully. Even this time of year, it didn't get dark that early.

Tony's next words explained it. "I think there's a storm coming."

I stood by the sink, holding my mug and looking out the window. "Is it too early to go to bed?"

He chuckled. "After the day you've had? No, Kell. I think you've earned a nap."

I loved the sound of his chuckle. It was a completely different sort of sound than when he threw his head back and laughed out loud. Both were beautiful sounds. I couldn't remember ever loving anything about Finn the way I loved those two sounds. A drop of water dripped on my hand, and I realized my cheeks were wet. I was crying.

Tony came up behind me silently and wrapped his arms around my waist, letting me face away from him, but still wrapping me up in his scent. Keeping one arm around my middle, he stroked my hair with his other hand. It was an awkward movement, what with my back against his chest, but he managed it. He made soft noises, the sort you make when a baby is crying. And I realized, again, what a great father this man was going to be.

I turned in his arms and hugged him back. I mumbled something against his chest, something that might've been disgustingly sentimental. Something like, "I love you." Fortunately, my face was pressed into his shirt, so hopefully, he couldn't understand what I said. I didn't want to set a precedent where we said such things to each other. I might be pregnant, but that didn't mean we needed to get all mushy.

He smelled good, warm and homey, and I stood on my tiptoes, reached up and pulled him down to me for a kiss. When someone knocked on our door, I growled bitterly.

He grinned. "Hold that thought. I'll get rid of them." Which was a nice thing to say, but odds were that knock meant some other catastrophe just struck that needed our attention.

When Tony opened the door, I caught Ethan's scent. Yup. More catastrophes.

"Hey, sorry to bother you." In Ethan's voice, I heard embarrassment. Was it that obvious that he was intruding on a private moment? I sighed and went to Mr. Coffee, pouring the last of the pot into two fresh mugs. I carried one to Tony and held the other one out to Ethan.

"Come on in, brother," I said, heading for the table again.

"Wow, you haven't called me that since we were kids." Ethan sat down across from me, leaving Tony the seat next to me.

"Yeah, well, between stress and hormones, I have no idea what the fuck I'm saying." Which was true.

Tony pressed his mug into my hands. "You need it more than me," he murmured. Which was probably also true. I still felt really shaky, after seeing Finn die and all.

Ethan held the coffee, but didn't drink it. "I really didn't mean to bother you. I just wanted to let you know, Maya told me that all's well at the border." He shrugged uncomfortably. "Don't know why she reported to me, like I could do something about it, but I guess none of us knows who to report to with Finn and Janus… Anyway, looks like they are both going to be okay. Janus is actually already heading back to his cabin. Finn got hit a little harder, it looks like, so he's still in the infirmary. Not by his choice, but Simone threatened to tie him to the bed to make him stay."

"Is Simone all right, then?" She didn't look too peppy the last time I saw her.

"Yeah, I think so. She says they all just need rest. No more magick for a little while. Which should be fine, if they really did bind Gina's powers."

"They did." I remembered the way they both collapsed at the same time. "They held on until they finished. I'm sure of it."

"All right, well. Good." Ethan looked extremely uncomfortable, like Tony and I were sitting there, tongue-kissing or something. "Well, I'll go, then. Get some rest."

"What needs to be done?" I forced myself to ask. There was always something that needed to be done, and with Finn out of commission, there were probably lots of somethings that needed doing.

Ethan smiled a little and shook his head. "You two take the rest of the day off. Like I said, Janus is back at it, and the younglings are all just as exhausted as we are. I've got most of them sacked out in the rec room, watching a movie. Cat and Dirk are on their way to take over border patrol from Valentine and Liam. Smack's keeping Gina company. It's all good. Get some rest."

Gina. She could probably use some therapy right about now. And what about Tia? Was she out in the forest, keeping Valentine company? Was she wearing a hat and mittens this time? Tony put his hand over my leg, as if he could feel me about to get up and check on the younglings. "Thanks, E. You know where to find us if you need us."

I waited until Ethan was gone before I shoved Tony's hand off my leg. "I should go and-"

"No." Tony's voice held a finality to it that chafed the same way his possessive hand on my leg did. "Ethan said they have it under control." He took my hand in his, laid it palm up and started tracing patterns on my palm with his finger. I shivered and all my indignation melted. "Stay with me," he said softly.

I did.

Chapter 17

KELLAN

Despite the excitement of Gina's magick lessons and the damn good sex with Tony as a winter storm raged outside, I slept like crap. The next morning, I felt tired and groggy and sore. I even had a headache. I never get headaches. When I mentioned it to Tony, he kissed my forehead. He was already showered, dressed and on his second cup of coffee. I was still nursing my first cup, dressed in the tank top and shorts I pulled on when I dragged my ass out of bed. He stroked my cheek, then kissed me again. "It's probably stress. Or maybe hormones? Give yourself a break. I'll tell anyone who asks that you're sleeping in. When you feel like joining the world, maybe go for a workout rather than looking for a job to do."

I didn't really have a job. Janus put me on inactive duty. I needed to convince him that pregnancy wasn't a terminal disease. But not right now. Taking the morning off sounded a little too good.

Tony left for his first class and I went back to bed. I dozed a little, but didn't really sleep. Galen settled beside me and I curled my body around him, breathing in his scent and relaxing. Idly, my mind wandered to Gina and Smack. I wondered how they were doing. And just like that, I was too awake to stay in bed. I began to fidget, until Galen raised his head and looked me in the eye. Whatever he saw there prompted him to stand up, shake himself and jump off the bed. He stood beside the bed and stared at me, waiting.

"When you're right, you're right, big dog." I pushed myself upright. I still had a little bit of a headache, but overall, I felt better. After a hot shower and a quickly downed cup of coffee, I felt like I could face humans. I remembered Tony's suggestion that I go work out. I decided to check in with Gina and Smack, see if they wanted to join me.

As soon as I stepped out the door, I knew something was wrong. The air buzzed with nervous energy. Younglings stood around in small clusters, looking tense and even afraid. I saw Tony standing near the door of the infirmary, and cold fear settled behind my breastbone. I started to run.

When I got there, I was out of breath and my heart felt like a baby bird, clumsy and twitchy. "Gina?" I asked Tony.

He shook his head. "It's, um, it's Finn." He wouldn't meet my eyes.

I could smell Tony's fear, like rancid sourdough. He wasn't going to tell me anything. I pushed past him into the infirmary, where Simone and Janus stood outside Finn's room. Tony trailed behind me, still reeking of fear and worry. The scent mingled with Simone and Janus's...grief. That was the only word for what I smelled.

"What happened?" I demanded.

They turned slowly and looked at me. Both were wide-eyed with shock. "What happened?" I said again, my voice rising not only in volume, but by several octaves, so I sounded foreign to my own ears.

Simone spoke. "Sometime during the night, he just...slipped into a coma. I tried to heal him, but it...it didn't work. I don't...I don't know..." Her voice was tight, like she was fighting back tears.

What was happening? How could this be real? How could they just be standing there, doing nothing, when Finn was on the other side of the door, comatose? "Fuck you both. Get in there and save him."

"Kellan, I can't." Simone's voice broke. "He's not responding."

She sounded so final. Like she'd given up. My hands formed fists. Anger. Anger was so much better than anything else I could feel. "What does that even mean?"

"It means he's slipping away, and there's nothing I can do to stop it."

For fuck's sake, she brought him back from the dead just yesterday. Now there was nothing she could do? Magick was useless.

"It is not your fault," Janus said quietly. He laid a hand on Simone's arm. "I should have known how weakened he was."

If I had to listen to them whine for one more second, I would start punching people. I pushed my way past them and entered Finn's room. He looked like he was sleeping. He looked normal. Except he was so very pale. Finn was never pale. His skin always looked golden even this time of year, in the dead of winter, and now he looked like, well, like a normal white guy in January. The longer I stood there, the more I noticed. His breathing was shallow.

His hair looked limp and oily, which it never was, it always shone. His scent, which reminded me of earth, was like dried-up dust in the middle of a drought. Barely even there. Fuck. This was real.

Tony's scent started to overwhelm Finn's barely-there scent. I couldn't bear that, so I stepped further into the room and closed the door in Tony and Galen's faces. Then I locked it, a flimsy little doorknob lock that was only slightly better than nothing, security-wise. I needed privacy. I needed to breathe in Finn's scent. While it was still here.

I felt the ever-present tears leak from my eyes. I let them stream down my cheeks without any annoyance, because this moment deserved tears. The pregnancy hormones might've been the reason I cried so easily, but it felt right in that room. I refused to consider what it meant that I was crying over Finn. None of that mattered.

Sitting in the chair by his bed, I reached out and brushed his hair back. He wouldn't want anyone to see him like this. I wished I could wash it for him. Would that even help? Or did the shine that normally lit him from within come from his magick, and without that energy, it was gone?

I let my fingers trace down his cheek, then took his hand in mine. And then…I felt a jolt, like something reached inside me and grabbed hold of my center, then started tugging on it. Instinctively, I tried to drop Finn's hand, but now he held mine tight and I couldn't break free. Why couldn't I break free? I was stronger than Finn, much stronger. But I couldn't break his hold. My vision started to go grey around the edges, I started seeing spots, and then the spots got bigger and bigger until they blotted out the whole room and everything went dark.

TONY

I stared at the closed door, feeling a flicker of anger down deep. Even if she didn't want me in there, it was just cruel to shut Galen out. The poor dog paced, whined, and scratched at the door, clearly confused by Kellan's abandoning him. He didn't deserve that.

Then something changed. Galen's ears perked, he seemed to listen for a moment, then he started howling and scratching at the door like he was trying to break it down. I didn't know what was wrong in that room, but I knew I needed to get inside.

The door was locked, of course. Fucking stubborn wolf. I kicked it open, glad the infirmary doors were thinner than the cabin doors or the door to the mess hall. Then I stared at the sight in front of me. Kellan was slumped on the floor, but she was holding Finn's hand. No, wait, she wasn't holding his – he was holding hers, even though he still looked unconscious.

Galen ran to her first. When he touched his nose to the side of her neck, like he was trying to wake her up, he yelped and jumped back. I went to try to help her, but Janus came up behind me and said sharply, "No, do not touch her."

Simone moved into the room, hovered over Kellan, but didn't seem to know what to do.

Just then, Finn's eyes fluttered open and he dropped Kellan's hand. Galen sniffed her experimentally, then once again pressed his nose to her neck. I took that as a sign that she was safe to touch, and knelt beside her, checking her pulse. It was barely there. I looked up at Simone, but my voice wouldn't work. Then I noticed Galen sniffing Kellan's pelvic area, and I saw something even more alarming.

"Blood," I whispered. No one seemed to hear me, so I shouted, "Blood."

That got them moving. Simone went to work. She made me stop touching Kellan, saying that any external touch could interfere with her healing. So I knelt by Kellan's head, one arm wrapped around Galen to keep him at my side, and we watched every move the healer made, completely ignoring the other men in the room. To Galen, Kellan was the only thing that mattered. As for me... Whatever was wrong with Kellan, it was Finn's doing, and I didn't trust myself to look at him, much less speak to him right now.

I couldn't see what Simone did – whatever she was healing was deep inside Kellan's body. But I watched as Kellan's cheeks gained some color, while Simone's drained of it. Finally, Simone dropped her hands and looked up at me. "Are you able to carry her?"

I nodded, a large lump in my throat preventing me from speaking. Then I stared at Kellan, worried that if I moved her, she would start bleeding again.

"It's okay," Simone said quietly. "You can pick her up. Do me a favor and carry her to the room at the end of the hall. You and Galen wait with her there. I'll be there in a moment."

Nodding again, I slid arms under Kellan's limp form and stood. She was so light, like she would blow away in a stiff wind. Finn said something as I carried her out. I kept ignoring them, him and Janus. This was their fault, somehow. Kellan almost died because of something they did. Maybe it was wrong to lump Janus in with Finn, but it felt right. Someone should've known something could happen. Someone should've warned her. And I was afraid if I acknowledged them, I might have to kill them.

I managed to open the door to the private room at the end of the hall without dropping Kellan. I looked at the nice, clean bed, then at Kellan's blood-soaked pants. Should I put her on the bed and soil the covers, or lay her on the floor? "Fuck it, we've got more sheets." I put her on the bed and eased off her boots, socks, yoga pants and underwear. All heavy with blood. God, how much did she lose? How much did she have left? Galen watched my every move. I couldn't blame him. I figured he was as scared as I was.

Simone came in just as I finished piling the soiled clothes on the floor. She handed me a packet of baby wipes, then opened one herself. We cleaned the blood off Kellan's legs, then slid her under the covers. Only the top blanket was dirty, so I pulled that one off, added it to the pile of bloody clothes, and tucked the other covers around Kellan's sleeping form. Unconscious form? Sleeping. I chose to go with sleeping. I didn't look at Simone as I said, "Do you need to examine her?"

"No. I – I got a good feel for what was happening to her as I healed her. She's going to be okay. She'll sleep for a while, but she'll be fine."

I wanted to lay down beside her, get as close to her as I could, feel her body ride each breath. I settled for pulling a chair over to her bedside and holding her hand. Looking at her hand in mine, I flashed back to the scene in Finn's room, him clinging to her hand as she bled on the floor. I almost dropped her hand. But I didn't. I wanted to give her comfort, if she had any awareness at all. "What the fuck happened in there?"

Simone sighed, a weary, worn-out sound that drew my gaze. She looked like she aged a couple centuries in the last hour. Since there was only one chair in the room, I moved to sit on the floor and let her take the chair. "Thank you." Another sigh. "Finn... siphoned energy from her. Life force. And he was able to siphon it from the baby as well."

Cold washed over my skin. "The baby?" was all I could say.

"I think she will also be okay. I did what I could."

Sudden relief made my muscles so weak that I had to drop Kellan's hand and let my hands fall to my lap.

I guess that answered the question of whether I wanted this baby. Regardless of who the father was, I already considered the baby mine. "The bleeding?"

"Kellan almost lost the baby. The child almost died. If it had gone on any longer, Kellan would've lost the baby and probably died herself."

Rage made me feel strong again. "Finn did this."

"Honestly, I don't think he knew what he was doing, Tony. He wasn't conscious, so this couldn't have been a conscious act. Kellan took his hand, his magick sensed her energy, and nature took its course. Kellan has an extraordinary life force."

I didn't care if he did it on purpose or not. Finn was alive, and Kellan almost wasn't. Her baby almost wasn't. In my opinion, probably in the opinions of most people she ever came into contact with, that wasn't a worthwhile trade. I let myself feel the rage, the hate that coursed through me for a long minute. Then, with a great deal of effort, I set it aside and looked at Simone. "Thank you. For saving them."

She smiled wanly. "Keep an eye on her, will you? I'm going to go take a nap."

She left and we were alone. Why Kellan? Why did it happen when Kellan touched him, but not Janus or Simone? Simone tried to heal him before Kellan ever went in there. Why did he have to choose Kellan? I knew Simone just told me that it wasn't a conscious choice, but if Finn had to choose someone to use up, it would be Kellan. He didn't care if she lived or died. Simone and Janus, he probably thought were too important to lose. Kellan was just a pain in the ass. Totally expendable. He must've known. That was the only explanation for why it happened to her.

Galen jumped onto the bed, and Kellan, still out cold, rolled on her side and curled her body around his. This was such a familiar sight that I felt tears press behind my eyes. I blinked them away, swallowed hard, and leaned forward, resting my forehead against the bed next to her head. Just then, there was a knock on the door.

I hesitated, not wanting to let anyone else into this little space. But they knocked again, louder this time.

I opened the door to see Finn standing there.

He was already on his feet. He went from almost dead to looking just fine, while Kellan was still unconscious.

"Tony, I'm —"

I shut the door in his face.

I drew the chair over to the head of the bed, stroked her hair and listened to her breathe while I waited for her to wake up.

Chapter 18

KELLAN

Tony. Galen. I drew those scents into my lungs as I came awake, feeling like I got hit by a bus, then run over by a garbage truck, then dumped on by a dozen seagulls. I didn't know why I felt so awful, but maybe it was a new symptom of pregnancy. Like the puking and the crying wasn't bad enough.

But as I opened my eyes, I realized Tony's scent wasn't his normal sleeping scent. He smelled angry. So angry. And when I looked around, I saw not our cabin, but one of the infirmary rooms. What happened?

Then I remembered. Finn. And then pain. Like something was tearing my uterus out. My hand went to my stomach. The cub? Was it —?

"It's okay." Tony sounded rough. I blinked up at him. The light was too bright, like I just entered the room from a dark hallway. "The baby is okay. Simone saved it. Saved you."

Relief poured through me. I guess I wanted this kid. "She's okay. You're – you're sure?" I was still having a fair amount of pain. Was that normal? "You're sure?" I said again. My voice sounded breathy, not at all like me.

A little of Tony's anger faded away. "I'm sure. Or at least, Simone is sure."

I nodded. If Simone was sure, then we were probably okay. Another wave of relief made me feel woozy. I closed my eyes because the light was too damn bright. "Finn?" I asked. I needed to know.

But that one word made Tony's angry scent quadruple, until I would swear that the scent singed my nose hairs. "He's fine."

"What – what happened?" I coughed. My throat felt so dry.

Tony got up, left the room, and returned with a mug of water. I would've rather had coffee, but he smelled so angry, I didn't want to make any special requests. I started to gulp the water. "No," he said, pulling the cup away from my mouth. "Simone said to sip it."

"What happened?" I asked again.

So much anger. I was pretty sure he wasn't angry at me. I didn't think I did anything to warrant anger before I blacked out, and I couldn't see how I could've done something after blacking out. Although I couldn't rule out the possibility. I did have a significant talent for making people mad at me.

"It's some magick thing. Basically, Finn sucked up your life force to restore his own." Tony said Finn's name like it tasted sour. "Yours and the baby's."

Sucked up my life force? What did that even mean? But it explained the anger. Tony blamed Finn for whatever the hell just happened.

Since I knew how overpowering anger toward Finn could be, I reached over and took Tony's hand in mine. His grip tightened on my fingers almost painfully. Yup. He wasn't mad at me. Now I could smell the worry under the anger. A confusing mix of sourdough and jalapeno focaccia. I didn't like this scent on Tony.

"But we're okay," I said, trying to redirect his attention.

He nodded, his adam's apple bobbing visibly as he swallowed hard.

"So everything's okay." I laid my other hand over his, so his hand was sandwiched between mine. Galen whined and nudged Tony's wrist with his nose. That seemed to pull Tony out of whatever thoughts were clattering around in his head. He looked at Galen, smiled, and scratched my dog behind the ear.

"Everything's okay." He didn't sound completely convinced, but he also didn't smell as angry. I took that as a win.

I didn't want to remind him of what happened, but I couldn't stop myself from asking, "How long was I out?" I had to ask. Any time I lost consciousness, I always wanted to know how long. Like I needed to know exactly how vulnerable I was.

Tony stiffened a little, but he rolled his shoulders and his scent stayed fairly chill. "It's been about four hours."

Four hours. Four hours, and my insides still felt like they'd slide right out if I moved the wrong way. I needed to talk to Simone. I needed to hear her say the baby was fine. And I needed to hear it soon, because I suddenly had to pee, but I didn't want to move an inch for fear I'd knock the baby loose. "Hey, Tony? Would you mind going and getting Simone?"

The scent of his fear slammed into me like a wave, oddly making the need to pee even worse. "Why? What is it? What's wrong?"

I was going to pee my pants. Except I wasn't wearing pants. Fucking hell. "Nothing's wrong. I just want to talk to her. Please?"

I didn't say please very often, so I think that worried him even more, but he left to go find the healer. By the time Simone walked through the door, I was whimpering with the need to empty my poor bladder. "Pee," I pleaded.

She nodded, ran out, and returned in moments with a bedpan. Tony tried to follow her back in. No. No way was I going to let Tony see me use a fucking bedpan. I pointed to the door. "Out." I thought about it for a minute, then added, "Take Galen with you. Give us three minutes, then you can come back in."

Then I squeezed my eyes shut, because some part of my brain thought that would help hold my pee-hole closed. Once we were alone, Simone helped me use the bedpan. I may have cried a little, it felt so good.

Then I opened my eyes and looked at her. She was looking at my pee, which was disconcerting. "What are you doing?" I asked.

"Checking it for blood." She gave me a little smile. "You're good. Blood free."

Why would there be blood? Did I want to know? No, I did not. "Awesome." I could've told her that I didn't smell any blood in the urine. But I suppose humans liked to check things themselves. I took a closer look at her. She had big circles under her eyes, and the corners of her mouth looked tight. "Rough day?" I asked.

She laughed. "That's one way to put it." The humor drained from her expression like water off skin. "How do you feel?"

I hesitated. I didn't want to sound like I was criticizing her healing skills, but… "It hurts. I'm…scared."

"Let me take a look." She sat beside me on the bed and placed her hands on my belly. She didn't look at anything, though. She closed her eyes and I felt the warmth of magick hum through me. I jumped and tried to pull away. Simone opened her eyes. "Kell, I'm checking the baby's vitals. Please hold still."

My logical brain understood what she said, but my animal brain said magick was bad. I didn't want it to touch me. But I forced myself to be still and let her do her thing. Tony came in just as she pulled her hands back and stood up.

Galen jumped on the bed, making me wince, not with pain, but fear that the movement might jostle the baby. Tony looked from Simone to me and back again. "Everything okay?"

Simone's mouth curved in what was obviously a forced smile. "Everything's fine. The baby feels strong. You have a tough little cub there, Kell. Just like her mama."

"Umm –" I glanced at Tony. "It still hurts. It feels…loose."

"The baby isn't loose. That's your fear talking. She's not going to slip out of you. Miscarriages happen for medical reasons, not because of loose tethers." Her smile still looked forced, so I felt like she wasn't telling me everything.

"Then why don't you look happy?" I said bluntly.

She sighed heavily. "Because it's been, as you said, a very rough day. Things are looking up, though. You're awake, the baby is well, and –" She stopped herself, glancing at Tony.

"And Finn's okay," I finished for her.

She hesitated, glanced at Tony again, then nodded. "Yes."

"You know what would really make today better?" I said.

She and Tony both looked at me expectantly.

"Pants. I'd love some pants. And some coffee. But honestly, first, pants."

Simone smiled. "Yoga pants or sweatpants – something with an elastic waistband. I have some we keep on hand for people who –"

"No," I said. "No offense, but I don't want community pants right now. I want my own clothes." I looked at Tony with big, begging eyes. "Please?"

My second please in less than an hour. Was this another unpleasant side effect of hormones?

"All right. I'll go get you some clothes." He kissed my forehead, then hesitated. "Simone, she feels cold."

Simone lay a hand on my forehead. "It's probably nothing. I think your body is continuing to replenish your blood supply. I'll get you some food and some coffee, and that will give you the fuel you need."

"Okay, well, I'll stay until you get back," Tony said.

I really, really wanted a pair of underwear. And maybe a moment or two alone, so I could wrap my mind around what just happened without people watching me and feeling their own feelings. "Tony? I'm okay. Please go get me some underwear and a pair of pants. Pretty fucking please with fucking cherries on top."

He snorted. "Maybe you are okay. All right. I'll be back in a minute."

"So will I," Simone said. They both left, leaving the door open. I didn't want the door open. Not when I was bare-assed. But I was too scared to stand up and close the door – I didn't quite believe Simone that the baby was firmly planted again – and Galen lacked the opposable thumbs required to work a doorknob. Which meant that any old person walking past could look in the room.

Except it wasn't any old person. It was Finn who stepped into the doorway and looked at me. "Hello, Kellan."

God damn it. I didn't want to talk to anyone. But most of all, I did not want to talk to Finn without underwear on. No. No, no, no. "Go away."

"Kellan, I just want to say –"

"I don't care what you want to say. I get it, it was a big fat metaphysical accident, you didn't do it on purpose, blah, blah, blah. Now go away."

"Kellan, please –"

"GO!" Galen punctuated my yell with a growly snarl of his own. Finn, who was a little afraid of Galen, retreated quickly. I looked at my dog and whispered, "Thank you."

A youngling appeared in the doorway. It was Tia. Valentine hovered behind her, a taller, silent shadow. "You okay, Miz Kellan?" Tia asked.

My heart was pounding a little too hard, but I forced my voice to be steady. "I'm fine. Everything's fine." I patted the chair beside me. "Come on, have a seat."

Valentine stayed in the hall like a bouncer, but Tia trotted over and sat on the chair. I noticed she had something crumpled in her mittened hand. "I made you a card," she whispered. Shyness smelled like warm milk with honey.

That scent, combined with the fact that no one ever made me a card before, brought an unwelcome dampness to my eyes. "You did?"

"Uh-huh." She hesitated, then handed me a piece of paper that was entirely covered in crayon scribbles. I stared at it, trying to figure out what it was so I wouldn't say the wrong thing. "It's flowers, 'cuz Vallie says you give people flowers when they're sick," she told me. She glanced over her shoulder at Valentine, then back at me. "But we don't have flowers 'cuz it's January." She pronounced January like it was two words, Jan-yary.

"These are perfect," I said around a huge lump in my throat. "In fact, they're better than perfect, because real flowers make Tony sneeze. These won't make him sneeze, so we can hang this up in our cabin."

"Oh, good. Okay." She studied me a moment, then darted in and kissed my cheek. "See you later, Miz Kellan. Feel better." Then she bounced from the room and Valentine closed the door, so when the tears fell, Galen was the only one who saw them.

Then, of course, Tony came in and saw me crying, and went into panic mode again. "What's wrong? Simone! Simone! Where the fuck is Simone?"

"No, no, it's fine, everything's fine." I held up the card, like that would explain everything.

Tony took it from me, stared at it with the same confusion I must've had on my face when I first saw it.

"Tia made me a card. No one's ever made me a card before. Then she kissed my cheek. And I started crying, because that's all I do these days. Cry and puke." I thought about that for a second. "Isn't that all babies do? Is that why pregnancy is like this? To get you accustomed to all the crying and puking?"

Tony sank into the chair with a suddenness that made me think his legs gave out. "I thought something was wrong."

"I know. I'm sorry."

He shook his head, then stood up and closed the door. "Let's get you dressed."

I let him help me dress, because that way, I could stay lying down without moving my pelvis any more than absolutely necessary. I didn't want to give that baby a chance to go anywhere, not for a little while longer. Just as Tony tucked the covers around me again, someone knocked on the door.

It was Gina this time, carrying a tray laden with sandwiches and two thermoses. "Don't get too excited," she said as she set the tray on the counter. "Only one of these is coffee. The other is soup."

I did feel a little disappointed at that. Thermoses should always mean coffee. "Thank you," I said anyway.

She poured some soup into a mug. "It's tomato. I brought a couple cheese sandwiches for you. Simone said you can worry about getting quality protein in a little while, first thing you need is just straight calories. And nothing says comfort like tomato soup and grilled cheese."

I disagreed. Coffee said comfort in at least six different languages. But she seemed like her normal self, and considering the latest magickal mishap around here, I didn't want to upset the delicate balance of her mood. So all I said was, "Thank you, this is perfect."

I managed to pull myself into a seated position without anything bad happening. Would my heart pound like this for the rest of the pregnancy, any time I had to move? Being pregnant sucked in so many ways.

As Gina handed me the mug of soup and half a sandwich, she avoided touching me. Did she worry that she might drain my energy, too? I didn't want that. Maybe I didn't understand how magick worked, but I didn't want Gina afraid of anything more. I was so scared, I felt like my insides were quivering, and it took every ounce of self-control I possessed, but I managed to grab her hand and hold it. "Really, Gina, thank you. You didn't have to bring this yourself. I appreciate it."

"Well, Simone really needed to sit down and eat something, so I offered to bring this to you." She stared at my hand on hers. It might've been my imagination, but I thought I could feel magickal energy on her skin. That made me start sweating in places I didn't know could sweat. She kept staring at my hand, like she was waiting for something to happen. When nothing did, she smiled a little and gave my hand a squeeze. "And you're welcome. Enjoy the food. I'll send someone with more coffee and some protein shakes in a little while."

After she left, I let out the breath I didn't know I was holding, and took a bite of my sandwich. "I really hate those protein shakes. Maybe I should try eating meat again." I didn't really mean it. But god, those shakes were nasty.

Tony sat down in the chair. "One thing at a time, Kell. For now, just eat the food you have."

"Have you eaten? I don't want to share my grilled cheese, but I could be convinced to part with the tomato soup." I never liked tomato soup all that much, though I wasn't going to tell Gina that.

"I grabbed a granola bar in our cabin when I picked up your clothes." He slouched a little in the chair. He looked tired.

"Do you want some coffee?" I really didn't want to share my coffee, given that it was only one thermos full, but he looked like he needed some.

"I'm tempted to say yes, just to see if you actually let me have some. But no, I'm all right. Just ready for an emergency-free hour or two." That sounded like he was aiming too high. At least for this week. But I didn't say anything. He poured me a cup and held it out to me as I drained the soup mug.

I watched him shift his weight on the chair. "That chair looks really uncomfortable."

"Well, it wasn't at first, but after this many hours, yeah, it's not great." He shifted again.

Slowly, carefully, I moved toward the edge of the cot. "There's enough room between me and the wall for another person. Just — try not to jar the baby," I said quietly.

He hesitated. "You sure?"

No, not at all. "Yeah, of course. Come on."

He stretched out with his back to the wall. Galen sniffed him, like he changed more than just his position. I just focused on breathing and holding still, despite the fact that my heart was lodged in my throat.

Another soft knock on the door. "Oh, fuck, what now?" I muttered. Behind me, Tony laughed softly. It was a good sound.

The door didn't open. I guess they were being polite enough to wait for an invitation. I was selfish enough to seriously consider withholding that invitation. But it might be another youngling, so I called, "Yeah, what?"

The door opened so slowly, so hesitantly, I was sure it was Tia, coming back for some other errand. It wasn't.

Janus stood in the doorway, looking small and old. Finn stood behind him, appearing to try to hide behind the much shorter man. Tony shot up, almost knocking me off the cot, and I clenched my thighs together in a panic.

"No," Tony said. "Not now. Kellan's tired, she's worn out, she doesn't need to hear whatever fucked up apology you feel obligated to dangle in front of her. She almost gave her life for you today, almost gave her firstborn child for you. That's enough. You don't get any more from her today."

Janus's scent warred between anger and worry. It smelled like burning sheets. I didn't like it, especially when the anger was pointed at Tony. I couldn't smell Finn at all through the strength of Janus and Tony's scents, but he looked so...cowed.

I knew Janus well enough to know that he wouldn't go away until he said whatever he wanted to say, but I knew Tony well enough to know that he wouldn't let the other men through the door. And I also felt an alarming dampness in my underwear that I couldn't ignore. "Tony?" I waited until he turned to look at me before continuing, "I need you to go find Simone, okay? I don't think anything's wrong, but I...I just have a question for her. Okay? Will you go find her for me?"

He hesitated, clearly torn between punching Finn's lights out and running for Simone. Finally, he nodded. "I'll be right back." He spat the words at the two men in the doorway. A warning. A threat.

Janus stepped back to let him pass, then entered the room and sat in the chair. Finn continued to hover in the hallway. I drained my coffee and tried not to think about what might be happening to the baby. The pain wasn't any worse. I focused on that.

"Hello, Kellan," Janus said belatedly. Now that Tony was gone, Janus smelled only of worry.

"Hi." I held out my mug and looked pointedly at the thermos of coffee on the counter. "Would you mind? I'm not moving so good at the moment."

"Certainly." Janus refilled my cup and handed it to me, then sat back down. Galen grumbled a little and glared at him. Through all this, Finn didn't speak, didn't move. Weird.

"Thank you." I took a sip. Gina made it strong. It warmed me and made me feel a little less scared, a little more like myself. "What do you want?" I asked. It was blunt, but I didn't really want to talk to them, and maybe bluntness would get this over with faster.

"Well, I wished to see for myself how you were doing." Janus looked me over. "You look much improved."

"From when I was passed out on the floor of Finn's room, covered in blood? Yeah, I suppose I probably do." I was edging toward crossing the border into insubordination, which was a fun place to visit, but never ended well for me. "Sir, Tony was right. I'm tired and worn and really lacking in social niceties right now. If you have some sort of motive for coming here with him –" I glanced at Finn – "then maybe you should just say it. If you don't mind."

Janus reached out like he was going to take my hand. I flinched. I never noticed before, but the old man had an aura of magickal energy that hovered around him, and I didn't want that energy to touch me.

I swallowed hard, that tomato soup threatening to make a reappearance. "Sir, no offense, but I'd rather not be touched right now."

That made him look sad. Fucking hell, I didn't want Janus to be sad. But if making him happy meant letting him touch me, I just couldn't do that. "Of course," he said. "I simply – well. Finlay wishes to apologize to you, and he seems to believe that you do not wish to speak to him."

Finn edged into the room, which surprised me until I saw the reason why – Tony was back and looming, taking up more of the hallway than I would've thought possible. I didn't want things to escalate again, so I said, "Thank you for the apology. But you're right, I don't really want to talk about it right now. I know none of this was on purpose, but..." My own anger flickered to life as I thought about all the magickal fuckups of the last several days. "You guys don't seem to know as much about magick as you thought you did. And I'd rather not be in the same room as you until I know for sure that my baby is safe. Thanks for stopping by. See you later."

Janus nodded stiffly, stood with dignified control, and left the room. Finn trailed after him like a dog that had been kicked too many times. I hated that. I hated all of it, but it wasn't my problem. Tony was right. I gave enough of myself to the Save Finn project for today. Finn needed to figure out the rest on his own.

Chapter 19

KELLAN

When they were gone, Tony came back and sat beside me on the bed. Simone followed him in. "What's wrong, Kellan?" she said, looking me over.

"I –" I didn't want to say it in front of Tony. "My…underwear is…wet. It's kind of freaking me out."

Simone nodded. "Lie down, I'll take a look."

"Could you –" Shit, how to say this? "I've had enough magick for today. Could you just look as a human, not as a healer?"

She looked at me with what I could only describe as kindness. "Kellan, I'm a healer whether I use magick or not, but I can do this without magick. No problem."

After examining me, she declared that it was just a little spotting, probably nothing, but I should rest quietly until at least tomorrow. Then she had a youngling bring in a sleeping mat with a sleeping bag and pillow so Tony could sleep on the floor. There wasn't room for another cot, not if we were going to be able to move around. I didn't offer to let Tony share the bed with me again. If he got startled and jostled me like he did when he saw Janus and Finn, I didn't know what might happen. I couldn't risk it. So Galen and I slept on the bed, Tony slept on a mat on the floor, and all was quiet.

For about two hours. Around five o'clock in the afternoon, I woke up, needing to pee again. Tony retrieved Simone, who helped me use the bedpan again. She again checked the urine for blood. Being part wolf, I recognized the usefulness of urine for marking territory, but I never had someone stare at my pee before. It was a little creepy and a lot disgusting, but I tried not to complain.

While I was awake, she insisted I drink a protein shake.

"This is a vicious cycle," I said. "I'm going to have to pee again in an hour."

"Yes, but your child needs the protein." Not "you need the protein," which might have prompted more whining from me. She made it about the cub, which meant I couldn't really complain any further. Damn it.

"When do you think she'll be able to get up and move around?" Tony asked.

Simone looked at me. "Hmm. If you were human, I'd want to keep you here at least a couple of days. But since you're a shape-shifter, your body has probably already healed everything that needs healing. But if you wait until tomorrow morning, I think you'll feel more comfortable with it, Kell, and that's hugely important. If you're tense and worried, the child will feel that. Bedpans suck, but so does worry."

Over the course of the night, Simone helped me pee three more times. By the third time, I resolved to not watch what she did post-urination. I just did my thing and then closed my eyes.

The next morning, I woke up to the combined scents of Tony and Galen, layered over the blood-and-disinfectant scent of the infirmary. Tony was stroking my hair, and it was oddly soothing. It made me wonder what it would feel like to have someone stroke my fur in wolf form. I never experienced being petted, probably because it was so much fun to scare the humans with my big ole wolf teeth. But if it was Tony doing the petting, I was willing to bet it would feel nice.

Of course, I only enjoyed it for a fraction of a second before I needed to pee again. "I'm going to try walking to the bathroom this time," I murmured.

"Do you want help?"

For the love of everything holy, fuck, no. I wanted to finally pee without an audience. "Um, no, thanks. I think I'll be good."

Everything went well. I may have been sniffing like mad the whole time I peed, searching for any hint of blood mixed in with the scent of urine. I may even have checked the toilet before flushing, just in case I missed the scent of it. There wasn't any blood. I breathed a sigh of relief, then returned to the room at the end of the hall. I very carefully avoided looking at the closed door of the room where Finn had been staying. Even walking past it caused my tummy to bubble with anxiety. That meant I threw up in the sink as soon as I walked into my room.

When I was done, I rinsed my mouth out and took the granola bar that Tony was holding out to me. "I guess it's a good thing you have an iron stomach," I said.

"I don't, actually, I'm just so used to watching you puke by now that it doesn't bother me anymore." The warm humor in his scent told me he was joking.

"Great, so glad I've managed to inoculate you against the sight of puke. At least something good has come from this."

Tony stepped up behind me and wrapped his arms around my waist, giving me a kiss on the back of the neck. "Lots of good things will come from this." He cleared his throat. "But maybe we should take you home so you can brush your teeth."

"Not quite as inoculated as you thought?"

He cleared his throat again and stepped back. "Maybe."

"Well, don't throw up or you'll get me going again." I finished the granola bar and sat down to put on my boots. There was blood on them. I stared at that blood and thought about what almost happened yesterday. My hand moved on its own to rest over my stomach.

Tony took the boots from me. "Sorry. I should've cleaned these yesterday. Stupid mistake. I'll go get you a different pair from the cabin."

"No, no, it's fine." It really wasn't fine. I was a hair's breadth away from hyperventilating as I thought of the cub. But I took the boots and forced my feet into them. "See? Fine."

"I'll clean them once we get back to the cabin." He was so upset, he was actually wringing his hands.

I stood carefully, took his hands in mine, and tried not to breathe on him as I said, "Tony, it's not like I'm going to forget what happened. This reminder? Sure, it hit me hard. But I'm okay. The cub is okay. We're all okay."

He nodded. "Let's go home."

Of course, before I could leave, I had to submit to another exam by Simone. I gritted my teeth and held my breath as she used magick to check the baby. I still didn't like being touched by magick, but I also really wanted to know how the cub was doing this morning. As soon as Simone was done, Tony came over and rested a hand on my shoulder. I guess I wasn't the only one who wanted a report on our cub.

Our cub. Was it our cub? Could it be our cub even if Tony wasn't the father? The worst part about this pregnancy was the waiting to find that out. Tony couldn't tell me for sure, not until the baby was born. Not until we found out who was the dad, not until he found out how he felt about that answer.

It sucked, six ways to Sunday.

"Your cub has a strong heartbeat." Simone looked at both of us as she said it. "She's doing well."

Tony's grip on my shoulder tightened almost uncomfortably. "That's great. That's good."

Should I read anything into the fact that he went from great to good that fast? No. Probably not. Maybe. "Thank you," I said.

"Sankha Simone?" someone called from the front of the infirmary. A youngling, it sounded like. Simone was needed, which gave me an opportunity to escape.

Dirk stood with Smack, Valentine and Tia. "I told you, it's fine," Smack said, sounding annoyed. But she was also holding her right arm funny. When Valentine tried to touch Smack's arm, she jerked away and then gasped in obvious pain.

"What happened?" Simone asked, going into healer mode.

Part of me wanted to know if Smack was okay, but mostly, I just wanted to get out of there, away from the scents of the infirmary and into the cold, fresh air. I could find out what happened to Smack later, I decided, as I snuck out the door with Galen. I heard Tony's footsteps on the snow behind us after a few moments. He probably stayed behind to make sure nothing life-threatening was happening. I really hoped he stuck around after this cub was born. He would be a much better parent than I.

He caught up to us and said, "Smack fell on the ice. Simone thinks she might've broken her wrist, but she's not sure yet. Good news is, Simone's back to full strength, so she'll be able to fix it with her magick rather than having to do things the human way."

"Super," I said, because it was, but I wasn't really thinking about Smack. I was thinking about Aza, and how many more times I had sex with him than I had with Tony. Tony and I only had sex a handful of times over the last several months. Aza raped me at least once a day for two whole months. If I was looking at this situation from a purely statistical standpoint, the odds were much higher that Aza sired this cub than Tony.

But god, I wanted this to be Tony's kid. I couldn't bear to lose him.

I was feeling shaky, not just from those thoughts rolling around in my head, but because that granola bar wasn't nearly enough to sustain me and the cub. "I should eat." I felt the cold sweat that always accompanied low blood sugar start to spread over my skin.

"Oh, shit, yeah, you need some protein. Want me to carry you?"

"No!" I stopped myself as I heard how annoyed I sounded. "No, thanks. I'll be fine." There, that sounded appropriately appreciative. "Maybe you could go ahead and mix up a protein shake for me, though?" Because that would keep you from watching me obsessively as I walk to the mess hall.

"Sure, yeah, okay." He took off at a run. He should probably be more careful, given the icy ground and the fact that Smack already broke her wrist. But I didn't say anything, because it was a relief to have a little privacy.

I appreciated Tony. As I said, I didn't want to lose him, but sometimes the constant watching-over grated on me. I understood it, especially in light of what happened with Finn. But he could be a little too hovery sometimes.

Of course, just because Tony was gone didn't mean I was alone. Three younglings waved to me, and then Ethan appeared at my side. "Hey. How's it going?" he asked.

I felt grumpy, sweaty, shaky and a little sick. In other words, normal. "Fine," I said bitingly. "Did Tony send you?"

Ethan blinked. "Well, he saw me in the mess hall." He was silent for three steps. "He was worried about you."

"Yeah. Of course, he was."

I saw Ethan slant a glance my way out of the corner of his eye. "You do look pretty shitty."

For some reason, that made me laugh. "Is that our resident therapist's opinion of my condition?"

He snorted. "No. Just an observation. From a guy who grew up with you." Another sideways glance. "Do you need a therapist?"

I thought back to my panic this morning at having Simone's magick touch me. And my more recent panic at the thought of my baby's parentage. "Nope." Probably a lie, but I really didn't want to talk about my feelings. I already did that way too much with Tony.

"Okay." He sounded relieved. "Well, if you change your mind…"

I gave him a thumb's up, because I was breathing a little harder than I should've needed to as we arrived at the mess hall, and talking just seemed like too much work. Tony met me at the door with a protein shake and several pieces of buttered toast. I could hear sounds coming from the kitchen, but no one else was in the dining room. I wondered what time it was, if breakfast was already over.

I sat down, with Galen, Ethan and Tony all watching me as I started to eat. I snapped at them, "I'll give you each a million dollars if you find somewhere else to be."

Ethan just nodded, waved and walked away, but Tony smelled like hurt for just a moment. Then his scent shifted to the white-bread scent of nothingness, which meant he didn't want anyone to know what he was feeling. He didn't smell like that nearly as often as he used to. I hated that smell even more than I hated the hurt smell, because it meant Tony didn't feel safe enough to let me know how he felt.

"Sorry, jeez, I'm sorry," I said quickly. "Thank you for the food. Please have a seat. You want some toast? You must be hungry."

He hesitated, like he was thinking about ignoring my words and leaving me there. Eventually, though, he sat down and took a piece of toast from the rapidly shrinking pile in front of me. Because I didn't stop eating, even as I waited for him to decide what he wanted to do. I still felt shaky and sweaty, and I needed those calories.

"Could you get Galen some kibble for me?" We kept a supply in the mess hall, just in case. Tony nodded and silently went to fill a bowl for Galen.

Tony returned, sat back down, and ate another piece of toast. He was quiet for a long time. Then he said, "I know I'm probably getting on your nerves. I just…yesterday was fucking scary."

And here we were again, talking about feelings. Lovely. "I'm sure it was. I know it freaked me out, and I didn't have to watch it happen." Besides, I was always infinitely more frightened when Tony was the one injured than when it was me.

Was that going to happen with the cub, too? Shape-shifter cubs tended to get hurt a lot because we had the impulses of a wolf prompting us to do a lot of reckless things that the human body wasn't meant to do. Great. Something else to look forward to. At least this cub wouldn't have a twin sister to get into trouble with. My mother always said Mal and I were more trouble than four of her other cubs put together.

But right now, the only trouble in front of me was Tony's hurt feelings.

I tried again to smooth things over. "I get it. When you were bleeding out, after Gina…" I lowered my voice, since Gina might be in the kitchen. "Well, after what happened, I've never been so scared."

"Not even when that nocturne attacked me last spring?"

I felt myself pale as I remembered that horrible attack. Tony almost died then, too. Why the fuck was I in a relationship with a human? They were so damn breakable. I wanted to cover up the memory of that fear, but then I realized maybe this was what he needed. To see how important he was to me. So I let my voice shake a little as I said, "Yeah, that was pretty bad, too. I spent the ride to the forest keeping your insides from falling out." I shuddered, then gave into the urge to break up the pathos in the air. "Of course, I didn't like you as much back then, so it's a little different now."

His mouth curved in an almost-smile. "You liked me just as much, you were just scared to admit it."

"Oh, them's fightin' words, Antony." But I smiled back, because he wasn't wrong. We didn't begin a physical relationship right away, but I knew my feelings for him started back then. Not that I would tell him that.

He stood up and kissed my temple. "I'm going to go get us some coffee. Drink your shake."

I'd been polishing off the toast and ignoring the shake, but he was right, I needed protein. So I drank the shake as fast as I could, trying not to gag as the gritty liquid slid down my throat. I really, really needed to find some different sources of protein.

When Tony came back with coffee, he carried the mugs on a tray along with another plate. I perked up, hoping for more toast. Instead, the plate contained several slices of sausage. They were a little burnt, but they also smelled odd. Not like there was something wrong, more like they were made with something other than pork. Venison? No, that didn't sound right, either. I was surprised when Tony set the plate in front of me.

"Um, I know I said I wanted to try eating meat again, but I wasn't really thinking of doing it now." I pushed the plate closer to him, though my mouth was starting to water.

"It's not meat." Tony took one of the two forks on the tray, then speared a piece of sausage and ate it. "It's some kind of plant-based meat substitute. Gina ordered it a few weeks ago, I guess, and she made some with breakfast for anyone who wanted to try some. I'll eat it all if you don't want any. She got the spicy kind, so I don't know if it'll sit okay for you right now."

I watched him eat another piece. My stomach rumbled, and he chuckled. But he didn't try to convince me to take some. Since I was pretty sensitive to the texture of whatever I ate at the moment, I wasn't sure it was a good idea to try something so similar to meat. But oh, my god, it smelled so good.

"I'll try a piece," I said quietly. Like if I said it too loud, my stomach might hear and protest prematurely.

"Want me to get a trash can, in case you gotta puke?"

That seemed like a wise idea, so I nodded. Once we had a small trash can at the ready, I picked up one of the forks and brought a small piece of the not-meat to my mouth. My eyes drifted closed as I chewed. It was the most delicious thing I ever tasted. I liked that it was a little overdone. It made it slightly dry and crunchy, like a meat-flavored cracker. And best of all, it chased away the taste of that protein drink, never to return.

Tony watched with a smile while I polished off the rest of the plate. "Does Gina have more of these?" I asked.

"I'm not sure, but I bet she can get more if she doesn't."

"How soon?" Maybe I'd never need to dip into the gritty world of protein powders again.

Tony laughed. It was a good sound that brought a smile to my lips and a little heat to…other areas. "We'll make it happen, don't worry," he said.

"Okay, good." I sat back, took a sip of coffee, and came to an uncomfortable realization. "I should go talk to Janus and Finn now."

Tony's joy vanished, muscled out of the way by two less fragile emotions: worry and anger. "Why?" he said flatly.

I sighed. How long was Tony going to act like this when the subject of Finn came up? Admittedly, I wasn't excited about seeing him, but Finn was a reality that I needed to face. And the sooner I could do it, the better, because with every passing second, I dreaded talking to him more and more. I told Tony exactly that.

"I'll go with you." He stood up, putting all our dishes on the tray.

"Actually…" What excuse could I give for not wanting him to come with me? Galen nudged my hand. Sending a silent thank you to my dog, I said, "I need you to watch Galen while I go. He hates Finn on a good day, and I have a feeling this isn't going to be a good day. Please?" There was that word again. I was turning into a polite person. It was downright disturbing.

Judging by Tony's expression, he recognized the excuse for what it was, but he agreed to take Galen with him to teach his first class, a weight-lifting and yoga class. One of these days, I really wanted to see Tony doing yoga. The thought made me smile.

Wondering how Tony thought he would accompany me to Janus's cabin when he was supposed to be teaching a class, I kissed his cheek, thanked him for the not-sausage, and left the mess hall.

Chapter 20

KELLAN

As I got closer to the cabin, my stomach started to do the jitterbug. I really didn't want to walk into that cabin, which was so full of magickal energy. I decided to make a last-minute detour, stopping at my cabin so I could brush my teeth, and maybe arm myself. I didn't need weapons, but they would make me feel steadier. I strapped knives to my forearms, stuck sheathed knives in my pockets, and slipped on the shoulder harness that held my katana. I loved the delicate/deadly Japanese blade. It sliced through things so smoothly. Through air. Water. Sinew. It was a great weapon.

There. I felt a little better. Still jittery, but prepared if things should go sideways. If anyone tried to touch me with their grubby, magick-loaded fingers, I'd just cut their hands off. It's all about being prepared.

When I walked into Janus's waiting room, Smack was sitting at the desk with one arm in a sling. Simone probably told her not to use it, just to give the wrist time to rest after healing it. Smack's eyes widened slightly as she clearly caught sight of the katana. That made me feel good. Maybe just the sight of the sword would discourage unwanted touching. I should wear that thing all the time.

"Hi, Smack," I said, smiling so she knew I didn't intend to use the blade on her. "How's it going?"

She shrugged. "*Asi-asi*." At my confused look, she said, "It's Spanish for so-so. Gina's been teaching me."

"Oh. Well, it's not *muy bien*, I guess, but better than nothing." I pronounced the Spanish words like a gringa who lived in Wisconsin for the last century and a half, but it made Smack snort a laugh.

"I'll let them know you're here," she said, and slipped through the door.

That meant they were both in there. My breathing and heart rate sped up. I reached into my pockets, loosened the knives in their sheathes so they would be easier to pull. Pointless, really, because those blades were like trying to quickly pull keys from the bottom of a purse. Whatever's attacking you will have more than enough time to finish you off before you manage to pull a weapon from a sheath in your pocket. But it was all about making me feel better.

Smack came back out, a strange expression on her face. I tried to read her scent, but that didn't help much. A mix of worry, confusion and...satisfaction? Weird. She muttered, "Serves 'im right." Then she looked at me, nodded, and said, "Go on in."

I wanted to stay, to sniff her more thoroughly and try to figure out the scent. But humans got creeped out when you sniffed them thoroughly. Okay, Tony didn't mind it when we were in bed together, but he was unusual in all sorts of ways. Every other human didn't like being sniffed. Besides, I wasn't here to talk to Smack. I headed for Janus's room, hands in fists so I wouldn't pull the katana as I stepped through the door.

My feet stumbled slightly as I took in the sight before me. Janus was kneeling by one of the armchairs that faced the fire. Janus never knelt. He spoke so softly, even my wolf ears could barely hear him. "Please, you must face her, all will be well. You will see."

Then I caught the scent of saltwater on sand, and the sound of quiet sniffles. Someone was crying, and it wasn't Janus. That meant it was...Finn.

Crying? Finn? Well, I guess I knew where the confusion part of Smack's scent came from. I suddenly wished Galen was with me after all. Katanas didn't do much good against tears.

I felt all the humanity in the room wrap around my chest, squeezing my ribcage until I couldn't breathe. I needed to get out of there. This wasn't my job. Finn crying wasn't in my job description. I was a fucking warrior, damn it. What was I doing here, anyway?

The need to shape-shift rose so fast and so hard, my vision blurred. Too much human. Not enough wolf. Too much. I wanted to run, but there was still the fear that the baby would slide out of me, so I walked as fast as I could while moving my thighs as little as possible. I bumped into the doorway hard enough that I knew I was going to bruise, but I didn't pause, needing outside, needing air and earth and fur and prey. I heard voices behind me, but I didn't care, they were human, more human, and I wasn't very human anymore.

Fear swirled inside me. I couldn't shift. The cub, needed to protect the cub. But I couldn't stand this skin! I hated human and all that went with it. Needed wolf.

I hit a wall. A wall with arms and a voice. "Kellan? Kellan! A youngling came and got me – what's going on? What's wrong?"

Mate. I couldn't think of his name, but I knew his scent. I looked up at him, but I couldn't form words. My brain wouldn't work. And then salvation stuck his cold nose against my palm. Little brother. I could lean on him.

I knelt in the snow, buried my face in the fur of my brother, and inhaled. I opened my mind, reached out to him, like uncurling a fist held too tight for too long, a little painful from lack of use. It had been so long since I did this. But it was easy with him, always had been, finding him was like finding a lost piece of my soul. My mind joined with my brother's, like taking his hand in mine, and I could see through his eyes. My nose smelled the richness of the day, the scents of all the humans…

No, no more humans. We needed wild places, wild things. I tried to walk beside my brother, but my body didn't move right. Hands under my arms pulled me up so I stood on my hind legs. My mate again. He spoke slowly and clearly. "I don't know what's happening, Kell, but I think you'll be able to walk better like this."

I didn't like it, didn't want to do things the human way, but it did feel better than trying to walk on four legs. I still couldn't speak, but I looked toward the forest and whined.

Mate pressed his lips to my temple. "Go. Yell if you need help. I'll be nearby."

I bared my teeth at him, fierce and happy. I couldn't run, but Brother could. Mate smelled uncertain, but he smiled back at me. "Have fun."

We entered the forest. I could feel the ground under Brother's paws, sharp and cold and crunchy. It was a strange sensation, having both my feet and my brother's paws, but I could feel them both. I found a downed log and sat on it, drawing a confused whine from Brother. He wanted to run. I pressed my forehead to the top of his head, and let him see the images I pictured. Me, staying put. Him, running for both of us.

He nudged me, and I felt how much he would prefer we ran together. But he obeyed. He took off through the trees, and I closed my eyes and let his senses fill my mind.

Prey. Brother found the scent trail, fresh enough to make our stomachs rumble. I could feel his excitement thrumming through him, which spurred my own. I threw my head back and howled. It was an anemic sound coming from a too-human throat, but I didn't let that stop me. Brother joined me with his own funny howl, not really wolf, but definitely not human and beautifully familiar.

He lowered his nose to the ground and snuffled around. Not a deer. Just a bunny. But bunnies were fun to chase.

Brother looked back in my direction. Our connection would allow him to pinpoint where I was, just like I knew exactly where he was. He whined one more time. I opened my mind further, strengthening our bond, like wrapping my hand tighter around his. *I'm here with you*, I was reminding him. *Go hunt.* Brother wagged his tail and took off.

I closed my eyes, letting his mind absorb mine so I could fully feel what he felt. He flushed the bunny from its hiding place and the chase was on. We whipped through bushes, dove over fallen logs, skidded to a sudden stop as the rabbit changed course, then off again, hot on its heels, until…we…were…almost…THERE!

When Brother's jaws clamped down on the bunny, he shook his mighty head and broke the creature's neck, ending its squirming. Then Brother trotted happily back to where I waited and placed the bunny at my feet.

The scent of the fresh meat didn't smell nearly as good close to my human nose as it did through his senses, and I came back into myself as I crawled away and struggled to keep my breakfast down. Galen – he was Galen again, my brain could form his name – approached tentatively. I was still connected just enough to know he felt bad, like he did something wrong. Didn't I want the bunny? Wasn't that what I sent him to do?

I turned to him and buried my cold fingers in his fur. I pressed my nose into the thick ruff on the back of his neck and reached out to him one more time. I didn't join with him fully, just enough to let him see that I was happy with what he achieved. His tail returned to wagging, and I stroked his coat. "Good boy," I managed to say. Human words still felt awkward on my tongue, but I didn't feel stifled by the fact that I was human. I could breathe again, the need to shape-shift completely gone for the time being.

But I was also tired. I felt like I ran down the rabbit along with Galen. I really wanted a nap in front of a warm fire.

We left the dead rabbit behind for something else to eat. Since Galen ate a full meal of kibble earlier, he was fine leaving it behind. I could've carried it to the kitchens, where someone would've added it to a stew, but it was clearly killed by Galen, and for some reason, humans preferred their meat taken down by an arrow or a rifle. It was one thing when Galen and I brought down a deer. They could overlook the fact that we tore the throat out and maybe snacked a little on one of the extremities. But a rabbit was kind of small – the tooth marks were a little too obvious.

Humans were weird that way, but what could you do?

Chapter 21

KELLAN

I used that link with Galen almost daily. One warm, rainy morning in May, we were returning from one of our runs, when my phone rang. I answered it happily. "Darcy!"

"Hey, how's my favorite mama-to-be?" He sounded happy, too, which made my happiness grow. Stupid hormones.

"Fat and gross." I was now roughly the size of a tanker truck. I was so grateful for the ability to meld with Galen. I missed running around with him, but that connection to his mind allowed me to feel wild for a little while, which kept me sane and kept me from shape-shifting and hurting the baby. "But I didn't puke when Galen brought me a rabbit just now."

"Oh, well, that's good." I heard the slightly horrified tones of a human who didn't know what to do with information that was a little too wolfy.

"How are you?" I asked.

"Same as always." Did his voice sound a little forced, a little too hearty? I wished he was here and I could smell his emotions.

"I miss you."

"Me, too. Maybe you can come visit soon?"

"Yeah, absolutely." Of course, in order to leave the forest to visit Darcy, I would have to talk to Janus and Finn, get permission. Permission wouldn't be an issue. They both still felt so guilty over what happened, they never said no to anything I wanted, including ordering Gina's not-sausage by the caseload. The problem was actually working up the courage to go speak to them. We had a few brief conversations, but I always escaped as quickly as I could. After hearing Finn in tears that day, I decided avoidance was a perfectly healthy way of dealing with things. I had enough on my plate. I was carrying a baby who might be the spawn of a faery referred to as the Horror. I was living with a human man who, on that same day as Finn's tears, saw me in a very nonhuman state. It freaked Tony out a little, and we had many conversations where I tried to explain what happened and he tried to understand. I'm not sure he really did, but he tried, and that meant a lot to both of us. I didn't need to be dealing with Finn, his feelings, or his desire to make things right.

The human on the other end of the line, of course, was too perceptive by half. "Still avoiding the big heart-to-heart with Finn, huh?"

I growled, and Galen glanced up at me with concern. I scratched his head and forced myself to sound normal, rather than annoyed. "I'm not avoiding. I'm prioritizing my energy."

Darcy laughed, which made everything worthwhile. I smiled as he said, "That's a good one. But you are avoiding. Just go talk to him, already. It's just going to keep weighing on you, the longer you put it off."

"I thought human males were supposed to be noncommunicative and never want to talk about their feelings. Why do I always get stuck talking to the ones who are all 'let's talk this out?'"

"Because you're drawn to the more evolved members of the species." He didn't sound at all bothered by my irritation.

"Or I'm just super unlucky."

"Or that."

I sighed, as Galen and I reached our cabin. "I don't know. I just don't want to deal with it. Their magick makes my skin crawl."

"I know, kiddo."

Kiddo? I refrained from pointing out that I was over a century older than he was.

"But if it means coming to visit me...?"

"Yeah, yeah. I'll go talk to them."

"Good."

"Smug is not a good look for you, Darcy Jameson."

"You can't see me, how do you know?"

I snorted a laugh, happy that he sounded so...Darcy. "I'll call you after I talk to them. Now go eat something healthy."

"Yes, Mom."

We hung up. My phone dinged with a reminder. I was supposed to go work with the younglings. I was teaching them self-defense, not hand-to-hand combat, but actual, practical ways to fight back against a bigger, stronger attacker. Specifically, a bigger, stronger attacker with rape on his mind. We had a class in half an hour. Not enough time to go talk to Finn and Janus. I wasn't avoiding. I was busy. I had just enough time to have a snack and feed Galen before going to meet the younglings in the muddy practice yard.

What really shocked me was that Finn and Janus allowed me to avoid them. Finn tried cornering me a couple times in the mess hall, but then Tony materialized at my shoulder and glowered at him, and Finn scuttled off. I also took to cutting up my little nonsausage patties with a rather large, very sharp knife, which may have discouraged unwanted table visitors. But given that they knew where I lived, they could've forced me to talk to them. They didn't, which was fine by me. I was going to enjoy it for as long as I could.

After working with the younglings, I wanted to catch Tony's yoga class, so the meeting with the bosses would just have to wait. I thought about Yogi Tony as Galen and I left the cabin, on our way to meet the younglings. He was a great teacher, which I knew, but he was also surprisingly adept at the graceful poses, despite his bulky muscle. And apparently, yoga was very good for pregnant women. This pregnant woman was not particularly good at yoga, but it gave me a chance to keep my muscles active when sitting at weight-lifting machines became too awkward.

We were almost to the practice yard, when I felt a sharp pain in my abdomen. Pain like nothing I ever felt before, and I'd been stabbed, flogged, fallen fifteen feet from a tree branch, and run through with a sword. Those were tickles compared to this. I screamed a stream of obscenities, and people came running.

Six younglings, including Smack, arrived just before Tony did. "I – it hurts," I managed to say, just as another sharp pain hit and my legs almost gave out from under me. Tony sent the younglings away, helped me to the infirmary, and he and Simone got me into one of the private rooms and helped me take off my boots and pants.

A lot of what happened next was a blur. There was a lot of pain, several different types of bodily fluid, and some really creative swearing. I do remember that Simone tried to make Galen wait outside, but I wouldn't let her send him away. I never would've gotten through the pregnancy without my little brother, so he was staying. He crawled up on the cot and squeezed between me and the wall, so I was able to have one hand in his fur while the other hand clenched around one of Tony's hands.

TONY

Kellan had a vise grip on my hand, so Simone was the one who caught the baby. I could tell instantly from the look on her face that something was wrong. As soon as Kellan released my hand, I walked around the bed to stand beside Simone.

At first glance, the baby looked beautiful. But then I saw them, and I knew. This baby wasn't mine. She belonged to Aza.

My chest felt tight. I couldn't breathe properly. I took several steps back, as far away as I could get, but still be in the room. I needed to think. I needed to breathe, and I couldn't seem to do either one. What would this mean for us?

Pull it together, I told myself. After all, I knew this was a strong possibility. But I couldn't seem to look at the baby again.

KELLAN

When it was over, I collapsed into the mattress like I just ran an Olympic race. My muscles were all goo. I couldn't move. Galen leaned over and started licking the sweat off my face. I gave him a hand to lick instead, so I could look around for the baby. I heard her start to cry, and a breath I didn't know I was holding suddenly whooshed out.

"Is she okay?" I croaked. My throat was so dry and raw. Swearing like that was hard work.

"Ah, she's fine." Something in Simone's voice made me struggle to sit up. My abdominal muscles wouldn't cooperate. I managed to awkwardly prop myself up on my elbows.

"What is it?" Nobody moved. "Show her to me!" I barked.

Simone brought the baby, wrapped in a towel, over to me. Tony was standing off to the side, not looking at any of us. Fuck. Fuck, fuck, fuck.

Simone lowered the cub into my field of vision. "Here she is. Your daughter." She shot a sideways glance at Tony, who still wasn't looking at us.

The cub was beautiful. Her skin was pink and healthy-looking, she had a dusting of dark hair on her head, and her eyes, when she blinked at me, were a lovely warm amber, just like mine. But...

I could tell there was something off about her back. The blanket just looked too lumpy. "Simone, just fucking tell me."

"Kellan, she, um, she has, well, she has what look like wings."

I blinked. "Wings? Like feathery angel wings?"

"Uh, no. More like...more like bat-type wings."

Well, fuck. That was unexpected. Why would she have bat wings? I didn't have wings, Tony didn't have wings, Aza didn't have wings, either. Where did the wings come from?

Clearly, though, this baby wasn't Tony's. There was no way he had anyone with wings in his ancestry. Aza, though? Plenty of faeries had wings. I even met a few that Aza was related to, while I was his prisoner. One might've been his sister, now that I thought about it. And her wings were pretty leathery, like bat wings.

Oh, my god. This was Aza's baby. I stared at her. She looked so innocent. Not at all like she was the spawn of evil. What if some of that lay dormant inside her, like a congenital illness, just waiting to blossom as she grew up? What if it was up to me to help her be a good person? Shit, we were both doomed.

Simone helped prop me up on pillows so I was sitting up enough to take the cub from her. Then she left, and I was alone with Tony, Galen and the cub. I held her carefully. She was naked, wrapped in a towel. I took a quick glance at the wings. They were leathery, yes, but the same shade of pink as her skin. The weirdest part about them was holding her – I worried that I would squish her wings and hurt her, but she didn't seem bothered by my grip. Galen sniffed her up and down, causing her to blink owlishly at him, but he clearly decided she wasn't particularly interesting, because he curled up by my hip and started snoring. He worked hard, helping me give birth. Plum tuckered out.

And still, Tony didn't say a word.

How was he not entranced by her? I couldn't take my eyes off her. She was teeny-tiny, but absolutely perfectly formed. Yes, perfectly formed, even though she had wings. They were part of her. Would she still have wings in wolf form, or would they be like her tail, only a visible part of one form, not the other? We would find out together, she and I.

How would she hide the wings from the world? It was one thing to be half wolf. You could still walk around looking human. But this little girl would never be able to pass for human, not unless we found some way for her to hide them. What were we going to do?

One thing was clear, though – it was a problem we would figure out together. I felt a connection to this tiny being unlike any pack connection I ever felt before. Stronger than the connection to Darcy, stronger than my mother or sisters, even stronger than Mal. This was the best thing ever, and Tony, still staring at the light switch by the door, didn't want to share it. That much was clear.

"It's okay if you want to leave," I said quietly. It wasn't okay, not at all. In fact, it made my gut twist in knots, just saying the words. But I didn't want him here if he didn't want to be.

"What?" He sounded surprised.

"If you want to leave, go ahead. We have our answer now. You're not the father. I understand if you don't want to stay." My heart thumped in my chest, not unlike one of the many rabbits Galen ran down over the last few months.

"You want me to go?"

Oh, for fuck's sake, did humans have to deliberately misunderstand shit? "Did I say that?" I snapped. The cub whimpered, and I took a deep breath to calm myself. "No, I don't want you to go. I want you to stay. But since you won't look at us or come near us, I assumed you didn't want to. It's awkward as shit, and I'm too tired and sore to dance around social niceties. If you want to go, then go. But if you don't, will you please come over here and talk to me?"

I couldn't get a read on his scent, possibly because my nostrils were filled with the scent of my cub. It was like hers was the only scent in the room, the alpha and omega and everything in between. The most important scent of my life, embedding itself in my brain forever.

I blinked, forcing myself to focus back on Tony. We needed to have this conversation. We needed to get it over with, because if I needed to grieve the loss of him, I wanted to get on with it as soon as possible, because it was going to be a lot of hard work.

"Are you staying?" I asked.

"I want to try."

Not exactly the resounding yes I was hoping for. Not a resounding anything, really. But if this was his answer, then... "In that case, come over here and look at our cub." I tried not to put too much emphasis on "our," like it was a natural thing to say, not at all a deliberate attempt to draw him into the pack unit.

He slowly walked to the bedside. He gazed down at her, but he didn't say anything about how beautiful she was or how she looked like me, none of those Norman Rockwell things. Instead, he asked, "Does Aza have wings?"

"No," I answered, "but someone in his family, maybe his sister, does. Maybe it's like coat color in labs. You get some puppies who are yellow, some who are black, all in the same family."

Tony looked at me in surprise, then snorted a laugh. "You just compared our little girl to lab puppies." He stumbled a little over "our little girl," but he said it, and like a stupid bloody female, my heart swelled, hearing those words.

"Well, she will have a tail when she's in wolf form." I hoped. Maybe the wings would impede the tail, or she had wings instead of a tail. What would she wag if she didn't have a tail? How could she show me she was happy? Of course, some dogs didn't have tails, and they just wagged their butts, and it didn't seem to stop them from looking happy. Maybe...

I shook my head before I went too far down Speculation Road. She wouldn't shape-shift until she started crawling or possibly walking. I'd have to ask Mal about that, but I was pretty sure it didn't happen until the cub could move around on her own. We'd find out then if there was anything else unusual about her.

"So she doesn't look like Aza?" Tony's voice sounded tight, and I managed to pick up the sourdough scent of anxiety.

"No, she doesn't look anything like Aza. Thank god. He's an ugly motherfucker."

Tony looked at her, then looked at me. "What are we going to call her?"

Relief flooded through me, followed immediately by a drowning wave of exhaustion. "I dunno, can we decide later? I'm dying to take a nap."

Tony took the cub from me, awkwardly at first. "Support her head, right? That's what the books say."

"Mmm-hmm." He was the one who read those books. They just sent me into more panic attacks, so I figured I would learn as I went along. But supporting her head sounded like a good thing.

"And I guess try not to crush her wings."

"Mmm." My eyes drifted closed, and that was that.

Chapter 22

KELLAN

When I woke up, Tony was asleep on the floor beside a bassinet. The cub, inside the bassinet, was awake and starting to whimper.

I pushed myself upright and picked her up, hoping to calm her before she woke Tony. I didn't think Tony slept much the last few days, so I wanted him to rest. I nestled her in my arms.

"She's probably hungry," Tony murmured.

"Oh. Shit. I was hoping not to wake you."

"'S okay." He looked up at us from his nest of blankets. "I'm sorry I had a hard time."

I pulled my t-shirt up, exposing my breasts. I didn't know what to do next. I should've read some of those stupid books. "You don't need to apologize."

"Maybe, but I want to anyway." He smiled, still looking a little sleepy. "Try squeezing your breast. See if a little liquid comes out, then brush it up against her mouth. With a little luck, she'll take it from there."

I stared at him. "You researched how to breastfeed." I was slightly appalled.

He shrugged unapologetically. "I heard it could be difficult to get it started."

I tried his advice, and it worked. The cub latched onto my tit like a vacuum.

Tony smiled. "I can't believe I thought even for a minute that I didn't want to be here for this."

I rolled my eyes, but inside, I felt so happy to hear him say that. I would miss him so fucking much if he left. I couldn't tell him that, though, so I said, "You just want to look at my boobs."

He chuckled and propped himself up on one elbow. "Do you need anything?"

"Coffee would be nice."

With another laugh, he got up and headed for the door. "Anything else?"

"Maybe some of that not-sausage? And pancakes. With lots of syrup this time. You're usually stingy with the syrup."

"Pancakes? It's four o'clock in the afternoon. Never mind, I'll see what I can do." Tony circled back and leaned down, kissing my mouth like I was made of spun sugar. So careful. "I love you, Mama Wolf."

I know the important part for most people would be those first three words, but for me, hearing him say, "Mama Wolf," in his rumbly bass voice while my cub nursed at my breast was…mind-blowing seemed too mild a term. So much so that I said without thinking, "I love you, too."

His face blossomed with the biggest smile I've ever seen. "Lots of syrup," he said, and left.

Not five minutes later, the door opened again. "That was quick," I started to say, but then I caught the scent in the air. Not Tony's, though just as familiar.

Finn's scent, which always reminded me of earthy smells, now had a tinge of moldy leaves. I didn't know what this scent stood for, and I didn't really want to know. He hesitated in the doorway. "Hi. Congratulations," he said quietly.

I tried to cover myself with the blanket, but between Galen lying on the blanket and my arms being full of baby, I couldn't manage it without dumping all of us on the floor. So I gave up and glared at him. "Tony's going to be back soon, and he won't be happy to see you," was my answer.

"You don't seem particularly happy to see me, either." A wry smile. "I suppose I can't blame you for that."

"Although you would if you could."

He nodded. "Yes, I probably would, wouldn't I?"

Self-awareness wasn't Finn's style. It was disturbing, and the cub seemed to pick up on my unease, releasing my nipple and whimpering slightly. I made soft, comforting noises and directed her back to my breast. I expressed a little of the fluid, which looked a little too runny to be called milk, rubbed it on the areola, and the cub clearly caught the scent, her nostrils twitching as she latched on. She had a good appetite.

"Well, I don't wish to bother you. I just wanted to stop by and give you this." Finn held up a small package wrapped in brown paper. "I believe traditionally the paper would be pink, but this is all we had on hand."

He brought me a gift? What the fuck was happening here? "Who are you and what have you done with Finlay?" I asked.

He ran a hand over his hair, slicked back in its usual ponytail. "I know you don't wish to hear my apology. I understand. What I did was...truly unforgivable. While I did not intend...No. I will not try to make excuses. I will simply give you this gift for your cub, and wish you well."

He set the package on the edge of the bed. Galen twitched, obviously not liking how close Finn got. I hoped he didn't go after Finn. I couldn't exactly restrain him at the moment. I looked down at the cub, and switched her to my other breast. "I'd open it, but my hands are kinda full right now."

"Of course. Well, you can open it at your leisure."

I heard myself say, without my permission, "I'd rather open it now, while you're here." Was I really prolonging this visit when he seemed perfectly willing to go away? Apparently, I was. "Maybe you could open it for me."

Finn's scent warmed, lost that moldy tinge, becoming the more familiar smell of rich, loamy earth. Healthy earth, the earth of a summer garden. "I would be happy to." He picked the package back up, prompting another twitch from Galen, but a twitch was as far as it went. Finn carefully opened the paper, gently pulling at each piece of tape in the most excruciatingly slow example of present-opening in the history of time.

"Tony will be back soon," I reminded him.

His hands faltered for a moment. "Yes, of course. Here." He ripped the last little bit and out fell a pink...something. The light was too dim and the object was too shapeless for me to tell what it was.

"Oh. That's very nice." Whatever it was.

That wry smile again. "Allow me." He picked it up and held it out, and I saw that it was a knitted blanket. It looked soft and intricately stitched, with cables in a pattern that looked like –

"Wolves," I whispered.

"Yes. They aren't perfect. I couldn't find a pattern, so I had to make my own. But if you can tell what they are, that's a good sign."

"You made up a pattern. A wolf baby blanket pattern."

"Yes, well, the pattern can be applied to many things, not just baby blankets." Yeah, because the part of all this that shocked me was the baby blanket part, not all the rest of it. But Finn kept on talking. "Sweaters, hats, scarves. It's possible some of the younglings might wish to use it. I plan to offer it to them."

"Wow. Um, thank you." I paused, still too shocked to really know what to say. "I'd give you a hug, but again, my hands are kind of full."

He smiled, nodded, and said, "Perhaps a rain check, then. I should go before Tony returns. I'll let you explain where the blanket came from."

That was going to be a fun conversation. But it would be a lot easier without Finn in the room, so I said goodbye to him and he left.

As I waited for Tony, I realized Finn didn't ask to hold the cub. Wasn't that what all humans did when faced with an infant? I supposed Finn must've known I would say no, and his pride probably wouldn't allow that. I decided that must be it, because looking down at the little being in my arms, I couldn't imagine not wanting to touch her.

By the time Tony returned, Baby Wolf was done feeding. Her eyelids looked heavy, but she struggled to keep her eyes open and take in her surroundings.

The smell of the coffee perked me up and seemed to grab Baby Wolf's attention as well. As Tony set the tray down on the counter, her nostrils twitched and she fisted her little hands, like she wanted a mug. Tony laughed. "She recognizes the true mother's milk, looks like."

"Yeah, well, I think it'll be a few years before we let her try a cup of her own." I handed her off to him and attacked breakfast with the same enthusiasm as my cub did hers. "Mmm. Oh my god, food never tasted this good before. Never."

"I'm glad." Baby Wolf's eyelids finally won the fight, and as she drifted off, Tony seemed to notice the blanket. "What's that?" He started humming softly, an unfamiliar, but pleasant tune.

"Oh, yeah, that." I ate the last of the pancakes, because they were hot and fluffy and delicious and I didn't want this conversation to ruin the taste of them. "Well, Finn stopped by."

Tony froze mid-hum. "Did he." His voice was as cold and flat as his expression, and while the lack of question mark at the end might've seemed like it gave me permission not to answer, I knew I needed to do it.

"He didn't stay long. He just wanted to say congratulations and give us the blanket. He knitted that for her himself."

"Interesting how he managed to show up at the one time when I was out of the room."

I hadn't really thought about it, because I didn't really want to think about Finn. But yeah, it was awfully convenient. It was a very Finn move, watching for Tony to leave before he stopped by. And the angry heat radiating from Tony's scent showed that Finn made a wise choice. Galen twitched again at the scent. Pretty soon, my dog was going to lose it. There was just too much testosterone happening today.

The cub stirred in Tony's arms, whimpering a little. Did she need to be burped? Or did she smell his anger? "Here, I'll take her. She's probably gassy." Regardless of whether it was gas or not, I wanted to get her a little further from Tony's angry scent. I didn't want her to associate him with anger.

I put a cloth over my shoulder and tried burping her like people always do in movies. Nothing happened, but maybe it was because I couldn't pat her back very hard without squashing her wings. It immersed her in my scent rather than Tony's, though, giving him time to cool down.

"I don't like it," he said suddenly.

I figured he was talking about the blanket. "Well, it's a lot more pink than I would've chosen, but it was a nice thought."

"No, I mean – I don't like that he came in here. Which is stupid. He's our boss, sort of. He can do whatever he wants." He blew out a sigh. "I can't help it. I don't want him anywhere near you."

I started to argue, started to say he didn't come near me, and I wouldn't let him do anything I didn't want him to do. But a part of me understood that Tony didn't want me to argue. He knew these things, or at least, he knew that I was more than capable of defending myself against Finn in most circumstances. But I couldn't defend myself against his magick when it mattered the most, could I? That's what scared Tony, and it was what scared me, too.

Our conversation was interrupted by a knock on the door. The door opened without my permission, which made my temper flare. This time, Galen growled. Not good. "Hello," Janus said, sticking his head through the barely open door. "May I come inside?"

A very naughty part of me imagined slamming the door shut and severing his neck, causing his head to bounce like a basketball. His eyes widened, so he must've seen my Looney Tunes-esque mental image.

"It's not a great time," I told him.

"My apologies," he said smoothly. Any shock over the sight of his head as a basketball seemed long gone as he stepped in the room. "I do not wish to intrude upon your family. I merely wanted to meet the little one, and extend my congratulations." He smiled almost shyly. "It has been such a long time since we had a baby here."

Did Janus like babies? Since Mal and I were the last two born here, this was the first time I was seeing him with a baby. Curiosity won out over annoyance, and I held her out to him.

He beamed at her. That was the only word for it. Beamed. "Welcome, little cub," he said, and his voice held power. Magickal power. Oh, fuck, no. I started to snatch her back, but before I could, she spit up all over him.

Not laughing was the most difficult thing I ever had to do.

Tony recovered before I did. "Oh, sorry, sir. She just finished eating. We were just about to burp her when you – very sorry." He didn't look sorry at all as he took her from Janus.

"Oh, such things happen with babies." Janus picked up one of the towels sitting on the counter and wiped himself off. "I will not take any more of your time. But..." He looked me in the eyes. "She looks just like you, Kellan Alastrina Faolanni." As he said my name, his voice once again held that magickal power. I wanted him to leave before it got any stronger.

"Thank you, sir. Now I think I need to change her diaper, so if you don't mind..."

"Of course. Congratulations." He leaned down and kissed my cheek, and it took all my self-control not to flinch away from the magick that surrounded him like an aura. Was he always like this, and I only noticed it now, after what happened with Finn? I hated it.

It was a good thing I had my hand wrapped around Galen's collar, because my dog started to leap off the bed to attack. Dogs could sense power, and Galen now associated that power with Enemy. Really, really not good.

After Janus left, Tony sniffed the cub's back end. "I don't smell anything. You sure she needs a change?"

I couldn't breathe. That magick, so close, and I let it touch me. Again. Fear gripped me, and I found myself flashing back to the dark, dank cell where Aza kept me for two months. I let it happen. My fault.

No. One trauma could trigger memories of another. That was something all the younglings said. I wouldn't go back there. There had to be a way to make life easier. "Maybe we should move back to the city for a while," I said, surprising myself.

Tony's head snapped up. "What?"

I didn't mean to say that, but now that I said it, it sounded really good. "Well, I mean, maybe a little distance would be good for us. Just until things are a little less raw. We've been trying to avoid them, but we can't avoid them forever, because you're right. They're everywhere here."

"Are you serious?"

I couldn't tell from his tone if he liked the idea or not. "Yeah. I didn't think of it before, but yeah."

"I don't – how would I be able to teach? I'd have to be here before dawn and stay until after full dark. I'd never get to see you."

"Maybe we could work it out that I'd come with you some days. I've been working with the younglings, too, you know. Maybe we could come to camp three days a week to teach, and the other days, we could be in Madison, doing our own thing." I was really warming up to this idea, picturing seeing Darcy on a regular basis, maybe starting up my dog-walking business again. I could walk dogs with Baby Wolf strapped to my chest. Humans did shit like that all the time. The big draw was Darcy, though. I pictured his face when I told him he was an uncle. He'd eat that shit up.

Well, and not being surrounded by magick one hundred percent of the time. That was a pretty big draw, too.

Tony seemed to be a little slow taking in the idea, which wasn't like him at all. "Has anyone ever done things that way before?"

"No, not that I remember." I shrugged. "So what? If I can't dictate my own rules after Finn almost drains the life from me, when can I?" I tried to say it lightly, but my voice shook. I could tell from Tony's expression that he heard that tremor. "Seriously," I said, firmer. "Finn will back me, because he wants me to forgive him. And maybe Janus will go along with it, too. There's no good reason not to."

"Since when does he need a good reason to say no?" But Tony's expression was less perplexed, more relaxed. "Maybe we can work it out so they think it's their idea."

That kind of scheming was way above my skill level, and I said so. Tony smiled. "Not sure that's true, but I think I have an idea. Give me a little time to think about it." He kissed my forehead, then kissed the top of Baby Wolf's head. He laid her in the bassinet. "Why don't we put her in her bed and let you and Galen take a little nap?" He started to lay down beside her again.

"There's room on the bed," I told him. Not a lot of room, but we did it before.

"Are you sure?"

"Yeah, come on. But I get to be in the middle of the sandwich."

He smiled. I knew he understood what I meant, because we slept this way a lot – one of us sandwiched between the other and Galen. Tony lay on the bed with his back against the wall. I settled with my back to his chest, and Galen curled up against my stomach. If I stretched, I could just reach the side of Baby Wolf's bed. Perfection.

Chapter 23

KELLAN

Perfection only lasted a couple hours, before Baby Wolf woke us with shrill howls. I told Tony to go back to sleep, and Galen watched with rapt attention as I attempted to change her diaper. Onesies are nicely designed to allow for the changing of diapers, so that wasn't bad. Taking off the dirty diaper was easy. But putting a clean one on? Fuck. Diapers must've been designed by airplane engineers. Plus, I had to cut a little flap out of the front so it didn't rub up against her umbilical cord, and I had to make sure I didn't catch her wings in the back. By the time I managed to secure it in place, I was exhausted.

Galen was edging closer to the dirty diaper, but that seemed like a bad idea. I said firmly, "No." His head hung and he looked at me with sad eyes, and I caved. I carefully wrapped the diaper closed so he couldn't poke his nose in the contents, then held the bundle in front of his nose. He sniffed vigorously and, with a huff, looked from me to the diaper and back again, as if wondering at the human obsession with collecting poop. For years, I picked up his poop as soon as it hit the ground, and now I was collecting specimens from this cub. Not that this was poop yet, but still. He huffed again, as if to say, Weirdo. I snorted a laugh and tossed the diaper in the bin.

Before I snapped her onesie back in place, I took a little time to look at her wings. They mostly lay still against her back, although occasionally, they would shift or move, just like her arms and legs. Not movement with a discernable purpose, just little twitches, maybe simply because she could. When I ran my finger down her left wing, goosebumps rose on her skin. I wondered what that felt like.

Would they always look like this? What if she grew feathers on them? Or a thin layer of fur, like a bat? Would we have to cut holes in her shirts to accommodate them as she grew? So many questions, and I didn't have a single bloody answer, because I wasn't a faery. Well, not really. My sire was a faery, but I didn't find that out until recently. I didn't have any attributes of the fey. I was just a shape-shifter. Nothing special.

No, this was going to be a new experience all together. An utterly fucked-up new experience.

I fed Baby Wolf again, and this time, she burped right away. Then I set her in the bassinet and sat to watch her, idly petting Galen as I did. Tony's snores rumbled in the background, making this little room feel more like home than just about any home I ever had.

My phone buzzed with a text. I checked it, and saw it was from Mal's number. My heart skipped slightly. It seemed my sister's mysterious "source" within the Sankhain told her the good news. *Congratulations*, the text said. *Abby and I are so excited to meet her new cousin. I hope we can see her someday. Love you, little sis.*

My eyes grew damp, and I wiped them irritably. I was not going to miss the incessant tears that came with this whole pregnancy thing. It was absolutely obnoxious. But maybe I could forgive myself for getting a little emotional. I had my sister back, at least by way of phone. Another upside to spending more time in the city, I realized. I could communicate with Mal without fearing discovery. Maybe even see her.

I texted back, *Thanks. I hope so, too. Love you back.* Then, before I could even hit send, another text came in.

We're still working on that problem you asked for my help with. I thought we had a good lead, but it turned out to be old news.

Problem? Oh, shit. J.C. I completely forgot about him. Well, I didn't forget, not really. Not with teaching the younglings self-defense and talking about the importance of disclosure. He was always there in the back of my mind. Maybe not over the last several hours, though.

J.C. was still alive. I gazed at Baby Wolf, and felt glad that Tony was asleep, so I didn't have to admit out loud that I was relieved the boy was still alive. I didn't like feeling that. I wanted to hate him, but I still couldn't quite forget the sound of his sobs. Why the hell did emotions have to be so complicated?

I almost texted back, telling her not to hurry. Instead, I typed, *Okay. Be careful. I'll let you know if we find any leads on this end.*

I tried to think of something to say that would prolong the conversation. Apparently, I wasn't the only one who didn't want to say goodbye yet. *How's my little niece doing? Did you pick out a name yet?*

Not yet. Right now, I'm calling her Baby Wolf.

Laughing emoji. *That's catchy.*

Fuck you, I responded, but I was smiling.

What about the paternity? Did you figure that out?

So Simone didn't fill her in on all the details. Interesting. *Yes. Her sire was Aza, but Tony's her dad. She has wings.*

Silence for so long, I didn't think she was going to respond. Then, *Wings, huh? I wonder if she'll be able to fly, or if they're vestigial.*

Just one of many unknowns at the moment, I typed.

I'm glad Tony stepped up. It would've sucked if I had to come back to Madison and beat him up because he dumped you.

The fact that she would even think about doing that made my eyes damp again.

I gotta go. Love you, little sis.

Wow. Two love yous in one conversation. Maybe I wasn't the only one feeling overly emotive. I typed back, *Love you, shrimp.* Then I stuck my phone back in my pocket. That movement woke up Galen. Tony had him out a few hours ago, but as he looked at me, I realized I really wanted to take him outside. I longed to feel the wind on my face, feel connected to my pack with the smell of the outdoors. Not growing up Christian, our spiritual tradition said that when we burned the bodies of our loved ones, they spent their afterlife riding the wind, coming back to visit us or offer us comfort or guidance that way. Some people would say the wind was just weather, but it wasn't, not to me. I wanted to feel that. But I couldn't leave. I had Baby Wolf to think of now. I murmured an apology to Galen and tried not to fidget too much as I tried to go back to sleep.

I was unsuccessful both in my efforts to fall asleep and my efforts to be still so I didn't wake the others. Tony and Baby Wolf both stirred. Baby Wolf slipped right back into sleep, but Tony sat up and looked at me. "What's up?" he whispered.

I couldn't tell Tony the whole story right now. I didn't know who might overhear. So I just said, "Someone sent their congratulations." Then I showed him the texts.

I watched him puzzle over the message. I saw the moment he figured out what the "problem" was – his face and scent went blank. "Oh," he said. I wondered if he was relieved, too, that J.C. still lived. I didn't ask, just watched as he kept reading. I knew the moment he saw the part where Mal said she would've beat him up if he dumped me. A smile managed to stretch from his mouth to reach his eyes and warm his scent. "Her, beat me up? She's what, five feet tall?" he whispered.

"Five feet of shape-shifter strength. Yeah, she could kick your ass, my friend."

That smile grew and settled in to stay. He closed his eyes for a moment, then pulled a big breath into his lungs and stretched his arms over his head. "Well. Do you still want to talk to Janus about moving to the city for a while?"

I never thought I would be excited about living somewhere else, but I was. There were aspects of life in Madison that held a certain appeal. Was this what Mal felt when she broke away from the Sankhain? Not that I was going to do that. I cared too much about this place and the people here. But to have a little piece of life that was just mine, just ours, sounded really right.

I realized I was quiet for a long time, which might make it seem like I was having second thoughts. I quickly said, "Yes. Abso-fucking-lutely yes." At my tone, Galen wagged his tail and headbutted me.

Tony smiled. "All right. You want to come with me to Janus's cabin and bring the little one, or would you rather stay here?"

I decided we should all go. If we needed to remind them of how I almost died, I could do that better than Tony could. Nothing garnered sympathy like a woman holding a baby.

Of course, before we left the infirmary, Simone insisted on examining both me and Baby Wolf. Jeez, we really needed to come up with something to call her.

As if reading my mind, Simone asked, "Have you come up with a name yet?"

I shook my head. "I've been thinking of her as Baby Wolf."

"Lovely," Simone said with a grin. "But maybe not a good long-term solution."

I looked at Tony, whose cheeks were looking a little redder than usual. "Do you have an idea?"

He shrugged. "I mean, she's your baby."

"Fuck that. She's our baby, and anything's got to be better than Baby Wolf."

"Well, we could call her B.W. for short." The way he squinted his eyes told me he was struggling not to laugh.

"Oh, yeah? What do you got, smarty-pants?"

"Well…" Embarrassment smelled like cinnamon-sugar bread. "I was thinking of October."

I blinked. Of all the names he could've come up with, why that one?

"What I was thinking was, you came back to us in October. You were gone, and when you came back, you had her with you. It's when you started healing, started on this…shit, this sounds lame, but this journey. You know? So I thought, October." The longer he talked, the more embarrassed he smelled.

I looked down at the cub, and considered. It was a big name for such a little thing, but then, my mom thought my name meant warrior. Turned out it actually meant slender, which was a dumb name for a little girl, especially in today's skinny-obsessed culture, but I grew up under the pressure of a warrior's name. I liked the idea of naming her after my homecoming, but then again, would that forever tie her existence to the place I was coming home from?

"October," I said carefully, and traced her cheek with my finger. "It's better than Baby Wolf." But I didn't think it was really right.

"Well," Simone said, "it's a beautiful name, although she's going to wonder why you named her October when she was born in May."

Fuck it. I really didn't want to talk this through with an audience. This was a question for me and Tony, not a committee.

"I'm happy to say, you're both looking well. You didn't have any problems getting her to breastfeed?"

I snorted. "Nope. She likes her food, just like her mama."

Simone nodded. "Good. Well, if that changes, we can talk about it. But it sounds like you'll be all right."

Simone warned me not to do too much or lift anything heavy while I was healing, and reminded me that my body was going to be burning calories like mad, between the healing and the breastfeeding. She said my mother usually took a couple days off after birth before going back to work. I promised to be lazy, while thinking that I wasn't about to sit around on my duff anymore. I spent the last few months waiting for this baby to be born so that I could resume my normal life. But what Simone didn't know wouldn't hurt her.

That is, until I stood up and felt the gush of...ick between my legs. I was wearing the thickest, heaviest pad ever created, but it felt saturated within moments. Bloody hell. Normal life was going to have to wait, I guessed.

With our healer's blessing and our sort of named baby in tow, we left the infirmary. The sun was shining and it was warm, at least seventy degrees. Galen pranced and preened as we were stopped by a half dozen younglings on the way to Janus's cabin. He thought they wanted to see him. Fortunately, they petted him as they asked to see the baby.

Most of the kids were in the mess hall, eating dinner, which was the only reason we managed to cross the yard in under an hour. I was glad to see Valentine and Tia. Little Tia took a great interest in my pregnancy, and she squealed and bounced up and down when she saw October. It was the biggest, loudest show of emotion I ever saw from her, and I loved it. She was finally starting to come out of her shell, and it was beautiful.

After we disentangled ourselves from them, we finally reached Janus's cabin. My heart thudded in my chest, and October whined a little in a way that reminded me of Galen when he was nervous. She must be able to smell my anxiety. Galen echoed her worry with a whine of his own. I took a deep breath and tried to soothe my nerves. This was my first time stepping into this cabin since that day I ran out, when Finn was crying. Why was it that avoiding things always made anxiety worse instead of better?

I reminded myself that this wasn't my first time seeing Finn and Janus since it all happened. I saw them several times, most recently in the infirmary when they came to meet the baby. That didn't go so bad. Just a little magick. No big deal. This would be fine.

Smack sat at the desk, writing in a notebook. Ethan was encouraging her to write a journal, which I caught a glimpse of a little over a week ago. Most of what I saw was swear words, but maybe Smack found that therapeutic. I know I did.

She came out from behind the desk. I lowered October slightly so Smack could see her. "It's a baby," she said.

I snorted. "Um, yeah. What were you expecting?"

"I didn't know if she'd be a puppy or what."

I wondered how many other younglings thought I'd be giving birth to a cub with four paws. Probably didn't help that I called her a cub. "No, she's a baby. She won't be able to shape-shift until she starts moving around on her own."

"Oh. Okay. She's cute, I guess." After scratching Galen's ears, she went back to the desk, opened a drawer, and pulled out a small black object. "Here. Sankha Ethan said babies need to wear hats when they're born." Under her breath, she muttered, "And it ain't pink, so don't get your undies in a bunch."

Tony took the gift and turned it over. It was a little black hat, complete with skull and crossbones, just like the one Smack made for Ryder last year. I grinned. "Smack, thank you. It's perfect."

Tony settled the hat on October's head. "Her name is October and her first real article of clothing is a skull-and-crossbones hat. She'll be sleeping in a graveyard by the time she's five."

"You picked out the name. But don't worry. Much more likely she'll be sleeping curled up with Galen," I said. "Although a graveyard isn't the worst place to sleep. They tend to be very quiet."

"Not gonna ask how you know that," Smack muttered. In a more normal, respectful tone, she said, "I'll announce you. Please wait here, Sankha Tony. Sankha Kellan." After spending just a few seconds inside the other room, Smack came back out and said, "They'll see you now."

A part of me was hoping Finn was off getting lunch or something, but apparently, no such luck. Tony smelled as nervous as I felt, but in we went.

Chapter 24

KELLAN

Tony told me he would open his thoughts to Janus, let him see what we wanted. That would start the conversation, ease us into it better than if I went in there and told them anything. In other words, that would prevent me from putting my foot in it and ruining our shot at getting what we wanted.

I held onto Galen's leash and sang "Enter Sandman" in my head. It was one of my favorite Metallica songs, one of the first I ever heard by them and one that I knew I could keep in my mind for a long period. If Janus tried to get into my head, I didn't want him finding out about Mal. Metallica was a great way to drown out voices, inside your head or out.

Meanwhile, Tony held onto October. Yeah, she needed a different name. I didn't want her to ask where her name came from and learn that she was named for the month that I came back from Aza the Torturer. But for now, October was a better placeholder than B.W. or "the cub." Especially if people were expecting the cub to be a puppy.

Janus studied us with a slight smile on his face. Then he must've tuned into Tony's thoughts, because his smile sank into a frown as he tilted his head slightly. "You wish to relocate to the city."

Finn jerked like something invisible hit him in the face. "What?"

Janus rested a hand on Finn's arm, but kept his attention on Tony.

"Just part time," Tony said. I could smell cold sweat from nerves and was grateful Janus didn't have my nose. "I still want to teach. Kellan does, too. We just…this baby is going to take some getting used to. We need a little more time and space than we can get here."

"Plus, between me and Aza, this baby is, like, seventy-five percent fey," I said. "She has wings, for fuck's sake. I need fey help with her. And Raoul is the only fey I know who isn't a psycho killer."

Tony glanced at me sharply. I hadn't said anything to him about asking Raoul for help. Raoul was a faery prince who lived in the same neighborhood as my apartment. I also recently found out he was my father. Tony didn't smell too happy at the idea of me talking to him. Maybe because, when we needed a solution to the Aza problem, Raoul refused to help me. He didn't want to get involved. He was, at best, a neutral entity. He certainly wasn't a friend or ally. The thing was, I knew that, so I wasn't worried about approaching him. I wasn't expecting us to be a happy family. But the slimy bastard could help me with my child.

Janus studied me, but Finn stared at the table. I could smell Finn's scent, dark and earthy like the forest floor after a heavy rain. It was so strong, I could almost feel the weight of the dark clouds overhead. This was such a sad smell, it made me sad, too. Part of me wanted to reach out to Finn, but I didn't.

"You believe you can trust this faery?" Janus asked softly.

Trying to stay focused, I shrugged. "As much as you can trust any faery. He's not a bad guy. He's been…kind to me before. After a fashion. Look, I know you guys know magick. But not the kind of magick we need." I reached over and stroked October's cheek. "I need to be able to teach her faery glamour if she's ever going to have a chance at a normal life."

Normal. October stared at me with amber eyes. She and I would never be normal. Not with a wild animal inside. Nope, normal was too big a stretch, but hey, aim high. I returned my attention to Metallica.

"An ear worm. Is that the term?" Janus looked at me.

I returned his gaze. *Sleep with one eye open, hugging your pillow tight.* "Sir?"

"The song you seem to have stuck in your head. The song you keep repeating over and over. That is an ear worm?" He said the words precisely, like they were genus and species.

"Not sure Metallica really qualifies as an ear worm, sir, but yeah, I've got it stuck in my head." Now Finn was staring at me so hard, I had a feeling he was trying to penetrate my thoughts. Fortunately, he couldn't read minds. Unfortunately, his intensity was putting Galen on edge. I heard a low growl in my dog's throat.

With a glance at Galen, Janus nodded. "Very well. You are correct, Finlay and I cannot help you with faery magick. And your daughter deserves the chance to achieve normalcy. We will try this part time arrangement." Finn's eyes slid shut. I don't know what thought Janus read from Finn's mind, but I saw Janus's hand tighten on Finn's arm. "You will report to me in one month's time so we may evaluate whether it is working. In the meantime, you will spend Saturday through Tuesday in the city. You will be within the boundaries of the forest before daybreak each Tuesday morning. You may leave again just before daybreak each Saturday."

For some reason, my wolf didn't like that they were dictating the terms. This was my idea, damn it. "Friday night," I said, as anger burned through me like a flash fire.

Janus raised his eyebrows.

"There's no reason to stay here overnight on Fridays. We'll leave Friday night after dark and return Tuesday morning before dawn." I raised my chin and met Janus's gaze. What was I doing? I never did that, never challenged my alpha this way. But I didn't back down, didn't lower my eyes. If anything, I stood a little straighter, a little stiffer.

Janus studied me, and I realized I forgot to sing the song. Panic washed the anger away, and I resumed the mental music as Galen looked up at me and whined. I still held my head high, but my gaze faltered. I lost the staring contest as I checked Janus's scent for anger at my insubordination. Surprisingly, I didn't find anything. Instead, it smelled like freshly washed sheets hung in the sunshine. His happy scent. Why was he happy?

"You make a valid point. For now, you may leave Friday night. As I said, we will evaluate in one month's time whether to continue this arrangement."

Friday. What day was it today? Tuesday. Nope, I didn't want to wait until Friday. I wanted to see Darcy now. I wanted a giant bear hug from him, and I wanted to see his face light up when he heard me call him Uncle Darcy. That couldn't wait four days.

"I think that Tony and I need the rest of this week off for maternity leave. I'd like to go to the city tonight. Like I said, we need to figure out how to do this, and it will be easier if we have peace and quiet. Things are never peaceful or quiet here."

"Sir –" Finn began, but Janus interrupted him.

"I have doubts that peace and quiet are in your near future," he said, looking at October. "But I understand the need for solitude. You may leave once full dark settles over this evening, which shouldn't be long. Then you will return next Tuesday before dawn. Will that be acceptable?" His voice and scent were warm, like he was amused.

I looked at Tony, who was uncharacteristically quiet. He just smiled at me and waggled his eyebrows. The show is yours, his expression seemed to say. "Yeah, okay. Thank you, sir."

Janus nodded. Finn took a breath like he was going to say something, but again, Janus didn't give him the chance. "You may go," Janus said. "Perhaps you would like to start packing. And we have allocated funds for you to provide for your little one." He reached into his pocket and handed me a black credit card. "Whatever you need, you shall have." Then he turned away, leading Finn toward the armchairs by the fire. Tony and I skedaddled.

When we stepped outside, Galen sighed as if in relief, and Tony shifted October into a one-armed hold and pulled me close. He planted a kiss on my lips. "I love you."

The sudden heat in his scent made my knees a little wobbly. "What was that for?"

"You have any idea how hot it was, watching you stand up to him like that?" His voice was the softest whisper.

"I'm not sure what got into me. But I'm glad you enjoyed it." I breathed in his scent, then said regretfully, "I'm sorry, but I just pushed a watermelon out from between my legs. I heal fast, but I don't think I'm ready for sex."

He laughed. "That's okay. When you're ready, maybe I can show you how hot I thought it was. But for now..." He kissed me again, slower and more thoroughly, until I was really regretting the no-sex thing.

We went back to our cabin and started packing.

"Listen, about her name," Tony said. Right now, October was laying in the same bassinet that she was using in the infirmary. Simone or one of the younglings must have dropped it off at our cabin while we were with Janus and Finn. I looked around. We really were going to need more baby stuff. Clothes. Diapers. A stroller, so we didn't have to carry her everywhere. Which meant going shopping. My heart started to pound as I pictured going into a store, with all the people and aisles and limited number of exits. I was phobic about stores.

Maybe we could just order everything online.

"Kell?"

"Hmm? What? Sorry, I was thinking about something else."

"I think we should talk about her name. I liked it when I was thinking of it as a celebration of your returning to us, but after what Simone said...I don't want her to ever feel like her name is connected to Aza."

Her very existence was connected to Aza, but I understood what Tony was saying. "Agreed. Any other ideas?"

His scent immediately turned embarrassed, which told me he did have another idea. "It's probably a stupid idea," was all he said.

"Stupider than Baby Wolf? Because if we're not calling her October, then Baby Wolf is the only other name in contention at the moment." Why was he embarrassed?

Except he wasn't embarrassed anymore. Now, his scent was a mess, anxiety and hesitation, sadness and hope, all jumbled together to form something my brain labeled as "vulnerability." "I told you, it was stupid."

"It's not stupid, it's important to you. I can smell it. So please, just tell me." I focused on packing, hoping that if I wasn't watching him, he would come out and say it.

"Well…" I heard him shuffle his feet, but I didn't look up, keeping my attention on knives I was packing in my duffel while I waited for Tony to 'fess up. "I was thinking. Maybe we could name her after my mom."

I dropped my matching set of Scottish dirks, and they hit the floor with a clatter that made me jump and made Baby Wolf whimper. "What?"

"See, I told you, it was stupid. Just forget it. Look, I'm going to go and –"

"Tony, stop, please. It's not stupid, it just surprised me." He smelled so raw, I wanted to give him a hug, but I had a handful of throwing knives now. It wasn't a good idea to hug people when your hands are full of blades. I dumped them in the duffel bag, grateful that the cub was still too young to go rooting around in drawers and duffel bags. Where was I going to put all my blades once she started crawling?

After a few moments' silence, Tony said, "What did you mean, you could smell that it was important to me?"

"Well, you know, I can smell things. Emotions and things. Part of being a wolf."

"No, I know that, but what's it like? If I'm going to help raise a shape-shifter baby, I need to know these things."

"Oh." I thought about that. "Well, it's hard to explain."

"Can you try?"

I hated explaining wolf things to humans. It never translated well, and I always ended up feeling like a freak. But Tony really wanted to understand. He wouldn't have asked if he didn't. Galen trotted over and sat beside Tony, and both males looked at me expectantly. Grr. "Okay. Well, for example, anger smells spicy."

"Spicy?" He smiled, like he was laughing at me.

I shoved him in the shoulder. "You want to know or not?"

"Yes, yes, I'm sorry. I want to know. What does spicy mean?"

"Well, your anger smells like jalapeno focaccia bread."

That surprised him. "I smell like bread?"

Of course, he thought that. Humans always took offense when you told them they smelled like something. Even something nice, like bread. "No, you…see, I can't explain this."

"Please?" He looked so serious, so earnest.

I sighed. "You don't smell like bread. You don't smell anything like bread. You smell like…your deodorant, and your shampoo, and the gunpowder from the time you spent doing target practice three days ago. But underneath all that, someone like me can smell your scent, the scent that means you. And, well, my brain associates your scent with fresh bread. That's the picture that comes to mind."

"Like yeast?"

"No," I snapped. "Like home. It's a homey smell. Nothing more homey than fresh baked bread."

He squinted at me. "So your brain tells you I smell like home?"

I shrugged, deeply uncomfortable with this whole stupid conversation. "Yeah. I guess so." My stomach rumbled. All this talk of bread. "Would you make me a protein shake?"

"Sure." He went about it, still seeming deep in thought. As he handed me the shaker bottle, he said, "Home. Wow. That's nice."

And that was all he said. He didn't tease me or call me a freak. I shouldn't be surprised, but I was. I downed the shake, just as Baby Wolf started fussing. She was probably hungry, too. I settled on the bed with the cub to feed her.

"So what did I smell like when I said that earlier? Not jalapeno focaccia."

I'd hoped that conversation was over. "No. You didn't smell angry. You smelled…" Would he take offense if I told him he smelled vulnerable? Well, too fucking bad, he insisted on talking about this godforsaken subject. "You smelled vulnerable. Like dinner rolls."

He snorted a laugh. "Dinner rolls?"

I growled and glared at him, wishing I could kick his ass but too busy feeding a baby. This whole motherhood thing was turning out to be incredibly inconvenient.

Tony's laugh softened to a crooked half smile. "Please, Kell, I'm sorry. I know this is hard for you. Please, help me understand?"

Maybe it was the double please, but I caved again. I took a deep breath and tried to translate scent into words. "Dinner rolls. Soft, squishy, easily smooshed. Not heavy, kind of light and airy and a little sweet."

"Oh. Okay. Sure, that makes sense."

It did? "It does?"

"Yeah, given what I was feeling, you pretty much got that spot-on." He sounded impressed, which annoyed me.

"Of course, I did. I know how to interpret scents. I just don't know how to explain them to dumbass humans who don't get wolfy things."

He leaned over and kissed my cheek, while Galen watched and wagged his tail. "Thank you for explaining to this dumbass human."

I shrugged again. "So now it's your turn. Explain to me why you want to name B-Dub after your mom."

Tony stiffened, and Galen looked from me to him. Maybe my tone was a little more abrasive than it should've been when I asked Tony to talk about his mother. It was a sensitive subject. I knew that because he never, ever talked about her. Which was why this was so strange.

"Listen," I said, softer this time. "You know I know this wasn't just some random, off-handed comment you made. You've been thinking about this. So explain it to me. We don't want to name our baby after my triumphant return from rape and torture. Why would we name her after the woman who – who sold you?" I forced myself to say those words, although I felt his flinch like a punch to the stomach.

That maelstrom scent was back. "I – she wasn't just that." He took a deep breath, like he was diving underwater. "I've been thinking about her a lot. You know? What kind of parent could I be, when the only one I ever knew sold me for drug money? Right? But that wasn't all she was. There were times…" His eyes had that faraway look that meant he was seeing something from long ago. "She wasn't high all the time. Sometimes, she tried to clean up. She used to take me to McDonald's for breakfast. She would get pancakes. I always got hashbrowns. That was all I wanted, was the hashbrowns. That made her laugh every time. And we'd stay up late, and she'd play her favorite blues albums, and she'd sing along. She had a beautiful voice. Actually, it was probably terrible, but to me, it was beautiful."

I didn't breathe, didn't move, for fear of breaking him. He smelled that fragile in that moment.

Galen must've picked up on it, too. He leaned against Tony, the way he always did with me when I was losing my shit. Tony petted Galen absently for a minute, then shook his head. "No. It's a bad idea."

Since he seemed to be out of the memory, I risked saying something. "It's not a bad idea at all. I think it's probably important to honor those memories."

He glanced at me, then shied away. "I haven't thought about that in so long. I couldn't. You know? It was more important to hate her. Because the bad shit was so bad. But she was my mom, too. She was my whole family. And – and she never hurt me. Not really. She tried to be a good mom. She just…was too fucked up to do it right."

Shit. I could relate to that. I was terrified I would fuck this up. "Please don't tell me her name was Beulah. I'm not sure I could saddle a little baby with a name like Beulah."

He laughed a little, which was the only reason I said it. "No, not Beulah. Her name was actually Rhonda, but everybody called her Sky."

Something inside me clicked into place, and I looked down at our baby. "Sky."

"Yeah. But it's –"

"Tony, so help me god, if you say that it's stupid one more time, I'm going to make you change Sky's diapers from now until eternity."

He blinked. Surprise lightened his scent. Like the dinner roll was slathered in butter and honey. All he said was, "Well, hopefully, she won't be in diapers until eternity."

"Whatever. Now, it looks nice and dark out. How about we hit the road?"

Chapter 25

KELLAN

Because of Simone's warning earlier, Tony tried to take all the bags. But he also had to carry the bassinet, and so I convinced him to let me wear the backpack that carried Galen's favorite toys, food and dishes. I also carried the baby, since Simone said I could pick her up as much as I wanted to. Well, that wasn't exactly what she said, and judging by the amount I could feel myself bleeding when I stood up with the weight of both backpack and baby, she definitely wouldn't have approved of this. But I was sick to death of being treated as breakable, and damn it, I wanted to carry something.

It was probably just as well that I wasn't carrying anything much, though. As we walked through the forest toward the outer border, I kept tripping over roots and fallen branches, because I was so busy looking at Sky's face. I knew that she wasn't a toy, that this was going to be a lot of work and difficult in so many ways I hadn't even thought of yet. But watching her fascination as she breathed in the scents of the forest, I knew that it didn't matter. It would be worth it, whatever it cost, just to see that look in her eyes.

Galen paused in his mission to mark every tree in the forest, looked up and wagged his tail, giving me a moment's warning before Cat dropped out of a tree a few yards away. She bowed. "Sankha Kellan. Sankha Tony. Galen. Are you leaving us?"

I put a hand on her shoulder and she straightened to look at me – and the bundle of blankets and cub in my arms. "We're going to live part time in the city. Don't worry, we'll be back. We just need some family time."

Cat studied Sky with the same surprise that Smack showed. Seriously, how many people thought my cub would have four legs? "All right. When will you be back?"

"Bright and early Tuesday morning. Spread the word, okay? I don't want anyone worried about us."

"Yes, ma'am." Cat bowed again, a smaller bend at the waist this time. "Safe journey."

It was a traditional farewell, but it felt a little silly, given that my apartment was about five minutes from the forest. "Thank you. We'll see you soon."

With a smile at me, then Tony, then a pat on Galen's head, Cat jogged back to her tree and scaled it so fast, it was like she disappeared.

As we passed under her tree, I called up, "Oh, and Cat? When you're spreading the word about when we're returning, do me a favor and tell everyone that the baby is a baby, not a puppy."

A laugh floated down from the high branches. "Yes, ma'am."

"In their defense, I wasn't even sure whether she was going to be a baby or a puppy," Tony commented as we exited the forest.

"Oh, for fuck's sake." I could smell his amusement. He liked that it bothered me, which made me rein in my irritation so he wouldn't see it. "Well, she's a baby."

"Yeah, I can see that now. Everyone else will, too. She won't be getting those looks for long."

"Right." That was what bothered me, I realized. I didn't like people looking at her like she was a freak. "Except she's also got wings."

He sobered as he unlocked the doors of my truck. "Yeah, there's that. You think Raoul can help with that?"

"The man's a fucking faery prince. He'd better be able to help with that."

"Okay, yeah, I guess what I should've asked is, do you think he will help with that?"

I settled in the passenger seat with Sky still held in my arms. Galen took his usual position in the in-between spot, and Tony climbed behind the wheel. Priority number one, car seat. And probably a vehicle that had more than two seats. And more than two seatbelts. Shit. I had a feeling that the limit on Janus's credit card wouldn't extend to a car.

Tony was looking at me, and I remembered that he asked me a question. "I'll get Raoul to help. He'll do it. Whatever it takes."

I expected Tony to drive to the apartment, so I was surprised when he got on the Beltline, the main highway that circled around Madison. "Where are we going?"

"Darcy's. Call him, find out if he's home or if he's at the library."

Excitement fluttered in my stomach as I fumbled with my phone. Darcy answered on the first ring. "Kell?"

"Where are you?"

"Library, why?"

"Are you guys busy, or could you take a minute to say hi?" I whispered to Tony, "Library," and he drove past the exit that would take him to Darcy's apartment, heading for the library where my friend worked.

"It's a pretty slow night. Are you really on your way here?"

"We are." I realized Darcy didn't even know Sky was born. I'd been a little busy – I forgot to call him.

"Awesome! Does that mean Tony's with you, too?"

"Mm-hm." I decided I didn't want to tell him about Sky – I wanted to surprise him. This was so not who I was, but fuck it. I knew it would make Darcy happy, and it would be fun for me, too. I noticed a soft smile on Tony's face – he clearly figured out we were going to surprise Darcy.

"Great! I'll see you soon."

"Very soon," I said and hung up, as Tony pulled off the highway and turned right, rumbling down the block that led to the library.

"You didn't tell him?" Tony asked.

"I thought it would be fun to surprise him. Humans like surprises, right?"

"Some humans. I suppose Darcy's probably one of those people."

I figured he probably was. I fussed with Sky's blanket, making sure no part of her wings stuck out from under her onesie. It wouldn't do to have the mundanes seeing her feyness. "Maybe we should've gone to see Raoul first."

Tony glanced at us. "Kell, if glamour is something she's going to have to learn, it's not like she's going to be able to do it right now. It'll be fine. Remember, people see what they expect to see most of the time. As long as she doesn't unfurl her wings and fly across the library parking lot, I don't think anyone will notice a thing."

"Okay." Still, the excitement turned to nerves that made my blood feel electrified.

Tony parked the truck. "Let's go introduce Sky to her uncle Darcy."

And just like that, I was grinning and excited again. Uncle Darcy. He was going to love that.

I wasn't disappointed. Darcy saw us enter and started walking toward us. Then I saw the moment he realized what I was carrying. His eyes went wide, his steps stuttered momentarily, then he broke into a run, skidding to a stop in front of me.

"Pretty sure you're not supposed to run in a library," I teased him.

"I'm a librarian, we're exempt from the rules. Can I –" He couldn't seem to take his eyes off of Sky.

I laughed and said, "May I introduce our daughter, Sky. Sky, this is your uncle Darcy."

His gaze shot up to look at me, then at Tony, then back at me. "What did you say?" he whispered, his eyes starting to shine with tears.

"Uncle Darcy. That's who you are, right?"

His adam's apple bobbed as he swallowed hard. "Yes. Yes, that's me, Uncle Darcy." He smelled happy, but his smile looked like such a fragile thing. Was I wrong? Did he not want to be called Uncle Darcy?

"I mean, if you want. We don't have to call you that."

With a sudden frown, he reached out, gently took her from my arms, and snuggled her to him. "No takebacks. I'm Uncle Darcy." And with a more solid smile, he started cooing and rocking her.

I looked over at Tony, and his scent washed over me as he came to stand beside me. Slipping an arm across my shoulders, he smelled like Gina's cinnamon, raisin and pecan bread. The kind of bread a person could live on. Happy, solid bread. And I felt a part of me relax further. He was really still here. He was really staying.

Since Darcy was supposed to be working – and since we had to leave Galen in the truck – we didn't stay long. Just long enough for Darcy to extract a promise to bring Sky for a visit on Thursday, which was his day off. I left, feeling lighter and happier than I felt in months.

"All right," Tony said as we pulled into the apartment parking lot. "I'm going to go to the store, get some food for us and other supplies. The books said she should sleep in something like a bassinet for a while. She's really too small for a crib, so we don't have to rush to get one. But we need diapers, clothes, a stroller. Unless you wanted to help me pick that stuff out."

I did want to have some say in what sort of things we bought for our cub. But I was also feeling exhausted and a little woozy from all the bleeding I'd been doing. I must be starting to heal, but I still felt a gush when I got out of the truck at the library. And I was a long way from ready to brave a store. "Promise me you won't pick out anything pink, and I'll trust you to buy what we need."

He grinned. "I don't know. There are some pretty cute pink onesies out there. But I'll do my best."

I must've looked as wobbly as I felt, because Tony insisted I stay in the truck with Sky and Galen while he ran the bassinet and bags upstairs. Then he returned, carried Sky and walked Galen while he followed me up the stairs, probably wanting to make sure I didn't keel over, which felt like a distinct possibility. "I should've picked up some drive-thru for you," he said when we reached the apartment. He frowned at me, smelling like sourdough worry.

"We have canned soup in the cupboard. I'll heat up some of that."

"I'm pretty sure all your soup has meat in it."

Shit. I didn't even think about that. "Ummm…"

"I'll be back in ten minutes with food for you. Then I'll go shopping." He kissed me. "Shit, your skin is starting to feel chilled. Ten minutes, I promise."

"I'll be fine." Probably. Maybe.

"Just sit down and rest. Even if she starts crying, it won't be anything that I can't help with when I get back. She's not going to die in the next ten minutes." The look he gave me told me he wasn't so sure about me.

"Just go. We'll be fine." I was starting to get annoyed.

He jogged out the door. I heard him pound down the stairs, and moments later, the truck roared out of the parking lot. Sure enough, the moment he was gone, Sky started to whimper. I didn't try to pick her up, because I didn't trust my arms at this point. My muscles felt like overcooked egg noodles. But I couldn't just listen to her cry, so I laid down on the floor beside the bassinet and stuck my hand inside, stroking her cheek. She took my finger in her mouth and started sucking. Poor kid was probably hungry again. Human newborns needed to be fed every two to three hours, so a shape-shifter infant probably needed to eat at least every hour. I was going to be shoveling in calories nonstop to keep up with her.

I must've fallen asleep, because the sound of the key in the door startled me upright. My head spun. Tony knelt beside me and handed me a bag. "Four grilled cheese sandwiches and a couple orders of fries. I'll be back with more substantial food soon." He left a large cola by my leg. "You gonna be okay?"

I stuffed a handful of fries in my mouth and gave him a potatoey smile. "I'm good. See you in a bit."

He snorted a laugh, relief flooding his scent. He must've been really worried. We'd need to work on that. I was chronically guilty of misjudging my blood sugar. His hair would be gray before his thirtieth birthday if he kept worrying about me like that.

As soon as I didn't feel like I was going to pass out, I stashed the bags of food on top of the kitchen counter and I fed Sky. I couldn't deny that I kind of loved this part. I wasn't going to become some earthmother or something, but being so connected to another being felt so good. Wolves loved nothing more than living as a pack. I spent so long with just Galen as my pack, I felt like now I was being showered with gifts. I got choked up, and before I knew it, tears streamed down my face.

Fucking hell, I thought that would stop as soon as the baby was out.

Maybe I should've read some of those pregnancy books, too.

Oh, well. Nobody was here to see it except Sky and Galen, and they wouldn't tell. So I let myself cry and shamelessly enjoyed the feeling of pack surrounding me.

After Sky ate her fill, I returned to my fast food. I put the bassinet beside my chair at the card table which sat in the tiny eating area off the kitchen. I pulled out my cell phone and looked at it. After thinking about pack, there was one person I wanted – needed – to reach out to.

I texted Mal. *We're staying in the Madison apartment. We'll be living here part time for the foreseeable future. In case anyone wanted to come visit us there.*

I held my breath, waiting for a response, which came after a few minutes. *Good to know*, with a smiley face. What did that mean? Did it mean she was going to come see us? I hated texting.

Sky fussed a little, and I used my foot to rock her bassinet. I looked around the apartment, taking in the smallness of it. It never seemed small when it was just me living there, but knowing that Tony and Sky would be sharing the space made me realize that we probably needed a bigger apartment, too. We could all sleep in the bedroom – it would be the same sort of arrangement as our living quarters at camp. But eventually, Sky would probably need her own space. I decided to set that problem aside, along with the car issue. For now, we could make due. Those bigger problems could be tackled when I was fully healed.

Once I was fed, I set up Galen's water dish and gave him some kibble. He emptied out pretty well while we walked through the forest earlier, but he would need another outing before bed. Maybe Tony could take care of that. I felt much better, but I didn't trust my legs to carry me too terribly far. I didn't want Galen to think that the new baby meant he wasn't going to get his usual number of walks. No, Galen wasn't going to be neglected. Tony would understand that and take Galen for a walk when he got home from the store.

Sky started fussing again, so I checked her diaper, which was wet. I paid attention to how the old diaper went on this time, so putting on the fresh diaper should've been easier. It wasn't. There were just so many things to be aware of. The first diaper had to be thrown away, because the part I cut out for the umbilical cord was too far to the left. I decided that as soon as I figured out exactly where to trim it, I was going to trim a bunch of other diapers so we'd be ready for the next changing. Which is what I was doing when Tony got home.

"Why are you mutilating those diapers?" He set a huge armload of bags on the floor and stared at me.

"Her umbilical cord."

"Her umbilical cord is on her back?"

I looked at the diaper in my hands. Fuck. He was right. That was the back.

"Maybe that'll be more comfortable for her wings," Tony said, and he carried the bags into the kitchen.

After bringing up two more loads of bags and a large box that contained the stroller, Tony fixed spaghetti. He looked as exhausted as I felt earlier, but he was the only one with cooking skills, so I just thanked him. Sky's bassinet once again sat beside the card table as we settled down to eat. The pasta smelled delicious, but mixed in with the sauce was something that looked suspiciously like meatballs. "They're plant-based protein, like the not-sausage," he explained. "If you don't like them, you can pick them out and pass them to me."

I knew I needed more protein than the processed cheese from the fast food sandwiches, so I resolved to try it, even though it didn't sound very appealing. Another protein shake sounded far less appealing, so maybe nonmeatballs wouldn't be so bad.

The red sauce wasn't marinara, but something Tony called arriabbata. It was much spicier than your typical spaghetti sauce, which meant that I didn't really taste the meat substitute. After the first couple bites, I devoured my serving and went for seconds.

"It's okay?" Tony asked. He was only halfway through his plate and sounded tired enough to fall asleep in his food.

"It's great. You're a genius." I gulped some water, then went back to eating.

He smiled. "It's nice to see you enjoying food again."

"It's nice to be enjoying food again." Over twenty-four hours without even a tiny bit of nausea. This was awesome. Now if only I could lose the tears, life would be perfect.

After we finished eating and washed the dishes, we were both sagging. I looked at Galen, then at Tony. I couldn't ask Tony to take Galen for a walk. He already braved the store and cooked us dinner. I could do this. Then I felt another gush between my legs, and I looked down, as if expecting to see a puddle under my feet. Tony set a hand on my shoulder. "I'll just take Galen out for a stroll. Then we can go to bed."

"You're tired."

"Yes, but I didn't just push a watermelon out from between my legs. Let me help."

My fierce independent streak wanted to say no, but I could tell my body was using up all the calories with healing and also producing more breastmilk. I just didn't have the energy to do anything else. "Okay. Thank you."

He kissed me and picked up a bag that still sat on the kitchen floor. "For you. There's something you forgot to pack."

I looked in the bag. Zombie DVDs! And he got the first and second seasons, which were my favorites. Tony really was too good for me. I didn't deserve him, not at all.

All of a sudden, the exhaustion and the emotion overwhelmed me, and I was ugly crying.

Tony and Galen raced in from the living room, where Tony had been putting on Galen's harness. "What's wrong?" he asked, then appeared to notice the discs in my hand. "I thought those were the ones you liked."

"They are." I blew my nose in a paper towel. "They're perfect. You're perfect."

"Oh. Okay." He still sounded bewildered. "So you're okay?"

I nodded, still leaking a few tears.

"'Kay. I'm going to take Galen out. We'll be right back." He watched me closely, like he was still waiting for me to give him a reason for the tears.

Good luck with that.

After checking Galen's harness to make sure it was secure, Tony left with my dog. I put the first disc into the DVD player – yes, I still used DVDs, thank you – and was happily settled on the futon, watching zombie hijinks, when Tony returned. I had the volume turned low and Sky slept in her bassinet by my side.

Tony unharnessed Galen, ran a brush through the dog's coat, then refilled the water dish. I guess I wasn't the only one who didn't want Galen to feel neglected. I listened to Galen slurping up water, then heard a crunching sound that sounded suspiciously like a milkbone being consumed. "We should save the treats for when he's interacting with Sky," I said softly as Tony sat down beside me.

He just grunted, leaned his head back and closed his eyes. "I think Sky would like us to replace this futon with a nice cushy sofa," he said, his voice already heavy with sleep.

"I like my futon. The first time we slept together was on this futon."

He opened one eye and looked at me. "The first time we had sex was in the kitchen."

"I wasn't talking about sex. I was talking about when we slept on the futon with Star Wars playing in the background." That was the night before we had sex the first time. Before Aza even entered our lives. Before I knew how bad – and how good – life could be.

He smiled. "I remember."

I turned off the TV. I wanted to lie down with Tony on one side and Galen on the other, just like we did that night. "Let's go to bed."

"You sure? They didn't get to kill any zombies yet." Tony knew those episodes as well as I did.

"There was that one at the beginning. And yes, I'm sure." I stood up, felt a trickle rather than a gush, and felt hopeful for my healing prospects.

While Tony settled the bassinet a few feet away from the bed, I changed the pad I was wearing. Then Tony and I both took off our shoes and just crawled into bed fully dressed.

"I've never been this tired," Tony murmured.

I grunted, too tired for words.

And Sky started to cry.

I got up, fed her, and settled her back in the bassinet. By the time I slipped back into bed, Tony was snoring. Galen curled up between us on the bed, and I fell asleep, listening to his contented sigh.

Chapter 26

KELLAN

Sky woke us up every hour or so. Tony helped with the diaper changes, but the feedings were all on me. Which meant that by morning, this caffeine junkie needed a fix in the worst way.

I fed Sky, then stood staring at Mr. Coffee, who burbled happily but much too slowly.

"Look, why don't you have a seat?" Tony said. "I'll fix us some eggs. Toast with butter and jam. Maybe a pound or two of that not-sausage?"

The only thing that sounded good was coffee, but I hadn't eaten since the night before and my stomach growled angrily. "Okay. Thanks."

"I think we should probably work it out that you eat anytime she eats," Tony said as he pulled out a pan and started heating it for the eggs. After a final glare at Mr. Coffee, I sat at the table. Sky slept in the bassinet, while Galen sat vigilantly by Tony's feet, waiting to see if anything dropped from above into his waiting maw.

"I should take Galen outside," I said, standing up.

"I took him out when you were feeding Sky. I'll take him out again for a longer walk after breakfast, but you should rest. Remember, Simone said a couple days to heal."

I resisted the urge to snarl at him, because he brought me a cup of coffee. The brew was hot and strong, and almost enough to make me feel alive again.

Then Tony's words registered. "Wait, you took him outside already?" I didn't even realize they left.

"You were busy." Tony started frying the not-sausage in another pan, and the scent made my stomach growl again.

"Did you feed him?"

"Yup."

"Oh." How did I miss all that? It wasn't like feeding a baby took a whole lot of concentration. Although I did seem to have a tunnel vision problem when I was holding Sky. It was hard to care about anything else.

Except coffee. Tony brought over a plate heaped with food and the pot to top off my mug. He was kind of amazing, this mate of mine. "I really don't deserve you," I said. He even put jam on my toast for me, a good, thick layer of it.

"No, you don't. I guess you're just lucky." He sat down with his own plate and cup.

I had a lump in my throat and my damned eyes were wet, but I washed the lump away with extra coffee. It truly was a miracle drink.

"How are you feeling?" he asked as he started eating.

"Okay. Still a little sore, but I don't think I'm bleeding very much anymore. I'm awfully glad I'm not a human. Can you imagine how long it would take to heal something like this?"

He swallowed, his mouth turned down at the corners like Galen when he was about to throw up. I guess Tony didn't really want to imagine.

"Probably a good thing you picked up those DVDs yesterday, though. I think a nice binge session is just what I need to finish healing the rest of the way." What I really wanted was to go out for a walk with my dog and my cub, but Tony would just say no to that. Maybe if I suggested a day of zombies, he would be more amenable to us getting the hell out of the apartment.

"Yeah, good thing." He pushed his eggs around his plate for a moment before pushing his plate toward me. "You want this? I'm full."

Poor guy. Maybe mention of healing lady parts, followed by mention of zombies, was too much for him. With a sigh, I said, "If you're really done eating, would you mind taking Galen out for a good long walk? I feel so bad for him. I've been so wrapped up in Sky, I just haven't been giving him the kind of attention he's used to."

Before you could say "zombie," Tony harnessed Galen and was out the door.

"Well, kid, I guess it's just you and me," I said quietly, not wanting to wake Sky. I ate my food and drank the rest of the pot of coffee. I figured Tony would be gone a while, and I could make another pot when he came back, if he wanted some. Then it was – shockingly – time to feed the baby again. Afterwards, Sky and I fell asleep in the living room with zombies frolicking in the background.

TONY

Galen and I walked for miles. We went up to the Henry Vilas Zoo, and I sat on a bench while Galen sniffed around the base of it. I watched people – mostly women, but a few men – pushing strollers and holding the hands of toddlers as they walked through the gates of the zoo. We could bring Sky here, I realized. We could do normal things like that if we were living part time in the outside world. I loved being a Sankha, loved the forest and the younglings, but I also loved the idea of having a life of our own, a life together without any interference from Janus or Finn. Would I ever be able to forgive Finn for almost killing Kellan? Nope, probably not. Fortunately, he seemed to know that, and avoided me pretty readily, so I wasn't forced to try.

When Galen tried to eat a discarded hamburger that he found at the base of the nearby trashcan, I decided it was time to get walking again. "Come on, bud. Let's leave that for the raccoons, okay?" I tugged him away from his would-be treasure and we headed for home.

It was a beautiful morning, warm and sunny with no humidity or mosquitoes. The kind of day we only got a handful of here in southern Wisconsin. I could feel my allergies kicking up a little bit, but I didn't care. I was outside with Galen, and there were no zombies anywhere or women talking about their healing vaginas.

As we approached the corner of our block, I saw a familiar figure step from behind a tree. "Raoul."

"Hello, friend," he said, looking at Galen. His voice sounded like windchimes, and the dog trotted over to him with a happily wagging tail. "Welcome back. It's been a while." Then he looked at me. I was used to Kellan greeting Galen before me, but it was a little annoying that Raoul did the same thing. Like father, like daughter, I guessed. He nodded a hello to me. "How you been?" Now he sounded like the urban disguise that he wore to hide his faery self.

"Great. You?"

"All right." He glanced at Galen. "And your girl?"

Was he asking me or the dog? "She's good."

"I saw you and her last night. You, um, had a little package with you." He looked at me expectantly.

"Yup." I didn't really want to have this conversation without Kellan. She knew Raoul much better than I did, she would know how to get him to agree to help. But it would be awkward to just not mention it. "Yeah, that's Sky. Our little girl."

His expression didn't change, but somehow, I sensed relief in the way his breath eased out. "Your little girl."

Suddenly, I was glad I got to be the one to impart the good news. I held more of a grudge than Kellan did about Raoul's indifference toward the Aza situation. I dropped my eyes to study a scraggly weed beside the sidewalk. "Yeah. Well, she's not mine. But we're – we're trying to work through it. It's been hard. What with her being the product of rape and all. It's not easy for Kellan to look at her and see…him."

Raoul's sharp inhale was very satisfying.

"Yeah. She was thinking she might need to ask for your aid. What with the baby having…wings," I whispered. "But I told her not to bother. I mean, you wouldn't help her with that fucker who raped her. Why would you help her with his offspring?"

When I looked back up at Raoul, he looked otherworldly. That was the only way to say it. His eyes were bright green, his skin seemed to glow, and I could almost see an aura of light around him. Then I blinked, and he was back to normal.

"If she wishes my assistance, I will be happy to give it." He might look normal, but his voice was the soft, courtly fae, not the street-corner hustler. "Whatever she requires."

I smiled, letting him see my self-satisfaction. Fae never offered help without trying to weasel something for themselves. I just got him to agree to help, and he didn't even blink, much less try to make a deal. "Thanks. I'll let her know. Have a great day, Raoul."

He narrowed his eyes at me. "You –" Suddenly, he burst out laughing. "Well played, human. I can see why she likes you." He was still chuckling as Galen and I walked away.

KELLAN

I woke up when Tony came inside, sneezing his head off. Unfortunately, Sky woke up, too. "Fucking tree pollen," he muttered, and accepted the box of kleenex that I took from the coffee table to hand to him. "Sorry, did I wake you?"

I didn't see the point in lying, so I said, "Yes. Did you have a nice walk?"

"Yeah." He sneezed again. "Until the end. Gimme a second, I'll go take a couple antihistamines and be right back."

"Sure." I gave Galen a nice rubdown, then picked up the crying baby and prepared for a feeding. When Tony returned, I had my shirt and bra off and a baby attached to my boob.

"Wow." He stared. "I don't think I'm ever going to get tired of seeing that."

"Stop ogling, you perv, and go make us some coffee."

He leaned down, kissed me, and headed for the kitchen with a big dumb grin on his face. "We ran into a friend of yours on his street corner," he called. I could hear the sweet sounds of coffee being prepared. "He asked how you were doing."

My heart thudded. I'd wanted to be the one to talk to Raoul. Faeries had a tendency to expect tit for tat when they agreed to something. I wanted to be the one to bear the burden of any tit Raoul might demand.

Ick. That just sounded so wrong, especially considering the old faery was my father.

As Mr. Coffee started burbling again, Tony came back and sat next to me. "Seriously, we need to get a couch."

"There's the armchair. Go sit on that." I was getting a little tired of defending my futon. It might be old, broken down and hard as a rock, but the old gal and I had been through a lot together.

Fucking hormones. I was getting sentimental about a trash-picked futon. Jeez.

Tony nudged my leg with his knee. "He said he'd help. Whatever you need."

"And what did he ask for in return?" I reminded myself to breathe while I waited for his answer.

"In return? Nothing. He was happy to agree. Especially after I told him how hard it was for you to look at the baby and be reminded of the rape that he refused to help you avoid."

I stared at him. "You – you said what?"

"Well, I knew you wouldn't twist the knife like that, and really, I wanted him to feel bad. So I just embellished a little. Don't worry, I also smiled at him and told him to have a great day. He knows I was yanking his chain."

Tony was so damn good, sometimes I forgot how smart he was, too, and what a talent he had for using words to his advantage. "Wow."

He blew his nose again, then pushed to his feet. "I'm going to get myself a coffee. You want one?"

"Am I awake?"

He chuckled. "So, yes, then."

"Yes, then."

I watched him walk away, appreciating the view. Kind, hot and devious. Really, he was damn near perfect.

After lunch, when my bleeding had all but stopped, Tony agreed that I could go outside for a short walk with him, Galen and Sky. I handed him a bunch of Kleenex, which he stuffed in his pocket obligingly. "Is that going to be enough?"

He stuck his tongue out at me.

I carried Sky downstairs, with Galen's leash wrapped around my wrist, because Tony was carrying the enormous stroller that he bought the night before. The thing had pouches all over the place and even a cup holder in the little awning. It was a little fancier than I would've liked, but at least it was a nice shade of gray and there was no pink anywhere. Sky's onesie was pink, but I found it difficult to be annoyed, because it said "Daddy's Little Girl" on it, and, well, I kind of loved that. I just wish I could've been there to see Tony picking it out.

I have never felt pride like the pride I felt walking down the street, pushing that stupid stroller. I was turning into a cliché. Honestly, I was going to have to kill something soon, because otherwise, I would find myself wearing a sweater set and drinking herbal tea to raise my vibrations.

We kept the walk short, not by my choice, but because my body demanded it. Only halfway around the block, I started dragging. Clearly, despite my best efforts, I wasn't eating enough. When we got back to our building, we left the stroller in the entryway temporarily, because Tony had to carry Sky back upstairs. Once again, I could barely manage to get myself up the stairs. Which made me cranky, because I wasn't feeling like myself, and all I wanted was to feel like myself again.

Tony started a pot of coffee before going back downstairs to retrieve the stroller. I perched on the futon and glared at the world. Not even looking at Sky could make me feel better. Which oddly made me feel more like myself, and gradually, my ire began to ease.

I settled back on the futon and started playing with Sky's fingers. She made cooing noises that brought Galen over to investigate. I was enjoying watching my dog and my baby when Tony dragged the stroller inside.

"I'm telling myself that it's good this thing is so heavy, because it means it's sturdy and will protect her," he muttered. He glanced over at us. "Oh, good."

"Oh, good, what?"

"You don't look homicidal anymore."

I growled at him, but all he did was laugh.

After collapsing the stroller, Tony fixed me a PB&J – "Because it's quick" – and a large mug of coffee. I inhaled the sandwich and sat back to sip the coffee. He made it extra strong, strong enough that I had a feeling he wouldn't drink much of it. I must've really looked pissy when we got home.

"Thank you," I said as he settled in the armchair.

"You're welcome." He blew his nose and sipped his own coffee. I saw his face almost fall into a grimace, but he wrangled it and maintained his usual quiet calm. I loved that his masculine pride wouldn't allow him to grimace, no matter how hard it was to swallow the brew. "Strong enough?"

"Almost," I said, which made him smile. "Is it wrong that I'm ready for a nap?"

"You got about an hour of cumulative sleep last night, so no, I think that's pretty understandable."

Right on cue, Sky started fussing in that way I was coming to know so well. She was hungry, too. I fed her, then placed her back in her bassinet, where she fell asleep. I curled up on the futon and did the same.

That was how our days went. A week ago, if anyone told me how I'd be spending my time, I would've thought I'd be bored to tears after twenty minutes. But I wasn't. For one thing, babies were a lot of freaking work. For another, I was enjoying our domestic bliss to an embarrassing degree. I loved being surrounded by my pack, their scents continuously permeating my consciousness. This was the happiest I'd been since before my mother and sisters died when I was a little kid. I finally had the feeling of pack again, a true pack, not just the human one of the Sankhain, but a pack connected to me by blood and whatever bond made my wolf call Tony my mate and Galen my brother.

Sure, I grew up with Mal, but when you spent your first nine years sleeping in a wolf pile, feeling the safety and comfort and sheer joy of that connection, it was hard to make due with just one other wolf. I wasn't sleeping in a wolf pile, not yet, but having my little pack all crammed in a small one-bedroom apartment felt almost as intimate. I loved it.

And of course, there was Uncle Darcy, too. On Thursday morning, Tony dropped me off with Sky. Tony liked Darcy, but he didn't share the same connection to him that I did. And there might still be a part of Tony that resented the fact that I chose to give myself to Aza to save the other man. That resentment now paled in comparison to the way Tony felt about Finn, but it was still there.

While Sky and I visited Uncle Darcy, Tony was going to take Galen for a run on one of Madison's many bike trails. He would be sneezing all night long, but I didn't point that out. He knew it, I knew it, and since he didn't care, I was trying to let it go. I just hated seeing him suffer, but he accepted it, so I needed to do the same.

I told myself to focus on the sheer joy on Darcy's face. For an adult human, Darcy was shockingly incapable of guile. He wore every emotion like a comfortable pair of pajamas. And today, he was as happy as I'd ever seen him.

Darcy became my friend when he was trying to get to the Spring, so he could save his sister. She was dying of cancer, and she was his only family. When Darcy and I bonded, I became a surrogate sister to him, just like he became a pack brother to me. But I could tell that me calling him "uncle" meant more to him in light of his sister's death last year. He must've mourned the fact that he would never play with his own nieces and nephews, after losing his sister so young.

Which gave me an idea. Sky had a first name, but not a middle name. I hesitated to ask the question, but I couldn't remember the answer, so I had to if I was going to follow through on the idea. "Darcy, what was your sister's name?"

His head jerked up, so he went from gazing lovingly at Sky to looking at me with understandable surprise. "Um, Gwen. Guinevere. Why do you ask?"

Of course. Darcy's mom was a librarian, too. She named Darcy after Jane Austen's Mr. Darcy, and his sister after King Arthur's great love. I hesitated again. His sister was such a sensitive topic. I didn't want to hurt him. But I hoped he would like my idea. "Well, Sky needs a middle name. I thought, you know, maybe we could use your sister's name."

He stared at me, his eyes wide and overly bright with tears. I knew that feeling, when you widened your eyes more and more in an effort to make room for the tears that gathered there. Like maybe if you created enough space, the tears wouldn't spill out. It never worked for me, and it didn't work for Darcy, either. As he started to cry, he said, "You really mean that?"

Fuck, now I was going to start crying. I couldn't catch a cold from a human, why the fuck did tears have to be contagious? As my own tears spilled over my cheeks, I spoke with more annoyance than anything else. "Of course I mean it, dumbass."

Fortunately, that made him laugh, and soon we were both laughing and wiping away tears. Sky gurgled happily, which seemed to banish Darcy's tears for good. "Sky Guinevere. I think that's the most beautiful name I ever heard." His happiness smelled bright, like Earl Grey tea with a triple dose of bergamot, and I found I had a couple more tears that needed to be wiped away.

Chapter 27

TONY

It was Monday night. Tomorrow, we'd be returning to the forest. And for the first time ever, I didn't want to go there.

I wanted to see the younglings. I was looking forward to getting back to my classes, because I enjoyed teaching. It fed me. But this window into domesticity was about as close to perfect as my life had ever been. I didn't look at Sky and see Aza's baby anymore. She was my baby. Our baby. And now, we needed to take her back to within the reach of Finlay. The man who almost stole her and Kellan from me.

Before the scent of my anger could pull Kellan out of her much-needed sleep, I carefully pushed out of bed. Galen raised his head to look at me, but I whispered, "Shhh," and he lowered his head with a sleep-heavy sigh. Out in the living room, I stared at the street below, lit by streetlights and peopled with the neighborhood's night denizens. I let that anger grow for a moment, let it be what it was, before taking a deep breath and letting it go.

Finn was a reality of our life. I needed to accept that. I needed to forgive him.

An image of Kellan on the floor of the infirmary, bleeding out, while Finn came to after draining her life force.

I stepped back from the window, as if I could step away from the memory. Warm hands wrapped themselves around my forearms, which felt cold. I looked down and saw Kellan standing in front of me.

"What on earth are you thinking about that made you that angry?" she asked quietly. "I could smell you all the way in the bedroom."

"Shit, I'm sorry." Shame washed over me. I needed to be better than this. I was the calm one, the reasonable one. Kellan was the hothead, and she needed me to balance that out. It'd been months since she almost died. Why wasn't I over it already?

"That doesn't answer my question." She squinted at me, and her eyes started to glow gold in the dark. "What bee crawled in your bonnet and died there?"

I snorted a laugh at the slightly jumbled metaphor. "It's no big deal. Come on, we should go back to bed before Sky wakes up."

But when I tried to lead the way back to the bedroom, Kellan dug in her heels. "Did I do something?"

I sighed, and the last of the anger slipped away. "No. No, Kell, I just – I don't want to go back."

"And that made you angry?" Her forehead creased with a frown, then smoothed out as understanding seemed to hit her. "Oh. Is this about Finn?"

I smiled ruefully as I heard the sounds of Sky starting to fuss in the bedroom. "You go get her. I'll heat up some pizza for you." We ordered takeout the night before. "Want coffee, too?"

"Um, yes. Always yes to coffee."

With familiar tasks to occupy me, I felt a little more solid in myself. I liked this. I liked caretaking, I liked that I could make coffee for her and give her food she enjoyed. It was so easy to make her happy. How could Finn not appreciate that? How could he have treated her the way he did, used her and made her feel small every chance he got?

That thought stopped me, with the bag of coffee clutched in one hand. Was that where some of this rage, this hate, was coming from? The fact that, for over a century and a half, Finn and Kellan were lovers, and because of the way he treated her, her self-esteem was pretty much nil? Oh, she had confidence and self-esteem in some areas of her life. She knew she was good with a blade, she was a talented hunter and fighter. But in relationships, she thought she was worthless, disposable. It was why she hid the pregnancy from me for so long. She was sure I would drop her when I found out.

And then, when Sky was born and it was obvious that she wasn't my biological daughter, I had a moment where I almost did.

Maybe it wasn't just Finn I hated. Maybe some of that hate belonged to me.

Kellan carried Sky into the kitchen, cooing and murmuring to her, and I felt love so strong, it was a pain in my chest. As they passed me, I reached out, wrapped my arms around them both so that Sky was sandwiched between us, and lowered my face to bury it in Kellan's hair. I might not have a wolf's sense of smell, but the scent of her shampoo, of just her, said home to me the same way she said my scent did to her.

I straightened and looked down at her, at them. Kellan's eyes were wide, like she was scared. Maybe she was. "What was that for?" she asked warily.

"I'm sorry."

"For what?"

I took a deep breath and forced myself to say it. "For thinking, even for a minute, that I might leave. For letting you think I could leave you."

She cocked her head to the side. "I'm way too sleep-deprived to understand where this is coming from. But you don't have to apologize for that. Even if you did leave, I would've understood."

"I know, and that's the problem." At her ever more confused expression, I struggled to find the words. "You're important. You're worth staying for. Just you. No matter how long it took me to accept Sky, no matter how long it took me to make peace with Aza's impact on our lives, I never should've considered leaving you."

After another moment of frowning, she shook her head. "I know I should probably say something like, wow, thank you, that's so sweet. But it's not. I don't want you to stay because you think you should. I want you to be here because you want to. You needed to figure that out. It's a big deal, raising the daughter of your mate's rapist. It's especially big for someone who grew up like you did. So I don't want you to apologize for needing to figure it out. I'm glad you made the decision you did, but if you didn't, if you went the other way, that would've been okay. I mean, it would've sucked and I would've missed you like crazy, but I still would've accepted it."

"Yeah, but I mean, Finn always made you feel disposable, and then I —"

"Whoa, whoa, whoa." Kellan shifted Sky to a one-armed hold so she could hold up her hand. "Don't ever compare yourself to Finn. That's like comparing yourself to Aza. Finn used me to scratch an itch, sure. But I used him the same way. We cared about each other as much as we were capable, but... This thing between you and me? It's a whole different beast. It's like saying ground beef and Grape-nuts are the same thing, because they look about the same. But if you put Grape-nuts in spaghetti sauce, you're gonna find out real quick that it's so not the same thing."

I burst out laughing at the messed-up, but somehow sensical imagery. "That's one of the most disgusting things I've ever heard of."

"I heard Valentine trying to explain to Tia once that her Grape-nuts weren't going to taste like ground beef. It stuck in my head." As if that explained it. Which it kind of did.

"All right. Look, I'm going to take that to mean you're hungry. So have a seat, get Sky feeding, and I'll bring you some pizza."

"Now you're talking." But she still stood there, staring at me. "Are you okay?"

"No. But I'm okayer than I was." I thought so, anyway. "Maybe I need to have a few sessions with Ethan."

She stretched up on her tiptoes to kiss my cheek before she went to the table to sit down and feed Sky. "I'm starting to think maybe we all need to have a few sessions with Ethan. But don't tell him I said that. The man has a charming lack of ego, and I wouldn't want that to ever change."

Laughing again, I returned to preparing the coffee. Definitely okayer now.

KELLAN

Predawn was one of the few times the neighborhood was quiet, so when it became clear that we weren't going to fall back to sleep, we loaded our belongings in the truck, then took a short walk. We let Galen lift his leg several times, so the neighborhood would remember in his absence that this was his turf. I wasn't surprised when Raoul stepped out from behind a building and stopped to stand a few feet away.

"So this is my grandchild, hmm?" he asked in his soft, windchimey fey voice.

"I guess so," I said, although I still wasn't completely comfortable with the idea of having a father. I just spent so long only having a mother, that this father figure thing felt foreign, like speaking Cantonese from a script.

He stepped closer, and I felt Tony tense beside me. But then he actually took a step back and let Raoul stand beside me instead.

"We're about to leave for camp, so whatever you want to say, say it fast," I grumbled.

Raoul smiled at me, then looked down at Sky. "Hello, little cub," he said. "I hear you will be needing my help. I will see you soon. For now, though..." He reached down and placed his hand on her forehead. I had to tense every muscle in my body to keep from tackling him. He wouldn't hurt her. I knew he wouldn't, because he must know what I would do to him if he did.

He straightened and met my gaze. "Your eyes glow, little wolf," he told me.

"So do yours." I pointed to his bright green eyes.

"Like father, like daughter." He smiled.

"Yuck. Look, what did you just do to my baby?"

"I gave her a little boost of glamour. It's rather difficult to get a spell to sustain itself, but this will last long enough for you to return to your forest dwellings. It will hide her otherness for the time being, allow you to enjoy your early morning walk without worry. A human could hold her in their arms and not realize she is…unlike them in any way."

It was a nice thing to do, which made me suspicious. "Thanks. I guess."

He bared his teeth in a grin that would make a wolf proud. "No strings attached, little wolf. That was the deal I made with your mate. I will help in whatever way I can."

"Super." Time to end this painful conversation. "Well, we better get going. If we're late getting to camp, there will be hell to pay."

"Mustn't have that." Raoul stepped back and assumed the mantle of his urban guise. "Be seein' ya." He melted into the darkness like he was never there.

"That guy's creepy," Tony muttered.

"Yup." We resumed our walk, feeling distinctly less peaceful than before. Raoul might say no strings attached, but somehow, I felt like he'd find ways to sneak a few strings into the deal. Necessary evil, I told myself. And I wouldn't let him hurt Sky, no matter what.

In the truck, Sky rode strapped to my chest in one of those baby-slings. It meant I couldn't use my seatbelt, which meant the whole arrangement was incredibly unsafe. We really needed to get a different vehicle. I vowed to speak to Janus about it the first chance I got.

We were just pulling into the parking lot of the forest when my cell phone rang. I blinked, recognizing Mal's number. I turned up the radio, just in case Janus was able to hear this far outside the forest, and answered the phone. "Hi."

"Hey. How are you?" She sounded a little breathless, like she'd been running.

"I'm okay. We just got back to the forest." So I needed to keep this short, I finished silently.

"Sure, I just had something to tell you quick." She must've heard what I wasn't saying, like she always did.

"Okay." I nodded to Tony, who got out and started hauling our bags out of the back of the truck. He took the first of what would have to be multiple trips into the forest. How did we end up with so much crap in just one week? Well, half of it was gifts from Uncle Darcy. But still. Jeez.

"I wanted to let you know that the problem's been taken care of. That lead that I told you about last week? Turned out not to be as old as I thought. We found him and eliminated the threat last night."

And just like that, a cold, clammy weight settled over my shoulders. J.C. was dead. The boy would never grow up into a man. I reminded myself of Smack, of the damage that boy had done. But I would never, ever forget the sound of his sobs. That would haunt me as much as the way Smack's dead eyes glared at me for my part in preventing her suicide.

"Kell? You there?"

I wiped my cheeks before I even realized they were wet. "Yeah. I'm here. Um, thanks."

I knew that she would hear the tremor in my voice. "What is it?" she said quietly.

And because it was her, because no one knows you like the person who shared a womb with you, I said, "When he was in the solitary cells, I heard him crying."

"Ah. And to your pregnancy-hormone addled brain, that made him a victim, too." Her understanding sounded an awful lot like dismissal.

"Fuck you," I said. I hated crying. I hated everything and everyone.

"Kell, I get it. In light of that, I'm glad I was able to take care of it for you. You shouldn't have to end a life that you feel empathy for." Shockingly, I heard no judgment in her voice. In fact, I heard that very same thing – empathy.

"That's why you did it, isn't it?" One of the reasons Mal left the Sankhain was because she secretly spared the lives of some of the former members she was sent to kill. "That's why you let Magda live?"

"Duh." Never let too much empathy or understanding get in the way of a good sibling conversation.

I took a shaky breath, then another one. "It's done?"

"It's done, little sister."

Done. No more wondering if there was any other way. He hurt people we loved, so he had to die. That was our world, our way of life. It was our form of justice, and it was what I promised Smack. It was done. "Then thank you."

"I was hoping I could get to Mad-town before you had to go back."

The subject change was jarring, but welcome. "I told you before, we're living there part time. We go back again Friday night, and we'll stay in the apartment until the wee hours on Tuesday morning."

"Oh. Yeah, you did say that. Sorry. It's been a busy week."

I let my brain skitter away from thinking about why her week was so busy. "Well, I suppose a little memory loss is to be expected at your age."

"MY age? May I remind you, you're only about a minute younger than me."

"Whatever. Shrimp."

We hung up, the sound of her laughter warming me.

Tony returned from hauling the last of our stuff into the trees. The sky was starting to brighten, meaning we needed to get across the border into the forest. But I needed to tell him about J.C. first. I couldn't walk beside him, pretending not to know this huge thing. Not again. Never again.

I motioned to him to join me in the truck cab. I left the engine running and the radio loud as I told him the news. He turned away from me to stare out the windshield and inhaled deeply. He seemed to hold that breath for an eternity before letting it out on a sigh. Still not looking at me, he said, "Okay. I guess that's good."

"No. It isn't." My voice sounded old and tired, and Tony glanced at me sharply.

"It isn't?" I recognized his scent as conflicted, the mash-up of sadness, anger, relief and confusion. It was a grief scent, because grief was all those things and more.

"No," I said. I stroked Sky's cheek to comfort her, then reached out to Galen, still my own comfort, my living, breathing security blanket. "It sucks. It sucks that we couldn't save him. I wish we could've saved him."

Tony stared at me. "You do?"

I didn't take his amazement personally. I was, after all, a killer. All wolves were. "Yes. It doesn't excuse what he did. But he was a kid. I wish we could save them all."

He took one of my hands, the one that wasn't buried in Galen's fur, and raised it to his mouth for a gentle kiss. "We better go," he said. So we did.

Chapter 28

KELLAN

Cat informed us that we needed to report to Janus's cabin, so we left our belongings with a couple of younglings who offered to carry them to our cabin. The baby sling was making me sweat, so I transferred Sky to my arms. I felt much stronger than I did a week ago, though I was already starting to feel hungry. I was learning, though – I had a protein bar in my pocket. I handed Sky to Tony and ate while we walked.

The sunrise was starting to color the sky. It was going to be a perfect spring day. Except for the fact that I now carried another death on my conscience, and I needed to figure out how to tell Smack about it. I knew she wasn't sleeping well. Would this help? Tony always told me that killing Aza wouldn't take the nightmares away, but I still believed it might help. It certainly wouldn't make anything worse. I gave many people my word many times over that I wouldn't hunt down Aza, but I could give Smack a little of the relief that I was denying myself.

Except how to tell her, and how to explain that Janus can never know?

Smack was working the reception desk, which would make it easy to find her, at least. She announced us, and Janus welcomed us into his quarters with an expansive sweep of his arms. I braced myself to feel the prickle of his ever-present magick, but it wasn't too bad. Or maybe I was just distracted, because the table was laid with coffee, scones, eggs, not-sausage, pancakes…a full breakfast spread. It seemed Janus didn't really have any reason for summoning us. He wanted to welcome us back.

I was surprised to see a bassinet alongside the big table, right next to the spot where I usually sat. I glanced at Tony, a little unsure of this big celebration. In all the years I spent living in Madison, Janus never threw me a welcome home party before. What was different now, other than a baby?

"Sit, sit, eat," he said manically. I smelled a strange scent in the air. Like an almost rotten plum. Still sweet, but only barely. Like it was just on the verge of turning. What did that mean? Janus wasn't angry. It was almost like he was...

Afraid. Afraid of losing me, the way he lost Mal.

Even though I wasn't sure what I was feeling, I forced myself to smile at him and sit at the table. "Thank you, sir. This is perfect. I was just thinking how hungry I was."

"It's true, sir." Tony sat down beside me. "She ate a protein bar as we were walking here, but you know those never fill her up. They're a band-aid on a bullet wound."

"Yes, so true. Your mother always ate ravenously when she had a newborn cub to feed." Janus beamed at me, and as weird as this was, I couldn't help feeling warm and fuzzy under the force of that smile. "When she was feeding both you and..." He blinked. "And Amalea, she almost could not keep up with the need for calories. She lost twenty pounds over your first six months of life."

I never knew that. "Why didn't anybody tell me these things before I popped out a baby?"

The old man's smile turned sad. "We have neglected many things, I fear. However, I wish to rectify that going forward. Now, tell me how your little one is doing. Is she sleeping?"

We spent the next hour talking, filling him in on our week. I remembered to tell him we needed a different vehicle, and he said we could choose one from the few that we kept for Sankhain use. Those cars were pretty crappy, but they would do for now.

Next, Janus gave us updates on each of the younglings. The whole time we were talking, I couldn't help but notice that Finn wasn't there. Finally, I worked up the courage to ask where he was.

"Ah." That one syllable carried so much weight, it seemed to fall flat on the table. "Well. Young Gina is...struggling a bit." I started to get up, to go looking for Gina. What was happening? What was wrong? Janus motioned for me to sit back down. "No, no, all is well. We simply decided that Finlay needed to spend more time working one on one with her. Her magickal abilities seem to grow exponentially by the day. Our containment spell does not seem to work anymore. She seems to use magick without thought, which then frightens her. But with Finlay's help, she is learning to recognize what it feels like as it comes upon her. She will be fine."

Judging by how tightly Tony's hand held mine, I didn't think either one of us was completely sold on that. But at least they were dealing with it and helping her. Gina was tough, I reminded myself. Even when I was nine months pregnant and hell on hormonal wheels, the girl still admonished me for taking the Lord's name in vain. If she could chew out a hormonal wolf, she could do anything. It would just take time.

Not that I would take Janus's word for it. I intended to check on Gina as soon as I could. But he was right. She would be fine, eventually.

"Now, you are probably wanting to go get yourselves settled. And you should, because the younglings have left you a surprise in your cabin. No, no, I will not tell you what it is," he said, as though we were begging him to spill the beans. Even though we didn't say a word. "But they are quite eager for you to see it. You should go. Antony, you have this morning off as well. You need a little extra time to make sure all is well for the baby. I have called home two of your Sankhain brothers to help with the teaching over the next few months."

Tony blinked. I wondered how he felt about that – he loved teaching and took a lot of pride in his work. If we were going to be living in Madison part time, they needed somebody to cover the classes while he was gone, but would he be okay with someone else teaching his classes? Oh, well. If he didn't like it, we could reevaluate the Madison plan.

"Thank you, sir," Tony said finally. He looked at me. "The younglings left us a present."

Hopefully, it wasn't pink. Darcy refused to listen when I said that Sky didn't like pink, and he showered her with pink stuffed animals of all sorts. Sky was already pretty attached to an improbably pink badger. Where Darcy found a pink badger, I would never know. I didn't really want to know, and hoped that I never needed to go visit a place that produced pink badgers. Badgers were tough, scrappy animals. They'd be horrified to be reduced to a cotton-candy pink baby toy. It was disgraceful, really.

I forced myself to return to the current conversation. "Yeah, I guess we better go see what it is. Thank you again, sir, for breakfast. That was delicious."

"You are very welcome. Welcome home, child." He rested a hand on my shoulder, which was Janus's version of a peck on the cheek. We hurried out before things could get any weirder.

And saw Smack sitting at the reception desk. "Smack, I'd like to talk to you." Might as well get all the emotionally awful moments out of the way at once. Immediately, I could smell her anxiety, but she nodded. I poked my head into Janus's office, where he was standing before the fire, staring at nothing that I could see. "Sir? Might I borrow Smack for a moment? I want to check in with her."

He nodded distractedly and waved me away. I wondered what he was doing, but I could feel magick growing thicker in the air, and I decided I wanted to get away. Right now.

I picked up Smack, Tony, Galen and Sky, who were all waiting by the reception desk, and we went to one of the vacant cabins. I wanted privacy for this.

Smack sat down in a chair by the table and looked at us with a fairly inscrutable frown. She still smelled a little nervous, but otherwise, she was very contained. "What?" she said.

I glanced at Tony. He and I sat on the bed, since there was only one other chair in the cabin. I didn't really have a plan of what to say. How was I going to explain knowing that someone killed J.C.? Who could I tell her hunted him down? Janus was right when he said I was a terrible liar. Tony was better at spinning words, but he didn't seem inclined to say anything. I decided to just keep it simple. "Look, I have something to tell you that can't leave this room. You can't tell anyone. Not Gina, not one of the other younglings. Definitely not Janus or Finn. Not even Ethan. Do you understand?"

Her frown deepened, but she nodded.

"Okay." Even knowing I was going to tell the truth, I still didn't know where to start. "I reached out to…a friend, and asked her to help me find J.C." Smack jerked, like I hit her, but then a moment later, she was still. Not the calm stillness of meditation, more like the tightness of a body full of clenched muscles. Galen walked over to her and nudged her knee with his head. She began petting him, and her posture relaxed slightly.

Good dog, I thought, and went on. "She found him, and, well, she took care of him. He's dead, Smack. He's gone for good."

Nothing. Not a word, not a movement, not even a breath. Smack was so devoid of reaction, I wondered if she heard what I said. "He's gone, Smack."

"I heard you. Anything else?" She stared down at her hand on Galen's head.

"Are you okay?" I asked.

She snorted, and that sounded so much like her, I felt the tension ease inside my gut. "That's a dumb question," she said.

"You're right, it is. But are you?"

She lifted her head and met my gaze. "I guess. I don't know. It's kind of hard to know right now." Which made perfect sense. "Why can't I tell anyone?"

Tony spoke up. "This friend of Kellan's isn't a Sankhain-approved friend."

Smack glanced at him before fixing her gaze on me again. I wondered what she saw there. Then I decided I probably didn't want to know. "All right, I guess," she said. "I should probably get back to work. I still have fifteen minutes on my shift."

"Okay," I said, not knowing what else to say. I wished I could loop Ethan in on this, but he'd never be able to keep a secret from Janus. One look from the old man and Ethan would crumble. I felt like there was something more I should do for Smack, but I didn't have a clue what that something was. I looked at Tony. He shrugged. I guess he didn't know what the something was, either.

Smack was almost to the door when she paused. "Thank you, Sankha Kellan. Please thank your friend for me. I think – I think I will be okay. Eventually, ya know."

I felt like my heart broke and swelled at the same time. I was so proud of her. "I'm glad. And I'll be sure to thank her for you."

Smack glanced back at me. "You know Janus has me keepin' an eye out for Mal's aliases, right? As part of my computer duties?"

I froze and forgot how to swallow for a second. "Uh, no. I didn't realize that."

"Yup. Too bad I'm just not having any luck with it. And I guess I won't have any luck with it, ever. Maybe you can tell your friend that, too." With that, Smack left.

"Jesus fucking Christ," I whispered. "How did she know?" I needed to tell Mal to never, ever use any of the aliases that the Sankhain provided for her. Shit.

"Well, you said 'she,' and your only other friend is Darcy, and he's a dude." Tony shifted Sky in his arms. "Don't worry. Smack can keep a secret. And it doesn't seem like this one will weigh on her, the way the secret of the rape did."

Oh, god, now I was forcing the poor kid to keep a huge secret, after I spent the last few months drilling the younglings with how important it was to keep everything out in the open. I really sucked at responsible adulting.

Tony stood up and Galen trotted over to nose his leg. "Wanna go see what the kids left for us?"

I focused on Galen, on Tony, on Sky. "Yeah." We left the vacant cabin and started walking to our own.

As we stepped inside, I noticed a strong scent of varnish. I frowned, confused. Nothing in our cabin was freshly varnished. Then I saw it.

"Oh," I breathed.

We crossed the room to the crib now standing beside our bed. This was a real crib, hand-carved with wolves running across the guardrail. Inside was a tiny mattress covered in soft sheets, piled high with blankets and stuffed animals. None of which were pink. Galen sniffed it suspiciously, as he would anything that mysteriously appeared in our home. Apparently deciding it wasn't a threat, he huffed and walked away to sniff around the cabin, leaving us two-legged folks to stare at the gift.

The ever-present tears pricked behind my eyes yet again, but I wasn't alone – I could smell Tony's tears, as well. "Wow," he said in a voice rough with emotion.

"Yeah." I ran my fingers lightly over the carvings. "Wow."

"Ryder must've designed this." Tony rubbed his cheeks. "I should go find him and thank him. He's going to be dying to know if we like it." Ryder was a youngling who suffered a major head injury before he came to us. He wasn't good at math or reading, but he was brilliant at other things. I knew he could fix just about anything, but I didn't realize he liked woodworking, too. Because of his learning issues, he didn't have a lot of self-confidence, but he was as sweet as could be.

"We should both go." I picked up Sky and clucked my tongue at Galen to tell him to follow me. We opened our door and found Ryder and Smack waiting outside, surrounded by all the other younglings. I saw Gina standing in the back of the group, too. She looked tired, but okay. She smiled at me, I smiled back, and with a wave, she left.

"See," Smack said. "It really is a baby, not a puppy."

"Oh, for fuck's sake," I muttered. "I thought you had work to do."

"Sankha Janus excused me from my shift so I could be here." She came over and gave us a little smile. I saw the things she didn't say, the secrets we held between us and how she was okay with them, in that smile. She ran a finger over the top of Sky's head.

"We decided to call her Sky, by the way. Not October."

"Good. October was a stupid name for a baby born in May." Smack didn't even bother to say it under her breath, she just said it for everyone to hear, with a broad grin on her face.

"Yes, thank you." I kept my tone dry, but inside, I was dancing a jig. Smack was herself. She would be okay.

I looked at the other younglings. "Thank you so much for the beautiful crib." Seeing their faces, each healing their own wounds, I got all choked up again.

Tony put a hand on my shoulder and squeezed. "We love it. When did you find time to work on that? Obviously, we haven't been working you hard enough."

Scattered laughs and giggles met his teasing. He was so amazing with them. I couldn't wait to see how he was with Sky as she grew up.

"We had to work on it in our free time," Ryder said shyly. "I've been eating my lunch and dinner superfast for weeks, to have time on meal breaks to work on the sanding and stuff."

"I bet you have. Well, it turned out just gorgeous." Tony gave Ryder a one-armed hug. "I almost don't want to put the baby in it. She's just going to puke on it, ya know."

"We varnished it so it's real easy to clean," Ryder was quick to assure him. "Don't worry. Babies can be messy, but this is built to handle it. Now, you know she's not big enough to put in there yet, right? And you have to take the stuffed animals out before you put her in. That's really important. She could…"

Ryder kept talking, but I stopped listening. Instead, I heard one sentence in my head, over and over again. *Babies can be messy.* Well, that would fit in with the rest of my life just fine. With tears once again streaming down my cheeks, I smiled at Tony and Galen and Sky and all the younglings. My mess. My family. My pack.

About the Author

Carrie Newberry discovered her passion for fantasy writing two decades ago when a shapeshifter named Kellan sparked her imagination. She is the author of the Eternal Spring, Invisible Forest series. The series includes Pick Your Teeth with My Bones, Wolf is a Four-Letter Word, and When the Fur Hits the Fan, Duck. Carrie studied creative writing at the University of Wisconsin but left academia to focus on her craft. By day, she's a Madison dog groomer; by night, she teaches and workshops at AllWriters' Workplace, sharing her boundless enthusiasm for storytelling.

Need something new to read?

If you liked When the Fur Hits the Fan, Duck,
you should also consider
these other EDGE titles...

Pick Your Teeth with my Bones
(Book One of the Eternal Spring, Invisible Forest series)

by Carrie Newberry

The Fountain of Youth is at Risk…

Its location is a closely guarded secret and the society itself is shrouded in mystery.

Kellan Faolanni, a single, lives-alone, drives-a-truck kind of woman. She's the girl-next-door type. Innocent looking and easy to get along with. You'd never know she's a battle-scarred shapeshifter.

That's until the existence of a traitor is revealed, and a leaked document containing the history of her people threatens to expose her, her fellow Sankhain guardians, and the secrets they keep.

With a fellow protector (and her faithful dog Galen), Kellan sets out to unravel the mystery of the compromising documents.

By using her unique senses that have kept her alive for two hundred years, Kellan follows the trail deep into the forest. But the truth she uncovers challenges everything she thought she knew and forces her to choose between her leaders and the dictates of her own conscience.

Everything they've sworn to protect is in jeopardy. Failure to locate the traitor is not an option.

Wolf is a Four-letter Word
(Book Two of the Eternal Spring, Invisible Forest series)

by Carrie Newberry

What do you do when the nightmare is real?

That's the question facing Kellan Faolanni.

Following the betrayal of her sister at the end of the previous book, Kellan Faolanni must set aside her own emotions and thwart an enemy who seems to have the upper hand at every turn.

Kellan, a member of a secret society called the Sankhain, is a shapeshifter, half-wolf, half-human. Kellan's superiors have discovered a man killed by what appears to be a wolf pack, a rare sight in modern-day Madison.

The Sankhain task Kellan to investigate and discover who seems to be leaving this message for her. Meanwhile, Kellan's friend, Darcy Jameson, a human with no ties to the Sankhain who was also victimized by Kellan's sister, reveals to her that he's being stalked. Kellan learns that the killer and Darcy's stalker are one and the same: a faery named Aza. But Aza is a high-ranking member of the Shadow Court, and to kill him would start a war with the fey, a war that Kellan's superiors want to avoid at all costs.

Kellan must find a way to eliminate the threat and save her friend. Her solution could cost her everything, including a new relationship with another Sankha, Tony, as well as her sanity.

For more EDGE titles and information about upcoming speculative fiction please visit us at:

www.edgewebsite.com

Don't forget to sign-up for our Special Offers

www.ingramcontent.com/pod-product-compliance
Lightning Source LLC
Chambersburg PA
CBHW030024200726
48283CB00012B/837